*The Dog Sitter Detective
Takes the Lead*

By Antony Johnston

The Dog Sitter Detective
The Dog Sitter Detective Takes the Lead

The Dog Sitter Detective Takes the Lead

ANTONY JOHNSTON

Allison & Busby Limited
11 Wardour Mews
London W1F 8AN
allisonandbusby.com

First published in Great Britain by Allison & Busby in 2024.
This paperback edition published by Allison & Busby in 2024.

10 9 8 7 6 5 4 3 2 1

ISBN 978-0-7490-3025-4

Typeset in 11/16 pt Sabon LT Pro by Allison & Busby Ltd.

By choosing this product, you help take care of the world's forests.
Learn more: www.fsc.org

FSC
www.fsc.org
MIX
Paper | Supporting
responsible forestry
FSC® C171272

Printed and bound by
CPI Group (UK) Ltd, Croydon, CR0 4YY

For rescue workers and foster carers everywhere

CHAPTER ONE

I missed the first phone call from Crash Double because I was upstairs trying to dig myself out from under my mother's old clothes before I suffocated under a pile of wool and plastic.

Honestly, Monday mornings.

My phone was on the kitchen table and set to silent because I wasn't expecting anyone to call. With a couple of hours to spare until rehearsal, I was determined to make a start on my mother's seemingly endless wardrobe. She had never been an extravagant figure, and I didn't remember her wearing half of the clothes I now stood facing. But there they were, row upon row of dresses and blouses and skirts and more, gathering dust and packed so tightly they threatened to burst out of the wardrobe in this third-floor spare room. There could have been a passage to Narnia back there and I wouldn't have seen it. After she died, my father could never bring himself to discard her clothes, so he simply shrouded them in plastic. I sometimes thought he expected me to wear them but that was about as likely as me twirling down the King's Road in a tutu.

So I reached in to remove a dress from the rail, because if I've learnt anything from fixing up the house I inherited it's that you have to start somewhere, and they did. Burst out of the wardrobe, that is. With me underneath.

As I clambered out from under the squeaking plastic, it was becoming clear that sorting out this tailored abundance would take more than a quick hour or two. I abandoned it with a promise to return when I had more time, because today I had an important rehearsal to attend.

Not that all rehearsals aren't important, but this was to be my first major role since coming out of retirement. I'd given up acting to care for my father, and assumed I'd never go back. But when he died after a decade of illness, it turned out he'd burnt through all the money he'd made in the City, and there was nothing left. I'd have to resume working, which was easier said than done for a sixty-year-old woman who hadn't been in front of a camera or audience for ten years. Nevertheless, I was determined to give it a go, and since landing a new agent I'd had several auditions. Mostly for the role of 'quiet grandmother who has one good line if she's lucky', admittedly, but work is work. And now I'd landed a meaty part: Melanie, frustrated daughter of Margory and long-suffering mother to Michelle, in a new play at the Sunrise Theatre called *Mixed Mothers*.

After freshening up and changing into a standard rehearsal outfit of pullover, slacks and flat shoes for comfort, I returned downstairs to gather my things. That's when I finally picked up my phone and saw a call from an unknown number.

I didn't think much of it. There had been a time when my friend Tina was the only person I could reliably expect to call my mobile, while calls on the house phone had invariably been doctors or officials discussing my father's care. Those calls ceased with his death, and I'd considered removing the landline altogether because now everyone lives on their mobiles, don't they? I did, especially as I'd also begun dog-sitting to make ends meet (auditions are all very well, but they don't pay). My number had quickly spread through the dog owners' grapevine and now calls from strangers weren't unusual.

Normally, though, they left a voicemail. No such luck here, so I assumed it was a scammer and tossed my phone, keys and purse in my handbag.

I hadn't yet worked out how to get the towering piles of old *Financial Times* in the hallway to the recycling, so I stepped carefully around them and checked myself in the hallway mirror. Still short and grey, but not in bad shape considering. Then I stepped out onto Smithfield Terrace where a fresh spring breeze blew down the street. I took a sweet breath and smiled, my mind on nothing but making a good impression at rehearsals.

Which is why I jumped several inches in the air when

a familiar sharp voice behind me called out, 'Guinevere, my dear. Are you well?'

The black-clad Dowager Lady Ragley, my next-door neighbour and stalwart defender of Chelsea house prices, had somehow left her house and approached me without making a sound.

'Very well, thank you, my lady,' I said, forcing a smile. 'In fact, I'm going to first rehearsal for my next role. I'm appearing at the Sunrise, you see.' It was a small theatre, to be sure, but the Dowager was easily dazzled by celebrity. I lived in vain hope that she might one day be impressed enough by my career to stop badgering me about house repairs.

'How lovely,' she said, the information immediately dismissed. Instead, she gestured with a thin, white-cuffed wrist to my house. 'I wonder if you've given any further thought to your façade.'

I fought to stop my eyes rolling and stepped back to take in the frontage. Really, it didn't need that much work. OK, some of the window frames were a little worse for wear; yes, the guttering and drainpipes needed attention; sure, there was missing ironwork on the basement stair. But it was hardly threatening to collapse onto the pavement.

'All on my list,' I reassured her, tapping my head to indicate where said list was stored. 'Don't worry, I'll get to it before—'

A piece of first-floor render chose that moment to succumb to the spring breeze and claim its freedom. In

silence (mine aghast, hers triumphant) we both watched it break away and skitter down the stone, to land on my front step as if mocking not just my words but my very thoughts.

The Dowager faced me with a silent, stony glare. I almost would have preferred her to be smug.

'I'll call someone right away,' I said quickly. Unable to resist, I added, 'Unless you can recommend a builder personally, of course.'

Her nostrils flared, offended by the suggestion that she might deign to fraternise with tradesmen. She turned on her heel and said, 'I have full confidence you'll deal with it, my dear,' then disappeared inside her house, somehow slamming her door in silence.

Suitably chastened, I pulled out my phone and prepared to call a builder. Except, of course, I knew no more builders than Lady Ragley did. I'd have to seek a recommendation.

Trudging toward Sloane Square Station, the spring breeze seemed to have turned sour.

CHAPTER TWO

I arrived at the Sunrise ten minutes before rehearsals were due to start, yet somehow still felt late. Finding the communal green room empty, I dropped my bag and coat on a free table and hurried through corridors towards the stage. Voices sounded from out front. Had I got the time wrong? Being late to first rehearsal wouldn't make a good impression.

I weaved past stagehands in the wings and emerged to find the principal cast huddled with the director, Simon. He had his arm around the shoulder of a young woman, and everyone smiled while she took a group selfie on her phone. I was still very much on the outside of acting scene gossip, having ignored it altogether for the past ten years, so I had no idea if this was Simon's daughter, his latest wife, a PA, or whatever. But they were clearly on good terms, so I decided I should make an effort.

Ted, the actor playing the eternally patient husband Martin to my harrassed mother Melanie, noticed me step

on stage and discreetly cleared his throat. The others turned like a pack of startled meerkats then parted so I could approach Simon and his blonde companion.

I took the initiative and walked forward confidently. 'By my watch I'm early, but seeing you all here makes me wonder,' I laughed, and before anyone could contradict me, I put out a hand to greet the young woman. 'Good morning. You've met everyone else, so you might have already guessed I'm Gwinny.'

'Oh yeah, of course,' she smiled, handing her phone to Simon. 'This is so good of you, thank you. I'm Violet, obviously.'

'. . . Obviously,' I agreed, envying the confidence of youth. She probably had a million followers on social media, so why wouldn't it be obvious?

(I know what social media is, I'm not a Luddite. My new agent had suggested I create a profile and get involved, to let people see 'the real Gwinny'. But when I spent an hour looking around, it seemed what people *really* wanted to see was either beautiful young people posting pictures of themselves in sunny locations, or angry old people arguing with each other about today's tabloid frenzy. I doubted there was an audience for back pain, varicose veins and house renovations.)

'Let's begin,' said Simon, clapping for attention. 'Places, please.'

I reached for my lines then remembered I'd left my bag backstage. Ted and I weren't on until scene three, though, so I'd have time. As everyone scurried to position,

I passed him in the wings and whispered, 'I need to get my lines from the green room. Cover for me, I'll be back in a minute.'

Before he could reply, a stagehand handed me a stack of pages. I thanked her and flipped through to scene three, only to find it wasn't there. 'Darling, I think you've got these mixed up,' I called after her. 'These are for—'

'Places, Gwinny, places!' Simon bellowed from his seat facing centre stage. 'Get with it, you're in scene one now.'

Confused, I turned back to the opening pages and scanned in vain for my character. Had there been rewrites already?

'Sorry, Simon, I don't see Melanie in the opener. Are these definitely the latest sides?'

'What? No, you're Margory. Violet is playing Melanie.'

I was so still I could have won a prize. Vaguely aware that everyone else had frozen too, I glanced over at Violet. She stood in the wings, suddenly fascinated by her own script.

'Say that again?'

The director sighed theatrically. 'You're playing Margory now. The grandmother. Violet is playing Melanie, the mother. For heaven's sake, didn't anyone tell you?'

Blood rushed to my cheeks. I fought to keep my voice steady as I walked downstage to the footlights and said,

'Who, Simon? Who exactly would have told me? You're the director.'

'Yes I am, and that's why I've made the decision to recast with someone closer to the character's age. Now don't fuss, Gwinny. Find your mark and let's go.'

I did, and proceeded to stumble my way through unfamiliar lines and an unfamiliar headspace for the first run-through. I kept reminding myself that I was no longer a star, or even much of a recognisable character actor. I should have known that landing a central role so soon was too good to be true. This was what I'd dreaded most about resuming my career: having to start back at the bottom of the ladder, like a struggling young actress all over again but with several decades of accumulated aches, pains and wrinkles to contend with.

I didn't blame Violet. Assuming she wasn't sleeping with Simon, she'd done nothing more than be a pretty *ingénue*. Yes, she was twenty years too young for the part, but make-up could take care of that. In her position I would have done the same.

At lunch break I found a private area and called my agent, 'Bostin' Jim Austin.

'Bostin Agency,' he answered in his thick Brummie accent. *Bostin* was a nickname he'd acquired at school in Birmingham, apparently local slang for *brilliant*. It takes all sorts.

'It's Gwinny. What the hell's going on with *Mixed Mothers*? They want to recast me!' Furious, I related

what had happened while Jim patiently tutted in all the right places.

'Believe me, I would have told you if I'd known about it,' he said when I finally paused to breathe. 'But I don't think there's much I can do.'

'Surely it's a breach of contract,' I sputtered. 'Margory has a quarter of the lines Melanie does. Are they at least going to pay me the same?'

He hesitated. 'Now there's an idea. Leave that with me. The thing is, do you really want to cause a fuss?'

There was that word again. 'I'm hardly being an unreasonable diva. I was cast in a role, and I expect to play it.'

'I get that. But now you've been *re*-cast, and a woman of your experience knows that sometimes happens on small productions. Especially when they can suddenly get a big name from TV.'

'She's practically a teenager. How has she been around long enough to be any kind of name?'

'Are you serious? Didn't you watch *Eastenders* last year?'

'Last year I was somewhat busy caring for my dying father.'

After a pause he said, 'OK, I apologise for that. But if we're going to work together, I need two things. First, you have to take more of an interest in the business. Second, if I can be frank, remember that you're basically starting over from scratch, and with a handicap. You don't want a reputation for making trouble.'

I seethed quietly at being called a troublemaker when none of this was my doing. But I knew exactly what 'handicap' he meant. There was no shortage of older women vying for stage parts, thanks to the lack of decent roles on TV. If word got around that I was difficult to work with, or even (gasp!) *ungrateful*, I'd be consigned to the do-not-hire pile.

'Five minutes,' came a shout from the corridor.

I pushed my anger deep down inside, took a long, slow breath, and said, 'All right, deal.' Struck by sudden inspiration, I added, 'By the way, I don't suppose you happen to know any good builders? My house needs a bit of work.'

'I do, actually. Just had our loft done, and quite reasonable too. I'll text you his number.'

Before I could ask whether Bostin Jim and I shared a definition of 'quite reasonable', he ended the call. I threw down my phone and reread grandmother Margory's lines.

At ten past four I stepped out of the stage door and was assaulted by a black Labrador. Thankfully it was a loveable attack, all wagging tail and lapping tongue, so I crouched to greet him and fuss his ears. 'Hello, Ronnie,' I said between licks.

Ronnie belonged to my friend DCI Alan Birch, retired, formerly a senior detective in the Met and presently standing behind his dog as it tried to drown me. Seeing Birch there, stoic and grounded, it struck me how like

a faithful Lab he was himself. We'd become friends by tripping over a murder case, when Tina had been accused of killing her husband-to-be. With Birch's help I uncovered what the police had failed to, unmasking the real murderer, and through it all his loyalty had never wavered. Tall and wide-shouldered, with grey cropped hair and a full moustache, he couldn't look more like an ex-policeman if he tried. But beneath a firm brow he had the most delightful bright blue eyes, and wasn't to be underestimated.

Nevertheless, glad as I was to see a friendly face, it was a surprise. 'I don't recall telling you when I'd finish today,' I said. I wasn't entirely sure I'd mentioned rehearsals at all.

'You didn't.' He tapped his nose and winked. 'Asked one of the staff.'

'Once a detective, eh?'

'Guilty as charged. How'd it go? Did you knock 'em dead?'

I almost laughed at his turn of phrase. There had been several times today when I'd have gladly knocked someone dead. 'To be honest, I'd rather not talk about it. Can we discuss something else?'

'Sorry, didn't mean to pry. Lesson learnt.' He looked like a scolded schoolboy, and I relented. Like most people who've never seen behind the showbiz curtain, Birch would never understand how mundane it is ninety-nine per cent of the time. If all you see is the final film cut, the TV broadcast, or the two hours spent onstage,

it's natural to think the entertainment business is, well, entertaining. But behind the performances lie hundreds of unseen hours of planning, auditions, rehearsal, logistics, administrative blather, bad food, more rehearsal, more logistics, worse food . . . not to mention the simple tedium of sitting around waiting for someone to shout '*go*' so you can finally walk on set and do your job.

Don't get me wrong, it's hardly digging ditches for a living. But the life of a jobbing actor is not filled with jet-set glamour.

'Tell you what,' I said, falling into stride beside him as we walked away from the theatre, 'if you promise not to interrupt, I'll regale you with the whole sorry story. Now, where are we going? St James's?'

'Right enough, then if Ronnie needs more, maybe over into Green Park.'

We continued on, and as promised I told him the whole story, from being buried under my mother's old clothes to my surprise recasting. I could practically feel him shaking with outrage on my behalf, wanting to interject. But he held it in, directing his grunts and gruff outbursts at Ronnie instead as the Lab pulled this way and that, sniffing at every square inch of his surroundings in case they were edible.

I finished my tales of theatrical woe, and admittedly felt better for having shared them with someone else.

'So that's my day,' I said. 'Please tell me yours was more normal.'

'Nothing but, ma'am,' he said briskly. 'Breakfast,

walk, lunch, walk, *Escape to the Country*, and here we are.'

Nobody would accuse Birch of being loquacious, but after forcing him to hold it in for so long I'd expected a verbal uncorking, not an appointment schedule.

'Who'd you have lunch with?' I asked, trying to get a little more out of him.

He responded with a confused look. 'Ronnie, of course.'

I sighed. After a lifetime in the Met, he was much better at asking questions than answering them. Much like how he couldn't stop addressing me as 'ma'am', because I apparently reminded him of his old detective chief superintendent.

It was nice that Birch didn't speak unless he had something to say, but it meant that I still didn't know much about him. He was a widower; he enjoyed the theatre; he lived in a modest, orderly house in Shepherd's Bush, over which his late wife Beatrice cast a long and enduring shadow; and that same shadow kept his wedding ring firmly on his left hand.

'Tell me something I don't know,' I said.

Without hesitation he replied, 'Most people think CID coppers automatically outrank uniform, but that's not true. For example, a desk sergeant is superior to a detective constable regardless of plain clothes.'

I laughed. 'I asked for that, but it's not what I had in mind. Tell me something about *yourself* I don't know.'

'Oh,' he squeaked. 'Um, well . . .'

Before he could answer, my phone spoilt the moment by ringing.

I pulled it out of my handbag to silence it, and recognised the same unknown number that had called earlier. 'Scammer,' I explained, showing Birch the *Unknown Caller* display on the screen. 'They already called me this morning—hey!'

Before I could protest, he took the phone from me, jabbed the Answer button, and growled angrily, 'Look here, this is DCI Birch of the Met. Delete this number immediately or there'll be trouble.'

Birch wasn't averse to occasionally using his old rank when it could be helpful, but I was in two minds about this response. On the one hand, even if he was tilting at windmills asking a phone scammer to care about the law, it was a gallant gesture; he all but puffed out his chest as he spoke, which I wasn't complaining about. On the other hand, he'd snatched my phone without asking and assumed I needed him to fight my battles, which is precisely the sort of thing I will happily complain about.

'Oh, very funny,' he continued. 'Pull the other one, sunshine.' Then he ended the call and handed my phone back.

'What on earth did they say?' I asked, curiosity winning out over annoyance.

'Claimed to be Crash Double. You know, Bad Dice singer. Classic band.'

After deciphering Birch's habitually clipped phrasing, I did indeed know who he meant. Bad Dice was an Irish

rock group from the 1970s, all long hair and loud guitars. Crash Double, their lead singer, was a notorious hip-swinger whom I'd briefly met once or twice at showbiz parties long ago. I realised this was something I did know about Birch. During a previous visit to his house, I'd noticed a collection of rock music records in his lounge, which had surprised me because to look at him you'd think he listens to nothing but marching bands.

'They still tour, don't they?'

'Absolutely. Saw them the year I retired. Great show. Not cheap, mind.'

'Why on earth would a scammer pretend to be an old rock star—*oh*.' Even as I said it, I came to my senses. 'Did it sound like Crash Double's voice? On the phone?'

'Oh, yes. Excellent impersonation.'

'And is Mr Double by any chance a dog owner?'

Birch shrugged. 'Unknown. Can't say I've seen him about.'

I was about to call the number back and find out when my phone buzzed again, displaying the same number. Staying well away from Birch's kleptomaniacal hands, I answered the call and wondered if I should ask for *Crash* or *Mr Double*. Fortunately, he spoke first.

'Look, is this Gwinny Tuffel or not?' asked a deep voice with a light Irish accent. 'I took this number on good faith, but if I've been set up for some kind of prank—'

'Not a prank, I assure you. Gwinny speaking, and I apologise for my *presumptious* friend.' I glared at Birch,

22

but he'd already turned away to focus on pulling Ronnie out of a bush. A squirrel popped out of the top and scurried up a nearby tree, completely unseen by the Lab.

'He's a nutcase, is what he is. Said he was a copper! Anyway, my name's Crash Double, I sing in a band called Bad Dice.'

'Yes, I know who you are, um . . .' I still didn't know how to address him. 'What should I call you?'

He laughed. 'Crash is fine. Listen, I need a dog sitter for Ace. Got a gig over the weekend, so I'll be away for a few days. Normally I'd ask my wife, but she went and got herself a boat cat.'

'I'm sorry, did you say *boat cat*?' Birch shot me a baffled look. No doubt, hearing only one side of the conversation must have been confusing. Mind you, I could hear both sides and wasn't much the wiser.

'Yeah. You know, a cat. On her boat. A boat cat. What would you call it?'

Fair enough, he had me there. Although what her boat had to do with it, I couldn't guess. I shook confusion from my head and asked, 'What dates, exactly? And whereabouts do you live?'

'On . . . a . . . boat,' he said slowly, as if talking to a child. 'In Little Venice.'

CHAPTER THREE

I've never been what you might call a water person. Some people long to cruise the world or imagine living out their days on a yacht. My father was a little that way; it's why he and my mother are now both scattered in the Tegernsee. But the most time I've ever spent continually on a boat was when that French musician came over in the nineties to perform at Docklands and I was invited onto a VIP barge for a close-up view. Naturally, this being London it promptly rained and blew a gale, and we could barely hear over the plastic rustle of our promotional rain ponchos supplied by the record label. Was the fact they had them prepared in advance sensible or suspicious? I could never decide.

Anyway, suffice to say I won't be joining my parents in a Bavarian lake. Bury me under a tree, at least that's useful.

So when Crash Double said he lived on a houseboat on the Regent's Canal, I wasn't as impressed as I think

he hoped. But I could use the money, and after Thursday morning's rehearsal *Mixed Mothers* paused for the bank holiday weekend anyway. I caught the Tube to Warwick Avenue Station and from there followed Crash's directions, walking a short distance to the main bridge junction at Little Venice.

To my right shone the triangular Pool where three canals meet. Tourist barges moved to and fro on the water but what caught my eye were the dozen or so narrowboats lined up side by side against the canal path, their occupants busily hanging bunting across their roofs. I had a sense of *déjà vu*, having seen something similar on my one previous trip to Little Venice many years ago.

Turning left took me onto Blomfield Road, then past the junction house and down to the canal path, finally to stand before a tall locked gate declaring this part of the canal for residents only.

I was a few minutes late, but so was Crash, assuming he was the tall, rangy man sauntering towards me along the path. Actually, *swaggering* is a better description; he had the confident gait of a singer, born of being worshipped for two hours onstage every night. Besides an occasional picture in the paper, I hadn't seen him for more than twenty years. I'm not much of a music person either, you see. It all tends to go in one ear and out the other.

Crash Double (Birch had told me with a tap of the nose that his real name was Shaun Donnelly, 'But even

his family calls him Crash,') wasn't a conventionally handsome man. Heavy eyebrows, a long nose, pointed chin and hair that had long ago flown the coop, for which he compensated with a white goatee. He was all bones, with barely a scrap of meat on him and, I couldn't help noting, no bum whatsoever. Flat as a billiard table. Nevertheless, he had the same bright-eyed presence as a good leading actor and a charisma that swept aside concerns about photogenic looks and made the simple t-shirt, scarf and faded jeans he wore seem like designer clothes. Come to think of it, they probably were.

Dog and owner were well-matched. By his side, collared but not on a lead, padded a dutiful Border Collie with a rough tricolour coat, mismatched brown-and-blue eyes, and asymmetrical ears. *Eine poppen, eine floppen* as my father would have said in deliberately comedic bad German. In a breed competition, Ace's non-standard features would only win a wooden spoon. But in combination with his canny expression, effervescent tail and enthusiastic grin, they somehow made a very charming dog.

'Gwinny,' said Crash with a smile, taking a key from his pocket to unlock the gate. 'Actually, have we met?'

'Many years ago, darling. Parties.' I slipped inside and crouched down to greet Ace as Crash locked the gate behind us. The Collie sat of his own volition and extended his nose to sniff me out – or more precisely the small bag of treats I'd brought in my handbag. 'Nothing wrong with your sense of smell, is there?' I looked to

26

Crash for guidance. 'Any allergies?'

'No chance. This one's a canine Hoover.'

I held the treat in my open hand and offered it to Ace. He was practically drooling for it, but didn't take it until I said, *Good boy, go on.* Then he scooped it off my hand with his tongue and swallowed it immediately. 'Did you even taste that? It hardly touched the sides!' I laughed and fussed him behind the ears. He fixed me with his bright blue eye, and grinned to give me an unexpectedly close and comprehensive look at his teeth. They were in excellent condition and his warm breath smelt fine. 'How old is he?'

'Six. Prime of his life, like us.' Crash winked and turned to lead me along the canal towpath. Ace forgot all about his ear skritches, hurrying to catch up and fall in alongside his owner. I wasn't surprised. Thanks to my father being a soft touch with the local rescue, our family had owned or fostered a full house of dogs over the years including a Border Collie named Daisy he'd brought home, enthusing about the breed's sharp intelligence. As if to prove him right, Daisy quickly divined that the ranking member of our household was in fact my mother and from then on hardly left her side.

'You don't keep him on-lead?' I asked.

'Never needed one,' said Crash. 'He's collared and tagged, but that's to keep the warden away. Ace would never run off.' We reached the first houseboat along the path, a large black structure. Crash stopped and turned to me. 'So, have you not been to Little Venice before?

You sounded unsure on the phone.'

'I attended the Canal Carnival once, years ago. That was very jolly, all the boats and bunting. Is that what they're doing over in the Pool today?'

'Bingo,' said Crash with a curled lip. 'You're about to attend your second Carnival, and you're welcome to it.'

'Not a fan?' I recalled the event as loud, colourful and happy. All the narrowboats had been strung with flags, buskers and street entertainers passed round the hat, fast-food vans kept everyone fed and many boats were opened to the public to educate them about this quintessentially British way of living.

'I hate every minute. Tourists everywhere, screaming kids, people gawping in your home. Luckily the bank holiday is the anniversary of our first proper gig in Dublin. So, every year we play two nights at the Olympia to celebrate, mostly fan club tickets. It's a great vibe and it gets me away from here while all this crap is going on.'

I had a sudden recollection of a past interview with Bad Dice on TV. 'Don't I remember you saying you were doing your last ever tour twenty years ago?'

'What can I say? It's a long tour.' He adopted a lopsided grin that had no doubt broken many a girl's heart.

'So these Dublin shows aren't your only concerts?'

'God, no. You must understand, sales aren't what they used to be, even for a so-called classic band like us.

It's all I can do to keep my head above water, pardon the pun.'

'Then you must go away often,' I said, alert to the possibility of a repeat client. 'Who looks after Ace normally?'

Crash gestured along the canal, lined on both sides with permanently moored houseboats. 'My wife's along there. She's always been up for it before but now she's got Lilith. The boat cat.'

I remembered the confusing phone call earlier but still felt unenlightened. 'Can we go back a few steps? You and your wife live on a boat, and you have a dog, but she's also gone and bought a cat? I'm not really a cat person, so you'll have to leave instructions for me while you're away.'

He looked puzzled, then laughed heartily. 'Ha! OK, we've got our wires crossed here. First of all, we don't live together. This is mine.' He rapped his knuckles on the side of the large black houseboat. 'She's my third wife, you see.' He smiled expectantly.

'Um, congratulations?'

'No, no,' he laughed. 'She's my third wife . . . and my first, and my second. Get it?'

The funny thing about fame and notoriety is that when you have it, suddenly everyone knows the intimate details of your private life. It's intrusive, and you wish they'd leave you alone . . . but it also means you can assume everyone you meet knows those details.

Of course, eventually the papers and gossip columns

lose interest and they really do leave you alone. Then you regain your private life, but at the cost of a serious blow to your ego.

Despite his fame, though, all I knew about Crash Double was that he sang in Bad Dice. I tried to let him down gently.

'Darling, I've been off the scene for too long. Caring for family, you understand. Indulge me.'

He produced a set of keys from his pocket. 'We're on our third go-around, for old times' sake. But if we tried living together again, we'd be onto the third divorce instead, you know?' I didn't, having never married let alone divorced, but nodded politely. 'I'm down here, she's up there, and she can't be looking after Ace any more. I'll introduce you later.'

The black houseboat occupied prime position at the head of the canal, and was also the largest. To be honest it barely resembled a boat at all, being a boxy shape and twice the width of a normal narrowboat. It was also twice the height, thanks to an unusual second-floor section along a third of its length. Crash saw me look up and shrugged.

'Eighteen months of fighting with the residents' association that took. Worth it, though. Grand views.'

He unlocked the front door and led me inside (or should I say *on board*?). It struck me that I'd never set foot inside a proper houseboat before. I'd been on a regular narrowboat once or twice, but this was on a different order of magnitude.

The most immediate and obvious difference was the front door, which opened from the side facing the path, and this narrow entrance hall into which we'd stepped, with stairs leading up to that second floor. But then Crash led me into the lounge (which he explained boaters call a *saloon*) and I gasped. First, because there was more space to move about in here than in the whole of a normal barge. Second, because you couldn't actually move about for the mountains of paraphernalia. Records, CDs, old videotapes, band memorabilia and more filled the room, threatening to trip anyone unwary enough to put a foot wrong.

A somewhat worn-looking sofa sat against one wall, while against another stood an upright piano, watched over by framed gold discs mounted on the wall. Facing it was a spirits bar with a polished wooden counter. In one corner stood a single bookshelf whose contents alternated between wellness guides and historical biographies: Churchill, Napoleon, Mandela, the usual suspects. There was no TV, I noted, so I resolved to bring a jigsaw puzzle with me for entertainment.

Opposite the sofa, tall French windows dominated the centre of the wall facing the canal. To one side of them was a stereo that looked worth more than my house. On the other side lay Ace's bed, on which he'd flopped down as soon as we entered the saloon and where he now methodically tore up pieces of cardboard.

'Every few days I get a box from Choudhury up the road,' Crash explained. 'When I go out, Ace dismantles

and shreds it to cope. Did you know collies can have autism? I can't be sure if it's that, but he definitely suffers from separation anxiety. Pity I can't give him a Xanax, you know?'

I nodded in sympathy. Separation anxiety is a hard thing to deal with, especially in Border Collies, who need mental stimulation as well as physical exercise. I noted with approval that Crash kept a plastic box of toys next to Ace's bed, including flying discs, ball launchers and even some puzzle feeders.

'Better he destroys a cardboard box than your sofa, eh?'

'Exactly. He loves having a job to do, and it gives him something to focus on instead of worrying. I'll walk up to Choudhury's and get a new box tomorrow morning to occupy him until you get here.'

Beyond the spirits bar lay an open-plan kitchen (the *galley*, apparently) where a chrome-top stove gleamed. Was Crash an assiduous cleaner or just someone who never cooked? The pitifully bare cupboards suggested the latter, holding little more than dog food, multipacks of crisps and energy bars.

Further on, a corridor led first to the bathroom and then Crash's bedroom. I braced myself for silk sheets and a mirrored ceiling, but to my pleasant surprise I found cosy rumpled bedclothes with a thick woollen throw, a spartan wardrobe and a second dog bed for Ace. On reflection, black satin probably didn't go well with a rough-coated tricolour dog. A dresser stood by

a window overlooking the water, piled high with male grooming products. Wedged into its mirror frame was an old paparazzi photo of Crash with a young woman on his arm. She looked familiar. A late-night Channel 4 presenter, perhaps? I didn't feel I knew him well enough to ask.

Finally, we returned to the entrance hallway, and I realised along the way that no windows faced the path. Aside from the front door, every view outside faced the water, presumably to maintain his privacy. So as we climbed the stairs to the second floor, where he'd boasted of 'grand views', I anticipated easy chairs, a sun lounger, perhaps even a yoga mat to fit my impression of him so far: an ageing rock star who left the business end to other people while he walked his dog, basked in gold discs and nostalgia, and did yoga every morning to feel better about takeaway the night before.

Don't get me wrong, I didn't begrudge him. He'd earned it, and God knows I wouldn't turn it down if it came my way.

But my expectations were confounded when I entered what appeared to be a hi-tech recording studio. Synthesiser keyboards lined the room, all hooked into one of those big recording consoles bristling with knobs and switches. Two large speakers stood on either side of what I assumed was the main desk, with a large computer monitor, a keyboard and more dials and buttons. Beside them sat a large mobile phone, in a photo case printed with a picture of Ace. Underneath

the desk stood a huge metal-cased computer and in front of it an expensive Aeron chair. Finally, a dozen different microphones stood around the room on adjustable stands, ranging from old-fashioned crooner models to the kind of high-precision 'shotgun' mics I was familiar with from TV.

'Are you sure you have enough equipment?' I asked cheekily.

Crash smiled. 'You can never have enough.' He pointed out a series of small mesh circles embedded in the walls. 'There are mics hooked up around the room, too, for when inspiration strikes.'

'I'll be sure not to sing in the shower, then.'

He laughed. 'Don't worry, they're not permanently recording. But it's an easy one-touch control. See?' He pressed a button on the desk to demonstrate, but nothing happened.

'I'm sorry, was that supposed to do something?' I asked.

'Oh, it did. Watch.' He pressed another button next to it, and suddenly I heard my own voice asking, *'I'm sorry, was that supposed to do something?'*

As I took all this in, Ace padded up the stairs, deftly squeezed past me and walked over to his third and final bed, nestled under one of the synthesiser stands, from which he watched us and lazily wagged his tail.

Crash laughed. 'Here, you'll enjoy this. Take a seat.' He gestured for me to sit in the Aeron. I did, watching him carefully as he leant over me to wake the computer

with a password, then tap and click on things. The desktop was a jumble of files, and when he started using some music software it all went entirely over my head. But Crash whizzed around the screen, very familiar and comfortable with it all.

Suddenly a traditional Irish reel began playing from the speakers. Crash stepped away as Ace's ears pricked up and the dog practically leapt off his bed to meet Crash halfway. He sat, waiting for a signal . . .

And then they danced.

Well, that's being kind and seeing it through a dog-lover's eyes, I suppose. But as I watched, Crash led Ace with a gesturing hand, turning around and weaving the dog between his legs, all in time to the rhythm of the music. It was a long way from Crufts, but it was delightful nonetheless and got even better when Crash began singing along in Gaelic. Neither he nor Ace missed a beat.

Abruptly the song stopped and Crash knelt down to give Ace a ruffle around the neck and ears. The Collie panted with delight but clearly could have gone for another song or ten. Crash gave him a treat, smiling all the time. Then he leant over me, put the computer back to sleep and picked up his phone.

'Something new I've been working on. All these years and I never did anything traditional, you know?'

'So you miss Ireland?' I asked as we returned downstairs.

'God, no,' he laughed. 'Miserable, cold, damp place.

I couldn't wait to get away. But the nostalgia kicks in as you get older. You'll see.'

I could have reminded him there was only a decade between us but whether he was merely being polite or really did think I looked younger than my age, I wasn't about to contradict him.

After seeing that mess of files on his computer, the state of the lounge made more sense. At least an agile dog like Ace could easily navigate the precarious towers of memorabilia. Crash unlocked the French windows with a key and pulled them open; they looked directly out onto the canal through an exterior guard rail.

'This room would be great for parties if you tidied up a bit,' I said. 'Do you have a cleaner . . . ?'

'Sure and I'll just call Bono round for dinner. No, I'm flattered, but my partying days are over and I like the place as it is. Although I should get that rail removed.'

'I assumed it was to stop Ace from jumping in the canal.'

Crash laughed. 'I suppose that's a bonus, but actually it was to stop idiots like Johnny from getting hammered and falling in.'

Presumably he meant the Bad Dice guitarist, Johnny Roulette. I remembered Birch enthusing about him after Crash had called me in the park.

'Has that actually happened?'

'More than once, until I had the rail installed. But like I say, those days are over.'

'The partying, or Johnny's drinking?' It was a

mischievous question, but I'd known enough actors who fell prey to the bottle over the years to understand the problems it could cause.

'Both.' He looked troubled for a moment, then his easy smile returned. 'Let's show you round the walk.'

We left the house with Ace in tow, and Crash looked up the path towards the Maida Vale bridge. Further along, a woman stepped off a boat painted in patchwork rainbow colours. Potted plants covered its roof and hung over the sides. She did something with a rope on the towpath, then saw us and waved. Crash waved back, and as I raised my hand to join in, Ace sprinted down the path. In the blink of an eye the dog was sitting obediently at the woman's feet while she stroked his fur.

'Your wife, presumably?' I said. 'I still can't get over the idea that you live on separate boats. Do you, um, alternate—?' I considered what I was about to say and stopped myself. 'Sorry, none of my business.'

Crash laughed anyway. 'The spirit is willing but the flesh is weak, Gwinny. No scheduling complications there.'

I felt my cheeks flush. It really wasn't my business, but Crash had so readily put me at ease that I felt I was chatting with an old friend, not someone I'd barely met before today.

'Can't live with 'em . . . can't live with 'em,' said a voice behind us, chuckling.

A man who wouldn't have looked out of place on a

picket line approached along the towpath. His square-shouldered coat was festooned with button badges, he wore a flat cap atop a wide head, and his jeans ended in two-inch turn-ups over heavy boots.

'I'll thank you not to cast aspersions on my good wife, now,' said Crash, looking the man up and down. I couldn't say why exactly, but this new arrival didn't look like a resident. I wondered how he'd got in through the gate and what he wanted with Crash. There was a tension in the air, like one of them might throw a punch. Both men looked about the same age, but I'd have put my money on Mr Picket Line any day.

Then they laughed and embraced in a half-handshake, half-hug movement and I felt foolish.

'This is Johnny,' said Crash, turning back to me. 'Johnny Roulette, meet Gwinny. She'll dog-sit Ace while we're in Dublin.'

'Sure and you're Gwinny Tuffel,' repeated Johnny, smiling. 'I remember you from the telly. Looking good, pet, are you well? D'you have your health? Course you do, you're grand. What brings you out here? Don't let this one play games with you, now. How are you?'

I wasn't sure which of this barrage of questions to answer first, or if he even expected an answer. Crash saved me by asking, 'What's the tale, Johnny? Early for you, isn't it?'

'That's a fine thanks for me making an effort. It's the big one, you know it gets me all excited. Have you

been rehearsing your words? We don't want Live Aid all over again.'

'For God's sake, that was forty years ago. Have I ever dropped a lyric since?' Crash stage whispered to me, 'He's showing off. One sniff of a girl and Johnny Roulette reverts to a spotty fourteen-year-old.'

Johnny gamely ignored this ribbing, while I made sure to keep Crash between the guitarist and me to prevent any such sniffing. Luckily by now we'd reached Crash's wife, who stood on the path fussing Ace as we approached. When she looked up in greeting, I had two sudden revelations. First, that I was looking at Fox Double-Jones, whose gardening programmes had been a guilty pleasure during the years of caring for my father. That explained all the plants on the boat's roof. Second, I saw now that she was the woman in the photo on Crash's dresser. She had indeed been a late-night TV host, young and glamorous, but unlike most of her contemporaries Fox had successfully reinvented herself as she aged out of the party girl bracket. She'd now been a celebrity gardener for decades longer than she'd been a starlet.

While watching her dig up borders and plant hedgerows, it had never occurred to me that Double was her husband's name (especially as it wasn't even his real name) or that she was a rock star's wife, thrice married to the same man. That's showbiz.

'Morning, boys,' she said brightly. A black cat poked its head out from the houseboat's open door behind Fox

as she offered me a hand. 'You must be—'

But our pleasantries were interrupted by sound and fury as Ace spied the cat and gave chase, barking furiously and scrabbling down the stairs into Fox's boat.

'Oh, no! Lilith, run! Ace, stop it!'

A frantic *meow* sounded from somewhere inside.

CHAPTER FOUR

'Ace, no! Leave!' Crash shouted, giving chase with Fox following close behind. Johnny and I looked at each other, then he shrugged and strolled after them with no sense of urgency. Rather than remain outside on the towpath like a spare wheel, I brought up the rear.

It took me a moment to get my bearings as the interior of Fox's houseboat was unlike anything I'd seen before, including Crash's place moments ago. This boat only had one floor but that was far from the main difference.

In some ways it was more like my own house, filled to the brim with what other people might call clutter but I call evidence of a life. Not that I don't intend to clear some of it out, but the minimal lifestyle holds no appeal for me.

Fox's house wasn't filled with books and jigsaw puzzles, though, or even piles of music memorabilia. Instead, it was full of plants. Plants in pots standing on the floor, plants in pots balanced on stools, plants in baskets hanging from wall brackets, plants in troughs

lined up on shelves. Even a large glass display cabinet was filled with yet more pots and plants of all shapes and sizes.

I could barely see the walls behind all this greenery, which may have been a blessing in disguise because they were a gaudy clash of purple and orange. Somehow it suited this crazed interior rainforest.

We found Ace standing on a hippy-chic sofa that, at first glance, I took for a pile of duvets. Back feet on the seat and front paws on the chair back, he gazed unblinking at Lilith the black cat. She hissed at the Collie from behind a plant pot, safely out of reach atop a shelf unit, protected by cacti.

'Ace, get down! *Heel*!' Crash called. The dog looked at him, looked back at Lilith, then realised he was on a hiding to nothing. Ace jumped down from the couch and returned to Crash's side.

In most other dogs I might have been surprised to see them give up so easily, but despite his wonky features, Ace was a Border Collie through and through. Our family house in Chelsea was as far from the herding-sheep farm lifestyle as a dog could get, but Daisy had also been capable of snapping from playful family pet to obedient working dog in a heartbeat. I handed Crash a dog treat from my pocket which he gratefully took and gave to Ace.

Then he took a bottle from his own pocket, unscrewed it and removed a pill which he swallowed dry. 'Anti-anxiety,' he said with a wink.

I was about to suggest he clip a lead on Ace, then remembered he didn't have one. To be fair, it didn't seem necessary; the dog now sat patiently at his owner's side, appearing to ignore the cat completely. I doubted that was truly the case but as long as he didn't act on it there was no harm. Lilith, for her part, remained atop the shelf, carefully grooming herself behind a spiny cactus while keeping one eye out for opportunist dogs.

'As I was saying, you must be Gwinny,' said Fox, sitting on the many-layered sofa. 'Crash told me you're looking after Ace while he's away. Have we met before?'

'No, but we were almost certainly at some of the same parties years ago.' I gestured to the array of plants. 'I watch your show, though. It was a big help to me over the past ten years.' I explained about my father and she took my hand.

'I'm sorry, but I'm also glad I could help. So you're a gardener too?'

'Heavens, no,' I laughed. 'Strictly wildflowers and a badly mowed lawn. But I like watching other people do it. Like those shows where a foolhardy young couple build a house halfway up an Italian mountain. I admire their ambition but preferably from the safety of my living room.'

'Sure and you've got a fan, Trips,' laughed Johnny.

'Why don't you give her the tour?' Crash added. 'Get some practice in for the weekend, like. Johnny and me need to talk about the gig.'

This was news to Johnny. 'For what? After thirty

years we can do it in our sleep. You probably have.'

'Ah, come on. Give the ladies some privacy.' Crash put a hand on Johnny's arm and guided him back to the door, taking Ace with them.

'"Trips"?' I asked when they were out of earshot.

'A silly nickname. Married three times to a man called Double, so Johnny says I should change my name to Triple-Jones. Cheeky sod, but it's his way.'

'I suppose being married to Crash for so long, you must have known Johnny all this time too.'

She laughed. 'They come as a pair, right enough. Don't you worry, I give as good as I get. Now let me show you around.'

The tour took in her whole boat, apart from a spare room which she said contained personal items. Every other room, and almost every flat surface, featured plants of some kind, from exotic bromeliads to common tulips and everything in between. Even with my layman's interest it all blurred together.

'I'm amazed you can keep track of what's where,' I said. 'You sound as if you've given this tour a hundred times before.'

'I have. During the Carnival I open the boat to visitors and take families around. I often practise on the residents, too.'

'Ah,' I said, understanding. 'That's what Crash meant about preparing for the weekend.'

'Not that I need it, but yeah. Kids always love these in particular.' She gestured to the glass cabinet I'd noticed

earlier, which I now saw was locked. 'My poisonous collection,' she explained. 'Deadly nightshade, monk's hood, burning bush, and so on. Always gets their attention.'

'I assume the key is safely hidden away?'

'Of course. Well, it will be.' Her glance flicked to a brightly painted jug on a shelf with a pair of gloves poking from its mouth. 'Don't worry, tomorrow morning I'll put that away in a cupboard, far from little hands. Do you have children?'

'Not even married,' I said. 'Although, these days one doesn't necessarily follow the other. You?'

Fox smiled. 'Just Ellie, but she's long flown. Lives in Tokyo now, married to a government minister. Her own form of rebellion, I suppose.'

'She didn't feel the pull of show business?'

'I think seeing two divorces and plenty of smashed crockery over the years put her off. But then, loving someone means giving them ammunition to hurt you, doesn't it? Anyway, she's happy. That's all I care about.'

I've seen enough eternally on-again-off-again showbiz partnerships not to pass judgement. Instead, I changed the subject.

'So you're a fan of the Carnival, I take it? Crash tells me he can't wait to get away.'

'That's because he's a miserable old sod,' she said. 'I've told them, they should get the band to put on a show, play on a barge in the Pool. People would love that, and it'd smooth the waters between him and Lucy.

But he won't miss the anniversary concert. Every year, like clockwork.'

'Who's Lucy?'

'The Carnival organiser. It's so silly, they're always at loggerheads.'

I thanked Fox for the tour, said goodbye to Lilith the black cat, and left with flashbacks to the rain-soaked Docklands concert running through my mind. Dublin anniversary aside, I couldn't blame Crash for not wanting to trust the British weather.

Climbing the steps to the deck, I heard low voices talking. Actually, more like arguing, in the quiet and urgent way people do when they don't want to be overheard. To my surprise the voices belonged to Crash and Johnny, standing close together on the path with their backs to me. I saw Johnny take something from his pocket but couldn't see what it was.

Then Ace noticed me and barked, the traitor. Both men turned hastily, now smiling and relaxed. There was no sign of whatever it was Johnny had been holding.

'How'd you like the tour?' asked Crash.

'Delightful,' I said. 'I'm sure lots of people will enjoy it during the Carnival too.'

He grimaced, earning a hearty laugh and a slap on the shoulder from Johnny. 'She's got the measure of you, Crash. Gwinny, a pleasure. You'll be here when we get back, won't you? Of course you will. Maybe you can get us a ticket to your next show, that'll be grand.'

'Do you live here on the boats as well?' I asked. Was

46

half the canal related to Bad Dice?

'Not at all, the water's not for me. I'm on the Crescent, a hop and a skip away.'

A thought formed in my mind. 'Then I wonder if you could recommend a good builder?'

I'd spoken briefly to Bostin Jim's man, a local tradesman called Darren who, in a stroke of uncommon luck, could actually fit me in on the condition he started early next week. He still hadn't supplied an estimate, though, so I wanted to have at least one fallback.

'Actually, I—' Crash began then stopped himself. 'Yeah, yeah, he probably does. Johnny?'

'Sure, and I had some people in last year. Give me your number, pet. I'll text you.'

'Hold on,' I laughed, 'I'll need to look it up. I can never remember my own mobile number.'

Crash rolled his eyes. 'I've got it, Johnny. I'll send it to you later. Go on, now.'

'Grand,' said Johnny. 'See you in Dublin.' He bent down to fuss Ace. 'Take care of the old man, now. Make sure he learns his lyrics, you hear?' Then he walked away down the path chuckling to himself.

'Shouldn't you unlock the access gate for him?' I asked Crash.

'Just watch.'

The guitarist reached the gate, gripped its railings, hauled himself up, and easily climbed over it. He made it look effortless.

'Told you he's a show-off. Runs around like he's still

twenty years old. And speaking of . . .'

I followed his gaze a few moorings down to a lovely, traditional-looking boat. It was another one twice the width of a regular barge but unlike Crash's was shaped in the traditional English style. It looked very well maintained, as did the man who stood on its deck and waved to us.

'That's Howard Zee,' said Crash. 'Not his real name, of course. He's . . . actually, I'll let him explain. He'd prefer that.'

Howard Zee was tall, athletically built, and proud of it. As we watched he lifted a heavy gas bottle and lowered it into a trapdoor, showing off his chest and arms under a fitted sleeveless vest. He wore a bulky computerised watch on one wrist but no other jewellery, and was completely bald with a bushy white beard. The overall effect made it hard to guess his age which I imagined was the point.

He closed and locked the trapdoor, wiped his hands on a rag, then reached for a plastic jug of dark green liquid perched on the roof. He swigged from it and smiled at us, leaning against the boat in a studied, languorous pose.

'Afternoon, Howard,' said Crash. 'This is Gwinny, she'll be looking after Ace for the weekend.'

'Gwinny Tuffel, of course,' he said, dazzling me with a made-for-TV smile. 'I didn't recognise you with the grey hair. It suits you well.'

'You've nothing on today?' Crash asked.

'Plenty, but I'm between sessions,' Howard replied. 'I did three this morning and I resume at half four for the evening. Can't start too early, they all want to have time with the children after they're brought home.'

'Brought home?' I asked. 'What do you mean?'

'Howard's yummy mummies aren't going to sit in school traffic themselves for an hour,' said Crash playfully. 'That's what nannies are for, isn't it?'

Howard took the ribbing in good humour. 'Those "yummy mummies" are some of my best-paying clients. Probably yours, too. Who do you think is paying three hundred quid for your VIP tickets, Crash? It's not a struggling teenage mother collecting her dole, is it?'

By now I was thoroughly confused, and frankly hoped I was getting the wrong end of the stick. 'Clients for what, Mr Zee? What do you do?'

'Howard, please,' he said, his expression turning serious. 'I'm a body and mind wellness guide. Don't you think today's modern world demands so much of us, Gwinny? It saps our ability to focus on the truly important spirit of our inner self and it's our collective responsibility as superconscious human beings to say "No!" The world is dying of thirst, but if we don't take time to replenish our own well, how can we offer water to others? I help seekers find their own unique path through yoga, relaxation and mental reassurance, guiding them to inner fulfilment and contentment.'

I waited for this well-practised spiel to end, then

asked, 'And how much does inner fulfilment go for, these days?'

'Eighty pounds per group Zoom session, or two hundred and fifty for a personalised guided experience on board,' he said without hesitation. He swigged more of the green liquid, which I guessed was some kind of health drink.

'But the first is always free, isn't that right, Howard?' said Crash, nudging me. 'Maybe you should sign up, Gwinny.'

'I'm perfectly content, thank you.' The truth of that could be argued but I had no desire to pay someone for the torture of having my limbs twisted into yogic knots.

'I don't think I could anyway, Gwinny. I only take clients over forty years old.'

I almost gagged at this transparent flattery, particularly after he'd already recognised me. 'You're too kind,' I said, and quickly changed the subject. 'This boat is lovely. Quite traditional compared to most of the other residents.'

'Which is ironic seeing as Howard's the new boy on the block,' said Crash. 'But you're right, she's a fine craft. Aqualine, isn't it?'

Howard ran a loving hand across the boat's lacquered exterior. 'She's my saviour, really.' He turned to me. 'Crash has been so welcoming, as has everyone else. This is such an intimate community. Are you considering life on the water, Gwinny?'

'The water's not for me,' I demurred, echoing Johnny's

response, 'but I can appreciate a good-looking boat. Crash, don't you think we'd better move on before Ace gets restless?' In fact, the Collie was happily lying on the path to watch ducks paddle by on the water, but he was a convenient excuse.

'Absolutely. We need to get you a set of keys, anyway. See you later, Howard.'

Howard beamed his smile again, parting the thick white beard and deepening his telltale crow's feet. In the afternoon light I now saw that even his baldness was fake. Stubble marks betrayed a shaved head, presumably befitting a guru.

'A pleasure to meet you, Gwinny,' he said. 'Do stop by again.'

'Not without a chaperone,' Crash muttered as we walked away.

I laughed. 'I don't think Howard is my type. Or that I'm his, despite the sales pitch. Fancy doing yoga sessions from his boat!'

'To hear him tell it, he didn't have much choice. Laid off, divorced, lost the house, so he came down here a couple of years ago and spent everything he had left on the boat. As for you not being his type, you're in the right half of the population and that's normally enough for Howard.' He quickly added, 'Uh, not that you're – you know, I mean . . . well . . . you're a perfectly fine . . .'

I enjoyed watching him squirm in the wake of his *faux pas*, but eventually spared him. 'No offence taken. Believe me, I've met plenty like Howard Zee before.'

'I don't doubt that for a moment. Here now, let's get you my spare keys.'

Crash stepped inside his houseboat and took a ring of two keys from a sideboard; one for the front door, one for the French windows. Then he walked back out onto the towpath, gesturing for me to follow. Ace tried to come with us too, but Crash firmly told him to stay. The Collie obeyed, sitting and watching us as we stepped outside and closed the door.

The singer shrugged at my quizzical expression. 'I was burgled a while back, so I had the locks changed.' He quickly added, 'Don't worry, they were donkey's years old. I reckon someone got a key copy from an old set somehow and tried their luck. Besides, they didn't take anything. There's nothing worth lifting.'

'I doubt that,' I said. 'Your band memorabilia, the record collection . . . not to mention all that equipment upstairs. So the police didn't catch anyone?'

'Do they ever? Anyway, these modern mechanisms are great.' He locked the door, and I heard the reassuring heavy click of multiple bolts engaging. 'But I haven't actually tried the spare keys yet, so go ahead. It'll do Ace good to see someone else unlock the door and go in.'

He stood back as I inserted the main key and turned it to unlock. Through the door's small windowpane Ace eagerly watched my every move, his wagging tail banging a tattoo on the floor. I pushed the door open and walked inside, then rewarded the Collie with another treat.

'Perfect,' said Crash. 'Be here for eight, and take Ace

for a walk when you arrive. He'll be ready for it by then and you can feed him when you get back.'

'Wait, you won't be here?'

Crash shrugged. 'I'm an early bird. I'll take Ace for his usual dawn walk, then get a cab to the airport. As long as you're here by eight he'll be fine.'

'And when do you get back?'

'Gig nights are Sunday and Monday, and I'll be on the first flight home Tuesday morning.' He looked around, as if running a mental checklist. 'Now, I've showed you the food, towels, his toys . . . I think that's everything?'

It was everything to do with Ace, but he'd hardly shown me anything about how to live here for the weekend as a human. I'd have to buy in some groceries, for a start. That wouldn't be a problem, though. Little Venice's isolation is deceptive; walk half a mile and you're back in regular old London.

'Yes, I think that's everything,' I said. 'Don't you worry about Ace, I'll take good care of him. We'll have a fun time while he's off rock and rolling, won't we, boy?' The dog looked from his owner to me. With Border Collies it's easy to imagine they really do understand every word. As if to confirm this, Ace padded over, sat down beside me and leant his head against my leg.

I said goodbye and walked back to Warwick Avenue Station, smiling in the spring sun. Notwithstanding the sheer amount of exercise that any Collie requires, I looked forward to a nice relaxing weekend.

How wrong could a woman be?

CHAPTER FIVE

The next morning, I woke to find four waiting text messages that sent my mood on a rollercoaster ride. The first was from Crash, sent the previous evening to tell me he'd given Johnny Roulette my number. The next was a few minutes later, from an unknown number that turned out to be Johnny, with the details for a builder. I added both to my contacts. The third text was from Crash again, this time sent an hour ago, to inform me he was setting off for the airport and trusting I'd take good care of Ace. I smiled at his concern and sent a quick reply telling him to break a leg, assuring him Ace was in good hands.

The final message was from Darren, the builder recommended by Bostin Jim, sending me an estimated cost that quickly wiped the smile off my face. Did he think everyone who lived in Chelsea was loaded? Did he not understand the concept of 'property rich but cash poor'? These were things I would have asked him in no

uncertain terms if he'd deigned to answer his phone, but after it rung out again on the third attempt I stopped trying and replied to the text using an emoji of a bundle of cash with wings flying away. This made me feel very modern and with-it, which cheered me up until I realised I'd have to continue gathering quotes and find someone I could actually afford. Thank goodness I'd had the sense to get a recommendation from Johnny.

Brushing my teeth, I wondered again if I'd have to take a pay cut on *Mixed Mothers*. If I was honest with myself, though, the indignity bothered me more than the money. Not that I hadn't been passed over for a younger face when auditioning before; every actress over thirty has experienced that. But to be replaced *after* casting was a new kind of embarrassment.

Still, I couldn't dwell on it now. Ace was waiting for me.

I guzzled some coffee, filled a tote bag with spare clothes, dog necessities and a jigsaw puzzle I'd bought for the occasion, then dashed out of the house. I locked up, popped the key in my purse and turned to find the Dowager Lady Ragley standing six inches away on my doorstep.

'Guinevere, my dear. You haven't forgotten the matter of the workmen, I trust?' She glanced upwards, as if I needed to be reminded of the crumbling render.

'It's a bank holiday, my lady,' I said, squeezing past her. I decided not to tell her about my failure to find someone so far, as it would invite further conversation.

'Oh, is it? How tiresome.'

'Don't worry, there'll be someone here to fix things before you know it. Must dash, bye!' And with that I rushed along the street towards the King's Road.

It was only when I arrived at Little Venice that I noticed the keyring Crash had given me didn't include a key for the residents' access gate. I called out, but nobody answered. Either they couldn't hear me, or nobody was yet awake. Or they were simply ignoring me.

But I couldn't stand there forever in the hope someone would emerge. Ace was waiting and it was now a couple of hours since the text from Crash to say he was departing. Remembering Johnny Roulette's antics the day before, I shifted the tote bag to put the weight across my back and gripped the gate railings. Then I hoisted one foot halfway up the gate, which for a shortie like me was no mean feat, and pulled myself up despite the metal jabbing painfully into my tennis shoes.

'Hey! What are you playing at?' shouted a man's voice behind me.

Startled, I lost my balance, tried to get a firmer grip, failed, and toppled backwards to the ground. Or I would have, if my inquisitor hadn't been so close that I actually fell on top of him instead. I both heard and felt the air being pushed out of him as he struck the paving, and I lay still for a moment trying to steady myself. Then I rolled off and pulled myself upright with the help of the gate, simultaneously explaining and apologising.

'I'm so very sorry, you startled me, and you see I'm actually house-sitting for someone whose boat is through here, but he forgot to give me a key to the gate, and hang on a minute, didn't I meet you yesterday?'

Howard Zee, the wellness guru, pushed himself into a sitting position and rubbed his winded stomach. He wore a hooded top, jogging bottoms and scuffed trainers, evidently returning from a morning run.

'I was pulling your leg,' he said weakly. 'Although I didn't mean to pull it on top of me.'

I helped him to his feet. 'I really am sorry. The only contact number I have for anyone on the canal is Crash himself, and obviously he's in Dublin. Or mid-flight by now, anyway.'

Howard unzipped a pocket in his jogging bottoms, removed a key, and used it to unlock the gate. After we passed through, he locked it again behind us. 'For all the good it does to keep people out, as you so aptly demonstrated,' he said. 'Listen, I've got a spare key at home. Why don't you borrow it for the weekend?'

'That's very kind. You're right, it's really not much security, is it?' Climbing the gate wasn't as easy as Johnny had made it look. The guitarist was bigger than me, undoubtedly stronger, and unlike my tennis shoes his heavy boots would allow him to clamber over without a second thought. But anyone determined and prepared enough could do it. No wonder the police hadn't been able to find whoever burgled Crash's boat.

As we walked along the path a procession of

narrowboats floated past us towards the Pool. 'Plenty coming for the Carnival, I see.'

Howard followed my gaze. 'If you're staying at Crash's, I warn you now that you won't get any peace. The price of being boat number one is you're within earshot of Rembrandt Gardens, just over the bridge, where they entertain the kids. Before Saturday's done, you'll be able to recite the Punch & Judy show from memory.'

I laughed. 'You're not a fan of the festivities either, then?'

'Heavens, no, I love it. Anything to bring some life to the area. The residents don't normally mix with the cruisers, you see.'

'But what's the difference? Surely you're all boaters?'

'Don't go saying that too loud around here,' he laughed. 'We tend to keep to ourselves . . . apart from during the Carnival.'

We reached Crash's houseboat, and through the door I saw Ace already lying in the hallway. 'New locks,' I explained to Howard as I opened the door. 'That's probably why the gate key isn't on this ring.'

I stepped inside and playfully shuffled Ace backward to make some room to walk past. 'Poor thing! Let me put these things down and then we'll go for a walk, OK?'

I thought that was a perfectly reasonable request, but Ace disagreed. He bounded past me, out of the door and onto the towpath, where he first cocked his leg up the bushes on the far side, then squatted down and unloaded

a substantial poo on the flagstones.

Howard watched with bemusement as Ace stood up, shook himself, and proceeded to sniff enthusiastically at the guru's ankles. 'You're really not used to being on your own, are you?' he laughed, and reached down to skritch the Collie's ears.

I opened the tote to find a dog bag and grimaced upon seeing the 1,000-piece jigsaw I'd brought along. The box had been between me and Howard when I'd fallen on him and was flat as a pancake. I'd deal with that later. For now, I tore off a bag to collect Ace's business.

'There's a bin outside the gate,' said Howard. 'You're definitely going to need that key.'

Murmuring agreement, I tied off the bag and for the time being placed it on the path outside the door, where nobody would step on it. Then I led Ace back inside and began emptying my tote in the lounge. Removing the dog bags, a lead and the crushed jigsaw left only my spare clothes.

I heard the main entrance close and looked up to see Howard Zee leaning in the lounge doorway. Rather presumptious, I thought. But a close-knit community like this was probably the sort of place where people walked in and out without waiting to be invited.

Meanwhile, Ace had found a flying ring, the doughnut type with a hole in the middle, and held it in his mouth for me to take. Howard looked down and smiled. 'Too smart for his own good, that one.'

'Yes, well, that's collies for you. *Give*,' I said to Ace,

who obeyed and released the ring into my hand. '*Sit.*' He did, and I popped the ring over his head to rest around his neck. 'In my experience, a well-trained Collie will do absolutely anything you tell it to – unless that thing is "relax and take a nap", of course.'

My clothes could wait. I clipped on the dog lead I'd brought along – Crash might be confident enough not to use one, but Ace and I were barely acquainted so I wasn't taking chances – and it was then I noticed the tiny shreds of cardboard scattered on the floor around his dog bed. Crash wasn't kidding about Ace's separation anxiety; the dog had made very short work of that morning's box.

I turned to leave, but Howard stood in my way. 'Before you go running around the park, why not walk with me to my place?' He placed a hand on my arm and gently squeezed. 'I'll give you my spare key, and maybe we could—'

Whatever else he was about to suggest was interrupted by a knock at the door. 'That'll be the postman,' I said, unsure if the post even delivered here but using it as an excuse to slip out of Howard's grip.

The knocking was immediately followed by the sound of the front door being opened, and a woman's voice calling out, 'Crash? It's only me. I called last night but you must have been busy, so I—*aah*!' She saw me, Ace and Howard step into the entrance hall and recoiled, jumping backwards out of the door and onto the towpath, mercifully missing the filled poo bag.

Clearly this was no postal worker. Instead, standing

on the path but now poking her head back inside the doorway was a strikingly elegant east-Asian woman, forty-something, wearing tweeds, Hunters and a hiking gilet over a sweater. The ensemble gave her an air of somewhere between 'country manor lady' and 'local government official', though I suppose there's no law against being both.

'Hello, Lucy,' said Howard, immediately stepping towards her. 'Don't worry, we're all friends here.' He placed his hand on her arm, much as he had with me, and I began to wonder whether Mr Zee was touchy-feely because he was divorced . . . or divorced because of his wandering hands?

Lucy, though, returned the guru's smile. 'Hi, Howard. I'm sorry, I've come at a bad time. It's an impromptu visit, Crash wasn't expecting me.' She raised her voice and called past me, 'I'll come back later, OK? No worries.'

'He's not here, and he won't be here later, either,' I said, ushering everyone out onto the towpath and locking the door behind us. 'He's in Dublin for the weekend, performing.'

'Gone at the crack of dawn, as usual,' said Howard. 'Do you know one another, by the way?'

The woman looked me up and down as if assessing me, and from the expression on her face I didn't make the cut.

'My name's Gwinny,' I explained. 'I'm dog-sitting Ace while Crash is away.'

'Lucy Kwok,' she said in a tone implying I should curtsy. 'Carnival Chairperson.'

'Yes, Fox told me. So I imagine you two must have an interesting relationship?'

The question seemed to catch her off guard. 'What do you mean?'

'Only that I gather Crash isn't the Carnival's biggest fan.' I'd clearly struck something of a nerve, so smoothed it over with flattery. 'Putting on a big show while not annoying the residents must take quite a balancing act.'

She relaxed again. 'Yes, well, some residents are more accommodating than others.' She turned to Howard. 'Actually, perhaps you can help with a bind I'm in. Do you have any actresses among your clients?'

'Not that I know of. Why?'

'I'm a woman down thanks to flu. If I can't find someone to play Mother of the Waters in the opening ceremony play, I'll have to double up.'

Howard laughed. 'Then it's your lucky day, dear Lucy. Gwinny here is an actress. She used to be on TV all the time; don't you recognise her?'

She obviously didn't but I wasn't offended. The last time I was regularly working, Lucy Kwok would have been in her twenties.

'No, I don't think so,' she said, which I took as confirmation until I realised she was talking about my suitability for the role. 'The Mother needs to exude authority and dignity.'

Now, if I had any sense I would have let that pass me

by. But the humiliation of being replaced by a younger model in *Mixed Mothers* still burnt inside me, and something snapped.

I pulled myself up to my full height – which admittedly isn't much, but posture is everything – and said, 'Young lady, I have played Elizabeth at the Globe, and a recurring headmistress on *Heartbeat*. Whatever the role requires, I assure you I can deliver. What sort of costume does it involve?'

Lucy reassessed me. 'Not a costume, a headdress.' She peered at my head, looking at it from both sides. 'You and I are about the same size, so it should fit . . . All right, I'll bring the script round later. It's only four pages, anyway. The Mother is a minor character.'

Inwardly I breathed a sigh of relief. I'd begun to worry I'd signed up for an hour of tedium, but of course an amateur community piece would only be a few minutes long. I was certainly capable of learning half a dozen lines for a minor character overnight.

'Call it serendipity, then,' I said. 'When and where?'

'Noon tomorrow on the dot. Be at the exhibition barge ten minutes before. Now, I really must get on. Goodbye.' Barely giving Howard or I chance to return the farewell, she hurried off along the path and out through the access gate. I noticed she had a key, but given her Carnival role that made sense.

I let Howard watch her go for a while, then gently elbowed him to get his attention. 'Is she always like that?'

He laughed. 'She's just getting started. Now, about

that key.' We walked to his house, the traditional narrowboat I'd so admired the day before, where he invited me inside.

I hesitated. 'Perhaps I should wait out here with Ace. I don't want to risk tying him up if he's not used to it.'

'Nonsense, Ace is welcome too. He's been in here before.'

I relented and followed him inside, to be once again surprised by a boat's interior. Behind the traditional exterior, this one was even more ultra-modern than Crash's place.

A large TV hung from a wall in the wide saloon with a camera and shotgun microphone secured to its frame. A dozen wires connected the screen to a cluster of computers and technical systems on shelves beneath. From these, cables snaked out to more cameras in the room; two mounted on tripods, one on the ceiling. I could tell from my own experience on sets that they were all positioned safely; no camera would be visible in the frame of another, all wires and cables clipped safely out of view. Finally, several studio lights were positioned on stands to properly illuminate the room.

In front of the TV, in the cameras' focus area, was the set itself; an exercise mat, keep-fit equipment within easy reach, plus a couch and table facing the screen.

'This is a very professional set-up, Howard.'

He beckoned me to follow him through to the galley kitchen. 'Coming from you, I'll take that as a compliment. But you should see the kit some of the YouTube kids

have got. I used to be an English teacher so this was all completely new to me when I started. Luckily there are lots of people online to explain how it all works and the signal strength around here is good enough to transmit out.'

'Crash with his recording studio, you with a broadcast set . . . what's next, does your neighbour run a mobile phone company?'

Howard took a spare key from a drawer and handed it to me. 'Were you expecting a bunch of hippies?' He selected fruit and salad vegetables from the fridge, then removed the lid from a large blending machine on the countertop. Ace immediately perked up, sniffing the air. I noted stacks of protein and health supplement packs lined up against the splashback.

'I wouldn't put it like that . . .' I said, even though 'a bunch of hippies' is exactly what I'd expected.

'It's OK, I did too before I moved here. But what I found was a community of independently minded people. It's true, some are anti-establishment but it's also a perfect lifestyle for an entrepreneur. Can I interest you in a smoothie?' He piled the fruit and greens into the blender, and I remembered that he'd been jogging. I was interrupting his morning exercise routine.

'No, I'll let you get on. I'm sure Ace is ready for a good runaround. Thank you for the key.'

'My door is always open, Gwinny. Well, except when I'm working, but you know what I mean. Feel free to drop in any time.'

Ace and I left, my emotions about Howard now mixed. He was clearly vain but was that surprising in a man who'd decided to become a keep-fit instructor? I still had misgivings about his touch-feely nature but he'd been consistently friendly and polite.

I unlocked the access gate with Howard's key, then took Ace across the bridge to Rembrandt Gardens, overlooking the Pool.

On my umpteenth throw of the ring for this tireless Collie, I remembered Lucy Kwok's expression when I'd asked about her relationship with Crash Double. His star may have faded but Crash remained a celebrity. If he wanted to, I had no doubt he could find a friendly journalist to write a hit piece about the Carnival. Lucy probably had to handle him with kid gloves, and my sympathies shifted a little in her favour.

I wondered, though, if her surprised look had been something else. Had she thought I meant her relationship with Howard? They were obviously friendly and, age gap notwithstanding, they'd make an attractive couple. She an elegant, professional woman; he a rough-hewn guru *artiste*. Heaven knows it's a common enough combination. But I'd also noticed Lucy wore a wedding ring, so if they were carrying on in secret their shared innuendo was understandable.

The canal community was proving to be a fascinating little microcosm. I wondered what other secrets I might learn during my stay.

CHAPTER SIX

When Ace was finally ready to rest, we returned to Crash's boat where I fed and watered him before unpacking my clothes for the weekend. Then I checked the galley kitchen again and found it still empty. Even the fridge contained little more than some cheese and butter. I'd have to nip to the local shop; if nothing else, I'd offered to cook Sunday dinner for Birch and it would pay to get familiar with the cooker. I wondered if it had ever been used.

In the saloon, I finally opened my new jigsaw puzzle. One thousand pieces now bent and warped thanks to Howard Zee. But I was relieved to see it wasn't as bad as I'd feared. The box was crushed and the lid needed flattening out, but only about a quarter of the pieces were affected. I examined the lid picture. It was a painting of Little Venice's Pool with narrowboats moored along its edges, ducks in the water and the grand white houses of Blomfield Road overlooking it all on a beautiful spring

day. It had seemed appropriate when I found it in town, and a thousand-piecer would keep me occupied for at least a few days, though I was confident I'd be able to finish it before I had to return home.

Ace padded into the room, having finished his food. I sent him on his corner bed for a post-exercise nap while I sifted through the jigsaw pieces, folding bent lugs back into place. It was quite zen, really, and my mind began to wander. Perhaps that's why I finally noticed something I'd missed in my previous coming and going through the saloon; one of Crash's gold discs, mounted directly above the piano, was askew. I went over and stood on tiptoes to adjust it but somehow made things worse and had to catch it from falling altogether. Holding it in my hands, though, revealed why it had been wonky in the first place. Mounted in the wall behind it was a safe.

Never mind the value of the audio equipment upstairs. Surely this would be far more enticing to any burglar who knew it was here. But how would they? Crash hadn't mentioned it to me and I didn't imagine wall safes were a common feature in houseboats. It was the type found in a hotel room, shallow and wide with a keypad. Hardly Fort Knox but enough to secure important papers, like . . . a passport, of course. Crash must have taken his out in a hurry and failed to straighten the disc properly before he left. Satisfied at solving this mini-mystery, I hopped up on the piano bench for a bit of extra height and carefully rehung the framed disc.

Ace was now firmly in his post-meal snooze, and I knew I might not get a better chance to leave him here while I stocked up. According to my phone's map, Choudhury's was a short way past Warwick Avenue Station; I didn't know if it was technically the closest grocer, but it made sense to use Crash's regular shop. I left Ace sleeping, locked up and set off.

I was there in less than five minutes; Little Venice was proving to be a surprisingly compact place with everywhere only a short distance from anywhere else.

Choudhury's was styled like a boutique, all rustic untreated wood and handwritten signs, but it was still just a fruit and veg shop. I headed directly for the chilled section for a couple of pints of milk, then picked up some onions, mushrooms, a few apples . . . the usual necessities that Crash somehow did without.

A middle-aged Asian man, presumably Mr Choudhury himself, awaited me at the counter behind a beautiful old manual till with pounds-and-shilling pop-up numbers. It was for show, of course. A bleeping electronic touchscreen, mounted out of view under the counter, did the real work as he totted up my basket.

I was debating whether and how to introduce myself when he asked, 'Looking forward to the Carnival tomorrow?'

'Very much,' I said, taking advantage of the opening. 'In fact, I'm staying on Crash Double's houseboat, looking after Ace while he's away.'

'Ah! Such a well-behaved dog. How is he?'

'He's fine, though I think the oddity of the situation is making him more anxious than usual. He's already torn through the box you gave him this morning.'

Mr Choudhury looked puzzled. 'Not this morning. I haven't seen Crash since Tuesday.'

I chided myself for making assumptions. Ace hadn't been surrounded by tiny shreds of cardboard because he'd made short work of a new box; he was still tearing up Tuesday's box into ever smaller pieces.

'Crash planned to get a new box from you,' I explained. 'He must have forgotten entirely. Maybe that explains why the fridge is empty, too.'

Mr Choudhury suddenly dropped to his knees, rummaged under the counter, then popped back up, smiling and holding a sturdy cardboard box. 'I've been keeping this one back,' he said, placing my shopping inside it. 'Good, thick card. Ace will have his work cut out.'

'That's very kind, thank you. Does the Carnival bring you much trade?' I gestured at a small selection of premade sandwiches behind the counter glass.

'A little, but I mostly enjoy attending. Anything that brings the community together is always a good atmosphere, don't you think?'

I agreed, paid and thanked him again before returning to the houseboat. Ace had woken up in the meantime and once again lay in the hallway, but this time all thoughts of toilet were forgotten when he saw me carrying a cardboard box. He bounced up and down

in circles, anticipating the destruction to follow, and his mismatched eyes watched my every move as I unpacked the shopping. Then I found a broom and dustpan to sweep up the old cardboard shreds, which he found equally fascinating. Finally, laughing at his eagerness, I carried the empty box through to the saloon and placed it on the floor.

Crash hadn't told me the normal routine but I assumed Ace was smart enough to correct any 'mistakes' I made. Sure enough, he gripped the box with his mouth, lifted and placed it on his bed then looked back at me for permission.

'*Go on*,' I said, nodding, and without further encouragement he ripped into it with claws and teeth, deftly dismantling it to a flattened state before settling down to tear and chew on the pieces. If nothing else, it reinforced that a wolf still lives inside every dog. Those teeth could just as easily have ripped someone's skin if Ace was so inclined. I let myself imagine Simon the director's face on the box for a moment, then tutted at myself for being petty.

After brewing a cup of tea, I sat at the coffee table and began searching for jigsaw corner pieces to make a start. After all, come the evening I'd be too busy learning my lines for tomorrow's opening ceremony. At least Lucy Kwok was willing to put her faith in me for a role.

CHAPTER SEVEN

That afternoon I walked Ace around Little Venice, getting to know the area and enjoying the sight of dozens more narrowboats entering the Pool to line up side by side against the path, ready for the Carnival. Everywhere I looked bunting was being strung and shouts of greeting between boats mixed with invitations to dinner and drinks. It was all quite heartwarming. I didn't see what Crash had against it.

In the evening I fed Ace, cooked myself dinner, then settled in to continue the jigsaw. The houseboat's lack of a TV struck me as odd. I wasn't a telly addict but I liked to have it on in the background while I puzzled and I'd certainly never before been in a home without one. Mind you, I'd never been on a rock star's houseboat either. Music appeared to be Crash's sole concern; the stereo was impressive and there were enough albums, CDs and tapes here to last for a very long time.

A chiming sound startled me from my thoughts, and

prompted Ace to shoot off his corner bed into the hallway. I hadn't known the boat had a doorbell, but it was obviously well used enough for the dog to recognise it.

I opened the door to find Lucy Kwok now wearing something more like a businesswoman's power suit, complete with heels, which can't have been easy to negotiate on the path's uneven flagstones. I wondered what she actually did for a living and resolved to ask Howard.

'Good evening,' I said.

She thrust a sheaf of papers into my hand, said, 'This is very good of you, thank you so much, got to run, lots to do, bye,' then turned on her precarious heels and left.

'. . . Noproblemthankyou?' I suggested to her dwindling back, unsure whether she'd heard me. I fussed Ace, who sat patiently at my feet. 'Lots to do, and all of it more important than talking to me, it seems.'

Back in the saloon, I settled on the sofa to read the script.

'The Welcome of Water': A Fable
The Opening Ceremony Dramatic Presentation of
the Canal Carnival
Written by Lucy S. Kwok
From a story by Lucy S. Kwok
Directed by Lucy S. Kwok
Copyright © Lucy S. Kwok

Half-expecting page two to be a credit for Lucy S.

Kwok's typing skills, I turned over. There were definitely more than three pages here. Had she given me multiple copies?

Before I could concentrate on that question, I was distracted by a pair of mismatched eager eyes in my peripheral vision. Instead of returning to his corner bed, Ace now stood by the couch staring at me. I looked at Crash's bookshelf of Great Men biographies and wondered if this was part of an evening routine; reading on the couch with Ace at his side. But he hadn't actually said whether the dog was allowed on the furniture.

Remembering the bedroom, I commanded '*Stay*,' and dashed along the hallway to quickly retrieve the cover throw I'd seen the day before. I needn't have worried; when I returned, Ace remained sitting exactly where I'd left him. I spread the throw over the couch, sat down, said '*Good boy, come*,' and patted the thick fabric beside me. He leapt up, thanked me with a lick on the cheek, then curled up in a position that allowed him to keep an eye on me. I picked up the script again, and this time turned straight to the back.

That's when I noticed *Page 35* in the top corner and groaned. I'd completely misunderstood what Lucy had meant. This wasn't a four-page script with two lines for the Mother of the Waters; it was a thirty-five-page script, with what I now saw was four pages of monologue for me to learn in a little over twelve hours.

Perhaps sensing my despair, Ace cocked a sleepy ear at me. I rubbed his head and began to read.

* * *

By ten o'clock my eyes were glazing over. The opening three pages were a narration monologue from my character to welcome the audience and set the scene. I didn't speak again until the final page, when I had another monologue to bid everyone farewell. It ended:

So as our story reaches its joyful and delightful end,
We bid you enjoy the waters' bountiful gifts, dear
friends!

It was all like that, but to be honest I've recited worse. *The Welcome of Water* was a broad-strokes fable celebrating water as the source of all life, with an allegorical cast: Mother of the Waters, the Husband of Brent (as in the river), the twin Springs from which the river flows, and so on. For some reason Lucy had composed the entire play in rhyming couplets which should have made it easier to learn, but choices like rhyming *canal* with *diurnal* and *water* with, well, *water* didn't help matters. Still, I was determined to show Lucy I could handle it, even if I now regretted volunteering at such short notice. Dodgy memory or not, I bet Crash Double never had to learn the lyrics to a brand-new song the night before a concert.

That did give me an idea, though.

I climbed the stairs to his home recording studio, followed by a suddenly very awake and curious Ace. Reaching the top, I looked out the wide windows and finally understood what Crash had meant about it being a

grand view. From here he could look over and down the length of the canal, past the other houseboats towards the Maida Hill Tunnel. Moonlight reflected on the water, tree branches swayed overhead, and it was all very peaceful. But I could also understand why the other residents had fought him over building this second floor. It was high enough that, if not for their curtains, I'd have been able to see inside half the other boats. If I'd been in their shoes, I would have objected too.

I sat in the fancy Aeron chair and shuffled it toward the desk. Two small spotlights detected my movement and automatically shone on the computer keyboard. How very high-tech! A press of the spacebar lit up the screen . . . and then a box popped up, demanding a password.

I hadn't been deliberately watching Crash as he unlocked the computer the day before but it was hard not to notice that the first letters he'd typed were *e-q-u*. I tried *equine*, *equine123*, *equestrian* and more along those lines but nothing worked. I wondered if I was completely on the wrong track. Crash was a dog lover but he hadn't mentioned horses at all.

Frustrated, I took out my phone and called him. It was late, but surely a rock 'n' roll man like Crash would be awake. I began to concoct a story in my head about wanting to dance a jig with Ace but decided instead to be truthful. He might dislike the Carnival, but surely he'd understand.

He didn't answer, though, going straight to voicemail instead. I left a message reassuring him it was nothing to

worry about but asking him to call me back as soon as he could.

Ace lay on his bed, his upright ear twitching at my every noise and movement. I've never known a Collie who could actually fully relax. I thought of sharks, who sleep while they're still swimming because if they stop moving they'll drown. Was that right? Or was I confusing them with the birds who sleep while they're gliding?

My mind was wandering and Crash hadn't called back. Feeling frustrated, I phoned Birch instead.

'Everything all right?' he asked sleepily. I pictured him dozing on the sofa with Ronnie while the TV quietly showed . . . snooker? A programme about steam trains? I really had to find out more about what this man did when he wasn't dog walking.

'Yes, don't worry. I wondered if you might be able to help me with a question about Crash Double seeing as you're a fan.'

'Delighted to. Fire away.' Now he sounded fully awake.

'Can you think of a word associated with him that begins with *e-q-u*? I assume he doesn't own a racehorse.'

Birch thought for a moment, then chuckled. 'His daughter. Of course.'

'No, that's not right. His daughter's name is Ellie. Even if that's a shortened form, "Eleanor" doesn't contain a q.'

'Ah, but it's not Eleanor. Her birth name was Equilibrium, if you can believe that.'

I groaned. 'I suppose I can. Who'd be a rock star's child, eh?' I typed *equilibrium* into the password field, and

77

hey presto, the computer desktop appeared.

'Anything else?'

'No, thank you – wait, actually, yes. First, give Ronnie a fuss from me. Then tell me, what are you doing?'

'Oh. Um, well, now you mention it, watching an old *Classic Albums* I have on tape. About Bad Dice. Long time ago. Forgot I had it until this week, you know.'

Suddenly I felt sorry for him, in a way. Here I was sitting in Crash Double's home, but it meant nothing to me. Meanwhile, Birch would have been doing cartwheels but he was in Shepherd's Bush. I almost invited him over for the night then remembered there was only one bed. I hadn't even risked asking him for a kiss yet. Leapfrogging directly to an invitation between the sheets would probably give the former policeman a heart attack.

'Birch, why don't you come over tomorrow morning instead of waiting until Sunday? You can see inside Crash's house and we can walk around the Carnival together.' I suddenly had a brainwave. 'In fact, you could look after Ace while I'm performing in the opening ceremony.'

'Beg pardon? You're what?'

'It's a long story. But do come over, I'd love to see you.'

'Right you are. Good night.'

I clicked around Crash's computer, searching for a way to record myself. Like his house, the desktop was chaos; a jumble of files and shortcuts with cryptic names I didn't understand. Some had dates, some looked like abbreviations. Song titles, maybe? Without opening them I couldn't tell, and I didn't want to go snooping.

Then I saw one titled with yesterday's date and a familiar time. I prepared to kick myself and opened it up.

'*I'm sorry, was*—' My own voice blared from the room's speakers before it was suddenly interrupted by a burst of garbled digital noise. Then it returned, ending, '*do something?*'

I went ahead with the self-kicking, having forgotten all about the one-touch recording he'd shown me yesterday. Mind you, I was glad I checked; clearly something had gone wrong if it couldn't even record five seconds of speech properly.

Then I remembered that when Crash had played it back for me, it sounded fine. As an experiment I found the button on the desk, pressed it, and recited, '*All the world's a stage, and all the men and women merely players; they have their exits and their entrances, and one man in his time plays many parts.*'

A file immediately appeared on the computer with today's date and time; I played it back and this time it had recorded perfectly. How strange. Still, I couldn't trust it. If it went wrong again, I didn't have the time or knowledge to fix it.

Before I left the computer, though, something caught my eye; a folder in amongst the chaos of other files titled *Lucy*. I double-clicked it to open it and found myself faced with another box asking for a password. I typed *equilibrium* but it didn't work. I wasn't about to sit here and try to guess again so I closed the box and now saw three other similar folders; one each titled *Fox*, *Johnny*

and *Howard*. I tried them all but they all required a password.

Even by my standards this was getting uncomfortably nosey, so I closed everything and turned off the screen.

Ace watched patiently from his bed. No doubt he'd spent many a late night up here with Crash, too. 'It's a wonder he hasn't got you on backing vocals,' I told him. He cocked his head, trying to understand, and I laughed. Most dogs lying on their bed would roll over and ask for a belly rub, but not collies. The slightest sound from a human and they assume it's time to go to work.

I got down on the floor and fussed him anyway. He really was an odd-looking dog but his constant eager grin more than made up for it.

From down here on the floor, I noticed something glint under Crash's desk. Not a light; a reflection. Thinking it might be a mislaid dog toy, I crawled over and used my phone's flashlight to peer under the desk. It wasn't a toy at all. One side of the computer was partly open, revealing wires, lights and metal parts. Some were disconnected but I had no idea if that was good or bad.

Was this why the recording was damaged? Had Crash attempted some computer DIY, messed things up and hastily left before going to Dublin? After all, he surely didn't expect a busybody like me to mess around with it.

Nevertheless, it gave me an idea. Originally, I'd thought I could use the computer to record myself performing the monologues as an *aide-mémoire*. I could use it to learn them by ear, almost like they were songs. I didn't trust the

computer to do it properly any more, but in the spirit of DIY I could use my phone instead.

So I hauled myself up with the help of the desk, then propped my phone on the window sill and opened the camera to make a video recording. Standing in front of it, I held up Lucy's script and performed both monologues. Then I stopped the recording, pocketed my phone and led Ace back downstairs where I made a cup of tea, sat on the sofa, and played back the video.

I thought I'd opened the wrong recording. I could hardly see a thing. Then I heard myself talking, even though the picture remained dark. Finally, I caught reflected moonlight on water and movement in shadows and understood. I'd used the wrong camera. Instead of recording myself perform a dramatic monologue inside, I'd taped the scene outside through the window where I'd placed the camera. It looked directly down the canal path, past all the other boats and towards the Maida Hill Tunnel, and while it was a lovely nighttime scene, it wasn't at all what I'd intended.

'Silly old Gwinny, eh?' I mumbled to Ace, who groaned sleepily in agreement and pressed his back into my side.

Oh, well. I could still hear myself, which was the important thing. I went back to the start of the video, pressed play and turned off the screen to save the battery.

Two hours of recital later, I had it down. A night's sleep and a couple more practice runs early in the morning would properly fix it in my memory. Feeling pleased with myself, I nipped Ace outside for a final toilet then locked

up for the night and climbed into my pyjamas.

Ace dutifully went on his bed while I brushed my teeth, but the moment I got under the covers he leapt up and stretched out beside me. I suddenly panicked, remembering the throw was still on the couch. Still, I'd intended to wash the bedclothes before Crash returned home anyway. A few dog hairs wouldn't make any difference. With one hand stroking Ace's soft fur, I held my phone in the other and played the video one last time in the dark.

But now, I saw something strange.

Because I'd made a mistake, I hadn't really been paying attention to the video that first time. But now, in the dark of the bedroom, I could make out things I hadn't seen before. Things like Fox, wearing a hooded top, emerging from her boat carrying a tartan-patterned holdall. Instead of walking along the path towards the access gate, though, she ran directly to the fence facing Blomfield Road, tossed the holdall over onto the path, then leapt the railings to follow it.

How very odd.

Of course, it was none of my business – but it was distracting enough that I hadn't been paying attention to my own voice. I started playing the recording again and switched off the screen.

CHAPTER EIGHT

I woke with a grunt to find Ace standing over me, licking my face. I shooed him off and sat upright, wondering what I'd heard falling over. Then I realised it was my phone hitting the floor because I'd fallen asleep with it on my chest as I listened to the recording over and over.

It buzzed as I blearily leant over to retrieve it, and to my surprise the screen told me Johnny Roulette was calling.

'Johnny? Can I help you?' I answered.

'I hope so, pet. Has he left?'

'Sorry, has who left what?'

I could almost see him pinch the bridge of his nose. 'I'm in Dublin, but there's no sign of Crash and he won't answer his phone. Are you sure he's not sleeping off a bender, now?'

'If he is, darling, I can assure you he's not doing it here. I've been on his boat since yesterday morning. Crash texted me early to say he was off and nobody's

mentioned seeing him in Little Venice. Are *you* sure he isn't already in Dublin in a pub somewhere?'

'I wish I was,' he said. 'Listen, if you see that overgrown kid, tell him to call me immediately, understand? Christ, we'll have to charter a plane . . .'

He ended the call before I could retort, which was probably just as well given what I might have said in response to his brusque tone. Nevertheless, I hoped Crash was OK and simply sleeping off a hangover. If they did this same concert every year, by now it probably needed minimal input from the band themselves before showtime anyway.

Besides, he'd hardly be the first performer who liked a drink. If Crash was all that stable, would he be on his third marriage to the same woman?

I fed and toileted Ace, then myself, while deciding what to do with the bright spring morning. It was an hour until Birch said he was going to come by with Ronnie and a further hour until the opening ceremony. When I opened the French windows, though, the noise from the Pool made it clear the Canal Carnival had already begun. A small green tugboat drifted by with a giant orange contraption mounted on its front to scoop up leaves and floating debris from the water's surface as it went. It was all rather idyllic so I decided to have a look around the Carnival myself.

Ace still wasn't used to being on-lead, but he didn't complain. I led him out through the residents' access gate

and under the junction bridge to the Pool.

The noise was as much from the boaters as the Carnival-goers. More had arrived overnight, filling every remaining gap around the Pool's edge. It was now a solid mass of boats and bunting with yet more flags still being strung up.

A queue of people waited at the permanent café boat for coffee and pastries. Next to it an exhibition barge, open to the public, offered families a chance to see inside a narrowboat and learn about the canal's history. Lucy Kwok was there, talking to a young man in a high-vis bib who stood on the rear deck taking payment and issuing tickets. She waved at me, so I waved back, then realised my mistake when she shouted something about cash floats and the bank, and a woman wearing a matching bib emerged from behind me to talk to her. Faintly embarrassed, I let my hand drop and moved on.

The beautiful boats gleamed in the sunshine. I imagined every owner had been hard at work cleaning and polishing before they arrived, and now they stood proudly on deck chatting to the public. Here was a woman my age, selling her paintings of the canal; there was a grizzled old man, demonstrating a tiller mechanism to three fascinated young boys; further on, a younger man sold straw hats from his deck.

'A boater selling boaters,' I said to Ace as we passed, chuckling at my own joke.

I was in quiet awe of the ease with which the owners moved about their barges; climbing up and over the

sides, walking on the roof, shimmying around the edge. I stopped to watch one young woman, barefoot in a flowing skirt, hold the lip of her boat's roof with one hand while her toes gripped the gunwale, where the hull met the housing. With her free hand she reached down into the water. It was a little precarious for my liking and I wondered what she was doing.

Suddenly she plucked something from the water, pulled herself upright in a single move and returned to the rear deck with practised ease. I moved closer and saw she was another artist selling her work, but these were different to the landscapes and friendship bracelets others were flogging. Her pieces were sculptures of barges, made from bits of metal and plastic hammered and moulded into shape. In fact, what she'd retrieved from the water was a floating piece of plastic.

'My material source,' she explained. 'They're all made from things I find discarded in the canals.'

'How meaningful,' I said, admiring the striking sculptures. I was so absorbed I didn't notice a news reporter suddenly begin talking nearby.

'Now, look at this. Amazing creativity and the sort of thing that truly makes the Canal Carnival worth visiting. Let's take a closer look. Excuse me!'

That last was directed at me, or so I assumed from the reporter's subtle elbow jab in my ribs. I quickly stepped aside, but stumbled over a coil of mooring rope on the path and lost my footing.

I flailed, windmilling my arms in vain as I fell

backwards, and all I could think was that if I fell in the water, I must remember to let go of Ace's lead so I didn't drag him in with me.

But I was saved by a strong hand and a firm grip that caught me halfway and kept me mostly upright. I turned to thank my hero and was mildly surprised to see a short, broad woman with a stern face holding my arm.

'Are you all right, madam?' she asked. 'Have to be careful around here, all sorts of hazards about.'

'Yes, thank you. I tripped because I was trying to get out of the way of . . .'

I trailed off, finally seeing who had shoved me aside. It wasn't a news reporter at all; it was Violet, the actress who'd taken my part in the play! She held up her phone as if taking a selfie with the boat, yammering away like she was doing a field report and completely oblivious to me or anyone else around her. Violet was recording herself, I realised; and this was all that stopped me from giving her a piece of my mind there and then. Ace, however, had no such compunction and barked loudly at her.

Her smile fixed and her gaze never wavering from the camera, she said, 'Sorry about the noise you can hear, but that's life among the people! Not everyone can keep their dog under control.'

Camera or not, I wasn't having that. 'Or their elbows, eh, Violet? You nearly put me in the water.'

She stopped recording, lowered the phone, and turned to me with eyes blazing. 'You were in the way!

My followers don't want to see you, they want—hang on, do I know you?'

'Very possibly, considering we've been in rehearsals together all week,' I said, taking a deep breath.

Her eyes lit up in recognition. 'Glenda!'

'Gwinny.'

'Yeah. So great to see you, hold on.' She raised her phone again and tapped a button. 'Hey everyone, look who I met at the Carnival! This is Glenda Tubby, who's got a bit part in *Mixed Mothers*, playing the grandmother. Say hiiiiiii!'

'Gwinny Tuffel,' I said, leaning into the camera. I may no longer be able to compete with Violet's flawless skin and flowing hair but what I do have is decades of experience holding an audience's attention. 'Playing Margory. We're on at the Sunrise Theatre all next month, five nights a week, so don't miss it.'

'It's going to be so amazing,' Violet gushed, 'Proper theatre and everything. I play Melanie, a character who's really emotionally complex, yeah, and almost, like, traumatised . . .'

She wandered off into the crowd, still talking to the camera, having already forgotten about me, Ace and the boat sculptures.

'Friend of yours?' said the sculptress, laughing.

I sighed. 'If we'd had these phones forty years ago, I doubt I'd have been any different. Now I really must thank—oh.'

The good Samaritan who'd saved me from an

unexpected bath had done her own disappearing act and was nowhere to be seen. I decided to keep an eye out in case our paths crossed again, so I could thank her.

Suddenly Ace yanked on his lead, pulling me backwards. I half-stumbled, half-turned to see what had caught his attention, and for the second time in five minutes found myself held by a firm grip. This time, though, I was more than happy to find the hand belonged to Alan Birch.

'Steady on, ma'am,' he said. 'Dogs keen to say hello, that's all.' He nodded down at our feet with his bright blue eyes.

I would have gladly looked into those eyes for another minute or two but as this was the first time Ace and Ronnie had met we had to make sure they socialised properly. They happily sniffed one another, tails wagging upright as they moved in a circle and tangled their leads like a maypole.

'Well, I don't think we need worry about them,' I laughed as we unwound the leads. 'Come on, I'll show you Crash's boat.'

We made our way through the crowd and under the bridge towards the residents' area. The access gate was now open and crowds of people milled about on the narrow path, especially around Crash's place.

'Is it always this busy?' asked Birch.

I groaned. 'I forgot, they open it to the public for the Carnival. It's why Crash goes away every year, to escape this lot.'

Tourists stood against the singer's houseboat, alternately posing for selfies and trying to peer in through the door. One young man with a sculpted beard and tattoos stood at the back of the crowd, focused not on the boat but on a handheld gizmo with a telescopic antenna. A high-pitched whine sounded from above, and both Ace and Ronnie became agitated, looking up at the sky. I followed their gaze to see a small flying drone buzzing around the windows of Crash's upper floor studio.

Tapping the young man on the shoulder, I said, 'Is that thing yours? The noise is bothering our dogs.'

'Go away, then,' he said with a filthy look. 'I'm here for BuzzFeed.' I had a vague recollection that this was a website, and as he returned to looking at his controller I now saw it contained a screen. As I watched, the image panned over the boat's upper windows, looking into the studio. The drone had a camera.

'Problem?' said Birch, eyeing up the reporter.

'Just the usual celebrity gawping,' I said, ushering him away. 'Let's come back later, when the crowds have gone. Hopefully they'll lock the gate again—'

Suddenly someone grabbed my arm from behind, startling me. I was getting tired of this and turned on my harrasser with fury.

'For God's sake, what now?!'

Lucy Kwok faced me with an icy expression. 'The opening ceremony begins in ten minutes. Follow me.'

CHAPTER NINE

Birch graciously offered to take Ace, and my handbag, while I hurried after Lucy. She cut through the crowd with practised efficiency, leading me to the exhibition boat.

I'd anticipated a troupe of bored housewives, harangued into taking part because Lucy wouldn't take no for an answer, but I was wrong. The half-dozen people standing on a flat-decked barge next to the exhibition boat all looked happy and excited. A couple of housewives, to be sure, but also a middle-aged man, two teenage girls and a young boy. Each wore a piece of elaborate headgear to identify their character: the Girl of the Waters, the Husband of Brent, the two youthful Springs, and so on. The barge was decorated with water-themed scenery, behind which hid two trunks filled with props and a small PA system connected to speakers at the barge's corners.

'I say, she was telling the truth!' said the man, fastening his chin strap and looking wide-eyed at me. 'It's Gwinny Tuffel!'

The housewives turned to see and smiled in recognition. I don't get recognised often, as Lucy had demonstrated the day before, but she'd evidently told them I was taking part and some were old enough to remember me. It was a pleasant salve for my bruised ego. The youngsters hadn't the faintest idea who I was, of course, but they smiled politely.

'Hello, everyone,' I said. 'Thank you for inviting me to take part. Let's all break a leg, eh?' I wondered if the children might ask confusedly what I meant but they nodded and continued dressing. They start them young in Maida Vale.

Lucy picked up my headgear, a sort of helmet with metal prongs shaped like waves radiating out and a small microphone, presumably connected to the PA system. She was about to hand me the headdress, then thought again and rammed it directly onto my head. I steadied it with my hands while she fastened the chin strap. Lucy had the same stressed-out look all directors get five minutes before curtain-up and I knew in her mind she was running through a checklist of a hundred different things that could go wrong, hoping she'd done everything to ensure they wouldn't. Even rampant egotists get stage fright.

'Don't worry,' I said quietly, 'it'll be fine. I learnt my lines last night.'

'Of course you did,' she replied, giving me a strange look. I couldn't tell if she was complimenting my professionalism or couldn't conceive that I wouldn't do

what she'd requested. It didn't matter. The show was about to begin.

'So,' I asked, 'do we gather everyone around on the path, or—*oh*!'

My question was answered by the ground, or rather the barge, moving beneath my feet. I grabbed its rail to steady myself as the man playing Brent held the tiller, guiding us to the centre of the Pool. Lucy retrieved a handheld microphone from behind the scenery and began welcoming everyone to the Carnival. People on the paths stopped to watch and listen. I spotted Birch standing at the water's edge with Ronnie and Ace, and Mr Choudhury from the grocer's stood nearby.

Lucy was a good speaker: confident, clear and well-rehearsed. I was especially impressed that she had no problem addressing people from a moving platform, because the barge was now turning circles around the Pool to ensure everyone got a view.

Then it was time. Lucy said, 'And now we present our dramatic presentation to officially open this year's Canal Carnival: *The Welcome of Water*. It begins with the Mother of the Waters.'

That was my cue. With one arm clutching the rail just in case, I swept the other in a grand, beneficent gesture to the audience.

> *'From fissures cracked low and springs gushing high,*
> *I bring you all clear flow and abundance of life.*

From everywhere, in everyone,
I am never the same, yet all as one.

I wander the land, but I am not aimless.
I have many bodies, yet I am shapeless.
I have no feet, and yet I run;
I am all life, yet carry destruction.

The water welcomes you—'

I thought it was off to a good start, but clearly someone disagreed because I was interrupted by a loud, piercing scream; all the more so for being both right next to my ear and broadcast through the barge speakers.

Startled, I turned to see one of the Spring-playing housewives screech in horror and point at my feet. No, not at my feet. I followed her panicked gaze down to the canal, where something long and pale had floated to the surface in front of the barge as we slowly circled. It bobbed and turned, rotating lazily, and then *everyone* screamed.

Welcomed by the waters, Crash Double's dead eyes stared up at the sky.

CHAPTER TEN

Needless to say, the show did *not* go on. I shouted for someone to call the police, forgetting I was hooked up to the barge's PA speakers. The entire Carnival heard me and now even people who'd shown no interest in the play ran over to rubberneck.

The Husband of Brent was on his feet, waving his arms around and shouting, 'Everyone stay calm! Stay calm, please! Everyone stay calm!' until it became so much background noise.

For her part, Lucy Kwok was so calm she didn't move. She stood at the edge of the barge, transfixed by the sight of the body. I removed my costume headdress so as not to broadcast to the world, gently shook her shoulder and said, 'Take us to shore, quickly.'

As if speaking from somewhere far away she said, 'Lakes have shores. Canals have banks.'

'Then take us to the bank, the path, dry land. I don't

care what you call it but make sure you give the body a wide berth.'

She took the tiller, and as we moved away I looked at Crash's upturned face. What on earth had happened here? He was fully clothed, even still wearing trainers. His hands were empty. His skin was deathly white and I saw no obvious injuries. How did he end up in the water? Why wasn't he in Dublin?

I was still watching the body when the barge bumped into the bank and a familiar voice said, 'Take my hand, ma'am, let's get you off there.' Hearing Birch's reassuring tones, I turned to face him with my arm extended – only to see him take Lucy Kwok's hand and help her disembark.

He then turned to me, but I'd already stepped onto the path unaided, and made a point of greeting Ace before him. The former policeman reddened slightly at his *faux pas*. I wouldn't make him suffer any further, though. There were more important things to worry about than my bruised ego.

'Birch, did you see anything before he floated to the surface?' I asked, retrieving my handbag. 'Did anything happen?'

'Nothing out of the ordinary. Rum do.'

'It certainly is, considering he was supposed to have caught a plane yesterday. Did you call the police?'

'No need. Fletcher was already here.'

A short, broad woman emerged from the crowd with a phone pressed to her ear. It was the woman who'd

saved me from falling into the water, now wearing an even more serious expression. Not that everyone here wasn't suddenly serious, but most didn't know what to say or do other than opine how awful it was, and that perhaps they should try one of the boat cafés up near Paddington instead. The crowds drifted away, the Carnival over before it had properly begun.

The woman finished her phone call and turned to Birch. 'The cavalry's on its way, but as I'm already here and there's a celeb involved my boss has requested I handle it. Looking forward to it, if I'm honest. Work out some rust from the old gears.'

'Then it's in good hands,' he said, and introduced us. 'DCS Fletcher, Gwinny Tuffel. Fletcher's at the Carnival with family,' he explained.

'Not any more. Hubby and grandchildren have sensibly scarpered to get some peace. Still, the cream'll sour in a bottle.' I wasn't familiar with that saying but before I could ask she said, 'Tuffel, Tuffel . . . have we met?'

'You saved me from falling in the canal earlier. You left before I could say thank you.'

She shook her head. 'No, I mean the name's familiar. Are you another copper?'

Birch laughed, a little too quickly for my liking, and said, 'From the telly, ma'am. Gwinny's an actress. She was in *Midsomer Murders* once.'

'That was a very small part,' I said, embarrassed. 'I didn't even get a close-up, you wouldn't remember.'

'No, I've got it. I knew a Kraut called Tuffel when I was in Special Branch. Advisor type. We used to call him Kaiser Henry!'

'Henry Tuffel was my father,' I said, nonplussed. 'You do know there hasn't *been* a kaiser for a hundred years . . . ?'

'A harmless nickname,' she assured me, as if that made everything all right. 'Our guv'nor liked him a lot,' she added quickly.

It was no secret that my father had, well, secrets. I knew he'd done favours for the Foreign Office when called upon, and his funeral had been attended by a surprising number of politicians and City bigwigs. I made a mental note to press DCS Fletcher for details later, if she could manage it without invoking Dunkirk and 1966.

Then something clicked into place about this woman. 'Hang on – are you *Birch*'s old DCS?'

'Calls me "old", does he?'

'Sorry, I mean "former". He speaks well of you but I assumed you'd also retired.'

DCS Fletcher narrowed her eyes at Birch. 'Some of us aren't ready to hang up the uniform and be idle all day,' she said. 'Now, here come the woodentops.'

Uniformed police had arrived, directing some people away from the area while ensuring others stayed. They began erecting a white gazebo on a wide section of the path.

'See?' said Birch. 'Knew you two would get along.'

Personally, I thought the superintendent and I had got off to a rocky start but Birch was often oblivious to things *not* said. So this was the woman I reminded him of! Physically we had little in common; it's often said a strong breeze would blow me over, whereas Fletcher could probably withstand a gale force. But there was a certain flinty steel in her eyes that I liked, and chose to believe that's what he saw in us both.

'This is Crash's dog, Ace.' I held the Collie's lead and quickly explained the dog-sitting situation. 'What are we going to do about him?'

Fletcher looked down at Ace, who was busy trying to understand why the humans were idly standing around instead of doing something interesting like walking or throwing his ring.

'I suggest you carry on as intended, madam, until the deceased's family decide what to do. I'm sure they'll have a plan.'

I didn't share her confidence. A surprising number of people don't account for pets in their will, blithely assuming they'll outlive their cats and dogs. But the mention of family did remind me that someone important wasn't here.

'Has Fox been told?' I asked. 'She's been in her boat all morning, giving tours. She's along there in the residents' area in a rainbow-coloured barge with plants covering the roof. Someone should inform her before she hears it from the public.'

'A bird in the woods is the last to know,' said Fletcher

and began walking towards her colleagues. 'Please don't either of you leave, I'll want to talk to you later.'

'Perish the thought,' said Birch. We stood together on the path watching uniformed police and men in wetsuits pilot a barge to retrieve Crash from the water. 'Fletcher's a good one,' he reassured me. 'Talks nonsense, but she'll get to the bottom of it.'

Considering his comparison of us, I wasn't sure how to take that. 'You assume there's something to get to the bottom of,' I said.

'You think he might have slipped and fallen in?'

I hesitated, then said, 'No, actually, I don't. He'd lived here for years and seemed to know every inch of the place. Plus, he was still running around onstage, wasn't he? So even if he did fall in, surely he'd have been able to swim back out.'

'Heart attack, then? While walking the dog, maybe.'

I pictured Crash walking Ace by the Pool at dawn, suddenly clutching his chest and tumbling into the water. But one piece of that image didn't fit.

'Hang on, though. If he was walking the dog and fell in, how come Ace was waiting for me inside the houseboat when I arrived?'

'Smart dog. Could have squeezed through the gate, opened the front door.'

'What, and locked it behind him as well? Even the smartest Collie doesn't have opposable thumbs. So why was Crash out walking by himself after he'd already texted me to say he was taking a cab?'

Birch's moustache twitched. 'Texted you? When?'

'Yesterday morning, around six.' I took out my phone and showed him.

'Let's inform Fletcher. Significantly narrows down time of death.'

I agreed. We approached the gazebo, where the DCS was talking to Lucy Kwok.

'Sorry to interrupt, but I remembered that Crash sent me a text yesterday morning.' I showed her the message, and this time noticed something odd. 'Oh, look. I texted him back, but it says here my reply couldn't be delivered.'

Fletcher nodded, reading the screen. 'So the deceased texted you at oh-six-hundred but when you replied at oh-seven-ten the phone was offline.'

'I also tried to call him last night but he didn't pick up. He must have already been in the water.'

'Assumes the phone is still on his person,' said Birch.

In the Pool, police divers lifted Crash's body out of the water and onto the barge. Fletcher radioed them and asked but the answer came back negative.

'*Pockets empty. No phone, no keys, no wallet.*'

She looked at the text again, read Crash's number off the screen, then dialled it. There was no answer. 'Voicemail. Likely, then, that everything fell out when he submerged, but point of entry could have been anywhere along the canal so we may never find it. At least we know he died sometime after six.'

Lucy's hands flew to her mouth. 'Oh my god, I think I saw the killer!'

We all looked at her, waiting. She had a thousand-yard stare; I could almost see her mind working overtime to reassemble the memory.

'I live on Blomfield Road,' she finally explained. 'My bedroom overlooks the canal. I was coming out of the bathroom when I heard a cry. I looked out and saw someone climbing over the access gate, to leave the residents' path.'

'Is that unusual?' asked Fletcher, scribbling in her notebook.

'Of course. Residents all have keys. I assumed it was a thief, or burglar.'

'Crash was burgled recently,' I agreed.

Lucy nodded. 'So they came back to kill him then escaped over the gate! Oh, how awful!'

'Let's slow down for a moment,' said Fletcher. 'What time was this?'

'Six o'clock. I'm an early riser, especially during Carnival when there's so much to do.'

'Can you describe the person you saw?'

'Not really. There was a spring mist yesterday morning and all I saw was someone dressed in black.'

'Or it looked black through the mist,' offered Birch.

Fletcher nodded. 'The cry you heard: male or female? Did you make out any words?'

'No, just a cry of pain. I think it was a man but I can't be sure.' Lucy looked shocked again. 'Perhaps it was Crash! Oh, I heard him dying!'

'Slow down,' said Fletcher again with much more

102

patience than I could have mustered. For a woman who normally appeared so self-possessed, Lucy was dangerously close to losing her composure. 'You might simply have heard this person slipping and hurting themselves as they climbed over the gate, and the person in question could be unrelated to Crash's death.'

I suddenly remembered the video I'd accidentally taken last night of Fox jumping over the fence. But mentioning it would only throw suspicion on her and confuse matters. Instead I said, 'Besides, why wouldn't a killer simply hop over the fence into the road? It's a more direct route, not to mention a couple of feet shorter than the gate.'

Lucy looked at me with a strange expression. 'That doesn't matter. Whoever I saw *did* climb over the gate.'

'And around the same time Crash sent that text message,' said Fletcher. 'Thank you, Ms Kwok. We'll be in touch.' She handed Lucy off to a uniformed policewoman, who gave her a cup of tea.

'So someone might have killed Crash right after he texted me, then escaped,' I said.

The superintendent shook her head. 'There's no clear evidence that this was intentional. It could have been misadventure; a heart attack while walking the dog, perhaps.'

'I don't think that's very likely.' I explained that Ace had been locked inside the house when I arrived. 'Why would Crash be walking around by himself when he was expecting a car to drive him to the airport?'

'Perhaps he was meeting someone. Lot of people here this weekend.' Fletcher gestured at the assembled narrowboats with her pen as if I hadn't noticed them before. 'Or perhaps he was mugged, and things got out of hand.'

'Yet nobody saw him fall in the water? What about CCTV?'

'Road junctions only, I'm afraid. Nothing here on the canal.' She flipped her notebook closed in a gesture of finality. 'Leave it with us, Ms Tuffel, and we'll get to the bottom of it. We always do, eh, Alan?'

Birch nodded, clearly on the side of his old boss. Feeling betrayed, I turned on my heel and walked to the water's edge. The barge carrying Crash's body was being carefully guided back to the path.

I sensed Birch approach and stand beside me, but kept my gaze on the water. He didn't try to make conversation, to his credit, but that only made me more frustrated. I should have known police would stick together, no matter how flimsy their speculation.

Finally, I had to say something. 'It doesn't make sense, Birch. If he died out here, surely someone would have seen or heard something. And if Lucy is right, Crash was targeted. Why else would anyone go to the trouble of climbing over the gate?'

'It'll all come out in the wash,' he said, then quickly added, 'Um, so to speak. Fletcher knows what she's doing.'

'Really? She doesn't seem very willing to contemplate

104

that Crash might have been murdered.'

He was quiet for a moment, then said, 'Perhaps best if you don't stay in the houseboat any more. Potential killer on the loose, and all.'

I appreciated his concern, but it was misplaced. 'I don't think he died on his boat. There's no blood, toppled furniture, or any sign of a struggle. Besides, what kind of killer locks the door behind them when they're escaping?'

'To stop the dog from chasing?' Birch looked down at Ace.

The Collie keenly watched the police carry Crash's body off the barge and into the gazebo, which had been enclosed on three sides. I wondered if he could still recognise Crash's smell, even after a day underwater.

'Let's get out of here in case Ace smells something he shouldn't,' I said, suddenly feeling awful for the dog. 'In fact, why don't we go and have a look in Crash's houseboat? If I'm wrong and he was killed there before being thrown into the water, there's only one place it could have been done.'

Birch coughed. 'Been a while since I picked a lock. Besides, that was always in the line of duty. Breaking and entering is out of the question.'

I dangled Crash's keyring. 'Hardly breaking in when we have the key, is it?'

He grinned, and we ambled away slowly, trying not to draw attention to ourselves. We needn't have worried. The public was focused on the police, and the police were focused on Crash's body. I led Birch along the path

and under the junction bridge to the residents' area. The access gate stood open and now I saw that not entirely everyone was watching the police. A crowd had gathered around Crash's boat, posing for pictures and calling their friends. I thought I heard a news reporter relating the story but once again it was an ordinary person recording themselves on their phone.

Birch walked ahead, gently but firmly moving people aside so we could get to the door. I sharpened my own elbows a little and the dogs also helped, with most onlookers retreating at the sight of Ronnie and Ace.

Finally, we reached the door. I unlocked it while Birch stood facing the crowd, dogs in hand to deter followers. Then he backed through the open door after me and I quickly locked it again. As if on cue the crowd surged forward, pressing against the door, trying to see who we were and what we were doing.

We entered the saloon, and Birch whistled at the untidy jumble. 'Looks like he was burgled after all.'

'No, it was already like this,' I said. 'I've been here since yesterday, remember?'

'Oh, yes. Of course.'

I let Ace off his lead and Birch did likewise with Ronnie, who let the Collie lead him to the water bowl on the galley floor. My stomach rumbled and it occurred to me I hadn't eaten since breakfast.

'I wasn't looking for anything untoward yesterday when I arrived, so it's possible I missed something,' I said, beckoning Birch to the French windows. 'Apart

from the front door, all the house's windows are on the canal side and only these are big enough for a person to fit through. Crash even said he had those railings fitted to stop drunk guests falling in the water.'

'So if he was killed in the house and dumped in the canal, it would have to be here,' said Birch. 'Much simpler than dragging a body outside, then dropping it in the water. Are they locked?'

'Yes, but so was the front door – oh, hang on.' I weaved back through the piles of records and tapes to check the sideboard in the hallway. The crowd was still peering in but I ignored them and returned to the saloon. 'Crash's keys are missing. Perhaps that's why they weren't found on his body; the killer used them to lock up when they left.'

'If they were in here at all,' said Birch. 'Think you're right. No signs of a struggle I can see. No blood, nothing obviously knocked over.'

It would be difficult to have a fight in this saloon and *not* collide with a tower of records or a stack of DVDs. Even if Crash had been killed elsewhere, carrying a dead body through the room without disturbing anything would be impossible.

I unlocked and opened the French windows, then examined the floor and frame. 'I don't see any marks to suggest a body being dragged . . .' Leaning out to check the railing, I heard a high-pitched buzzing from above. A tiny drone descended, probably the same one from before. I would have swatted the nosey parker away,

but it wisely stayed out of my reach so I ignored it and continued looking. 'Nothing on the railing either. No chipped paint, no fabric caught on the metal, nothing. Here, take a look.'

'Tricky,' Birch said from behind me, punctuated by barking from Ronnie and Ace. I turned to see him straining to hold both dogs back by their collars, as they tried to attack the buzzing drone outside.

'Get lost,' I shouted at the hovering contraption. 'Have some respect!' Not that I imagined the reporter could hear me over its infernal buzzing. I was about to retreat inside and close the windows, but saw Ace's box of toys by my feet and had an idea. I grabbed a plastic ball launcher, leant out over the window railing and smacked the drone with it.

I only wanted it to fly away but I must have hit it in a particular spot. Something inside the drone went *bang*, and smoke curled out of the top. It swayed from side to side, flipped over twice, then plummeted into the water with a splash.

'Well, serves them right,' I said, closing the windows. 'They shouldn't be poking their noses in.' Birch coughed quietly. 'Oh, shush. It's different; we knew Crash. Well, I did. Well, I did a bit.' Suddenly feeling awkward, I was glad the drone was no longer recording.

Then I had a brainwave. 'Follow me,' I said, walking past Birch into the hallway (where the crowd still pressed against the door) and up the stairs to Crash's studio.

'Stone the crows,' said Birch, taking in all the high-

tech recording equipment. He put the dogs on Ace's bed while I sat at the computer. Then he watched me enter the password *equilibrium* and said, 'Ah.' It was amazing how many emotions he conveyed in that single syllable.

'I wanted to use it to rehearse my monologue,' I said defensively.

'Of course you did. No question at all,' he said in a tone implying there were in fact many questions.

I found the recording of me from Thursday afternoon and played it for him, garbled static and all, explaining what had happened. 'Now I want to see if he recorded anything after that,' I said, scanning the mess of files on the desktop. 'He may not have died here but you never know what he might have recorded. There could even be something from Friday morning.'

'Good thinking,' he said, peering over my shoulder.

Unfortunately, my hopes were in vain. Not that it was easy to find anything in the chaos, but I saw no files with Friday's date.

'Hang on, though. Here's another from Thursday afternoon, after I'd left.' I opened it, and we listened to Crash and another man talking. Unfortunately, this recording was also damaged:

[Static]
Crash: '. . . *could have phoned, you know.*'
Unknown man: '*Not likely. Listen, we just want to talk. She*—' [Static] '. . . *very generous offer*

to resolve this once and for all. At least—'
[Static]
Crash: '. . . *making your own generous offer to
the likes of Vicki—'*
[Static]
Unknown man: '. . . *serious. Nine o' clock, all
right? Don't be late.'*

'Well!' I said. 'What do you think that was about?
Who was the second man?'

'Search me,' said Birch. 'Definitely not Johnny or
anyone else in the band. I'd know their voice.'

'It didn't sound very friendly, did it? But that talk
about "generous offers" makes me wonder. A recording
contract? Someone who wanted to buy the boat? Hardly
a recipe for murder.'

'Not to mention he wasn't killed until the next
morning,' Birch reminded me. 'Let's pass it on to Fletcher.'

'For all that she'll care,' I snorted. 'Hardly convincing
evidence of a murder, is it?'

That question would be answered sooner than
expected because as I walked back down the stairs I
came face to face with an angry DCS Fletcher, standing in
front of the crowd outside and hammering on the door.

CHAPTER ELEVEN

There was no point trying to hide, so I let her in. Upon opening the door I was greeted by a wall of noise: shouting, jeering – a few people were even laughing for some reason. They all held up their phones to take pictures which I wasn't especially happy about, but they do say no publicity is bad publicity.

'Come in, Superintendent,' I shouted over the din. Then I turned to the crowd and said in my best dog-obedience voice, 'The rest of you, *stay*!'

To my surprise, they did. Fletcher and a uniformed policeman whom she introduced as Constable Wright slipped inside and I quickly locked the door behind them again. As I did, my phone buzzed with a call from Bostin Jim. On a Saturday? How unexpected. But I didn't have time to talk to him. I declined the call and ushered everyone into the lounge away from the gawping public.

We stood amid the piles of records and memorabilia. Sitting felt inappropriate somehow. Ace went onto his bed,

while Ronnie took a great interest in Constable Wright and proceeded to sniff every inch of the policeman's legs.

'Don't tell me you carry sliced ham in your pocket too?' I laughed. The confused constable shook his head. Birch called Ronnie over and produced a strip of cooked meat from his own pocket which the Labrador greedily chomped.

'So this is where you whacked that young man's drone, is it?' said Fletcher, looking out of the French windows.

'How on earth do you know about that? It happened a few minutes ago.'

The DCS sighed and took out her phone. 'You've gone viral, Ms Tuffel.'

She played a video headlined 'Crash! Former Actress Goes Mediaeval on Our Drone in Dead Singer's Home!' I watched myself lean out of the boat's French windows, ball launcher in hand, and whack the camera. The shot swayed and flipped before plunging head first into the canal. That drone must have been transmitting live and the whole thing had been recorded. I was apparently the top-trending video on BuzzFeed.

'The owner has made a complaint and wants you to compensate him with a replacement as the equipment is necessary for his work. I'd say you don't have a leg to stand on. The film clearly shows you destroying his property.'

'His property?' I blurted. 'What about Crash's privacy? Those vultures have been buzzing around this place all day, and now he's dead there are twice as many.'

'Isn't that like the deer mocking the rabbit's tail? At least they're standing outside, while you've broken into the place for a sniff around.'

While I tried to piece together another of her garbled aphorisms, Birch spoke up. 'No breaking and entering needed, we have keys. Gwinny's dog-sitting for Crash, remember? Besides, not a crime scene. No evidence he was killed here.'

'Actually, it seems Mr Donnelly wasn't "killed" at all,' said Fletcher. 'Preliminary examination of the body reveals no signs of foul play. My first assumption remains that he slipped and fell into the canal, though we also can't rule out suicide.'

'He'd lived here for years,' I said. 'Now suddenly yesterday morning he falls in the water, but nobody sees or hears him, and he doesn't swim out to the nearest boat? There must be a hundred in the Pool this weekend.'

Fletcher nodded sagely. 'Unfortunately, everyone was sleeping off the night before. Apparently, it's tradition to hold parties most nights of the Carnival and Thursday was no exception. Come Friday morning, Mr Donnelly could have gone in the water or even cried out without anyone noticing.'

'Might even strengthen the case for suicide,' said Birch unhelpfully. 'He figured nobody would see him and attempt a rescue.'

I protested. 'If it's suicide, why not do it here in his house? Why bother hiring me?' I crouched down and fussed Ace, who was listening intently and waiting for

words he recognised. 'Crash loved this dog. His phone case was a big photo of Ace, for heaven's sake. He wouldn't have gone without making arrangements to rehome him. Besides, where's the note?'

'Suicide notes are a myth,' said Fletcher. 'Even in very clear cases there often isn't one. As for going in the water, if he'd died at home he might not have been found for days. This way, as you point out, he knew his dog would be looked after.'

'I don't buy it. He had no reason to kill himself.'

The superintendent smiled sympathetically. 'In this country, the single group most at risk of death by suicide is men over fifty. The evidence, or should I say the lack of it, suggests Mr Donnelly may have been one more number in that sad statistic. You simply had your part to play.'

What she said made sense but I could hardly believe it. Could Crash really have hired me so he was free to kill himself, knowing Ace would be taken care of?

While we talked, Constable Wright had been rifling through the kitchen cupboards, then moved on through the rest of the boat. Now he returned from the corridor with a pill bottle.

'Found this in the bathroom waste, and there are at least half a dozen more in the cabinet.' He read the label. 'Xanax, private prescription.'

DCS Fletcher turned to me. 'Is that yours?'

'No, it's Crash's all right. He said he suffered from anxiety.'

'Interesting,' she said, taking out her notebook. 'I understand you also found the body?'

I didn't like where this was going. 'I was closest when Crash floated to the surface but that's a coincidence. There were several people on the barge.'

She consulted her notebook. 'The barge that was doing circles, yes?'

'That's right, and which was in full view of the public at all times,' I added with a certain amount of pique. 'Perhaps the barge stirred up the waters, bringing him to the surface. Crash wasn't even supposed to be here. In fact, their guitarist called me this morning because he hadn't turned up in Dublin and now we know why. He hadn't left Little Venice, let alone the country.'

My phone buzzed; Bostin Jim was still trying to call me. I declined again, hoping he'd get the hint and leave a voicemail. Much as I was delighted I now had an agent prepared to work hard to get me roles, the day's events put things into perspective. The police seemed so sure, I began to wonder if I was wrong. Had Crash really decided to end it all, even with all his fame, success and gold discs?

'What about his safe?' I said, suddenly remembering the disc above the piano. I pointed it out. 'That frame was askew when I arrived. I assumed Crash took his passport from the safe in a hurry, but maybe someone tried to break into it? He was burgled recently. You might get some fingerprints . . . *ah*.' I watched Fletcher put on a pair of gloves to remove the disc from the wall. 'Or not,

because I wasn't wearing gloves when I straightened it. Sorry.'

'You weren't to know,' said Birch. 'What was taken in the first burglary?'

'Nothing, apparently. I found that odd, given all the expensive studio equipment upstairs.'

'Not to mention these records and tapes,' said Birch. 'Plenty here would fetch a bob or two from collectors.' He looked like he fancied a chance at them himself.

'So what if they were only interested in the safe?' I wondered. 'Who knows what's inside there?'

DCS Fletcher removed the gold disc, revealing the hotel-style keypad. 'Simple enough to find out. Standard model.' She ordered Constable Wright to fetch 'the gizmo' and to station another officer outside to disperse the crowd. Finally, she turned to me and said, 'Thank you for your help, Ms Tuffel, but now I must ask you to leave. Police business, you understand.'

I did understand but I wasn't done. 'Before we go, there's something I need to show you. Or rather, play for you. It's upstairs, in the studio I mentioned.'

With dogs in tow, Birch and I led Fletcher to the second-floor studio. I sat at the desk and woke Crash's computer.

'You know his password?' said Fletcher, surprised.

'He was very trusting,' I squeaked, trusting Birch to stay quiet. I explained the one-touch recording system, the damaged files and the disconnected computer cables. Then I found the file from Thursday afternoon, of Crash

116

talking to an unknown man, and played it.

'The Irish voice is Mr Donnelly's?' Fletcher asked.

'Correct. We don't know who the other man is. Birch says it's not one of his bandmates.'

The former policeman shrugged at the surprised look from his old boss. 'Long-time fan,' he explained as we heard the police re-enter downstairs, followed by beeping noises.

'Perhaps the same person tried to break open the safe and then damaged these recording files,' I said. 'It must have been done after I left here on Thursday afternoon, you see.'

Fletcher didn't immediately dismiss the thought but I could tell she wasn't convinced. 'They could have been talking about someone owing a fiver for the biscuit tin, though. Without the full recording we'll never know.'

The beeping from downstairs stopped and was followed by a cheer. A shout reached us: 'Safe's open, ma'am. You'll want to see this, all right.'

CHAPTER TWELVE

Our expulsion momentarily forgotten, Birch and I crowded into the lounge behind DCS Fletcher to see what her officers had found. Unfortunately, everyone there apart from the dogs was taller than me, so my view was completely blocked. I stood on tiptoes, one hand on Birch's shoulder for balance, and could just make out the superintendent removing items from the safe. Constable Wright whistled, impressed.

'What's in it?' I asked.

'Passport, set of keys, notebook,' she said, while Constable Wright took notes. 'A substantial amount of money, too. That must be, what, a few thousand?'

'At least,' said the constable.

'So much for Crash protesting he was broke,' I said. 'All this time he had money stuffed away in his safe. No wonder someone tried to break into it.'

Fletcher opened the passport. 'This is definitely Mr Donnelly's. The keys look well used.'

'Probably his old house keys, from before he had the locks changed,' I said. 'What's in the notebook?'

The DCS flipped through it and shrugged. 'Poetry.'

'Poetry?' said Birch, his ears pricking up like a dog hearing a whistle. 'You mean song lyrics?'

'Well, Crash was a singer,' I smiled, nudging him. 'Surely that's not unusual?'

The former policeman shook his head. 'But there's been no new Bad Dice material for twenty-five years.' He gasped. 'A new album?' He said it with such wide-eyed excitement that I immediately pictured him as a long-haired young man, sitting on the floor and listening rapt to a hi-fi. Birch could be so gruff and, well, *old* at times that I hadn't imagined him as a young man before. It was a pleasant thought.

'Seems like overkill to put them in a safe,' said Fletcher. 'Mind you, it was his livelihood.'

'Could I see?' Birch asked. 'You, um, never know. Bit of knowledge can't hurt.'

Fletcher saw through this transparent excuse but passed him the notebook anyway. 'You'll never get to hear them now, so go ahead. Glove up.'

Birch donned a pair of latex gloves supplied by Constable Wright, then began to leaf through the pages. I thought of the studio upstairs and Crash and Ace dancing together. *Something new I've been working on*, he'd said.

The notebook was about half-full of lines and lyrics, all scribbled, scratched out, underlined and circled. There was no need to ask Birch if this was all new material; it

was plain from his wide-eyed expression.

The police were understandably distracted by the more pressing matters of Crash's passport (the presence of which confirmed he hadn't been en route to the airport) and the bundles of cash, so I whipped out my phone, made sure it was on silent and started snapping pictures of the notebook. Cottoning on, Birch grinned and leafed through the pages, pausing briefly on each so I could take a photo. We reached the end of the lyrics and he turned over a few blank pages before flipping it closed. But as he did, I saw something and nudged him to open the back page again.

It wasn't like the others. Instead of scrawled lines and margin doodles, this page contained several lines of random letters and numbers, like '*JOW-1000T-434206913IAFCLSHER*'. Then underneath was the name of a management company and an email address. It meant nothing to me, but maybe it had something to do with his studio upstairs?

'Birch, how are you getting on?' said DCS Fletcher suddenly. I took a final hasty photo, then hid my phone behind my back as she turned to us and held out a hand for the notebook.

'Confirmed all new, as far as I could see. Damn shame.'

I wondered about the idea that the notebook was in the safe because it was Crash's livelihood. Were his lyrics really that valuable? Or was there more to this than met the eye?

Fletcher sealed it inside an evidence bag while I tried to ignore Ronnie licking my hand behind my back. He must have thought I was hiding a treat from him. Knowing Labradors, if I wasn't careful he might try to eat my phone.

'I really don't think he killed himself,' I said, pretending to look for a tissue in my handbag so I could surreptitiously slip my phone back inside. 'Crash was in good spirits. He was writing new lyrics, making new music and looking forward to the Dublin concerts.'

'It's a funny thing,' said the superintendent. 'Suicidal people are often said to have been in a good mood right before they do themselves in. The shrinks say it's because they've finally made up their mind and feel free of responsibility at last.'

'That's terrible,' I said. 'How depressed must someone be to think that way?'

She grimaced. 'By definition, enough to kill themselves. You can't get much more depressed than that.'

Ace had padded over to see what Ronnie was so interested in. Now I reached down to stroke his head, wondering what would become of the Collie in the long term. Fox couldn't take him in, not with her new 'boat cat'. Ace would have to go to a local rescue.

'You don't have pets, do you, Superintendent?'

Fletcher looked at me with surprise. 'What makes you say that?'

'It's hard enough saying goodbye to a family pet when it's their time to go. I can't believe anyone who's been

through that would kill themselves without making arrangements for their dog to be rehomed.'

'In my experience, motivations are rarely so neat or clearly thought out. Whether or not this was suicide or an accident, I fear we may never know. But it will take a lot more than what we have so far to convince me it was anything else.'

Well, I do love a challenge.

CHAPTER THIRTEEN

After collecting Ace's throwing ring from the saloon, I led Birch and the dogs outside and over the junction bridge to Rembrandt Gardens, leaving the police to finish their work.

That morning the park had been full of people but now it was deserted. The Punch & Judy tent stood empty and unoccupied; there would be no more shows today. I looked out over the Pool and saw a few people milling about, but it was nothing compared to the earlier crush and most of the boaters had retreated inside. If I'm honest, I was a little surprised it wasn't more lively precisely *because* a celebrity had been found dead.

We let Ace and Ronnie off-lead, and Birch kept an eye on them while I finally returned Bostin Jim's call.

'Gwinny,' he answered, 'I've been trying to get hold of you. Is it true you're at Little Venice? Where Crash Double turned up dead?'

'Correct on all counts, Jim. How did you—oh, you've

seen that video, haven't you? I can explain . . . '

He laughed. 'Save it for the agency who just called me. They saw it online and want you to play a crotchety old woman in a new campaign.'

'A campaign for what?'

'No idea. Don't think they know themselves, but that's not the point. Got to strike while the iron's hot, haven't we? If we can keep your profile up I might book you some panto this year too.'

First a crotchety old woman, now an ugly sister? 'Darling, I'm a serious actress.'

'With serious cashflow problems. Listen, if it's good enough for Priscilla Presley it's good enough for Gwinny Tuffel, know what I mean?'

I mulled over this unexpected comparison and watched Ace try to herd Ronnie, who remained completely oblivious. This naturally only made the Collie more determined. Ronnie was a lovely dog, but like most Labs he had no more brains than the sheep Ace so fervently wished he was. Birch ran after them, waving his arms in vain as he tried to calm them down.

'I'll want to see what the agency is advertising, first. But so long as it's not a stairlift or incontinence pants, I'll consider it.'

'Can't say fairer than that. I'll get details. Any joy with Darren, by the way? The builder I sent your way?'

'Oh, I'm afraid he was too rich for my blood. Thanks, anyway.'

I ended the call and related the news to Birch, who by

now was red-faced and out of breath.

'Sounds like it's all going to plan,' he said between gasps. 'This time next year you'll be in *Les Mis*.'

I grimaced. 'I sincerely doubt that. Nobody wants to hear me sing.'

'All the same.'

His belief in me was charming, even though it was mostly based on what he'd seen of me twenty-plus years ago on TV. I laughed as Ace, presumably seeing my hands empty, ran up and nudged at my leg.

'On the other hand, someone definitely wants to see me throw a ring. All right, boy.' I took it from around his neck and prepared to toss it, but Birch held up a hand in defeat.

'Think we'll pass,' said Birch. 'Ronnie's tuckered out.'

To be honest, they both looked ready for a lie down somewhere. I sympathised. Even a boisterous dog like Ronnie couldn't match the energy reserves of a Border Collie. Then I remembered that Ace would soon have to go into rescue for rehoming and felt sad all over again.

'Birch, put your copper's head on for a moment—'

'Never off.'

'No, I suppose not. What do you think to this suicide theory?'

'Not impossible. Empty pill bottle's suggestive. Lack of witnesses is significant either way. Whether suicide or murder, someone troubled themselves to make sure it wasn't seen.'

I considered that again. 'If you were going to end it

all and didn't want witnesses, wouldn't you do it at night rather than waiting until daylight? I do wish there were cameras on the canal itself.'

'Mmm,' he murmured and gestured back towards the road. 'CCTV on junctions and crossings, though. Be easy enough to see anyone coming and going from the area, even at night.'

'If Fletcher bothers looking.' I fussed Ace, who sat eagerly waiting for the humans to finish making noises and start throwing things instead. Once again I thought how unlikely it was that Crash would leave his beloved, kooky-looking dog with an uncertain future. I made up my mind and said, 'After I've run Ace for a while, I'm going to pay Fox a visit. She knew Crash better than anyone, and seeing Ace might raise her spirits a little. It's probably better if I go alone, anyway.'

'Right you are. Dinner's off tomorrow, then? Sure you won't need a hand taking things back to Chelsea?'

'Oh, rats. In all the fuss I'd completely forgotten about dinner, sorry.'

I also hadn't considered where I'd be sleeping, but Birch was right. The police wouldn't take kindly to me staying at Crash's place any more. I'd have to return home and take Ace with me until his fate was determined. I hadn't made any preparations for Birch to eat at my house.

'Can we postpone? How about we do our usual walk and I'll buy you lunch at the café instead?' We'd fallen into the habit of meeting at the Kensington Gardens

bandstand on Sunday mornings to walk Ronnie. It was where we'd first met – and where I'd given Birch a thorough ticking-off for not keeping the Lab under control.

'Right you are. See you at eleven.' He was obviously disappointed, but it's not like I could have anticipated a dead body wrecking our plans.

I watched him leave the park, taking his tired dog up the low ramp instead of the steps, until Ace nudged my leg again. I dutifully threw the ring but was so distracted I completely messed up the throw. Instead of sailing the length of the grass, it hooked to the left and got stuck on a bush halfway down. Ace chased it anyway, trying to jump for it, but it was too high. After a couple of attempts he lay down on the grass, looking alternately at the ring and me.

Annoyed with myself, I stomped over to retrieve it. As I stood on tiptoe and reached up, I heard a familiar voice speaking quietly from the other side of the bush.

'. . . wondering if he left any instructions? No, I don't mean his will, I understand you can't disclose that yet . . .'

I leant forward a little to peek through the branches and saw Lucy Kwok standing on the narrow path between the Gardens and the Pool, shoulders hunched as she spoke on her phone. What on earth was she doing there? During my Friday walkabout I'd tried that path but found it narrow and treacherous, used solely by boats moored on this side of the Pool. It was much easier and safer to walk through Rembrandt Gardens, which

had exits to the canal at either end. Besides, Lucy's own exhibition boat was less than a hundred yards away.

She continued, 'You know . . . any *other* instructions. In the event of his death. Well, he has a dog. Yes, *had*, sorry. So I thought there might be some provision for that, and maybe some other . . . I see. No, I understand. Of course. Thanks for your time, Mr Patwari.'

Suddenly Ace barked, startling me. I turned to see what had set him off but trying to crane my neck while still leaning into the bush wasn't my best idea. I stumbled, slipped, and fell over in a tangle of limbs and branches. The impact dislodged the throwing ring, which fell from its adopted branch and landed on my chest. Ace pounced on it, knocking the wind out of me, and ran off with the disc in his mouth.

Breathless, I looked up to see a large-chinned man with big, fuzzy white hair looming over me. Then I realised I was looking at Howard Zee but upside-down, like everything else from this angle. Beside him was a young, dark-skinned woman I didn't recognise.

'Gwinny,' he said in a level voice. 'May I ask what you're doing down there?'

'I was wondering the same thing,' said Lucy, leaning in from the other side.

I sat upright and took a moment to replace the air that had been knocked out of my lungs, as well as my dignity. Forcing a smile I said, 'I was retrieving Ace's ring,' and gestured at the Border Collie now doing laps of the Gardens with it in his mouth. 'But he promptly stole

the evidence. If you've ever wondered why dog owners keep separate "dog-walking clothes", you're looking at the answer.'

'How are you holding up, Lucy?' asked Howard over my head. 'Such a terrible business. If there's anything you need, anything I can do before tomorrow evening, don't hesitate to ask. I'm only over the road.'

I stood up and brushed myself down. 'Yes, such a shame about the Carnival,' I said. 'All that hard work you put in, wasted because of this tragedy. You had event insurance, I hope?'

Lucy looked at me like I'd grown two heads. 'On the contrary, tomorrow morning we'll resume as normal. I'm sure the police will be out of our hair by then, considering Crash apparently killed himself.'

'But you said you'd seen his killer. On Friday morning, remember?' I was taken aback by this cold change of heart.

'Oh my God, really?' said the young woman accompanying Howard. She had a fast-paced American accent. 'Who was it? What did they look like?'

'Hang on,' I interrupted. 'What's happening tomorrow evening?'

'My last ever session with Howard, not that it's any of your business,' said Lucy. 'Now I must be getting on.' She walked away along the narrow path, back towards the junction bridge.

Ace bounded up, ring in mouth, to ask for another throw. Howard's American companion flinched and

moved to put him between her and the dog. He smiled and reassured her, 'Nothing to worry about. Ace is perfectly friendly.'

I quickly threw the ring, to my relief managing a straight flight this time. 'He really is, don't worry,' I said to the woman. 'Howard, you haven't introduced us.'

'Of course, how rude of me. Gwinny, this is Latesha Michaels. My new business partner.'

Latesha waved rather than offered a hand, keeping her distance as Ace returned the ring. 'I'm with Zabok+ in LA,' she said, as if I should know what that meant. 'We're pivoting to streaming on-demand wellness and Howard will front our P1 strand.' I understood most of that, though, and wondered if she'd descended into TV lingo to bamboozle me, or if it was how she always talked. You can never tell with executives.

'So your lovely boat's going to be famous,' I said to Howard.

He laughed. 'Goodness, no. We're off to LA this week to begin production, and I doubt I'll be back. I feel the universe pulling me to California and who am I to resist?'

Especially with a large cheque and a pretty girl waiting for you, I thought, but who could blame him?

'Crash's death brings things into focus, doesn't it? *Carpe diem*, as they say. So have you already sold your boat?'

'It's in hand,' he said, putting an arm around Latesha. She gave him a dazzling smile in return.

'What do you think he was doing out there, Howard?'

I said, throwing Ace's disc again. 'From what I saw, Crash barely left the house without his dog. Why would he go for a walk alone, right before he was due to catch a flight?'

'Didn't that woman say the cops called it suicide?' said Latesha. 'There's your answer.'

'I don't accept that. I think someone killed Crash.'

'What do the police think?' Howard asked. 'Are they looking into it?'

'No,' I admitted. 'Apparently there are no injuries on the body, so they're not looking for a suspect.'

'They can look somewhere else, anyway,' said Latesha. 'I know how cops work, always trying to pin something on somebody. But Howard was working Friday morning and we've got video to prove it.'

That took me by surprise. 'Why?'

'The live streams are automatically recorded,' she explained. 'After the show launches, we're going to pull second-strand material from them. So you tell the cops he's got an alibi, OK?'

'That's not really how it works . . .' I began, but she was already walking away, offended at any suggestion that her golden ticket might be tarnished.

Howard turned to follow, then stopped and turned back. 'Gwinny, remember that you only met Crash for a few hours. People on the canal have known him a lot longer, and . . . well, we all have our darker side, don't we? I tried to help him focus on his inner light. So did Fox, as much as he'd let her. But this isn't a huge surprise

to the community. You know yourself what it's like being in the spotlight for years, only to have it fade away.'

He hurried after Latesha before I could respond to such an offensive remark, although I couldn't deny it. Even before I retired to care for my father, work had been drying up for a while as I aged. When Fox had faced a similar problem she'd successfully switched from young starlet to an older, friendly face. But it was too late for me to do the same, and besides, I didn't have useful skills like her. I doubted audiences would run home to watch *Gwinny Solves Jigsaws* on BBC2.

It was time I paid the widow a visit. If Crash really had committed suicide, surely Fox would know why better than anyone.

CHAPTER FOURTEEN

The residents' access gate was now locked again and Constable Wright stood guard outside Crash's boat. I nodded politely as Ace and I passed but kept walking towards Fox's boat.

As we neared the unmistakeable rainbow-and-plants combo, Lucy Kwok emerged from within looking harassed.

'Are you still here?' she demanded, seeing me. Remembering her panicked distress that morning at the thought she might have seen Crash's killer, I wondered how much of it had been an act for the police's benefit.

'I've come to see Fox,' I explained. 'How is she?'

'She's fine. Goodbye, Gwinny.' Lucy turned to go and I remembered something else: she didn't live on the canal but in one of the lovely, white-painted houses on Blomfield Road overlooking it.

'Which is your house, by the way?' I asked.

'Why do you ask?'

'I hoped you could recommend a builder. I need some work doing but I'm at something of a loss.'

She blanked for a moment, blindsided by the change of subject. 'Um – yes, I suppose. Number thirty.' She pointed to a house back towards the junction bridge, then thought better of it and said, 'But don't call. My husband wouldn't like it. I'll look up the number for you later.'

'If he's anything like you, I wouldn't like it either,' I murmured as Lucy strode away.

She turned back. 'Sorry, was there something else?'

'No, nothing. See you soon.'

I wrapped Ace's lead around my hand to make a short hold, then stepped on board Fox's boat. 'Fox?' I called out. 'It's Gwinny. Can I come in?'

There was no answer. Which wasn't a definite 'no', so I decided to take is as a 'yes' and walked down the steps.

'I've got Ace with me but he's under control,' I called out into the gloom. 'Where are you?'

'In here,' Fox replied quietly, then sniffed and blew her nose. I threaded my way through the towers of foliage and found her on the duvet-slash-sofa, clutching a tissue to her red-rimmed eyes. A low table held a cup of tea and a tray of cookies. Lilith looked balefully out from the shadows of a bookshelf, pinpoints of light reflected in her cat's eyes. Through the lead I felt Ace tense up but trusted he could tell she remained out of reach.

The room's only other seats were wooden stools being used as plant pot stands, so I sat next to Fox on the sofa. Ace immediately flopped to the floor between us and

rubbed his furry head against Fox's feet, which made her smile. She reached down and fussed him.

'How are you, Gwinny?' She took a cookie and delicately bit into it.

It struck me that she was the first person to actually check I was OK. But much as I appreciated her consideration, it felt wrong that Fox of all people would be the one to ask after my well-being.

'Never mind me,' I said, 'how are you coping?' I took a cookie then thought to ask, 'Is there chocolate in these? I'm sure Ace would love one.'

She smiled ruefully. 'There isn't but best not anyway. It'd make him ill.'

I decided to keep it for myself instead but, despite my hunger, I dropped it in my pocket for later. I wasn't about to put her to the trouble of making more tea.

'Thirty-five years,' she said, gazing out at the water. 'That's how long we'd been together. Sounds a long time, doesn't it? But it feels like we met yesterday.'

'At a party, I assume?'

'No, he invited me to the Royal Albert Hall when they played. Apparently, he used to watch me on TV.'

'Crash had green fingers?' That took me by surprise. He hadn't really seemed the type and I hadn't noticed any plants on his houseboat.

Fox laughed, sniffed, then blew her nose again. 'This was before the gardening shows. No, he used to watch *me* on TV. Short skirts and long boots, you know the sort of thing.'

There was no easy way to ask but I couldn't think of a better time, so I plunged in. 'Fox, is there any reason you can think why he might kill himself? Was he ill?'

'What, mentally? He's a lead singer, Gwinny. They're all a bit special.'

Many would say the same about actors but it wasn't what I meant. 'No, physically. Cancer, perhaps? Something terminal?'

She munched on her cookie. 'Not as far as I know. I mean, whatever was going on in his mind, I guess you could call that terminal. But I didn't – I never thought . . .' She trailed off, holding back tears.

'He told me the Dublin concert was the highlight of his year.'

'It was. He'd never admit it but the older he got, the more he missed the place.'

I took a deep breath. 'Which is why I don't think he killed himself. Or that it was an accident.'

'No, no,' she said, looking puzzled. 'The police said it was.'

'Fox, nothing fits. Why would Crash text me to say he was leaving for the airport, then lock Ace in the boat and jump in the water? How come nobody saw or heard him? Who was the stranger climbing over the gate at six in the morning?'

She sat up a little straighter. 'The what? What stranger?'

'Lucy saw someone from her bedroom window. She couldn't tell who it was, but if they had to climb over

the access gate, then it obviously wasn't a resident . . .' I suddenly remembered what I'd seen on the phone video I'd taken accidentally. 'Although not everyone uses the gate, do they? Why did you jump over the railings last night?'

Fox reeled, her expression turning to outrage. 'I beg your pardon? How is any of this your business?'

I'd pushed too far but there was no going back now. 'Well, for a start it looks like I'm the one who'll have to rehome his dog. You can't take Ace on, not with Lilith here. Why did you go and get a cat right before the Dublin concerts, anyway?'

She leapt to her feet. 'I will not sit here and be interrogated! Get out!'

I got up too, followed by Ace, his head ping-ponging back and forth between us. 'But don't you see? If someone murdered Crash, they're still out there. They must be stopped.'

'You're the one who has to stop! It's bad enough he's dead, but you want to run around shouting murder? How dare you!'

'Now, what's going on here?' said a man's voice from behind us. I turned to see Johnny Roulette descend the steps into the saloon. 'Fox, I flew back as soon as I could. Come on, pet.' He approached her with open arms and Fox gratefully collapsed into them, sobbing. Johnny frowned at me over her shoulder. 'What's this nonsense you're talking to upset her?'

'I'm sorry. But I don't believe Crash killed himself,

and if I'm right then someone has got away with murder.'

Johnny opened his mouth to say something, then decided not to and closed it. 'Maybe you'd better leave.'

I did, leading Ace through the plants and up the steps. The afternoon was getting on but the day was still bright and pleasant, and by Collie standards the poor dog had barely exercised. I decided to give him another run around before collecting my things from Crash's boat and heading home with my own tail between my legs. Lucy wanted nothing to do with me, Howard thought I was naive, I'd upset Fox, and Johnny understandably took her side.

Besides, I hadn't been inclined to argue with him. When he'd wrapped Fox up in his long arms, the guitarist's sleeve rode up to reveal a sticking plaster on his right forearm that hadn't been there on Thursday. Somewhere between then and now, Johnny had cut himself.

CHAPTER FIFTEEN

People were returning to Rembrandt Gardens, though the half-dozen families sitting on benches were a sorry sight compared to how full and lively the park had been that morning.

I threw Ace's ring over and over, thinking about Crash's death and wondering: was I wrong? Had he really decided to end it all? Or had he fallen in? No matter how hard I tried, I couldn't convince myself of either possibility.

If I was right, though, it posed an even more difficult question: who would murder Crash, and why? A random mugging at six in the morning was unlikely, and surely even people sleeping off a hangover would have been woken by a cry for help.

Did Crash have a stalker? Crazed fans, who feel somehow betrayed and decide that if they can't have you nobody can, are more common than you might think. But wouldn't he have warned me, in case they'd

turned up at the houseboat? Besides, most stalkers stab or strangle the objects of their obsession, not shove them in a canal. Perhaps that part of it could have been an accident. Crash argued with his stalker, they fought and he fell into the water. But then why didn't he swim back out?

'I think he's waiting for you, pet.'

Startled, I turned to see Johnny Roulette approaching. Then I saw Ace, sitting at my feet with throwing ring in mouth, patiently waiting while I'd been lost in my thoughts.

I tossed it for him and said to Johnny, 'I really didn't mean to offend Fox.'

'She'll be fine. It's a shock, you know? For her, me, everyone. Crash had his moments, sure we all do, but this is out of the blue. Then you come along and cry murder, so it's no wonder she lost her rag. Who wouldn't? What makes you think that, anyway? The police are positive it's either suicide or an accident. And there's no proof either way, so best let it rest. Don't you think?'

I waited for him to finish this characteristic wall of blarney, wondering how much I should say. I wanted to ask about the plaster on his arm, not to mention the argument I saw him and Crash having on Thursday. But I didn't want to risk Johnny walking away in a huff as well.

'You're right,' I said, 'We'll have to wait for the police's final verdict. Hopefully I'm barking up the wrong tree . . . which reminds me, do you know if Crash had any plans for Ace if he died?'

The guitarist puffed out his cheeks. 'Now that's a good question. He didn't mention anything to me.'

Standing there, throwing discs in the park for the second time today, I remembered Lucy's phone call and decided to take a chance. 'What about Mr Patwari?'

'His solicitor? How would he know?'

'Owners sometimes write a letter of wishes in addition to their will,' I explained, feeling pleased with myself that I'd guessed the mystery man's role correctly. 'It states what they'd like done with any surviving pets. My parents always updated theirs as dogs came and went in our house.'

Johnny shrugged and took out his phone. 'Worth a try, isn't it? Hold on, now . . . here you go. Not sure if he'll be working Saturday.' My phone buzzed as he texted me the number.

'Oh, I have a feeling he already is,' I said. 'Would you keep Ace occupied while I call him? No time like the present.' I stepped away, leaving Johnny to dutifully throw the dog's ring.

Mr Patwari answered himself, sounding harrassed.

'I'm sorry to bother you,' I said. 'My name's Gwinny Tuffel and I'm currently looking after Crash Double's dog. I wondered if he left any instructions in the event of his death?'

'His dog? That's a new one. Where are you, the *Mail*?'

'No, I promise you, I really am his dog sitter. That's why I'm calling, to find out what happens to Ace.'

The solicitor sighed. 'I really don't think Mr Donnelly

expected to die before his dog. You're by no means the first to ask if he left any special instructions and I'll tell you what I told all of them: none whatsoever. However, there is the will and the matter of his estate and properties which I expect will be protracted. So I'm sure you can imagine I have a lot to do. Unless there was anything else . . . ?'

'Wait, hang on, yes. You said "properties", plural. But I thought Crash only owned the houseboat in Little Venice. Did he have a holiday home as well?'

'No, nothing like that. A small concern on Penfold Mews that he rents to a boutique management firm. Actually, thank you for reminding me as I'll have to inform them. Good day.'

He ended the call and I let my brain run in circles for a while as I watched Ace do the same. The dog obviously adored Johnny, but then they'd probably spent a lot of time together.

Questions swirled in my mind, a morass of puzzle pieces in search of a connection. Why had so many callers asked if Crash had left instructions in the event of his death? Why did Crash tell everyone he was broke when there were thousands of pounds in his safe, and now it turned out he also collected rent on a second house?

High-pitched shouts and cries shook me from my thoughts. On the far side of the Gardens, several children shouted and screamed while Ace ran around them and Johnny tried in vain to call the dog to heel. The children's parents yelled at him to 'call off his vicious dog', threatening all sorts of lawsuits and recriminations.

It was naughty of Ace to herd children but it was also pretty normal behaviour for a Border Collie. I ran over, putting myself between them so the dog couldn't avoid eye contact and called out, 'Ace, *stop*!' with a sweeping gesture of my hand. He paused, eyeing me warily, so I stepped away from the children – but not towards him, to show that he was the one who had to approach – and pointed down at my feet. '*Come. Heel.*'

His eyes flicked between me and the oh-so-tempting children, but I held his gaze and waggled my hand again, to keep his attention. Finally, he slunk over to me, tail drooping and sat by my side. I quickly clipped on his lead and turned to the children.

'Ace was just playing,' I reassured them. 'He wanted to pretend you were sheep, that's all. Collies will be collies.'

They stared at me for a moment, before one wailed and burst into tears. The others immediately joined in. Dealing with children has never been my forte.

'You're the mad woman from that video!' One mother jabbed a finger at me as her weeping daughter clung to her legs. 'It shouldn't be allowed!'

'What shouldn't, exactly?' I protested, confused. 'Did you miss the part where I brought my dog under control?'

But, like an angry audience on opening night, I'd already lost them. Other parents followed, berating me for traumatising their children, and nothing I could say would placate them.

Johnny put a hand on my back and ushered me towards the exit. 'Come on, pet, we're not wanted here.'

'You don't say. Let's go to Westbourne Green, and hope they don't follow.'

'Oh, we can do better than that,' he said with a twinkle in his eye. 'Let me treat you to a cup of tea and a private park, eh?'

I was still wary of Johnny. That sticking plaster on his arm worried me. But the braying parents were a much more immediate concern, and at least he was offering a method of escape.

'Darling, you know all the right things to say to a girl. Lead on.'

CHAPTER SIXTEEN

'I assume this means the end of Bad Dice?'

Ace and I followed Johnny past Warwick Avenue Station. My question was a little tactless, but I couldn't help remember Birch's remark about the band's lack of new material when we found Crash's notebook.

'Hard to say, pet. There's others who've carried on, you know? AC/DC, New Order, even Queen. But it's too early to think. Plus, Fox might have an opinion, of course.'

I hadn't previously considered what Fox might stand to inherit. 'Does she take over his music rights, then? Those must be worth a penny or two.'

'There's less than you might think. But I wouldn't want to upset her, you know. Maybe . . .' Johnny shook his head. 'Like I said, there's a lot to think about.'

We were chatting comfortably so I decided now was a good time to slip my real question into the conversation. 'What happened to your arm, by the way?'

He looked confused, then said, 'Oh, the plaster. Changing a guitar string, can you believe it? The thing whipped up and cut me. Not deep but it bled like billy-o. That's why I normally have my tech do it,' he added, laughing.

'Why didn't you this time?'

'I was worried where Crash was, you know? Sure, you remember I phoned you. Nothing de-stresses me like fiddling with the guitar.'

It was a plausible explanation but was it the truth? Johnny was hard to read. I'd already seen that his cheery and gregarious demeanour hid a more serious side, and while I've never been on a music tour, I've performed in enough travelling theatre productions to know that you don't survive fifty years on the road by being happy-go-lucky.

We passed a side road of shops, Choudhury's the grocer among them, and then entered the Crescent proper; a long, gentle arc of beautiful white-fronted houses with columned porticos. As we mounted the steps to Johnny's place I remarked on the area's tranquillity.

He turned from the door and said, 'What's that?'

'I said it's so peaceful around here. This is a very lovely house.'

Johnny led us inside. I kept Ace on-lead; the dog might know this house but I didn't, and I feared if I unclipped him he might gallop upstairs and leap on Johnny's bed or go ten rounds with the loo roll.

'It wasn't always like this,' he said. 'Sure the BBC's

down the road but after the war it was hardly *des res*. It's only when the likes of muggins here stepped off the boat that they put the prices up.'

It was hard to believe this house had ever been cheap. Even the hallway featured a twelve-foot ceiling and miniature chandelier. Like Crash's houseboat, the walls were lined with gold discs, concert posters, and—

'Good lord, is that . . . you?' I asked, taken aback by a life-size statue of Johnny playing guitar. Hooks were attached all over its surface, holding hats and coats.

He laughed and slung his jacket over a hook erupting directly from the statue's forehead. 'A gift from the architect who did this place up. I could hardly say no, and then after a while I got used to it. Now, let's get a tea brewing.'

I had a sudden attack of concern. 'Johnny, are you sure? I don't want to impose, and after what's happened . . .' Here I was, gawping at his spacious home like a pint-sized Loyd Grossman, when it was Johnny who'd lost what must surely be one of his oldest friends.

'Nonsense, pet, it'll do us both good. Come on.'

He walked on through the hallway, but I was quickly brought up short by Ace who was intent on giving the bizarre hatstand a thorough inspection. I wondered if he could smell Crash. Waiting for him to finish, I noticed an occasional table piled with incoming post. The topmost letter was to this address, *FAO Mr Jonathan Ormond-Wiles*.

Ace's curiosity satisfied, we proceeded into the

kitchen and I quietly upgraded my description of the house from *spacious* to *palatial*. This was another large room, all chrome and marble, with vintage American diner signs hanging from glazed splashback tiling and a large breakfast bar. It looked out over a wide expanse of green, sandwiched between another row of houses opposite and accessed by a door towards which Ace was already pulling me.

'You really are tireless, aren't you?' I laughed, winding in the dog's lead and directing him to lie at my feet while I took a stool at the breakfast bar. 'Wait a minute and then we'll see Johnny's park. Although it looks like you've seen it before.'

Johnny turned from the kettle where he'd been preparing tea. 'Milk and sugar?'

'Just milk, thank you. Has Ace been here before?'

'Sure, a few times. It's a good runaround, lots of folk with dogs.'

'But not you?'

He shook his head. 'Too much work and then I'm often not here, you know.'

I did. It was why I hadn't taken in a dog of my own after my father died, because I knew I'd be out for auditions and rehearsals all the time. It wouldn't be fair on either of us as I'd be forever handing the dog off to another sitter.

Not for the first time, I thought how ironic it was that the people who could most easily afford this sort of house, like Johnny or my friend Tina with her country

mansion at Hayburn Stead, were the least likely to spend much time in them.

He finished preparing the tea and sat opposite me, placing the mugs between us. 'It's a bad business, this,' he said quietly.

I remembered the notebook and the photos I'd taken. 'At least you won't be short of new material if you do carry on. Look at this.' I opened my phone's photo gallery and showed him the pictures. 'The police found a book of lyrics in Crash's safe. I'm told it's all new.'

Johnny's eyes almost popped out. 'Sweet Mary . . . in his safe, you said?'

'Not any more. The police took it for evidence but I snapped some photos before they took it away.' He raised an eyebrow at me. 'They didn't say I couldn't,' I protested, which was true but only because I hadn't asked.

'Can I see those?'

'Of course.' I handed him my phone and drank my tea as he swiped through them in silence. With perfect timing, I remembered Fox's cookie. I retrieved it from my pocket and began happily munching.

Johnny watched me sceptically. 'Tell me you're not eating dog biscuits, there.'

'No,' I laughed. 'Fox gave me this earlier, so I kept it for when I had a drink to go with it. Do you want a piece?'

He smiled and said, 'From Fox, you say? No, pet, you enjoy it.' Then he returned to looking at the pictures.

'Actually, I wondered if you could explain something,' I said. 'Keep swiping until the end.' He did, until he came to the page of random numbers and letters. 'This was on the last page, but it's gibberish to me. Is it something to do with his studio, perhaps? Who's this manager?'

He peered at the screen. 'Could be mix settings, sure. EQ and the like. What manager?'

I leant over and moved the picture on the screen, to reveal the name and email address underneath:

Don Christopher Management Ltd
dcm@top-emails.net

Johnny looked up and asked, 'Do you know who that is?'

My mouth was full, so I shook my head.

'Well, me neither. Maybe Crash met him at a party.'

'Oh.' I couldn't hide my disappointment. 'I thought perhaps you'd been writing new songs together.'

'Ha!' Johnny laughed bitterly. 'Chance'd be a fine thing. I've been writing by myself but this is all news to me.' He swiped back to the lyrics, reading them thoughtfully.

'Don't you think it's odd, keeping his notebook in a safe like that?'

Johnny looked up but didn't answer. Instead he said, 'Can I send these to myself, like? I don't trust the coppers not to lose the original.'

'Go ahead. I don't see what good they are locked up

in a police station.' I sipped my tea, pleased I'd had the impulse to take photos. New songs from Bad Dice really were more valuable than I'd assumed.

Ace barked, almost making me spill my tea. When I looked down I found him sitting upright, staring at me with his mismatched eyes, tongue out and expression hopeful.

'All right, all right,' I laughed. 'It must be at least fifteen minutes since you last had some exercise. Shall we take you in the park? Johnny, what do you say?'

I looked up as the guitarist passed my phone back. 'Thanks for that, pet. Come on, now, let's get the boy some exercise.' He took a keyring from a wall hook and opened the door to the rear garden with it. 'You can let him off-lead, it's all safe. Private park, remember.'

I didn't want to appear rude but I wasn't ready to take his word for it. Johnny had admitted he didn't have a pet himself. In my experience, people who've never had to worry about a dog bolting after a squirrel don't notice gaps and openings that to canine eyes might as well be lit with a neon sign. When we walked out, though, I saw that the park was truly private and fully enclosed. In addition to the row of houses opposite, more houses bound the top and bottom ends, ensuring the triangular green space was only accessible by the surrounding houses as a privilege for residents.

Satisfied, I unclipped Ace's lead and threw his ring. Johnny and I ambled across the grass as the Collie sped away, burning off yet more of his inexhaustible energy.

'Tell me about Crash,' I said. 'You two were obviously old friends, and he seemed quite normal for . . . well, for a rock star. Did you grow up together?'

'Sure, we were ten years old when we formed our first band. In Tullamore, for God's sake.' He looked wistful for a moment. 'Shaun got out first. One day when he was fifteen, straight out of the blue he said, "No! Enough." Packed his bag and caught the bus to Dublin that night. See, I thought he'd be back in a week.'

'But he wasn't?'

Johnny laughed. 'The fella went and got himself a job at the paper. He wrote to me, said come and join him. Well, I was doing nothing and hating every minute, so why not? Of course, when I got there, I found out he was the tea boy! We lived in one room with no heating until I could find a job. For a fair while after, too, you know.' Johnny smiled at the memory. 'But that was Shaun. Before he became Crash, like. Before all this.'

'Speaking of all this, if you don't mind me asking; how come you have such a beautiful place, while Crash was living in a houseboat?' His expression darkened, but I had to know. 'I mean, it's a very nice houseboat, but he was, well – no offence – he was rather more recognisable than you. Do your neighbours even know who you are?'

He looked at me with surprise. I winced, worried I'd pushed too far again. But then a deep, rumbling, full-body laugh built up and exploded like an erupting volcano from his big, broad frame. Even Ace, who'd once again dropped the ring at my feet, was caught off

guard and cocked his head at Johnny.

'I shouldn't laugh, not with everything,' he said between laughs. 'But there are two things you must know. First, just because Crash is up front shaking his arse, doesn't mean he wrote the songs. Sure, we wrote a few together and he got producer cuts from a couple of the early records. But most of our songs, certainly all the big hits, they were mine. And in this business, it's your name on the songwriting that gets you royalties, not pouting at the camera.' He paused for a moment, thinking. 'Used to be, anyway. With the Internet now, maybe it's the other way around, after all. Anyway, then your man married and divorced the same woman over and over. You know there was a time when Fox took eighty pence of every pound Crash earned?'

I hadn't. 'That seems excessive. But surely he wasn't still paying, now they were married again?'

'No, but historical, like. Never so good with money and the business side of things, was Crash. Not that Fox is much better, with her plants and rainbows, though she'll be right enough now. God bless her.'

A silence fell upon us as we walked. It wasn't uncomfortable, but it carried a certain weight that neither of us felt ready to lift. I certainly didn't think it was my place to move the conversation on, considering this man had today lost his oldest friend.

Then Johnny laughed again and said, 'You were asking if my neighbours recognise me. Probably not, it's the truth. But I don't know who they are either. They've

obviously got money and there's plenty of that washing around Little Venice, but it's still London, you know? A few weeks ago, I saw a removals van and realised what's-his-face from breakfast telly lived five doors down. You know, your man with the hair? Never seen him until that day.'

Ace returned with his ring, but as I bent down to take it, I overbalanced and stumbled, almost falling flat on my face. Johnny caught me and I looked down to see his hand gripping my arm. Or two hands gripping two arms, thanks to a slight blurring in my vision.

'I'm terribly sorry,' I mumbled. 'I feel a bit dizzy.' At least that's what I tried to mumble but I could tell from his expression that he struggled to understand me. That made me think of something else, something that felt important, but my head was spinning too much to think straight. I held onto his arm, hauled myself upright and took a deep breath. A moment later I took another, and slowly but surely the world steadied around me.

'I'd better take Ace home,' I said. 'Perhaps we both need some rest.'

'Grand idea,' said Johnny, smiling sympathetically. 'Everyone's had a long day, pet.'

We returned to his house, where I clipped Ace back on-lead and led him out to the street. The evening was drawing in and I suddenly felt very hungry. Had I eaten anything since breakfast? Had Ace? I couldn't remember. Wobbling slightly, I walked back to Blomfield Road and down to Crash's houseboat to feed us both.

Constable Wright had other ideas.

'Sorry, madam. Off limits, by order.'

'But Crash wasn't . . . wasn't killed in there,' I said, noticing with some alarm that I was slurring my words. 'Said that this afternoon, remember? Need to . . . feed the dog . . . get some clothes. Jigsaw.'

'Are you quite well, madam? What clothes?'

I rattled Ace's lead, then regretted it as I almost lost my balance and clutched at the policeman to steady myself.

'Dog sitting! God's sake . . . don't you remember? Call Fletcher . . .'

'The superintendent has left for the night, madam. I'd advise you do the same and sleep it off.'

Stupid boy! I couldn't make him see straight, though to be fair I was having trouble doing that myself. I resisted the temptation to shove the constable in the water because who would look after Ace while I warmed a cell for the night?

I swallowed my anger and trudged back to Warwick Avenue Station. At least at home I could relax and find something to eat, far from trouble.

I almost fell asleep on the Tube and missed my stop, but I fought the urge because I didn't want to risk Ace getting away from me. I wondered if he'd ever been on a train before. He boarded happily and sat at my feet but didn't seem at all relaxed. His head was in constant motion taking in the Saturday night crowd.

Finally, we emerged from Sloane Square Station onto

the King's Road and the fresh air gave me a second wind. Something nagged at me, something my mind was trying to make me notice or remember about Johnny. But I was too tired and it wouldn't come. It would have to wait until morning.

Turning into Smithfield Terrace, my thoughts were cut short by an unexpected sight. The dizziness returned as I walked down the road, and I couldn't be entirely sure I was seeing right but it looked like someone was having building work done. Seeing the assembled scaffolding, I wondered if I should pop round and ask them for a recommendation.

Then I recognised my own house.

A sign hung off one of the bars but I couldn't read it. The scaffold covered the frontage, taking up much of the pavement, and I couldn't seem to find a way through to my door.

'Guinevere, my dear. Could I have a word?'

I turned too quickly, stumbled, and steadied myself on an upright pole as I faced the Dowager Lady Ragley. She wore her customary black frock with white cuffs and stood on the far side of the scaffolding outside her front door. Her hair was scraped back in a tight bun, accentuating her severe expression.

'Good evening . . . lady,' I slurred. 'Who . . . did you do this?' I hadn't meant it to come out like that, but I was having difficulty forming words.

The Dowager was about to respond when she saw Ace, who first cocked his head at her, then without

breaking eye contact cocked his leg up a scaffold upright.

The normally composed widow practically vibrated with indignation. 'My dear girl, this abomination was erected by one of the rudest men I have ever encountered, and I once dined with the late Australian ambassador. When I asked him what he was playing at, well, I won't repeat his exact words. But he insisted I should "call Darren" to clear up the matter.'

'Must be . . . misunderstanding,' I tried to reassure her. 'Darren . . . said no. Shouldn't be . . . scaffold.'

'There most certainly should not be scaffold,' agreed the Dowager. 'Their van blocked the road for an hour, and the noise! Radio blaring, men shouting, and who ever imagined a Pole would know such Anglo-Saxon language? On a bank holiday weekend, no less!'

There was nothing I could do about it at this time or in my current state. 'No, of course . . .' I said, trying to soothe her. 'Call . . . tell him off, yes. Misunderstanding. Could you show me . . . front door?'

She finally noticed my shambolic state and looked appalled. 'Guinevere, are you *drunk*? Dear, oh dear. Whatever would your father think?'

'No! Tired . . . anyway, Daddy drunk plenty . . . but no! Just . . . door. Wherezit?'

I felt a tug on my hand and looked down to see my arm outstretched; at the end of it, my hand holding Ace's lead; and at the end of that, a tricolour Border Collie leading me through a canvas-lined tunnel in the scaffolding. I recognised my own front door at the tunnel's far end and

gratefully followed Ace while the Dowager returned to her house, muttering with disapproval.

It took a couple of minutes of wondering why my key didn't work to notice I was trying to open my door with Crash Double's keyring. Laughing at my silly mistake, I found the right keys, opened the door and fell inside.

The right keys. That felt important but I couldn't think straight. I closed the door and collapsed against it.

CHAPTER SEVENTEEN

Ace woke me again the next morning, standing next to the bed and whining plaintively. After shooing him away I glanced at the time. Quarter to nine! I shot out of bed, immediately regretting it as the world dizzily rotated around me. Thankfully, it cleared after a few seconds of holding on tight to the door frame and with bleary eyes I led Ace downstairs to the garden.

'Guinevere, my dear. I trust you've recovered since last night. Did you hear about this terrible business in Little Venice? A rock musician!'

In what was either a remarkable coincidence of timing or a remarkable display of patience, the Dowager Lady Ragley stood looking over the fence into my garden, her pinned-back hair as immaculate as her ivory cuffs. Had she even been to bed? I hadn't brushed my hair, let alone my teeth, and stood barefoot in my pyjamas with a plastic bag ready in hand while Ace went to the toilet.

'Really, my lady?' I said innocently, not wanting to

feed her salacious hunger for gossip. 'How curious. As it happens, this dog belonged to someone who died in Little Venice yesterday. We live in such dangerous times, don't you think?' I quickly bagged up Ace's business and made to return inside.

'Two? Two deaths?' she spluttered as I hurried back in. 'Is that what you're saying?'

I closed the patio doors, leaving her bewildered. I hadn't actually said it was a different person to the 'rock musician' but I enjoyed imagining her spending all day searching in vain for a mysterious second death.

The last thing I heard before the double glazing cut her off was a faint cry about builders. Hazy memories of the night before began to resurface. Hoping I might have dreamt the whole thing, I flung open the curtains in the front room and looked out. No such luck; the scaffolding was still there, as solid as the pavement on which it stood. Feeling miserable, I closed the curtains and returned to the kitchen.

Making coffee for myself and breakfast for Ace, I grimaced at the state of the countertop and remembered ravenously scoffing toast before collapsing into bed. The kitchen was the one room I'd managed to keep in good and tidy order while caring for my father, but now it was a mess of breadcrumbs, butter smears, opened loaves and unrinsed kitchenware.

While Ace ate his kibble I wiped down the surface, loaded the dishwasher and tied off the open loaf. Feeling a little more organised and righteous, I decided to unload

the rest of my frustration on Darren the builder and took out my phone to call him.

There was a text message from an unknown number waiting for me.

> *See for yourself and leave H alone*
> *I sent this to the cops too*
> *– L*

It included a link, which took me to a page of video recordings. Each thumbnail image was of Howard Zee's face, sometimes smiling, sometimes calm, sometimes sweating with exertion on his houseboat set.

L for Latesha Michaels. She'd got a bee in her bonnet about his alibi, and no doubt the video of Howard's class from Friday morning was somewhere in here. How did she get my number? I didn't recall giving it to Howard.

I really wasn't in the mood, so I closed the message and phoned Darren. I didn't expect he'd answer this early on a Sunday but I could leave a disgruntled voicemail.

He did answer, though.

'Hello?' said a gruff male voice with the unmistakeable tone of someone who had been woken from a perfectly good lie-in.

'Darren, it's Gwinny Tuffel on Smithfield Terrace. I don't know why you sent someone round to erect scaffolding yesterday but you need to take it away again. I declined your estimate so there's no reason for it to be here.'

'What are you talking about? I've already booked out the time, I start on Tuesday.'

'But I can't afford you. Why do you think I sent that emoji of money flying away?'

He sighed. 'I thought you were being funny, making a joke about the cost. You said you wanted me to start as soon as possible so I booked Mateusz.' He muffled the phone and I heard voices in the background. It occurred to me that he might have a whole family there and I'd woken them up. I felt slightly guilty about that but this had to be dealt with. He returned to the phone and said, 'If you'd wanted to decline you should have said so explicitly.'

'If I'd wanted to proceed I *would* have said so explicitly. You can't assume someone has agreed to have work done without checking.'

'Listen, you'll have to pay for the scaffolding, regardless. It's already up and whether they pull it down now or next week makes no difference. Mateusz's crew has done the work and they'll expect to be paid. Then you'll have to pay all over again when you find someone else to do your frontage and, by the way, good luck finding someone cheap enough to save that money compared to me. Plus, I'll have to charge you for at least one day of cancelled time anyway because I've already booked out the week to do this for you. So, do you still want to cancel?'

I felt frustrated, deflated and not a little extorted. Darren's quote was high enough to use up a substantial

chunk of my savings. Every builder claims nobody else can do it cheaper, but the work really did need doing and if I wound up having to pay half of it anyway as a kill fee, then pay another builder the same amount again, he was right; I'd be even worse off.

Someone would have to pay me for dog-sitting Ace, I decided, whether it was Crash's lawyer, Fox Double-Jones or the damned residents' association. And I still hoped that Bostin Jim could negotiate my original fee for *Mixed Mothers*, regardless of recasting. If I could win both of those battles, I'd be OK. More or less.

'Fine. Have it your way,' I said, and went to brush my teeth.

Staring in the mirror at my red-rimmed eyes, I tried to understand what had happened last night. In the cold light of day, the idea that I'd been exhausted and hungry didn't hold water. I might not jog the streets of London every morning like Howard Zee, but I was in reasonably good shape and no stranger to spending all day on my feet. True, Ace had the boundless energy reserves of any Border Collie but I'd kept pace with him.

So what was it, if not weariness? It had been a very long time since I'd felt so disorientated and fuzzy-headed. In fact, not since—

The last time I smoked dope.

I'm no innocent prude. You couldn't be in show business thirty years ago without encountering drugs of all kinds and I doubt it's any different now. So yes, I smoked a little, and once or twice tried something stronger, but nothing

ever took. Marijuana made me sleepy and hungry, which would explain stuffing my face last night. Other drugs just made me feel horrible, or rather made me feel like I became a horrible person, which had been confirmed whenever I'd remained sober while in the company of others buzzing off their heads. For decades, a drink or two had been my only vice.

Well, that and jigsaws. But they couldn't arrest you for driving after finishing a tricky thousand-piecer.

I tried to retrace my steps. Crawling into bed after scoffing toast; before that, a soporific Tube ride home; before that, slurring my words at Constable Wright; and before that, it all started with me stumbling around Johnny's private park.

Right after he'd made us both tea.

Had he spiked it? But why? He hadn't tried to take advantage of me; in fact, despite Crash's warnings, Johnny had been a gentleman. I didn't recall an odd taste or anything at all unusual about the tea, except . . .

The cookie I'd eaten with it. The one from Fox's tray which she'd warned me not to give to Ace.

I groaned, feeling very naive. Of course. Celebrity gardener Fox Double-Jones secretly grew cannabis, probably in the unseen locked room on her houseboat, and had baked some into the cookies she was eating when I visited. To cope with Crash's death? Or was eating loaded biscuits a regular habit? It would explain her mellow demeanour. Either way it seemed an innocent mistake, with no nefarious motive and no harm done besides the

butter smears on my kitchen countertop.

But what if it wasn't?

Had Fox hoped the cookie would disorientate me to stop me asking awkward questions? If I'd eaten it right away I'd have been reeling much earlier, perhaps even before I'd got round to mentioning her late-night leap over the fence.

Now another question formed in my mind, adding a new piece to this strange puzzle: what if Crash had been poisoned?

There were no injuries on his body; nothing to indicate he'd been attacked. But poison wouldn't leave a mark. A killer could simply wait for him to die, then throw his body overboard without a struggle. It would also explain why nobody saw or heard anything. At six in the morning anyone could stand on their deck with a coffee, seeming completely innocent while patiently checking the coast was clear.

Did that mean Crash had definitely been killed on someone else's boat? Or could it have been done in his own home after all? The killer might have called round for an early chat before Crash left for Dublin, spiked his coffee then tossed him out of the French windows without making a mess or leaving any trace of blood.

No matter where it happened, it would have to be someone Crash knew. He was mindful of his privacy at the best of times and I couldn't believe he'd invite a stranger in for coffee at six a.m. It would also explain Ace being at home; he'd either been left there when Crash visited the killer

or locked inside when the killer departed.

The puzzle piece that continued to elude me was motive. Money? The singer wasn't as broke as he'd claimed, with thousands in cash to hand and a premises he rented out. But nobody else knew that . . . did they?

Only one person I could think of in Little Venice fitted the bill. Someone who knew Crash; whom he would have readily visited or received at home early in the morning; who gained financially from his death; and with easy access to poisons.

Fox Double-Jones.

I was due to meet Birch at eleven for our regular Sunday walk, but I felt so lethargic after the night before that I considered calling it off. I didn't need to look in the mirror to know I had bags under my eyes and the energy to do anything about it was in short supply, but I felt obliged to make up for the lack of Sunday dinner. Besides, he appeared in no hurry to turn his own blue eyes my way so he'd have to take me as he found me.

While attempting to perk myself up with another coffee, I texted the former policeman to say I'd be a little late. Then I saw the message from Latesha Michaels again and it gave me an idea.

You can add yoga to the list of things that aren't really 'me'; many years ago, Tina tried to recruit me as her classmate but half an hour of what felt like a sadistic game of Twister convinced me I wasn't cut out for it.

Nevertheless, that was a long time ago and she still

swore by it. I could at least hope it would put a spring back in my step. So, five minutes later – after double-checking the lounge curtains were well and truly drawn – I placed my laptop on a bookshelf and stood facing it in my underwear ready to watch Howard Zee. Ace watched me with unabashed curiosity from the sofa but that didn't bother me; Sabre, our family's German Shepherd, had a habit of following people into the toilet if they didn't close the door quickly enough. There was no privacy with dogs.

Latesha's link contained dozens of videos going back several months. As she'd said, there were two from Friday morning, one starting at six and another at seven. I played the one that started at six, figuring I might as well check Howard's alibi while trying to inject some life into my tired body.

As the video began, I was once again impressed by his professional set-up and presentation. No wonder her company saw potential in him. I wondered idly if they'd add maintaining the beard to his contract; I'd heard of clauses that banned actresses from cutting their hair or mandated that leading men spend a minimum number of hours every day in the gym. It sounded exhausting.

Things started easily enough, with deep breaths and stretching. I had to cheat a little; the last time I could touch my toes without bending my knees was thirty years ago. We progressed to sit-ups, toe-touching and holding out an arm or leg while trying to stay balanced. So far, so good, though I was already beginning to sweat.

By this time Ace had come off the sofa and decided to join in, doing his own version of stretching on the carpet beside me.

When Howard asked me to stand on one leg and stretch out the other while touching it, I started to worry that perhaps I wasn't in such good shape as I'd thought. Finally, after a position that made me hop, stumble and almost crash into the TV stand – which sent Ace leaping back onto the sofa – I admitted defeat. Muscles I didn't even know I possessed felt stretched in ways never intended by nature and I was sweating all over. Was this meant to feel good?

'Don't worry, boy,' I said to Ace, breathing heavily. 'At least we got near the end, eh?'

I touched my laptop to see exactly *how* near the end and whimpered when I saw barely fifteen minutes had elapsed. I skipped ten minutes ahead to find Howard doing press-ups, his muscular arms flexing and bulging. It wasn't hard to see why he might attract an audience of older women, particularly if their husbands had lost interest now that they'd produced the expected two-point-four children. I skipped again, and again, grimacing each time as the exercises reached far beyond anything I was capable of, until I suddenly reached a black screen showing a countdown timer. I went back to see what I'd missed, and found Howard declaring a break at the forty-five minute mark. He turned off the camera, and the view changed to a five-minute countdown. I skipped forward until that was over, at which point Howard reappeared with a towel

around his neck and smoothie in hand, sitting on a stool and talking to the class. They were also visible now, smiling women in little boxes at the bottom of the screen.

The first question was something about chakras and my attention quickly drifted. It was horrible to think that at the very moment this was being recorded, Crash was dying nearby. In fact, if Lucy's mysterious climbing man was the killer then Crash had already been dead for almost an hour by now.

Could that man have been Johnny? Crash's death might cause a surge in Bad Dice record sales, and from what the guitarist had said most of the royalties would go to him. True, he was already loaded, but money is a powerful motive. His story about a guitar string sounded fishy, too. If he'd really cut himself while climbing the gate, and Lucy heard him cry out—

The doorbell rang, startling me. I turned to answer it, then remembered I was still barefoot in my underwear. Ace had already leapt off the sofa and ran into the hallway. The bell rang again and I hurried after him.

'All right, hang on,' I called out, grabbing a raincoat from the coat rack and hastily tying the belt around my waist. If the Dowager Lady Ragley insisted on calling at odd hours she'd get what she got and that was that.

In the split second it took to open the door, it occurred to me that the Dowager normally preferred to intercept me as I left the house. And it wouldn't be the postman on a Sunday morning. So who . . . ?

'Blimey!' exclaimed a wide-eyed DCI Alan Birch, retired.

CHAPTER EIGHTEEN

'Sorry, ma'am – said you'd be late – thought I'd call – save you – ah, that is—'

Birch turned a shade of red and averted his eyes. Not before I noticed he gave me a quick up-and-down, mind you. Ronnie and Ace wagged tongues at one another across the threshold.

I stood in the doorway, momentarily frozen as I realised I was sweating, still tired, *sans* make-up and currently resembled a street flasher. Oh, well. Birch would indeed have to take me as he found me.

'It's not the eighteen-hundreds, Birch. There's no need to be scandalised by my ankles,' I said, refusing to be embarrassed. 'I was just getting ready, so wait in the lounge and I'll be down shortly.'

Despite my bravura, I wasn't about to shed the raincoat in full view, so while he made his way to the sofa I hurried upstairs with it still tied around me. I'd expected Ace to stay with him and Ronnie, but instead

the Collie followed me and waited on my bed as I dressed and put on a face.

Ten minutes later, with Birch's complexion returned to a normal colour, we strolled through South Kensington while I explained my theory that Crash had been poisoned.

'Plausible,' he said. 'Hard to imagine Fox hefting Crash up and over the side of a boat, though. An accomplice, perhaps?'

'I wouldn't discount her on the basis of strength. You should see her throw bags of compost around on telly. But you're right that it would have been easier for someone like Johnny.' I told him about the plaster on the guitarist's arm.

'Hmmm. Suspicious. Would he have access to the poisonous plants?'

I thought back to Fox's cabinets. 'Yes, I think so. She practises giving her tour on local residents, and the key is kept in a nearby jug so it's not a closely guarded secret. He'd have to have got inside the boat without her knowing, though.'

'And while Fox is already there, too. Tricky.'

'The question I keep coming back to is motive. The one person who had any real argument with Crash was Lucy Kwok, but would she really murder him over the Canal Carnival?'

'People kill for less every day, I'm sorry to say. But first let's find out if Crash was poisoned. I'll talk to Fletcher, see what she thinks and if they've checked for toxins yet.'

We entered Kensington Gardens and let the dogs off to run around. Ace tried to herd Ronnie again, but

the Lab remained oblivious, being far more interested in the bushy-tailed squirrels darting in every direction. The Gardens looked lovely, as they always do in spring, with trees starting to leaf and flowers budding among the bushes and dewy grass.

Ace finally tired of trying to get Ronnie's attention and ran to me with an expectant look. I dutifully took the disc from around his neck and threw it.

'What if Johnny got that cut not from climbing over the gate, but from heaving Crash over the side of a boat?' I wondered.

Birch shrugged. 'Possible, but as you said, motivation's tricky. Crash and Johnny have had plenty of disagreements over the years, that's well documented. All in the past, though. Killing him now feels twenty years too late.'

I remembered that last night I'd been close to understanding something about Johnny, something about his behaviour, but I couldn't pin it down. By now we were approaching the Long Water and both dogs' tongues were happily panting, so we called them to heel and clipped on their leads.

'Jealous lover?' Birch mused. 'What if the feud between Crash and Lucy was for show? They were having an affair, Fox found out, slipped him some poison.'

'But why not simply divorce him again? Apparently, she took him to the cleaners the first two times, claiming almost all of his income.'

'True enough. Second divorce came about when he

shacked up with a Swedish model, who then dumped him anyway. Got a great album out of it, mind you. All heartbreak and bitterness.'

Once again the former policeman's tastes surprised me and I was glad of it. Talk about hidden depths.

'That reminds me,' I said, pulling out my phone. 'Let me send you those photos of Crash's notebook, with the new lyrics. I showed them to Johnny yesterday and he said he'd never seen them before. He didn't even know Crash was writing new songs.'

Birch smiled wistfully as I opened the photo gallery. 'Shame we'll never get to hear them now. Still, lyrics are better than nothing.'

But something strange had happened.

'I don't understand,' I said, distracted.

'Turn of phrase. I mean even if we can't hear Crash sing them, there's enough previous material to imagine—'

'No, not that,' I interrupted. 'The photos. They're not here.'

I scrolled through my gallery, wondering if I'd done something to make them show out of order, but the notebook was nowhere to be seen. I tried looking in my Favourites folder, then remembered that most of the recent pictures in it were candid photos of Birch I'd snapped while dog walking. Hearing a sort of strangled cough over my shoulder, I quickly scrolled down to save us both our blushes, but again: nothing.

'They were here yesterday. I showed them to Johnny, in his kitchen.'

'Beg pardon?'

'We were having a cup of tea,' I said defensively. 'He was amazed to see the new lyrics and asked if he could send them to himself. Of course, I said yes and gave him my phone . . .' I groaned. 'Ace distracted me while Johnny was holding it. Could he have deleted the pictures when I wasn't looking? Why would he do that?'

'Innocent mistake?' Birch ventured.

'Poppycock. He and Crash might be getting on, but they're no Luddites. Not like us!' I almost cried with frustration. 'What is it about this bloody notebook that's so valuable?'

Birch reached for my phone. 'May I?'

I let him take it, feeling rotten. I should never have let Johnny handle my phone but even with that cut on his arm, I hadn't been sure he was up to no good. Now, though . . .

'Look this way, ma'am?'

I did, to find Birch holding up my phone with the screen facing me. Then he tapped a few things and handed it back.

'There you go. All present and correct.'

He was right. The notebook photos were there, even including the last page with the technical recording codes. I stared at him in amazement.

'Not quite a Luddite myself,' he smiled. 'They were in your Recently Deleted folder, but it's locked behind facial recognition. Johnny couldn't access that, so wasn't able to purge it. I restored them.'

'I only understand half of that but I could kiss you all the same,' I said with delight, this time sparing him no blushes as I swiped through the photos. 'Next time I need help with a file that mysteriously disappears, I know who to—*oh*!'

'Beg pardon? Something else wrong?'

I stared at the photo of the page with the recording codes, and below those:

Don Christopher Management Ltd
dcm@top-emails.net

'Crash's solicitor said he rents out a place on Penfold Mews to a boutique management firm,' I explained.

'Is there much call for managing boutiques?'

'No, it . . . never mind. What are the chances it's this company? You're the music man, have you heard of them?'

Birch peered at the name. 'Does ring a bell, now you mention it. Where's Penfold Mews, then?'

'Let's find out.'

I opened my phone's map and searched for the street, expecting to be whizzed halfway across London. Instead, the pointer merely hopped north a small way . . . to a street in Little Venice.

CHAPTER NINETEEN

Finding Penfold Mews was easier said than done. Even with a map it took five minutes of searching before we located the road entrance because it was literally a street within a street; an old, narrow road that ran between two larger thoroughfares north of Warwick Avenue Station, tucked away out of sight.

Walking down its cobbled surface, my heart sank at the lack of any signage. 'Probably a residents' by-law,' I said. 'Should I call Mr Patwari again and ask which house it is?'

Birch gave me a disapproving look. 'Sunday, remember. Besides, he'd want to know why you're asking.'

Ace began pulling on his lead, which was unusual. Border Collies are all keen as mustard to get wherever they're going (even when they don't actually know where that is) but they train to heel well and Ace had quickly adapted his pace from Crash's long legs to mine. He hadn't forged ahead like this before.

'Something's got Ace's nose,' I said, giving his lead some slack. 'Let's see where he takes us.'

The dog moved directly ahead. Was he going to lead us straight out the other end of the street to a smelly rubbish bin? Then again, this didn't seem like an area where rubbish was left on the street, smelly or otherwise.

Ace veered left towards a nondescript door with a buzzer, where a card affixed inside its small windowpane informed us this was the home of 'DC Management'. There was no other indication of who was inside but it was enough.

'I remember now that when I asked Johnny to recommend a builder, Crash almost said something but stopped himself. I wonder if he was going to suggest whoever converted this place but realised it would blow his secret?'

'Why keep it secret is the question,' said Birch. 'Hiding assets in case of divorce, perhaps? As you said, he's been rinsed before.'

'Whatever the reason, I'm guessing Crash's scent lingers here and that's what Ace caught. *Good boy*,' I said, slipping the Collie a quick treat from my pocket. He panted with excitement, looking from me to the door with his tail going ten to the dozen.

Birch pressed the buzzer but there was no answer. He tried again. I strained to hear any reaction or sign of life from within, but it was quiet as a church.

I decided to be cheeky and try the door. It was locked. Pressing my face to the glass, all I could see inside was

an unlit set of stairs leading up. Mews houses commonly have a garage space at street level with the living space starting on the first floor. Crash had presumably converted the house upstairs to office space but left the garage as it was.

Ace suddenly reared up on his hind legs and began scratching at the door. I pulled him away, but sympathised with his eagerness to get inside.

'Can I help you?'

We turned to find a slim young man standing behind us. I suppose we did look a bit suspicious, although having the dogs gave us good cover.

'Oh, we were out for a walk and thought we'd call on Mr Christopher,' I said. 'Have you seen him lately?'

'This is a respectable street, you know.'

'I'm sure it is,' I said, floundering a little. 'But, um, we're old friends of his. From the music business.'

He looked me up and down with a scepticism bordering on outright hostility.

'All right, you got us,' said Birch, laughing. 'Not showbiz types at all, of course not. Look at us! Terrible cover story.' Before I could protest, he continued, 'Truth is, here on behalf of a client. To collect a debt, if you get my meaning.'

The young man softened slightly. At least Birch looked the part.

'If you mean you're debt collectors, then yes, of course I do.'

'Good. So, seen him lately?'

'Never.'

'Here much, are you? Might come and go when you're not around.'

The young man indicated a house on the other side of the street. It was a hairdresser's, with the garage space converted to a shop frontage.

'That's my shop, so I'm here all day long and I've never seen a soul go in or out of that house. Don't know why he bothers, what with the rents around here. Maybe that's why he can't pay his debts.'

With that he turned and walked to his door, taking a set of his keys from his pocket. I suddenly remembered my own escapades the night before, mistakenly trying to open my front door with Crash's keys, and gave an involuntary squeak.

'The keys were for here!'

Birch looked puzzled. 'Come again?'

'Remember the old keys found in Crash's safe? I assumed they were an old set from before he changed the houseboat locks. But why keep old keys if they didn't fit any more?' I pointed at the mews house. 'I think they fit this door, instead.'

'Suggests he's had the place a while. Is it likely, though? Very recognisable man.' He turned to the hairdresser's house, where a light had come on in the upstairs rooms. 'Surely even that chap would know him.'

'He'd have to see him first. Perhaps Crash visited when nobody else was around and he knew he wouldn't

be seen. If he brought Ace with him, it would explain why he's so keen to get inside.'

'Very plausible,' Birch agreed. 'Another thing to ask Fletcher.'

His loyalty to his old superintendent was admirable, but I was getting a little tired of it when she wouldn't take our suggestions seriously. Still, there was no sense in starting an argument.

I opened the final notebook photo again, noted Don Christopher Management's email address, then sent them a short message from my phone asking about their connection to Crash. Did they even know he was their landlord? Surely they would, being in the same industry. They might even know why he was so keen to keep this place hidden from family and friends, though I didn't mention that in the email.

Returning to the photo, a puzzle piece tentatively clicked into place in my mind. Not the management company, but the lines above it: what Johnny had said could be studio recording settings. Given his attempt to delete the pictures, I was no longer inclined to believe him. Instead, I had a new idea of what they might really be.

'Birch, I see a computer in our future. Let's get back to the canal.'

CHAPTER TWENTY

If I'd thought Crash's death would bring the Carnival to a halt and dissuade people from attending, I couldn't have been more wrong. Today was even busier, the tragedy seemingly forgotten by everyone clustered around the Pool.

The people gathered outside the residents' access gate hadn't forgotten, though. It remained locked, and presumably wouldn't open to the public again, but they wouldn't be dissuaded.

We pushed our way to it, helped once again by the dogs clearing a path. I spied Constable Wright still standing guard outside Crash's front door, which could be a problem after our unceremonious ejection yesterday.

'Hey, it's the angry drone lady!' shouted a voice in the crowd. All eyes turned on us as I fumbled with the key, trying to unlock the gate before embarrassment overtook me.

'You owe me a replacement,' called another voice.

The bearded young reporter whose drone I'd whacked pushed his way towards me with a furious expression. 'I've reported you to the police!'

'Why don't you use the money you made from that video?' I shot back, suddenly angry. 'I should be asking you for royalties!'

The reporter advanced. 'Do you have any idea what those things cost? The article fee doesn't even begin to cover it!'

Perhaps sensing the tension, Ace moved in front of me and snarled at the young man.

'Even her dog's vicious,' he called to the crowd. 'Shouldn't be allowed!'

'I suggest you step back, sir,' said Birch, taking a step forward himself. Before it developed into a proper stand-off, though, a loud voice behind us cut through the noise.

'Now, then, what's going on here?'

I practically fell through the gate as Constable Wright swung it wide open. Birch and the dogs followed, and we backed away onto the residents' path, leaving the constable to argue with the angry young man.

'Quick!' I whispered to Birch, realising that for the first time since we'd stepped onto the path, nobody was looking at us. While everyone focused on Constable Wright, I hurried to unlock the door to Crash's houseboat. We tumbled inside, and after closing the door behind us I made for the stairs. 'Like you said before, hardly breaking and entering when we have a key, is it? Besides, I still need to collect my things from in here. But we'll

deal with that later.' I led the way up to the second floor and Crash's studio.

'You said he really was working on new music?' Birch asked.

'He was, yes. But it's not the music I'm interested in.' I sat at the desk and unlocked the computer with the password. Then I clicked on the folder called *Johnny*, and was confronted with another password box. 'I tried to open these folders before, but couldn't get in. I already tried *equilibrium* and it doesn't work.'

'Others all the same, I assume.' He pointed at the three other folders named *Fox*, *Howard* and *Lucy*.

'Yes, but now I think the answer was under our noses the whole time.'

On my phone, I opened the photograph of the last notebook page and zoomed in on the strings of numbers and letters. 'I thought this was some kind of technical gibberish, and Johnny said they were settings for the recordings Crash was making.'

'Looks like a funny way to go about it.'

'Well, I wouldn't know. But listen: I'd guessed "Roulette" was a stage name, but I didn't know Johnny's real name. Until I went to his house, where I saw a letter for "Jonathan Ormond-Wiles".'

'That's right. Family of bankers, I believe.'

'Oh, so not the poor farm boy he'd have us believe? That's interesting. But now look at this first line.' I pointed to it:

JOW-1000T-434206913IAFCLSHER

Birch's eyes widened. 'You're thinking "JOW" is for Jonathan Ormond-Wiles. Could be a coincidence?'

'I don't think so. Look at the others.' There were three other lines underneath the first. They read:

FDJ-600W-411276138PSHGCKSRS
HZ-800M-916942461SDGFPUASN
LSK-500T-549134347ICNESOPXC

'Fox Double-Jones, Howard Zee and Lucy S. Kwok,' I said. 'You haven't met Howard yet, and Lucy is the Carnival organiser whom you so gallantly helped off the barge yesterday.' Birch nodded, oblivious to my gentle reproach. 'Still think this is a coincidence?'

'Point taken. But what are they?'

I directed his attention to the computer screen, still asking for a password to the *Johnny* folder.

He smiled, understanding. 'I'll read that first line out for you.'

I typed it in as he did, and hey presto, the folder opened.

It didn't contain much: a spreadsheet and several more recordings. I opened the spreadsheet. It was damaged somehow, like the recording from Thursday, and many lines were filled with garbled text and symbols. Not all, though. There was enough to see what looked like a pattern: weekly dates going back a little over two years,

with '£1,000' listed alongside each of them.

'What's going on here?' I wondered aloud. 'Some kind of regular transaction? If Crash was paying Johnny a thousand pounds every week, maybe he really was broke, after all.'

'Some exceptions, though. Varying amounts.'

Birch was right. A few dates listed '£2,000'. I leant closer to the screen, looking for a pattern. The amounts varied, but only between one and two thousand pounds. The dates . . .

'There, look,' I said. 'The dates are weekly but sometimes they skip a week, and the following date is always two thousand pounds.' I scrolled down the sheet to double-check. It was impossible to say for certain with the missing lines, but what we could see fitted that pattern. 'Crash and Johnny are bandmates living less than half a mile from each other. Why would they need to skip a week?'

'Touring? Could be dates when they were on the road.'

'But surely then they'd be even closer, wouldn't they? Let's listen to these recordings.'

I opened one of the audio files. It began with mechanical clicking noises, then after a few seconds of hiss we heard a muffled, low-quality recording of someone playing an acoustic guitar and singing. The tune sounded familiar but I couldn't place it.

'Do you recognise this?' I said and turned to look at Birch. He was listening intently. Behind him I saw Ace

sit up from his bed, ears pricked and alert. 'Oh, is this Crash singing?'

Birch nodded. 'Young Crash, at that. Voice hasn't been that light in years. Singing "Spin the Lady", an early hit. Doesn't sound like Johnny's guitar playing, though. Maybe it's Crash by himself. Old recording.'

Screeching static suddenly blared from the speakers, and Ronnie's ears pricked up to match Ace's. I lowered the volume, hoping there might be more to hear, but the static continued until the end of the file.

'So much for that one. Let's try another.' I opened a second file, *Red Riding Hood*, and we heard much the same thing; young Crash, playing another song by himself in between long bursts of static. Birch confirmed it was another of the band's hits and while a third file wouldn't open, its file name was apparently the title of yet another chart-topping song.

'Are they all like this?' I wondered. 'What does it mean?'

But the last recording file, which did open, was different. It began with the now-familiar static burst, then cleared into Crash talking with Johnny. This time, even I could recognise their voices.

[Static]

Johnny: '—*believe you. This isn't proof.*'

Crash: '*Don't talk rubbish, man. Any fan will know the truth as soon as they hear it, and then you won't be able to cover it up any more.*

Really, I couldn't believe my luck when—'
[Static]
Crash: *'Think how much hiring experts would cost you. Besides, you're coining it in every year. Cheaper to pay up and then nobody else has to know.'*
Johnny: *'How do I know you won't go to the press anyway?'*
[Static]
Johnny: *'I've a mind to throttle you right here. Toss you over the side.'*
Crash: *'Oh, Johnny. You're not smart enough to get away with it . . . and your Da can't help you now, rest his soul.'*

The recording ended. Birch and I were both stunned.

'Damning,' he said. 'Practically a confession from Johnny. Surprised he'd allow that to be recorded.'

'He might not have known,' I said, and explained the one-button recorder Crash had used on me when he first showed me around. 'I had no idea he was recording until he played it back. It's faulty now, presumably thanks to whatever happened to the computer between then and me arriving. But at the time it worked like a charm.'

'Crash secretly records Johnny making threats. Keeps it on his computer in a password-protected folder. Why?'

I thought about what we'd just heard. 'Johnny wasn't the only one making threats, was he? "Pay up and nobody else has to know", Crash said. And Johnny

was obviously afraid of Crash going to the press about something . . .' The answer struck me like a thunderclap. 'Oh! Silly us, we've got this the wrong way around. Crash wasn't paying Johnny a thousand pounds every week. Where did all that money in the safe come from?'

We looked at one another and simultaneously said, 'Blackmail!'

'This explains what I saw on Thursday,' I said. 'As I came out of Fox's boat, Crash and Johnny had their backs to me, arguing. Johnny took something from his pocket, but when they turned around it was gone.'

'Gone straight into Crash's pocket.' Birch nodded. 'Thursday, you said?'

'Yes, when Crash showed me around. This might also explain why Crash doesn't employ a cleaner. He wouldn't trust them not to snoop about.'

Birch pointed to the first few letters of the password. 'JOW-1000T, see? Jonathan Ormond-Wiles, one thousand, Thursday. A grand every week, in return for keeping a secret. Nice little earner.'

'It fits your idea of the missing dates being when they were on tour, too. There's no privacy on the road, so no way to keep the payments a secret. Better to wait until they're home, then pay double to catch up. And speaking of doubles . . .'

I closed the *Johnny* folder and clicked on *Fox* instead. Once again, the computer demanded a password. 'Read me the Fox one.' I typed it in as he did and the folder opened.

'FDJ-600W,' said Birch quietly. 'Fancy blackmailing your own wife for six hundred quid every Wednesday.'

'I'm sorry, Birch. This must shatter your illusions of Crash.'

'Not many left after almost forty years in the Met,' he said, but despite his brave face I could tell it hurt. He'd been a fan of Bad Dice for years but in the space of two days the singer had first been murdered, then revealed as a blackmailer.

I shuddered, remembering how I'd taken an immediate liking to Crash, largely because of his obvious love for Ace. He'd fooled us all.

The *Fox* folder contained another spreadsheet and several picture files. The spreadsheet was even more damaged than Johnny's, but it confirmed that Crash was collecting similar payments from Fox. The picture files were also in a bad state; only two would open and all they showed was part of Fox's houseboat from a high angle. The rest was bright green digital static.

'Shot from here, do you think?' said Birch.

I stood up and looked out the windows. The same view I'd seen the other night when recording on my phone, but bright and sunny. 'Yes, although it's zoomed in a lot. I wonder what he saw?'

'Impossible to tell from these. Something on her boat?'

'Oh, of course,' I said, remembering my morning hangover. 'It's the drugs. Fox is baking cannabis into cookies, and I think she's growing it in a spare room she doesn't show to the public.'

'Serious thing to have over someone. Consuming is a slap on the wrist these days but growing plants is a different matter. Dealing, even?'

'I hadn't thought of that. What a scandal that would be, the celebrity gardener dealing weed from her houseboat. If we're right, it would be a strong motive for her wanting Crash out of the way.'

Birch grunted. '*If* we're right. What's in the others?'

In the *Howard* folder was another spreadsheet, noting eight hundred pounds every Monday. Unlike the others, this one had a separate column for another day; every Wednesday, for five hundred pounds.

'Why do that instead of a single payment of thirteen hundred?' I wondered.

'Search me. What's in the photos?'

Most of them wouldn't open, and those that would were badly damaged. They appeared to be pictures of newspaper pages and screenshots of websites. I could make out the words 'scandal', 'reputation', 'substantial sum', and 'gave no comment', which could all have applied to many different things. Beyond that it was all indecipherable stripes of bright colours, like a TV set gone horribly wrong . . . apart from a blurry name on one photograph that looked like 'Vick'.

'Oh! It's Howard,' I said.

'Well, yes. Folder's got his name on it.'

'No, on the other recording. The one from Thursday. I'd hardly spoken to him when I first listened, so I didn't recognise his voice.'

I found the file on the computer desktop and played it again.

> [Static]
> Crash: '—*could have phoned, you know.*'
> Howard: '*Not likely. Listen, we just want to talk. She—*'
> [Static]
> '*—very generous offer to resolve this once and for all. At least—*'
> [Static]
> Crash: '—*making your own generous offer to the likes of Vicki—*'
> [Static]
> Howard: '*—serious. Nine o' clock, all right? Don't be late.*'

'So Howard's involved in a scandal of some kind with a woman named Vicki, involving a "substantial sum". . . and he invited Crash to meet her? How odd.' I made a mental note for later, to search online for anything about Howard and a woman named Vicki.

'So far, all three of them had motive to kill Crash,' said Birch.

'Yes, and to want these files destroyed. I'm sure now that the damage to this computer wasn't accidental. Especially with that gold disc over the safe being askew.'

Birch nodded. 'Killer broke into the premises, disabled

the computer and attempted to crack the safe.'

'But they *didn't* break in, did they? There was no forced entry, so they must have taken Crash's keys after killing him. Then they did half a job on this computer and couldn't get into the safe at all. Why go to all that trouble if you weren't going to follow through?'

'Fair point. Interrupted, maybe?'

'But by whom? If someone else had come in on Friday morning and seen the killer, surely they'd have said something.'

'Unless the witness is now blackmailing them, too.'

My head spun with all these possibilities, so I turned to the final folder.

'Lucy Kwok, five hundred, T for . . . oh, of course. Thursday again.'

'Could be Tuesday, though.' Birch suggested.

'I don't think so. Lucy called at Crash's place on Friday morning, shortly after I arrived. She was rather cagey about why.'

'Um . . . Friday doesn't begin with a T.'

'No,' I explained patiently, 'but she said she'd called the night before, on Thursday, and got no answer. Crash was probably out walking Ace.'

I looked over at both dogs, dozing together on Ace's bed. That was a mistake because they immediately pricked up their ears.

'Let's quickly look at Lucy's folder before this pair get restless again.'

But then I heard the front door open. The dogs hadn't

pricked up their ears because I looked at them; they'd heard someone at the door long before us humans, and now leapt to their feet.

'No, *stay*—!' I hissed, but it was too late. Ace and Ronnie bolted past us and galloped down the stairs, barking. Birch and I ran after them, and halfway down the stairs came face to face with DCS Fletcher. Again.

'Superintendent,' I said, forcing a smile. 'We must stop meeting like this.'

CHAPTER TWENTY-ONE

'Nobody was outside the door when we came in,' I said, which was technically true. Constable Wright stood behind DCS Fletcher, looking simultaneously embarrassed and angry while Ronnie and Ace both circled around his legs. 'Also, I need to collect my possessions. After all, I can't stay here.'

The superintendent remained unimpressed. 'No, Ms Tuffel, you most assuredly cannot. In fact, I'd be grateful if you'd hand over your keys to this property.' I did, reluctantly. 'Thank you. Now, have you collected all your possessions?'

My cheeks flushed a little, thinking of the barely started jigsaw on the coffee table. 'Not yet. I was distracted by something we found upstairs that I think you should see.' I began climbing the stairs again.

'Stop there,' said Fletcher. 'Tell us what to look for and we'll find it ourselves.'

I ignored her and continued up. 'Impossible, I'm afraid. You'll see why.'

She and Birch, plus the dogs, crowded into the second-floor studio after me. I quickly showed Fletcher the files we'd found, explaining my blackmail theory.

'There's one folder remaining,' I said. 'Birch?'

He read out the password to the *Lucy* folder.

'Where did you find these passwords?' asked Fletcher. 'You should have given them to us.'

Birch cleared his throat. 'Matter of fact, you already have them. Notebook you found in the safe. Gwinny took photos.'

Fletcher reddened and glared at me. 'Ms Tuffel, I've overlooked your prior actions out of respect for your father, but this is too much.'

'Steady on,' said Birch, stepping in before I could respond. 'You've had the notebook since yesterday, but you didn't find this, did you? Gwinny's the one who figured out they were passwords. Without her you'd be stumped.'

I sat a little straighter in the chair, pleased that he was on my side this time. Fletcher certainly wasn't pleased, but at least she took Birch seriously.

'Sometimes, Alan, you can be infuriating.'

He nodded. 'Not the first to say it. Surely won't be the last.'

Before they could descend into an aphorism-off, I said, 'Shall we see what Lucy's been up to?' and opened the spreadsheet inside the folder. It confirmed the payments. 'Look here, though. These dates start three years ago,

earlier than the others. Perhaps Lucy was the first person Crash blackmailed.'

'Must be something serious if it got him started down this path,' said Birch. 'What are the other files?'

There were two. One was an image, garbled enough that all we could see was part of the canal path at night, taken from a height. The second was another damaged recording. I played it:

> [Static]
> Crash: '—*fool me of all people, Lucy. Rock 'n' roll lifestyle [muffled]*'
> Lucy: '*So now what? [muffled] tell the police you'd have done it already.*'
> Crash: '*I still might. Unless of course we can come to a mutually beneficial—*'
> [Static]
> Crash: '—*small price to pay, don't you think? Sure and you must [muffled] already.*'
> Lucy: '*You scheming [muffled]. If you breathe a word of this to anyone, I'll—*'
> [Static]

'Good heavens,' I said when the recording ended. 'No prizes for guessing what was cut off there.'

'That sounded different to the others,' said Fletcher. 'Muffled, with lots of background noise. Like it was recorded outside.'

I nodded. 'If it was before this second floor was built, Crash wouldn't have had the easy recording set-up. He might have used his phone, in his pocket.'

'What was she so concerned about him coming to us about?' Fletcher mused.

'I don't know, but that's all of them. A rogues' gallery of blackmail victims, all with secrets to keep and a motive to kill Crash. Why now, though? This has been going on for years, with people happily paying up. Well, maybe not so happily. But what changed?'

'Something to do with the Carnival?' Birch suggested.

'Or maybe that was a convenient cover. Everyone expected Crash to be away for a long weekend anyway, and if his body hadn't surfaced during the opening ceremony none of us would be any the wiser. They'd be scouring bars in Dublin for him, not dredging Little Venice.'

Fletcher shook her head. 'You're leaping to conclusions again, Ms Tuffel. This material is damning, but it doesn't prove Mr Donnelly's death was murder.'

I could hardly believe my ears. 'After all this, you still think it was an accident? He was blackmailing four people!'

'Three of whom have alibis for the time of death,' said Fletcher, consulting her notes. 'At six o'clock Friday morning, Ms Double-Jones was on a video call with her daughter in Tokyo; six a.m. here is three p.m. there. Ms Kwok was at home with her husband, and you'll recall even volunteered information about someone she saw

leaving the canal. Mr Zimmerman ran an online class, then went jogging; his colleague sent us an archived recording to confirm the class and he can be seen on CCTV footage of the surrounding area. We haven't been idle in checking the facts,' she added with not a small amount of hostility.

'What about Johnny Roulette?' asked Birch.

'Mr Ormond-Wiles is the one person with no corroborated alibi. He was asleep at home by himself, although several neighbours did see him an hour later.' She flipped her notes shut. 'The fact is that even if Mr Donnelly was killed, which I don't believe he was, it was most likely a random mugging.'

I tried to take this all in. 'Johnny told me he hardly ever sees his neighbours. But now, on the day he needs an alibi, suddenly they can vouch for him? Have you considered he might have deliberately made himself visible to throw you off?'

'He was having tea in his garden, Ms Tuffel. Hardly the stuff of criminal masterminds. The point is, combined with preliminary results from the pathologist, we don't believe this was murder.'

Birch's moustache twitched. 'Preliminary results?'

'Water in the lungs.'

The superintendent looked very self-satisfied by this revelation, while Birch looked crestfallen.

'Why is that bad?' I asked, confused by their reactions. 'Doesn't it just confirm he drowned?'

'It means he was alive when he hit the water,' Birch

explained. 'Dead men don't breathe.'

'OK, so maybe someone whacked him over the head and threw him in.'

'But there are no wounds on the body, remember?' Fletcher was being unbearably smug, and it made me so frustrated that I couldn't resist.

'Well, I think he was poisoned.'

I might as well have suggested Crash was killed by the Mafia by the look on Fletcher's face. Undeterred, I told her about Fox's drug-laced cookies and collection of poisonous plants.

'Hmmm,' she considered. 'We searched Ms Double-Jones's boat yesterday and didn't find any cannabis. But even if you're right, she didn't poison her husband.'

'She literally has a cabinet filled with deadly plants,' I protested. 'And she's clearly adept at cooking them into food.'

'As Alan said, dead men don't breathe. If Mr Donnelly had been poisoned and then thrown in the water, there would be nothing in his lungs.'

'Suppose he wasn't dead? She might have given him just enough to paralyse him.'

Birch intervened. 'Poisons don't really work like that. Even if they did, paralysis would also stop him breathing.'

I scowled, furious he wouldn't back me up, then turned to Fletcher. 'What do you mean, *if* I'm right about the cannabis?'

'There might be an innocent explanation. Perhaps you had a funny turn.'

'A funny turn?!' I leapt to my feet, which was a mistake because Ace also leapt to his, anticipating yet more exercise. But I was incensed. 'I might say the same of you! There's a man lying in your morgue whose death was unexpected, whose manner of death is unexplained, and who was blackmailing at least four of his neighbours, one of whom is an expert on poisonous plants and stands to inherit his entire estate, including this very boat. How can you be so blind? Look at this!'

I pulled out my phone and showed her the video I'd accidentally taken of Fox leaping over the fence on Friday night.

'Now, isn't that suspicious? Doesn't it at least merit investigation?'

She regarded me with a sceptical look. 'You say you took this?'

'Yes!'

'On Friday night?'

'Yes!'

'So more than twelve hours after Mr Donnelly died, then.'

'Well . . . OK, yes! But what if Fox was disposing of evidence?'

'What evidence? Evidence of what? Her alleged cannabis plants? Really, Ms Tuffel.'

She began talking about alibis and autopsies but I'd heard enough. I returned downstairs and clipped Ace's lead on when the Collie followed me down. Birch hesitated on the top step, his loyalties split. I gave him a

single raised eyebrow, then turned and stomped out onto the path, startling Constable Wright.

DCS Fletcher had taken my keys to Crash's boat, but not to the access gate; that was Howard's, and still in my pocket, so I unlocked it and walked through. The crowd had finally gone, presumably giving up when they realised the police presence was here to stay.

Turning to lock the gate behind me, I was pleasantly surprised to see Birch step out of the boat and hurry in my direction. I softened a little and waited for him.

We walked in silence, Birch very sensibly understanding that I was in no mood for small talk. Instead of heading for Rembrandt Gardens we crossed the Grand Union bridge and turned down Delamere Terrace, heading for Westbourne Green. The Green was much larger than the Gardens and also well out of sight of both DCS Fletcher and the Little Venice houseboats, one of which I was convinced held a murderer. We stepped onto the grass and let the dogs off to run.

As usual, Ace began herding Ronnie and as usual the Lab remained oblivious. I envied him such calm but simply being here in the park with the dogs, and Birch, was helping my blood pressure. I took several deep breaths and wondered if I should take up yoga for real.

Birch finally spoke. 'Fletcher's just doing her job,' he said apologetically. 'Can't go off half-cocked chasing after a killer who might not exist.'

'I disagree, especially when someone like Johnny has no alibi. He's familiar with Fox's boat and would know

how to get into the locked cabinet. If only we knew what he was being blackmailed for, we might also have a better clue as to his motive.'

'Still, bit unfair to call Fletcher blind. *Ronnie, no!*' He ran after the Lab, who was trying to climb a tree to get after a squirrel.

'Bah. Blind, deaf and—'

I stopped dead in my tracks as an elusive puzzle piece finally fell into place.

'Oh, my goodness,' I cried out. 'He's deaf!'

'No, just obstinate,' said Birch, dragging his black Lab away from the tree. 'Red mist descends when he sees a squirrel.'

'Not Ronnie. I mean Johnny Roulette.'

He looked confused. 'Johnny can't be deaf. He's a musician.'

'Beethoven was deaf as a post,' I protested. 'I don't think Johnny's lost all his hearing. He hides it very well, but in hindsight it's obvious.' I thought back to when I first met Johnny, then to seeing him in the park and his kitchen . . . 'Several times now I've stood behind him, or he's looked away when I said something and he didn't respond normally. Even the first time we met, Johnny wasn't facing Crash and didn't seem to hear him say my name. It explains so much.'

Birch puffed out his cheeks. 'Suppose it's possible. Surely by now he knows the songs well enough to play without needing to hear.'

'Could it be what Crash was blackmailing him over?

202

The recording talked about a "scandal" if the fans found out. Being exposed as deaf could spell the end of his career. That's more than enough motive for murder.'

'Might also explain why he deleted the photos. Perhaps Crash was planning to record new songs without Johnny. So you don't think it was Fox, after all?'

'Or perhaps it was a team effort,' I said, as a very different thought took shape in my mind. 'I should talk to the grieving widow again.'

CHAPTER TWENTY-TWO

The Carnival was in full swing, the noise easily travelling from the Pool to the residents' area. We approached Fox's barge, with its roof plants and bright rainbow colours, and found the main door open.

I handed Ace's lead to Birch. 'Stay here, in case Johnny Roulette or anyone else comes to see Fox. Keep them occupied until I get the truth out of her.'

'Right you are.' He gripped Ace and Ronnie's leads. 'If she tries to run, she won't get past me and this pair.' I doubted Fox would try anything of the sort, but I let Birch have his manly moment.

I stepped onto the boat and peered through the doorway but couldn't see anyone through the mass of plants and flowers. I knocked and called out, 'Hello? Fox?' No answer. If she was out visiting someone, surely she wouldn't leave her front door wide open?

I decided to act like a local and stepped inside, treading carefully around the pots and plants. How Fox

could move around without knocking things over all the time I didn't know. Mind you, my own house was similarly cramped with my father's files, old *FT* copies and whatnot, and I managed. Fox probably knew the place well enough to navigate by muscle memory.

Unfortunately, so did her boat cat Lilith, about whom I'd forgotten until I felt something brush against my leg. I instinctively recoiled and stumbled over a stool, wincing as a plant pot crashed to the ground with a heavy thud. Thankfully it missed both Lilith and my foot by a hair's breadth. The cat sped away as I cursed and picked up the plant, wondering if I could scoop up the soil from the floor before Fox came in.

'Gwinny? What on earth are you doing?'

No such luck. I looked up to find her standing barefoot in a bathrobe, ready to thump me with a bright yellow watering can.

I raised my hands in surrender. 'I knocked, but there was no response so I came in to wait for you. I didn't think you'd be asleep at this time of day.'

She placed the watering can on a shelf. 'I—well, I haven't been sleeping much.' She said it implying grief, but I wondered if it was more of a guilty conscience. 'Why are you here?'

'Can we sit down? I think we need to talk. Before the police get involved.'

'The police are already involved. What are you talking about?'

A muffled *thump* sounded from the back of the boat.

Fox rolled her eyes and called out, 'Lilith, whatever you're doing, come away.'

But Lilith had retreated to her high bookshelf spot. I could see her eyes shining out from behind the cacti.

'Who's back there?' I said, not needing to ask why. Barefoot, bathrobe, too preoccupied in the bedroom to answer a knock at the door . . . 'Oh, darling, please tell me it's not Howard.'

Fox's disgusted reaction reassured me she wasn't completely doolally, but that left only one likely option; her partner in crime.

Sure enough, Johnny Roulette emerged from the bedroom with a small green bathrobe barely covering his wide body.

'Ah, Gwinny, is it,' he said with resigned nonchalance. 'How are you, pet?'

'Jonathan, what are you doing?' Fox admonished. 'It could have been anyone.'

He shrugged. 'Who is it we're keeping secrets from any more? The mean bastard's gone and nobody else cares. Wouldn't you say, Gwinny? Live and let live, isn't that right. We only get one go-around, you know. Man's time on earth is short and the heart wants what the heart wants.'

Overwhelmed by this barrage of clichés, I took a moment to gather my thoughts, took a deep breath, then plunged in.

'I know Crash was blackmailing you. Both of you.'

Fox and Johnny exchanged wary glances but said

nothing. I didn't want to name Crash's other victims; that would be their business to sort out with the police.

'Which means you both had a lot to lose and the opportunity to do something about it.'

'How—?' Johnny began, but Fox interrupted him.

'Jonathan, shush. Gwinny, why are you talking such nonsense? I think you should leave now.'

I held firm. 'Now that I think about it, Johnny wasn't the least bit surprised yesterday evening when I reacted badly to one of your cookies. I expect he knows all about the drugs in your spare room. Am I right, Johnny?'

'Spare room?' he repeated, seemingly confused. 'Sure you've lost me there. A few edibles and the odd spliff, so what? There's no harm in it.' He smirked. 'You were a proper sight in the park, though.'

'I'm glad you find it amusing. But while there may be no harm in imbibing, I'm reliably informed that actually growing cannabis is taken somewhat more seriously.' I turned to Fox. 'Serious enough for you to pay Crash six hundred pounds every Wednesday.'

Johnny turned open-mouthed to Fox. 'You what, now? I'll kill him. Well, I would have. You know what I mean. Fox, pet, say it's not true.'

Fox's expression turned from offence to confusion, then finally resignation. 'I'm afraid it is. Or, at least, half of it is.' She rounded on me. 'You're not as clever as you think. Yes, Crash was blackmailing me but it wasn't drugs. That spare room is where I keep Lilith's cat litter and dry my laundry. I'm not growing anything in there,

and you can ask the damn police if you don't believe me. They went over the whole boat yesterday and found nothing.'

Johnny took Fox's hand. 'Then what for, pet? The nerve of him!'

Seeing their intimacy, more puzzle pieces fell into place for me. '"The spirit is willing, but the flesh is weak." That's what Crash said when I asked him about you living separately. I thought he meant he wasn't capable any more, but perhaps he was talking about your infidelity? Did he threaten to divorce you, this time, rather than the other way around? There'd be no question you were at fault. You'd be left high and dry.'

'He knew about us?!' Johnny spluttered. 'All this time, he didn't say a damn word!'

Fox squeezed his hand. 'He didn't care, love. He just wanted the money and I couldn't risk being cut out of his will.'

'To hell with his will! I've got more than enough for both of us.'

'But for how much longer?' I said. 'Even a rich musician like you must feel the sting of paying a thousand pounds every week.'

Johnny scowled at me. 'Now listen, I don't know what you've heard—'

'Everything, Johnny. Unlike you, and that's the problem, isn't it? You're going deaf. Are you really writing new songs? You may know your old songs well enough to play them without hearing the stage monitors,

but recording and learning new songs would be much more difficult. Was that why you tried to delete those photos from my phone? Perhaps you couldn't bear the thought that Crash was writing new songs without you.'

Now it was Fox's turn to look aghast. 'Jonathan? Is this true?'

The guitarist looked frozen, like a deer in headlights. Then, to both Fox's and my surprise, he threw back his head and laughed heartily.

'Stage monitors! You should get out more, Gwinny, you and your pet copper. It's all in-ear, now, and I can hear fine with a pair of those plugged in.' He turned to Fox. 'I tried to keep it secret but Crash found out.'

'Was he really going to record new songs without you?' asked Fox.

He dismissed the idea. 'C'mon, who else would put up with his nonsense? No Roulette, no Dice. Crash knew that.'

'He also knew that Bad Dice is your life. I may be a music ignoramus but even I know the money these days is in touring, not record sales. You wrote the hits, but that's in the past. Without concerts your income would dry up.'

'It doesn't make sense,' said Fox. 'Jonathan's right, if he was forced to retire, people would stop paying to see them. It would have ruined Crash, too.'

I hadn't considered that, but it was easily explained. 'Even without Johnny's payments, he was still raking in other blackmail money. Plus, Johnny bowing out might

have allowed Crash to record his new songs without a scandal. I'd say that's more than enough motive.'

Fox looked confused. 'Motive for what?'

'Killing Crash, of course. You poisoned him, didn't you? And then Johnny threw him in the canal. Was it in here? Or did you visit his boat on Friday morning at six o' clock?'

I wasn't sure what reaction I'd anticipated but *giggling* certainly wasn't on my list. That's what they both did, though; after a moment of shock, Fox and Johnny looked at each other and sniggered.

'Friday morning?' said Fox. 'I already told the police, I had a video call with Ellie in Tokyo. I was nowhere near Crash, let alone poisoning him.'

'Convenient that you happened to get up so early on that day, isn't it? Poison takes time to act. You could have administered it before calling your daughter.' I turned to Johnny. 'How's that cut on your arm? Guitar string, indeed.' He tried in vain to cover the sticking plaster with the tiny bathrobe's sleeve. 'It was you that Lucy Kwok saw climb over the access gate around six on Friday morning, wasn't it? She heard you cry out in pain because you slipped and cut your arm . . . in your haste to escape after throwing Crash in the water.'

Before he could protest, I continued, 'You have no alibi until an hour after he was killed, when you were seen at home. But you live less than ten minutes away. When you called me from Dublin on Saturday morning, asking where Crash was, were you trying to deflect suspicion?'

'You stupid woman,' said Fox, her amusement turning to anger. 'First of all, I'm hardly a stranger to getting up early after thirty years of TV and gardening. Second, use your eyes. Why do you think Johnny snuck away without wanting anyone to see him? We're not all celibate like you, Gwinny.'

'Sure and I was here with Fox all night, then left before she called young Ellie. I went straight to the gate and climbed over,' said Johnny. 'I admit it, that's how I got the gash on my arm. But I didn't even look at Crash's place as I went by, and it was before six.'

'You can't prove that,' I said. 'You could have disposed of Crash first, then climbed over the gate after six like Lucy said.' I remembered that she hadn't been completely certain about the time but Johnny didn't need to know that. 'There are no CCTV cameras along the path.'

'But they're on the traffic lights, aren't they? If the police check them they'll see me strolling across by the junction house, and before six o'clock. There's your proof.'

DCS Fletcher had said they confirmed Howard being out jogging with those same cameras. It was plausible Johnny would be on them, too.

'Well – perhaps you doubled back,' I protested. 'You know this area as well as any resident. It would be easy for you to evade the cameras, return to Crash's boat and kill him. Fox leapt over the fence the other night, you could have come in the same way.'

'Not this again,' Fox sighed.

'Don't deny it, I have you on video.' I turned back to Johnny. 'And with Crash dead, I bet your old records will shoot back up the charts.'

His face darkened. He got to his feet and closed the distance between us, looming over me. I regretted not bringing Birch along, but I refused to be intimidated and stood up to face the guitarist.

'Lord knows how you found out about the blackmail, but I swear on my mother's grave I didn't lay a hand on him, and Fox here will swear likewise. We don't need to hide ourselves any more now, and you've nothing but supposition and innuendo. So I think you should do as Fox asked and leave us alone.'

We glared at one another for a long moment, but he was right. I had a theory that fit the evidence but no proof it was anything more than coincidence. Without a confession the police couldn't act, and it was clear these two wouldn't crack easily. I backed away towards the door, not wanting to turn my back on him.

'Mind the plants,' said Fox. 'You've done enough damage.'

I cursed inwardly and hurried up the stairs.

CHAPTER TWENTY-THREE

Seeing my expression when I left Fox's place, Birch suggested we have a drink on the open top deck of the Pool's café boat. The Carnival was winding down for the day, so getting a spot was easy and the dogs were welcome. Both now lay under the table, eagerly accepting occasional strips of sliced ham from the pack in Birch's pocket, while I despondently stirred a tepid cup of coffee.

'Lucy was both right and wrong,' I said. 'She did see someone climbing over the gate, and Johnny admits it was him. But he was leaving Fox's place after spending the night and he insists it was before six.'

Birch nodded. 'Safe to assume he's not lying when CCTV from the road junction will prove it easily enough. Perhaps Crash was killed earlier than we thought?'

'I don't see how. He texted me at six on the dot, remember?' I clenched my fists in frustration. 'I was so convinced! Johnny was being blackmailed by a man he trusted, over something that could end his career. He

admits climbing over the gate and the cut on his arm proves it anyway. Plus, he and Fox were having an affair and she knows poisons.'

'Can't say I'm surprised they want to move on, though,' said Birch. 'Everyone's blackmail secrets would have died with Crash if you hadn't found those passwords. Convenient for all.'

'I imagine that's why the killer tried to break his computer. Kill Crash, bury the truth and nobody need ever find out. Until we come along and royally mess up that plan, anyway. Now their secrets are out.'

'Not entirely. Still no idea what he had over Howard or Lucy. And much as I'm sure Fletcher would want to find out, they're under no obligation to tell her.'

I sipped my coffee, thinking. 'We know Howard is involved in a scandal with a woman named Vicki. On the recording it sounds like he owes her money. Could she be a loan shark? Does he have gambling debts?'

Birch smirked. 'Ironic to be blackmailed by a casino-themed band, then.'

'That would probably appeal to Crash's sense of humour.' On my phone I searched for *Howard Zee scandal Vicki*. 'Pity we don't know her last name. It would make finding her easier.'

I scanned down the meagre search results, none of which seemed at all related, then mentally kicked myself. 'Oh, Zee is a stage name, isn't it? What did DCS Fletcher call him?'

'Mr Zimmerman,' Birch recalled instantly.

'That's right. OK, let's see . . .' I retyped it as *Howard Zimmerman scandal Vicki*.

'Any joy?'

I laughed at the headlines. 'Not unless Howard is actually a Hollywood producer accused of cheating on his wife with a pornographic actress called Vikki. With two Ks.' I clicked on a *Variety* link and read the story, which was accompanied by photographs. 'Actually, I'm not sure if that's her name or her bra size.'

Birch coughed. 'Doubt that's our man.'

'Of course not. Howard's a former English teacher and already divorced. There's no sign of him in these search results but I suppose that makes sense. If it was a public scandal he wouldn't be susceptible to blackmail.'

My phone buzzed with a text message from Darren the builder, reminding me to move my car tomorrow so he could begin work on Tuesday. I groaned, feeling the energy drain from my body.

'Problem?' asked Birch, feeding the dogs another strip of cooked ham.

'The builder,' I said, tossing my phone onto the table in disgust. 'He's going to cost me a fortune. But I daren't tell him not to bother because it might take weeks to find someone else who can fit me in and they'll probably cost even more, and he was very belligerent, and if I send him away now he might bad-mouth me to all the other tradesmen in town and then none of them will want to work for me anyway.'

'Take a breath, ma'am. Look here.'

It took me a moment to realise he meant it literally. I looked up to find him holding my phone with the screen facing me, like he had in the park. Once again it unlocked upon seeing my face and he held a poised finger over it. 'Say the word, I'll tell this chancer to buzz off. Dealt with plenty of his type in my time.'

'Oh, my goodness!' I shouted, startling him, the dogs and a young couple sat two tables behind us to boot. 'Birch, you're a genius. Watch this.' Then I slumped in my seat with my eyes wide open and a slack jaw.

'Christ!' he exclaimed, jumping to his feet and knocking over what remained of his coffee. 'Gwinny, you're having a stroke! Can you hear me? Look at me and try to focus! I'll call an ambulance!' He began jabbing at my phone screen.

'No, no, give it here.' I snatched the phone from him before he could cause trouble. I was flattered by his concern, not to mention that he'd actually called me by my name for once, but this wasn't the time. 'I think we've been looking at this all wrong.'

'Wrong how?'

I resumed the slumped posture and let my head loll about. 'Do it again. Point my phone at me and see if it unlocks.'

He did, and it did, but he remained confused. 'Isn't that what it's supposed to do?'

'Yes, exactly,' I said, my mind working overtime. 'Now what if a killer did the same thing with Crash's phone, before they threw him in the water? What if the

text I got at six o'clock wasn't sent by him at all?'

Birch perked up, finally understanding. 'Killer unlocked his phone and sent you a message, pretending to be Crash, so we'd think he was still alive.' His expression darkened. 'Means the killer knew you were coming here to look after Ace.'

'Yes, and that confirms it was probably one of his blackmail victims. I met them all on Thursday. Well, apart from Lucy. Howard introduced us on Friday morning, by which time Crash was already dead. But she's obviously close to Howard, so he might have told her the night before.'

Two memories, one distant and one very close, clashed in my head. I checked the previous messages on my phone.

'Crash texted me at half past eight on Thursday evening, to say he'd given Johnny my number. Nobody except the three of us knew he'd agreed to do that, so it must be real.'

'Unless Johnny's the killer. Could have been setting up his alibi.'

'But then why not set one up for Friday morning, too, when we all thought Crash had been killed? Johnny's the one person *without* an alibi at that time, remember.'

Memories nagged at me. Something about Friday . . .

'Lucy! The box!' I shouted, earning another loud *tut* from the young couple behind us. They got up and moved to a table further away.

Birch threw up his hands. 'You've lost me.'

I leant down and fussed Ace's ears. 'Lucy tried to visit Crash on Thursday night but he wasn't in. Then there's the box from Choudhury's.' I explained about the singer's habit of collecting a cardboard box from the grocer for Ace. 'He said he'd pick up a fresh one Friday morning before leaving for the airport. But Mr Choudhury hadn't seen Crash since Tuesday. I assumed he'd simply run out of time.'

'Maybe he did, in more ways than one.'

'Exactly. I think this confirms that Crash was already dead on Friday morning, and in fact could have been killed at any time after half-past eight on Thursday.' I felt a sudden surge of anger. 'No wonder Ace couldn't wait to relieve himself when I arrived. He'd spent all night alone on the boat with nobody to let him out.'

'We're dealing with someone smart,' said Birch. 'Smart enough to plan ahead.'

I nodded agreement. 'And willing to kill to keep their secrets. It makes me wonder if anyone else is in danger . . .'

As we pondered this, my phone rang with a call from an unknown number.

'Another celebrity dog-sitting enquiry?' said Birch, seeing the display.

'Let's find out,' I said, answering the call on speakerphone. 'Hello?'

'Is that Gwinny?' asked a woman's voice.

'Speaking, yes. Who's this?'

'Is Howard with you, for some reason?'

That stumped me. 'I'm sorry, what? Who is this?'

'Lucy Kwok, of course.' Evidently, not being immediately recognised was an alien concept to her. 'I'm scheduled for a private session with Howard but his door is locked, his phone goes to voicemail and nobody's seen him.'

Birch and I both turned to look in the direction of the houseboats.

'Lucy,' I said, 'find the police. They might still be at Crash's place. We'll be there in two minutes.'

CHAPTER TWENTY-FOUR

When we arrived at Howard's boat we found Lucy trying to peer through the windows, but they were all curtained. Muffled music sounded from inside.

'Why did you think he might be with me?' I asked. Lucy now wore a sporting top, leggings and trainers. A rolled-up towel carried under her arm completed the look, even though I had a hard time picturing her working up any kind of sweat.

'I already asked everyone else,' she replied. 'I've been too busy with the Carnival to keep track of people. This is my wind-down time, to recentre my energy.'

Remembering Howard's offer to me of a 'personal one-to-one session', I wondered again what kind of relationship he and Lucy had. Was Crash blackmailing her over an affair with the guru? That didn't fit with his threat to go to the police, though. Adultery was scandalous but not a crime.

'What's going on? Howard's not picking up.' Latesha Michaels, Howard's American business partner,

approached and held up her phone as if to demonstrate the lack of answer. Other residents now began to gather, wondering what the commotion was for. A small crowd was even forming on the other side of the Blomfield Road fence, as people peered through the railings to see what the fuss was about.

'Aren't you both flying out soon?' I asked Latesha. 'Could he be renewing his visa at the American Embassy?'

'Howard took care of that weeks ago and we leave tomorrow. He should be here, and besides, he's never without his phone.'

'So much for tranquillity and escaping modern life.'

She either didn't get my meaning or chose to ignore me, instead stepping onto the deck and pulling on the door. It didn't open. She turned to the crowd and shouted, 'Someone call the cops! They need to break down this door.'

'I already called them,' said Lucy.

'Besides, we don't know for sure he's inside,' I pointed out. 'Anyway, I doubt he'd thank us for destroying his door if he's having an afternoon nap.'

'Afternoon nap?' Lucy protested. 'Impossible. My session should have started eight minutes ago.'

'That's right,' said Latesha. 'It's on his calendar. His last session before we leave tomorrow.'

Lucy reddened slightly. 'You can see his calendar?'

'Zabok+ is about to make Howard one of its leading brands. His business is our business. That's why I need someone to break down this door!'

One or two people standing in the road had begun to climb the fence for a better view, and there was still no sign of DCS Fletcher.

'For heaven's sake,' I muttered, handing Ace's lead to Birch. 'Take the dogs and keep those people behind the fence. I'll climb around and see if he's in.'

'Can you swim?' he asked cheekily.

'Such confidence you have in me.' I hauled myself onto the deck beside Latesha. Remembering how the Carnival sculptress had moved around her boat, I gripped the roof lip, placed a foot on the gunwale and swung myself out onto the water side. I looked over to see Birch approaching the fence, and the gawping climbers begin to retreat.

The music from inside became louder as I approached the saloon window. Holding onto the lip with one hand, I leant down and peered in. The curtains were open on this side, and apart from Howard's absence the room looked normal. His giant TV screen was turned off, but the camera and lights were in their usual place with some weights scattered around.

That gave me pause. I'd only been inside briefly but it had been tidy and ordered, and on the workout video I'd watched he carefully replaced every weight on the rack after use. But now two small weights rolled loose and the floor mat was askew. Nearby a plastic jug lay under a side table with what looked like the residue of a green mixture inside. One of his health smoothies, no doubt.

I pulled myself upright in time to see DCS Fletcher

finally approaching, with Constable Wright in tow.

'What's going on?' the superintendent called out.

'Lucy will explain,' I said and continued shuffling along the gunwale. Next was a window into the galley kitchen, with Howard's packs of protein and health supplement packs lined up against the splashback.

Beyond that, though, was a strange sight. I couldn't see much beyond the counter, especially from my precarious position, but on the floor lay what looked like . . . a pair of jogging pants? Howard's or someone else's? Were we interrupting a 'wellness' session with one of his clients? It would explain the loud music but it didn't seem likely Howard would have forgotten his appointment with Lucy.

A piercing whistle blasted my ears, startling me. One foot slipped off the gunwale and my fingers held on to the lip for dear life. The whistle was followed by someone shouting '*Where's your drone, Spider-Gran*?!' A tourist boat sped past on its way to Camden, carrying drunk Carnival-goers who shouted and jeered at me while filming on their phones. If I hadn't been clinging on to stop myself falling in, I'd have given them two fingers, but instead I had to be happy with merely staying dry and telling them to buzz off. I righted myself, caught my breath and resumed shuffling along.

'Seen anything?' Lucy shouted from the path, oblivious to my well-being. I looked over the roof to see her keeping pace.

'Something seems off,' I said, 'but no sign of Howard.'

'Well, get a move on, then.'

I fought the urge to growl at her and finally came to a window in the bow. Most boats had their bedrooms here and Howard's was no exception. The curtain was only half-drawn, leaving enough of a gap to see inside. It looked very much as I expected, with black silk sheets, a large mirror . . . and a hairy, athletic body, wearing nothing besides boxer shorts, sprawled on the bed.

Howard Zee lay unmoving, his eyes closed and head lolling towards the floor, with green drool dribbling from the side of his mouth.

CHAPTER TWENTY-FIVE

'Superintendent!' I called out. 'You'd better force the door after all. Howard's in there, but he's not moving.'

'No!' cried Latesha Michaels, with genuine concern. DCS Fletcher guided her back onto the path while Constable Wright prepared to force the door of Howard's boat.

Still looking through the window, I heard the crunch of splintered wood, a sudden increase in music volume from within (and an equally sudden silence when someone mercifully turned it off), then finally watched the police rush into the bedroom. Fletcher took Howard's wrist in hand, checking for a pulse.

In response, he sat bolt upright and vomited bilious green goo down her shirt.

Fletcher recoiled as Howard doubled over, coughing. He was obviously in distress and pain, but also obviously alive. I knocked on the window to get her attention and mimed sliding the window open. She

came around the bed and opened it to talk.

'Sorry about your shirt. As I passed the lounge I saw a half-empty smoothie jug that had fallen on the floor, and the drink in it was a very similar colour to what you're wearing. You should take a look.'

'Much obliged, I'm sure,' she grumbled. 'Some kind of allergic reaction, no doubt. If he was having difficulty breathing, it would explain why he shed his clothes.'

'Don't you think it's more likely he was poisoned? First Crash, now this.'

She rolled her eyes. 'Why don't you come inside and we'll discuss it?'

'I'm an actor, darling, not a contortionist.' I gestured at the one-foot-square window opening. 'Besides, the boat's now a crime scene, isn't it?'

'Only if—look, never mind. I'll see you outside.' She slid the window closed as Constable Wright helped Howard up and placed a bathrobe around his shoulders.

I took the short way around the front bow and hopped onto the path to relay the good news to everyone. Well, not exactly *good*, but certainly better than the alternative.

'Not sure you'll be catching that flight,' I said to Latesha.

'What are you, nuts? This is all the more reason to get the hell out of here. Some psycho is killing people and I'm not sticking around so they can try again. I've been working on this deal for months.'

'Killing people?' said Lucy, overhearing. 'Wasn't this an accident?'

I shook my head. 'First someone killed Crash, most likely with poison, and now they tried to do the same to Howard. The question is, why?'

'What do you mean, poison? Crash drowned. The whole of Little Venice saw it!'

Fox and Johnny, now dressed, had come to see what was going on. Johnny rolled his eyes. 'Gwinny thinks someone poisoned Crash on Friday morning then threw him in the water. In fact, she thought it was me, because of this.' He pulled up his sleeve to show the plaster on his arm.

Lucy took a step backwards. 'It was you I saw climbing over the gate! Right after someone screamed!'

'For God's sake, I didn't scream. I caught myself on the railing and yelled, that's all. Besides, you should check your clock. It was before six and Crash didn't die until after that, right?' He looked to me for confirmation.

Birch approached and handed Ace to me. I gladly took him, thankful for something to do with my hands while I broke this particular news.

'Actually, I'm not so sure. I think Crash's killer faked the text message to me, and if so, it means he could have been murdered on Thursday evening.'

'Never found his phone, did they?' said Birch, backing me up. 'Killer might have taken it.'

'Well, then someone call the bloody thing and listen for the ringtone,' said Fox.

'The police already tried that,' I said. 'It's probably at the bottom of the canal. What matters is that everyone's

alibis for Friday morning are now useless.'

'*If* this and *could* that and *probably* the other,' said Johnny in disgust. 'Such claptrap. You're obsessed, Gwinny, and it's not healthy, you know. Why would anyone kill Crash?'

It was almost like he was daring me to expose the blackmail in front of everyone, but I wouldn't. Fox and Johnny knew about each other, but nobody else knew the identity of Crash's other victims and I felt it best to keep things that way for now.

'Well, I can tell you Howard's out of the picture,' said Latesha.

'Because he had an allergic reaction to a health drink?' said Lucy. 'That doesn't make sense.'

'OK, first of all, no way is Howard stupid enough to mix in something he's allergic to. Someone tampered with his smoothie. But it doesn't matter because he had live sessions all Thursday night.' Latesha turned to me. 'You can see for yourself on the recording stream. So don't come at me with this murder nonsense.'

The police brought Howard out of the boat and sat him down. He took deep breaths, his head hung between his legs, looking seriously worse for wear. But at least he was alive. Latesha fussed around him. Everyone else dispersed, the emergency and excitement over. Fox and Johnny returned to her houseboat while Lucy took her towel and expensive yoga outfit back home.

'Damned good luck we all got here in time,' said

Birch. 'Another five minutes, who knows what the effects might have been?'

'That depends on what was actually mixed into his smoothie ingredients. But Latesha's right; if anyone around here knows their own allergies, or is careful about what they consume, surely it's Howard. Someone must have snuck into his kitchen and poisoned his ingredients.'

'Why, though?' he pondered. 'Doesn't seem likely to be related to blackmail. Something else that connects Crash and Howard?'

'Why don't we ask him?'

Now that Howard was no longer in danger of keeling over, the police had gone inside to check the boat, leaving him and Latesha alone on the deck. He smiled as we approached.

'Apparently, I should thank you, Gwinny. If you hadn't climbed around and looked in the window, I might be dead by now.'

'The superintendent thinks you had an allergic reaction,' I said. 'Is that likely?'

Before Howard could answer, Latesha said, 'I already told you, he's not stupid.'

'I'm not so sure of that.' He gently squeezed Latesha's hand. 'I don't have allergies, but I was obviously stupid enough to leave my door unlocked so someone could sneak in and tamper with my plants.'

'Plants?' said Birch, confused. 'Thought you were drinking a milkshake.'

'Smoothie,' I corrected him. 'Get with the times. Howard, what exactly happened?'

'I'd finished a quick workout and I had some time before my appointment with Lucy. It was to be our last ever, so I knew it would be an intense session. I made a kale smoothie to fuel myself before we started, and . . .' He shook his head, as if searching for a memory. 'I think I went into the lounge? I don't remember much else until I threw up on that policewoman.'

How 'intense' a session he and Lucy had in mind was neither here nor there for the moment. More immediate were two concerns. First, if it was a poisoned plant smoothie that had made Howard ill, Fox was well and truly back on the suspect list. The second concern, as Birch pointed out, was motive. What connected Crash to Howard besides blackmail?

'Your relationship with Crash,' I said, trying to impart as much meaning as I could without spelling it out. 'Is that something we can talk about in private?' I nodded toward Latesha, hoping Howard would understand.

He didn't. 'We have no secrets,' he said, squeezing her hand again.

'Even about . . . Vicki?'

He'd been pale already, but now all remaining colour drained from Howard's face.

'Who's Vicki?' asked Latesha warily.

'Someone Howard owes money to,' said Birch. He was bluffing a little, of course, but the recordings we heard between Howard and Crash certainly suggested that.

Remembering something else Crash said, I was struck with inspiration. 'I thought it might be gambling debts,' I said, 'but now I wonder . . . are you hiding out from your ex-wife to avoid support payments?'

Howard stared at me for a moment, then exhaled heavily and hung his head. His shoulders relaxed, as if he was glad to finally get it out in the open.

'How did you know?' he asked.

I glanced at Latesha, who was silently processing this news about her star-in-waiting. 'Crash said you'd moved here following a divorce. And I know that he's been, um . . . holding it over you for the past couple of years.'

Mild panic showed in his eyes. 'He told you that?'

'Not exactly. It's a long story. But I'm sure the police will want to discuss it with you in light of Crash's death.'

'He was the worst. Washed up, star fading and vindictive with it. But I didn't kill him! I was . . . too open with him when I first moved here. I thought a rock star of all people would sympathise but instead he saw me as a new source of money. Not like he was making any from his music any more.'

'Source of money?' said Latesha, quickly understanding the situation. 'Were you paying him off? Where is this ex-wife, anyway?'

'I actually don't know. She moved out of the old house and that's the last I heard. But Crash said he was in contact with her.'

'You should have come to me. We deal with gold-digging exes all the time.'

Howard smiled nervously. 'Well, she won't be able to follow me to the States, right?'

'If she does, she's gonna run right into our lawyers, and they don't mess around. You shouldn't worry about it.'

He squeezed her hand again. 'I was hoping you'd say that. I'm sorry.'

'This is all very therapeutic,' I butted in, 'but it doesn't explain why you arranged to meet Crash at nine o' clock on Thursday.'

The mild panic showed again. 'You said he didn't tell you anything.'

'Crash had a habit of recording things, including a conversation you both had on Thursday after I left. Parts of it are damaged but others are quite clear. The upshot is that you offered to make a "generous payment", Crash said you should pay Vicki instead, and you told him to meet you at nine.'

'Whoa, hold on,' said Latesha. 'Generous payment? I thought you were already paying him.'

Howard shrugged. 'I tried to buy him off completely. What else could I do? I wanted this over before I moved to America.'

That made sense. Handing over cash in person was one thing, but if Howard had to start wiring large amounts to Crash every week, it wouldn't take long for someone to notice and ask questions.

He turned to me. 'You misunderstand. We were going to meet at nine o'clock on Friday morning, not Thursday.

Now I know why he didn't show up, so I went jogging instead.'

'Hold on, though,' I said. 'By nine a.m. on Friday he should have been on a plane to Dublin anyway. Why would he arrange to meet you then?'

Howard shrugged. 'I don't know. He didn't mention that to me.'

This cast a very different light on things. It could mean that Crash never intended to fly to Dublin on Friday morning. Why lie? Was it somehow connected to his death?

DCS Fletcher and Constable Wright emerged from the boat. The young constable carried Howard's half-empty smoothie jug in a plastic evidence bag.

Fletcher placed a firm but friendly hand on Howard's shoulder. 'Mr Zimmerman, can I ask you to accompany me to the station and give a victim statement? It won't take long.'

'Why? I'm fine now. There's nothing I can tell you.'

'Even so, sir. For the record.'

'I'm coming with you,' said Latesha.

'Can I at least get dressed?'

Fletcher agreed and sent the constable to accompany Howard back inside the boat.

'Presume you're on board that Crash was murdered, now?' Birch asked the superintendent. 'Lucky this one didn't succeed, I'd say.'

Fletcher pursed her lips. 'There's no obvious connection between the two incidents, but I've seen

enough to make an arrest for this one. Looking twice is fifty-fifty, as they say.'

I wasn't sure anyone said that besides Fletcher herself, but let it slide. 'Who do you suspect?'

'Only one person had means and opportunity,' she said, already striding back along the path. We all knew who she meant.

'Note that she didn't mention motive, though,' I said as we watched her approach the rainbow-coloured boat. 'Why would Fox want Howard out of the way?'

'Mind of a killer can be hard to fathom,' said Birch. 'Fletcher may not see a connection, but the blackmail gave Fox motive. Perhaps after that she snapped.'

'How does him blackmailing Howard give Fox motive?' asked Latesha.

I wished Birch hadn't mentioned that, but the cat was now out of the bag. 'Howard wasn't Crash's only victim,' I explained. 'He was blackmailing Fox as well.'

Latesha whistled. 'His own wife? OK, this I have to see.'

Now dressed, Howard emerged from his boat and we walked along the path together, following the sounds of Fox and Johnny protesting her innocence. DCS Fletcher finally led the widow out, with the guitarist hot on their heels.

He saw me and shouted, 'Is this your doing? I've a mind to teach you a lesson!'

He loomed over me, all bluster and pointed fingers. Johnny was a big man; if he decided to thump me, I'd

know about it. I took a step back, and the space was immediately occupied by Ace. The Collie stood between us and barked angrily at the guitarist's raised voice. Then Birch reached out to block Johnny with a straight arm and gently but firmly pushed him back. For once I was glad of the former policeman's protective tendencies.

'Wouldn't advise that, sir,' he said quietly. Johnny glared at him but Birch held his ground. 'I expect the DCS has sufficient reason to make an arrest, and threatening others won't help Mrs Double-Jones's case.'

'Absolutely,' said Fletcher. 'One of the poisonous plants in her cabinet has had a leaf clipped. Good chance it'll match what's in that tampered smoothie jug.'

'But everyone knows where I keep the key to that cabinet,' Fox protested. 'It's hardly a secret.'

'Surely you'd have noticed if one of your plants was missing a leaf?' I said.

She turned to me and shouted, 'I've been kind of preoccupied with my husband's death, in case you didn't notice! If I was going to poison someone, do you think I'd use one of my own plants? How stupid do you think I am?'

DCS Fletcher pulled her away. 'I must remind you that you're under caution, madam. Anything you say—'

'Oh, shut up. I didn't do anything! Why would I poison Howard? I hardly know the man!' She turned back to me. 'Just like you! Think you're so clever but you don't really know me, or any of us! I hope you choke on your own self-righteousness!'

I was stunned into silence, which I suppose was the desired effect. Birch puffed out his cheeks as the superintendent led her to a waiting police car. Johnny accompanied her while Constable Wright guided Howard and Latesha after them. Within moments, we were alone.

'Rum do,' said Birch. 'Watch her on telly, you wouldn't think she'd say boo to a goose.'

'Who we are in front of a camera is often very different to reality. Even so-called factual presenters are still playing a part.'

'Do you think she did it?'

I pondered the question. 'Honestly, I don't know. She had motive to kill Crash and her alibi for Friday is useless now. But she's right; what motive does she have to kill Howard? He seemed as confused as anyone about why he was targeted.'

'Possible he wasn't the intended victim? Milkshake was meant for someone else?'

An idea formed in my mind. 'What if the killer knew Lucy was due to have a session with Howard and expected them to share the smoothie?'

'Bit thin, if you don't mind me saying.'

'It is, isn't it?' I conceded. 'Perhaps we can remedy that. Fox was right about something else, too: I don't know these people half as well as I'd like. Let's pay Lucy a visit.'

CHAPTER TWENTY-SIX

Number 30 Blomfield Road was a beautiful white-fronted home with a gleaming Audi parked in the driveway and a doorstep of immaculate checkerboard tiles. Looking at it with more than a little envy, I decided I should definitely get the number of Lucy's builder.

I rang the buzzer. Nobody answered. I buzzed again. Still no answer.

'She only left a few minutes ahead of us. Did she definitely come back here?' I asked Birch.

'Think so. Could have run in and back out again?'

'Not without changing first. Can you imagine Lucy popping to the shops in leggings?' He said nothing, but adopted the far-away look of someone trying to do just that. I nudged him and said, 'That's enough. You're literally old enough to be her father.'

Birch coughed, and I turned back to the door as it finally opened.

A handsome middle-aged man looked at me with an

expression bordering on disgust. He wore a standard weekend casual outfit of shirt, slacks, and pullover, though with the unexpected addition of a bright yellow domestic rubber glove on one hand.

'We're not religious,' he said automatically, putting paid to my initial thought that Lucy might employ a housekeeper. Then I wondered what kind of evangelists they got round here who brought their dogs along. Didn't seem practical.

'I'm Gwinny,' I said quickly as he made to close the door, 'from across the road. Well, sort of. I'm a friend of Lucy's. Sort of. Look, is she here? I'd like to talk to her, especially after what just happened at the boats. With Howard.'

That was the first thing I'd said that got a reaction and I wondered if he had the same suspicions about Lucy and Howard as I did.

'I'm sorry, are you . . . Mr Kwok?' I asked. He didn't look Asian but I wasn't about to judge.

'Obviously not,' he said in a tone implying he'd been asked many times before. 'Lucy kept her maiden name for professional purposes. But I'm her husband, if that's what you really meant to ask.'

That certainly told me. He hadn't invited us in, although with two dogs in front of him and what looked like a spotless house behind, I wasn't surprised. Perhaps he *was* Lucy's housekeeper, after all. A 'house husband', as they say. I didn't care, but if Lucy did, it might explain why she'd asked me not to call round.

'I assume you've heard about the recent attacks, sir?' said Birch, in the unmistakeable cadence of a policeman. Retired he may be, but I doubted that would ever leave him.

'Attacks? I know they pulled that singer out of the canal. What else has happened?'

'Oh, for God's sake, Geoff, haven't you got rid of them yet?'

Lucy appeared in the hallway behind him, still wearing her sporting clothes.

He looked back and forth between us. 'This policeman said there have been – I'm sorry, are you police? I assumed – but he said—'

'Yes, I'm sure he did, but he's retired.' Lucy approached, annoyed at both our presence and her husband's vacillating. 'I told you, Howard had some kind of allergic reaction to his smoothie, it's why I'm back early. Gwinny insists he was poisoned, though. She's an actress,' she added, as if that explained everything.

'He *was* poisoned,' I protested. 'The police, that is to say the not-retired ones, have arrested Fox. It looks like she added one of her toxic plants to Howard's ingredients. He might have died if you hadn't sounded the alarm.'

'Keep your voice down,' she hissed. Did they have children? Lucy seemed about as maternal as me, which is to say not at all.

'I'm not deaf, and I'm not stupid either, much as you might wish it,' said another voice from inside the house.

I didn't see anyone, but then Lucy stood aside to reveal an old woman standing directly behind her. Ninety if she was a day, the woman's back was bent and she used a stick for support, but her voice was clear and certain.

'I didn't want to worry you, *maa maa*,' said Lucy, glancing back to shoot daggers at me. 'It's nothing to do with us.'

'We-e-e-ell . . .' I pulled a face. 'I think Crash would have disagreed. Don't you?'

Daggers became longswords, and if looks could kill Lucy would have murdered everything within a fifty-foot radius.

'Oh, this sounds good,' her grandmother chuckled. 'Bring them in, I want to hear everything.'

Suddenly everyone spoke at once.

'No, I think it would be better if—'

'Absolutely not letting those dogs—'

'I just finished cleaning this floor—'

The old woman banged her stick on the ground. 'Then you can clean it again after they've gone, can't you? I'm not dead yet, so this is still my house. I want to know what's going on.'

Lucy deflated, admitting defeat. I actually felt a little sorry for her, knowing from personal experience the impossibility of defying a matriarch once their mind was set. My mother had been perfectly happy to let my father run the household, so long as he did everything she said.

Geoff stepped back and opened the door to let us in while Lucy and her grandmother retreated into the

lounge. Birch and I followed with dogs in tow. Ronnie wanted to sniff every inch of this new place, while Ace's head rotated this way and that to take in the environment. He didn't try to pull me in any particular direction, though, so I guessed he'd never been in this house before.

'Actually, could I use your bathroom?' I asked Lucy. 'All the excitement, you know.'

She reluctantly directed me upstairs. I handed Ace off to Birch and quickly went up, leaving them all heading into the lounge. I really did need to go, but I was also curious about this house now that I knew it didn't belong to Lucy. Presumably she was hoping to inherit, although I wondered why it wouldn't go to her parents instead.

Upstairs was as clean and sparkling as the hallway and frontage. Geoff could have made good money doing this for a living; I almost felt bad using the bathroom, it was so spotless. But telltale signs of the elder Mrs Kwok were everywhere. Helper bars mounted around the bath, a wet room floor conversion and a booster toilet seat folded away by the radiator. After ten years of caring for my own father, I recognised them all.

I finished and left, trying to leave the room as I'd found it. It was quiet up here; if Lucy did have children, they were either out or unrealistically well behaved. Mind you, if she'd had them young, they could have already left home.

I quietly opened the nearest door, just for a quick peek, and immediately regretted it when a towel fell on

me. It was a cupboard, one much less orderly than the visible parts of the house. Towels, bedding, a couple of brooms, canvas bags and cardboard boxes were all messily piled on shelves or sitting on the floor. I hastily threw the towel back on a shelf, closed the door, and decided not to push my luck any further.

Descending the stairs, something in my memory began to surface. It came to me as I entered the lounge, which was another shining example of Geoff's handiwork, lined with bright paintings and photographs of canal boats.

'I'm surprised you don't live on the water, given how much you obviously love it,' I said.

'I did,' said Lucy coldly. 'My parents still do. But some of us take our responsibilities seriously.'

I felt another pang of sympathy for her as I recognised more signs; a low, soft and comfortable chair, which matched nothing else in the room, was the elder Mrs Kwok's daily sanctuary. On either side stood occasional tables piled high with magazines, books, a reading magnifier, remote controls for the television and DVD player, and more. As I watched, the grandmother moved a newspaper to reveal a tin from which she took a piece of shortbread.

She popped it in her mouth and said, 'Come on, then, start talking.'

'Wait a moment,' I said, and took my phone from my handbag. Lucy snorted impatiently.

Then I found the right place and held up my phone for her to see. I played the accidental video recording

I'd made on Friday night, cued up at the moment the hooded figure left Fox's boat and leapt over the fence.

'This is you, isn't it? That tartan canvas bag is very distinctive, and you're sprightly enough to jump over the fence like that.'

'Rubbish,' she said. 'It could be anyone.'

'I'm sure that was the idea, yes. I even thought it was Fox, at first, as it's her boat you're leaving. But I just saw that same tartan bag in a cupboard upstairs, and this is you wanting to avoid the CCTV cameras at either end of the road. Is that why you made such a fuss to the police about seeing someone climb over the gate? Because you didn't want them thinking too hard about people jumping the fence?'

'What do you mean, in a cupboard? Were you sneaking around?' Lucy's voice rose. 'God, you're as bad as—' She stopped herself before saying any more, but I knew she was going to say *as bad as Crash*.

Mrs Kwok's eyes darted keenly back and forth between us but poor Geoff looked bewildered.

'I'm sorry, I don't understand,' he said. 'None of this makes sense.'

'It does if you know that Fox is well practised at baking cannabis into biscuits. Are you enjoying yours, Mrs Kwok? Good for your back pain, I imagine.'

The old lady popped another piece of shortbread in her mouth and grinned.

Lucy glared at me. 'This has nothing to do with Crash's death.'

'Doesn't it?' said Birch. 'Criminal escalation's a common pattern.'

'Do you remember when we met, Lucy? We were with Howard and you froze up when I said that you must having an "interesting relationship". I was talking about Crash and wondered if you'd misunderstood me, thinking I meant Howard. But now I realise you were actually worried I knew about your relationship with Fox. Because that's why Crash was blackmailing you, isn't it?'

Geoff looked ready to burst a blood vessel. 'Blackmail?!' he cried. 'What the hell?'

Lucy didn't take her eyes from me. 'Why would he tell you? He hardly knew you.'

'That's true. But you're right, I'm as bad as Crash. I've found recordings of you pleading with him not to say anything about the drugs to the police. Or, I assume, your husband.'

'Nonsense,' Geoff said. 'Of course I know about the drugs. But blackmail? The impudence of the man!' He looked ready to murder Crash all over again, if he hadn't been already dead. 'How long has this been going on?'

Lucy hesitated before she answered. 'About three years.'

'On one of those recordings you also threatened to, um, do something very nasty if Crash told anyone. Did you run out of patience? Or money?'

She swept the accusation aside. 'We're fine for money, thank you for asking. I told you, I didn't kill him.'

'Who else was he blackmailing?' said Mrs Kwok suddenly.

I turned to her. 'What makes you think he was?'

'They never stop at one, young lady. I grew up in Hong Kong, you know.' I waited for her to elaborate, but she said no more.

'It's true,' I said, 'There were others.'

'If the police have arrested Fox for poisoning Howard, maybe she killed Crash as well,' said Lucy. 'He knew she was baking the shortbread.'

I wondered then if Fox had lied to me about her own blackmail, letting me make wrong assumptions. An affair with Johnny was one thing, but much as the police might often turn a blind eye, cannabis remained illegal.

'Where do you get it from?' I asked, suddenly picturing Lucy's attic converted to a plant nursery but dismissing the thought. 'Surely your grandmother wouldn't want to grow them inside her own house?'

'From a dealer, like everyone else,' Lucy said with an air of resignation. 'I buy it, I give it to Fox, she pays for half and bakes the other half into cakes.'

'And you do all this late at night, coming and going over the fence to avoid being seen. Does the money from Fox go towards paying off Crash?' She nodded, and I continued, 'But not any more. With him gone you can turn what was a monthly cost into a tidy profit.'

'Do you really think I'd murder him over a few hundred pounds?'

'People have killed for less,' said Birch. 'Family

245

circumstances aside, the police wouldn't look kindly on your actions. Selling to Fox is *de facto* intent to supply.'

'You seem like a woman who cares a great deal about her reputation and standing,' I said.

Lucy all but sneered at me. 'Some of us have a standing to care about.' She laid a hand over the elder Mrs Kwok's. 'But more than that, I'm needed here. I couldn't put that at risk.'

'Is that why you killed him? Did you use your familiar escape route to come back home without being seen?'

'No, it's why I paid his filthy blackmail money. The first I knew about his death was when he ruined my play, floating in the water. If you could prove otherwise, I'd be talking to the real police, wouldn't I? So I think you should leave, and be assured that if you tell anyone about this I'll deny every word of it. We all will.'

I saw Birch bristle at the implication he wasn't 'real police' but caught his eye and shook my head. He looked furious, but Lucy was right. There was nothing to tie her directly to Crash's murder. Not yet.

Geoff ushered us out, ensuring I didn't do any more 'sneaking around', and we found ourselves back on the street. From the junction bridge we looked out at the Carnival boats and colourful bunting in the Pool, all enveloped in the warm glow of a spring evening as the sun began to set. Could Lucy be the killer? Hers was the one blackmail we'd found so far that was actually criminal, giving her a strong motive.

'Ought to call Fletcher myself, send the knock-knock

boys in,' said Birch suddenly. He was still seething from Lucy's dismissal. 'They can flush it all away, doesn't matter. Easy enough to find traces with the right kit.'

'I don't think that would help anyone. It would immediately put her in the frame, but if she didn't kill Crash then the real murderer will still be walking free, and all you've done is prevent Lucy from taking care of her grandmother.'

'Not a matter of help. Matter of the law. Can't let people go around selling drugs with no consequence.'

I laughed. 'Birch, if that were true half of the glamorous showbiz world you're so interested in would be locked up. Besides, where's the harm? She's giving pain relief, not running a gangland empire. We don't arrest landlords for serving beer and that's no better.'

He snorted. 'Different, though. Legal.'

'By some quirk of history, not because it's any less harmful. Some might say it's worse.' Birch said nothing, but his silence spoke volumes. I tried to make peace. 'Can we at least hold off on telling Fletcher until we know more about what happened? Keep our powder dry, as it were.'

'Whatever you say, ma'am. We'd best be getting along, eh, Ronnie? Come on, boy.'

'Birch, wait—'

He didn't. Instead, he crossed the junction without looking back, heading for Warwick Avenue Station. I refused to chase after him; Ace looked terribly confused but stayed by my side. Besides, I still hadn't collected my things from Crash's houseboat.

There was no point attempting subterfuge this time, so I asked Constable Wright to call DCS Fletcher. She agreed to let me inside, but on the condition that he supervised me while I gathered my possessions.

'What do you think I'm going to do?' I complained to her.

'For all I know, you might unmoor the boat and pilot it down the Thames singing the national anthem. It's with the constable or not at all, Ms Tuffel.'

I relented and went inside with the young policeman following. I took the groceries from the fridge and my clothes from the bedroom, then returned to the lounge and the jigsaw of Little Venice. So much for my plan to finish it before rehearsals resumed on Tuesday; I'd barely started it on Friday and had made no progress since. I'd have to puzzle like a demon to even half-finish it by tomorrow. On the bright side, at least there wasn't much to break down. I disassembled the corner I'd built, returned the pieces to the flattened box, and put that in my tote along with everything else.

Then I took what I assumed would be my last ever look around the place, marvelling at how its casual messiness disguised an orderly and calculated blackmail operation. What would happen to Crash's studio? To his gold discs? To the upright piano? They'd all go to Fox, or perhaps her daughter Ellie if she was in prison by then. Would Ellie simply auction it all off?

I led Ace out into the cool dusk. Somewhere nearby, Fox sat in a police interrogation room with

Johnny watching. Howard would be there too, for different reasons. Meanwhile, Lucy was tending to her grandmother.

Crash's death really had thrown a wrench into everyone's lives, mine included, because DCS Fletcher was right: Birch could be infuriating sometimes. I doubted he'd ever stop thinking like a policeman, but a little flexibility now and then wouldn't hurt. I was annoyed with myself for not being more sympathetic to his view, but much more annoyed with him for making a mountain out of a molehill and flouncing off.

I crossed the road and finally followed in his footsteps to the Tube station.

CHAPTER TWENTY-SEVEN

This time I navigated my way through the scaffolding with ease, and there was no sign of the Dowager when I let Ace in the garden after feeding him. Then I fixed myself dinner, took it through to the lounge and reopened the Little Venice jigsaw on my puzzle table. It was only an ordinary coffee table, but I hardly used it for anything else, so I called it my puzzle table.

A bit like Fox calling Lilith her 'boat cat', I supposed. I hoped she'd be OK. Johnny would check on Lilith while Fox was at the station, wouldn't he? Then again, was that so important with cats? Fox had said the spare room contained her litter box.

My thoughts were interrupted by Ace leaping onto the sofa and curling up beside me. As he snoozed, I picked at my food and tried to focus on the puzzle, quickly rebuilding the corner section but knowing I'd never finish the rest before rehearsals resumed. If only I could turn the calendar back a couple of days! At least now

I could return to the puzzle whenever I liked. Fletcher couldn't confiscate my own house keys.

That made me think about the house we'd found on Penfold Mews that afternoon, almost forgotten in the subsequent excitement. Birch had said the name 'Don Christopher' rang a bell but I wasn't about to call and ask why. After stomping off like that he could jolly well sit and stew for a while.

Realising I was sitting with an empty fork in one hand and a puzzle piece in the other, staring into space, I conceded defeat and tossed the piece back in the box before quickly scoffing dinner.

With that out of the way I retrieved my laptop and checked my email, but nobody from Don Christopher Management had replied. It occurred to me that I hadn't hidden my identity in my email to them and wouldn't know how even if I'd wanted to. Had I made myself a target? What if the mysterious Don Christopher was involved in all this and thought I knew too much? Was that why Howard had been attacked? But everyone already knew I was asking questions. How much difference could an email make?

Everyone involved in this tangled business had an adopted persona. Crash pretended to be everyone's easy-going friend when in fact he was blackmailing four of his neighbours – including his own wife! – and using an alias to hide an expensive property that none of them knew about. Johnny let everyone think he was a poor farm boy from Ireland, despite his family apparently being well off.

Lucy's public face was that of an upstanding citizen, a straight-laced pillar of the community, but behind it was a woman who bought and sold drugs and had been left by her own parents to care for her ailing grandmother. Howard pretended to be a successful fitness guru but owed his ex-wife so much money that he was hiding in Little Venice, hoping to escape once and for all by jetting off to America. And while Fox outwardly played the celebrity wife, behind closed doors she was sleeping with her husband's best friend.

Would any of them kill to protect their secret?

Taking a different tack, I searched the Companies House website for Don Christopher Management Ltd. They were easy to find, but my excitement faded when I saw the company's registered address was in the British Virgin Islands. A tax haven. Was that normal even for small companies in the music business?

Then again, did I know for sure they were small? There were no other addresses listed, but perhaps the Penfold Mews office was one tiny outpost in a vast empire.

I wondered if it might be a front for illegal activity, but that would require some activity in the first place. The hairdresser insisted he'd never seen anyone use the house at all. There was no phone number or website listed, and the correspondence address for Don Christopher himself was the same house. The whole business was as circular as Ace's throwing ring.

I stroked the sleeping dog's head and wondered: what if none of this had anything to do with Crash's death?

Could DCS Fletcher even be right, and it was merely an accident? That would mean there was no connection to the attack on Howard. But then why would Fox poison him? He was due to leave tomorrow anyway. What did Howard know, perhaps unwittingly, that made him a target?

I returned to the page of his recorded classes and skipped through the Thursday night session to check his alibi. It was much the same as the Friday class I'd watched, with a similar progression from breathing and stretches to lifting weights and balancing on his big toe. Once again, after forty-five minutes he ended the session, set a countdown timer, then returned after several minutes to talk with the class. Drinking a vegetable smoothie, of course.

That feeling of routine and predictability made me wonder. Everyone knew where Fox kept her poisonous plants and the key. She'd pointed out the jug during the tour, complete with gloves to safely handle them. Everyone also knew Howard made health drinks and smoothies. You only had to watch one of his classes, or see his kitchen countertop, to know that sooner or later he'd whip up some horrid concoction of kale and fermented yak's milk.

What if someone was trying to frame Fox and get rid of Howard at the same time? Kill two squirrels with one garden rake, as DCS Fletcher might say. Could Howard's attacker be working for his ex-wife Vicki? No, that didn't make sense. Dead people can't pay their debts.

Unless it wasn't meant to kill Howard, but to frighten him into coughing up.

I opened a new search window, then hesitated. Earlier, when I searched for *Howard Zimmerman Vicki*, all I got were results about a film producer. I tried *Howard Zimmerman English teacher London* instead.

That returned plenty of results but about the wrong person; there had been a Mr Zimmerman who died suddenly a couple of years ago, much missed by his colleagues and students. I clicked through to be sure, and verified the tall, skinny man in the photos clearly wasn't the Howard I knew.

I decided to give it one more try and searched for *Crash Double Vicki*, figuring that perhaps Crash had discovered Howard's secret because he already knew Vicki. It was a long shot and even more tricky without a surname. Crash certainly knew women called Vicki; the most popular results were stories of him being seen at parties over the years with actresses and models of that name.

After the usual gossip, though, was a paparazzi story of Crash leaving a club with Vicki Richards, who'd apparently made headlines by accusing a TV director of sexual harassment when she was a teenager. I'd completely missed that story, and she didn't look like a celebrity, so I wondered how she was connected to Crash.

Searching for *Vicki Richards TV scandal* found some old newspaper stories. The director in question was a

veteran of Saturday morning kids' shows. I try not to judge people by appearance but he certainly looked the predatory type, with a big mop of curly hair and large tinted glasses. I wondered if I'd ever met him at a party. If so, perhaps I had a lucky escape.

Nevertheless, this was all unrelated. Howard the wellness guru was nowhere in these results. To make sure I wasn't going mad, I searched for *Howard Zee fitness* and found some social media accounts. They were sparse, containing little besides promotions for his website and selfies of him in workout clothes. The photos didn't even show his face, focusing instead on his muscles. Simple vanity or, along with his stage name, another attempt to avoid his ex-wife?

'Come on, Ace,' I said, rubbing my eyes. 'Let's see if things look any better in the morning.'

I cleared away my dinner and let the Collie out for a late-night toilet, then we trudged our way upstairs. By the time I'd finished brushing my teeth and entered the bedroom, Ace was already curled up asleep at the foot. Envying him, I climbed into bed and stared at the ceiling, trying to sleep.

But my brain refused to slow down, trying in vain to make all these strange puzzle pieces fit into a complete picture. The harder I tried to stop thinking about it and relax, the more frustrated I became, and for what? Aside from looking after Ace for a while, none of this was anything to do with me. I had bigger problems, like learning my new, minor role in *Mixed Mothers*

and wondering if I should let myself be laughed at in commercials for the sake of money.

I suddenly found myself wishing I could talk it out with my father. Crotchety old man he may have been but he maintained a good perspective on things that really mattered. What would Henry Tuffel do?

He would tell me to focus on my own happiness, of course. But that required knowing what I wanted in the first place.

CHAPTER TWENTY-EIGHT

While brushing my teeth the next morning, my mind continued swirling. The idea of Crash Double being a blackmailer still wasn't easy to get my head around, but it explained how he could afford to build that second-floor studio and fill it with expensive equipment. I hadn't thought about that at first because it seemed natural for a singer.

The corrupted recordings on his computer were maddening. Vital details were missing, details that might have revealed Crash's killer. I was now convinced it was one of his blackmail victims, but who?

Fox Double-Jones: three times wife, living close but separately. Was she really being blackmailed over her affair with Johnny, so as not to risk Crash's inheritance?

Or was it in fact over her now-revealed drug use?

Johnny Roulette himself: bandmate and lifelong friend, also living close by, in an expensive house to boot. By all accounts those two *were* Bad Dice, yet now their

friendship stood exposed as a façade. Would Johnny kill his lead singer, and risk people not coming to their concerts, rather than pay up every week? He was surely making more than enough to pay for it from record and ticket sales, so why rock the boat? Did Johnny think he could do it all himself?

Something about that one bothered me but I couldn't put my finger on it.

Howard Zee: an ageing Lothario, divorced (presumably because of said Lothario tendencies) and so badly in debt he was forced to hide on a houseboat and take up an entirely new career. Howard said he'd tried to buy Crash off but the singer had been killed before they could meet. Now Howard himself had been targeted, but why?

There was a lie in there somewhere, too. I could feel it.

Finally, Lucy Kwok: imperious mistress of the canal, self-important would-be playwright, living a stone's throw from Crash. Was she having an affair with Howard? I didn't know for sure, and maybe it made no difference, but I did know about her blackmail. It made sense that she'd fear a visit from the police over her cannabis dealings, and Birch's reaction had reinforced how right she was.

But would she risk being taken from her grandmother to murder Crash?

Any of them could have done it, especially now we knew he was probably killed on Thursday evening. The

only person with an alibi for that time was Howard, who'd been teaching a class.

Latesha Michaels wasn't in that class, though. Could *she* have killed Crash, to protect her business interest?

A fluffy tail beat a steady rhythm on the hallway floor, bringing me back to the present as I stood motionless with the toothbrush stuck in my mouth.

'All right, Ace,' I apologised. 'Let's get you toileted and think about what to do with the day, hmmm?'

The Collie wandered around the garden while I ate breakfast and considered what might happen to him. Would Crash's daughter Ellie be willing to take him halfway around the world to Japan? Emigrating a dog was a tedious and expensive task at the best of times.

My phone rang. It was Birch.

'Morning, grumpy,' I said. Perhaps not the best way to solicit an apology, but I was still annoyed with him. 'What's up?'

'Kept thinking about yesterday,' he said. 'Couldn't get it out of my mind.'

'Go on,' I prompted hopefully.

'Well, um. Perhaps you'd better come round to my place.'

My heart fluttered in anticipation. Was this the moment? A candlelit dinner, a springtime punt on the Thames . . . ?

'Uncovered something important about Crash Double. Easier to explain in person, you see.'

My flights of fancy crashed down to earth. 'Was there

anything else you wanted to say, Birch?'

After a moment's thought he said, 'No, don't think so. See you soon.'

It took some persuading to get Ace into my old Volvo. I was confused by his reluctance until I remembered that Crash didn't own a car, and whenever he went on tour he left Ace with someone in Little Venice. It was entirely possible the Collie had never set paw inside any vehicle besides a boat, so I tempted him with treats and reassurance. He quickly got the hang of it; driving to Shepherd's Bush, I looked in the mirror and saw him taking in the passing world with keen, mismatched eyes.

Birch opened his door before I could even knock and, after Ace and Ronnie had sniffed their hellos, he ushered everyone into the lounge where I saw a collection of Bad Dice vinyl albums lying on the floor next to his stereo. Birch knelt beside them, grunting as his knees popped, and Ronnie lay down with him. Ace joined me on the sofa, his pricked ear alert and twitching.

'So, what have you found?' I asked.

Birch passed me a record. 'Been bothering me since Penfold Mews. Tip of my tongue but wouldn't come until I played one last night. Early stuff, you see.'

I didn't, not entirely, but dutifully examined the album sleeve anyway. Worn and creased around the edges, it was old and well used. I half-remembered the cover art from many years ago. The title *Something is Rotten* was scrawled over a photograph of four young men, standing

in a scrapyard. I recognised Crash Double and Johnny Roulette front and centre, looking stereotypically thin and sullen in wingtip collars and striped trousers.

'Good lord,' I said, laughing at the fashion. 'Birch, please tell me you never dressed like this.'

His cheeks coloured. 'Perish the thought. Now, back cover. Credits, bottom left.'

I turned it over. The sleeve back featured a track listing, more photos of the band posing next to wrecked cars and a block of small text.

Produced by Don Christopher for Wade Enterprises

Recorded at Regent Sound and Island Studios

Engineer: Tony Allom and Brian Humphries

Management: Nobby Wade, Wade Enterprises

All compositions by Johnny Roulette, except (3) and (7) by Johnny Roulette and Crash Double

All compositions published by Essex Music Int. Ltd

As I've said, music isn't my strong point. I was never the type to sit and pore over records in my bedroom, so whatever Birch was seeing sailed straight over my head.

'You'll have to be more specific. What am I looking for?'

He pointed at the first line of the credits. I reread it . . . and my mouth dropped open in surprise.

'Don Christopher! The management firm who

rent Crash's house on Penfold Mews. Which might be some kind of scam, by the way.' I related the company information I'd found last night, then looked again. 'It says here the band's manager was called Nobby Wade. So did they change to Don Christopher at some point?'

Birch smiled. 'No, they're still with old Nobby. Try again.'

I reread the credits but was no wiser. 'This record must be fifty years old. I'm surprised you could . . . um . . . well, what I mean is, jolly well done for remembering a detail like this.' I quickly moved on. 'They must be old friends . . . but wait a minute!'

'Yes?'

'When I showed Johnny the photo of Don Christopher's name and email address he claimed he didn't recognise the name.'

'And that was before he deleted all the pictures? Another lie, then.' He looked crestfallen.

'Oh, Birch. I know you love this band. It must be horrible to find out they're a bunch of rotters.'

'Can't hide from the truth,' he said, taking a deep breath. 'No matter where it leads.'

'Yes, and the lead we have to follow now is Don Christopher. I haven't had any response to the email I sent yet, though.'

'Doubt you will. I'm a big fan, remember? Read a fair amount about Bad Dice over the years. Enough to know these early albums were low-budget, self-produced affairs.'

'What does that have to do with the mysterious Mr Christopher?' I suspected I was about to get a musical history lesson.

'Well, for a start, the mysterious Mr Christopher doesn't exist.'

After a moment's confusion I understood what he meant. 'It's a pseudonym. So who is he really?'

Birch tapped his nose. 'Expensive chaps, producers. But back in the day, a band producing their own album looked amateurish. Made people think nobody was willing to invest in them. So when they did it all themselves, they used fake names.'

I was beginning to see the light. 'That way it looks like a record company *has* invested in them, which in turn persuades people they're worth listening to. Yes, that makes sense.' I might not know music, but everyone in showbiz understands the importance of a credible façade.

'Remember I told you what Crash Double's real name is?' Birch asked.

'Yes, it's come up a few times since his death. Shaun Donnelly.'

'That's right. Full name Shaun *Christopher* Donnelly.'

I looked at the credits, then at Birch's smiling expression, then back to the credits. 'Christopher Donnelly. Don Christopher,' I groaned. 'Now something else Johnny said makes sense – that Crash had "producer cuts" on some of their early albums.'

He nodded. 'Crash didn't write the big hits, but some

producers get a royalty on album sales. Johnny, too. Look here.' He took another record from the floor and passed it to me, pointing once again at the credits.

'*Producer: Willy Ormond*,' I read. 'Because Johnny's real surname is Ormond-Wiles, isn't it? The banking family, you said?'

Birch smiled, enjoying showing off his knowledge. 'That's right. Tales of being a poor farm boy are, ahem, embellished. Minor scandal when it came out that his parents funded Bad Dice for years before they were signed.'

'So even the band aren't the plucky underdogs their legend claims. But why would Johnny lie about not knowing who "Don Christopher" is? Does this mean that Crash rents the mews house to . . . himself?'

'Odd, isn't it?' he agreed, taking back the records and carefully replacing them on shelves near the stereo. 'Should take this to the DCS. Let her look into it.'

'Pfft,' I snorted. 'Odds are she'll say it's a matter of his estate, nothing to do with his death and we should forget about it.'

'Don't have much choice. Can't break into the place and snoop around, can we?'

'Why not?' I said, smiling conspiratorially. 'You said you know how to pick a lock.'

He frowned at me. 'By the book. That's how Fletcher likes things.'

'All right,' I sighed, conceding. 'Let's pay Little Venice one last visit.'

CHAPTER TWENTY-NINE

We bundled into my Volvo, once again tempting Ace in with treats, though he was more keen than before. Collies are nothing if not fast learners. Ronnie had already leapt into the boot without prompting, but looked pathetically bereft until I gave him a treat as well.

'I wonder how much the solicitor knows,' I said as we set off. 'About the management company, I mean.'

'Good question. You think it's not real?'

'It's real in the sense of being registered, and presumably pays rent every month. Mr Patwari even said he'd have to inform them about Crash's death. Does that mean he doesn't know Crash is behind it? Or was he pretending for my sake? Perhaps it's a scam or a tax dodge.'

'Money laundering. Lots of dirty cash coming in. Use it to pay "Don Christopher's" rent, it goes through the system, comes back to Crash clean as a whistle.'

I considered that theory. 'Mr Patwari wouldn't even need to be involved, would he? It could all be Crash,

deceiving everyone. It seems he was very good at it.'

We fell silent as I turned onto the Westway. Then Birch said, 'Spoke to Fletcher last night.'

'Oh, Birch, no.' It hadn't occurred to me before now that he'd still have the superintendent's number but I shouldn't have been surprised. I envisaged a dawn raid on Lucy Kwok's house, with the police breaking down her door and terrifying her grandmother. Not that Mrs Kwok seemed the kind to scare easily. I revised the vision to include her whacking an unfortunate policeman over the head with her stick.

'Thought you'd want me to,' he protested. 'Asked about checking for poisons in the bloodstream. She said they're already testing, should have results this morning. Shows she's listening, see? Told you she's a good sort.'

I was relieved, but before I could thank him for not ratting out Lucy over the drugs, his phone rang.

'Ma'am,' he said, answering. No prizes for guessing who was on the other end. 'Hold on, driving. I'll put you on speaker.' He did, raising a finger to his lips to signal I should stay quiet. 'Go ahead.'

'You'll be pleased to know we received the toxicology report this morning and it confirms our hypothesis. Mr Donnelly didn't ingest poisonous plants at all. We found high levels of alprazolam in his blood.'

'That's Xanax, isn't it?' he said for my benefit. 'Like in his bathroom?'

'Correct. So you see, whether it was suicide or misadventure, his death has no connection to what happened yesterday with Mr Zimmerman.'

I protested silently but Birch waved for me to be quiet. 'Doesn't that make the attack on Howard even more suspicious?'

'If it even was an attack,' said Fletcher. 'We're not ruling out an accident there, either.'

'*House*,' I mouthed as we turned off for Little Venice.

Birch understood and (without mentioning me) told the superintendent about Don Christopher Management, the house on Penfold Mews and the possible scam of it all.

'Should take some uniforms. We, uh, that is Ronnie and I, can meet you there, show you which house. Break in if necessary.' He winked at me.

'Break in? What on earth for? Birch, I must say I think Ms Tuffel is exerting a bad influence on you.'

He bristled. 'Just trying to get to the bottom of things.'

'I warned you retirement wouldn't suit you. You're not a copper any more, Alan. I know Beatrice is gone, but you can't fill your days meddling in official business.'

The mention of his late wife incensed him. 'Uncalled for!'

'Is it? Anyway, assuming you're right and Mr Donnelly has an interest in that property, it'll all come out in the will.'

'Could be weeks away,' he protested. 'Trail will have gone cold by then.'

'There is no "trail"!' she shouted. 'I won't take a brigade of coppers to break down the door of someone's office because you think they have a funny name. Good day.'

She ended the call, leaving Birch fuming. This was

the closest I'd ever seen to him losing his temper. Being dismissed by his former boss was evidently a step too far and if she imagined bringing up Beatrice would help, she clearly didn't know him as well as she thought. He'd wear that wedding ring to his grave.

I turned into Blomfield Road, found a parking spot and turned off the engine. Birch stared out of the window, as below us the last day of the Carnival got underway at the Pool. People wandered along the paths, greeted heartily by the boaters. I saw Lucy darting about, organising things, eternally busy.

'Let's hope she doesn't summon another body from the depths, eh?' I joked, hoping to rouse Birch. It didn't work, so I stepped out and opened the boot to let the dogs down. He finally joined me in silence as we clipped on their leads, then crossed the junction bridge and descended the steps to the residents' path. As we reached the access gate, Howard was returning from a jog.

'You're obviously feeling recovered,' I said.

'Eighty per cent,' he smiled. 'Wild horses couldn't keep me, though. I fly out in a few hours.' A thought struck him. 'You know, Gwinny, this may be the last time we see each other, so thank you again for yesterday. I do wish we'd met under better circumstances.'

'I'm sure you're not the only one. Come to think of it, I should return your gate key.' I began rummaging in my handbag, but he waved it away.

'Won't need it, will I? Keep it, and consider yourself an honorary resident.'

He continued on, taking a wide berth – or as wide as the canal path would allow him to – around Fox's boat, where Johnny Roulette stood on the deck. The men exchanged scowls but nothing was said.

Curious about the guitarist's presence, Birch and I approached. We were greeted with a similar scowl.

'What are you doing here, Johnny?' I asked. No point beating around the bush. 'Is Fox still with the police?'

'She's right here, no thanks to you,' he grumbled. 'Coppers weren't willing to make an arrest and she's to meet Ellie at the airport later. Do everyone a favour and leave us alone.'

'Not yet, sorry. I want to know why you lied to me and deleted my photos of the notebook.' I decided not to mention we'd recovered them, to see how he might react. 'Birch here has all your albums, you see. Even the early ones produced by "Don Christopher" and "Willy Ormond".'

Johnny's shoulders sagged a little. 'It's band business and you've no right to be poking around in it. Don't you see it's over for us? No more concerts, no more tours. It was Crash who held the audience, there's no lie in that. But now maybe some West End eejit with more money than sense wants to make a tribute musical or something, right? Think how much those lyrics could be worth! And here's you, with them saved on your bloody phone.'

Fox emerged from the doorway. 'Tell her to go away, Jonathan. We have nothing to say.' Then she

remembered he wouldn't hear her and tapped his leg to draw his attention.

'What's up, pet? I was just telling this pair to get lost.'

'Good. You do that.'

Fox retreated into the dark interior, followed by Johnny. Birch and I beat our own retreat, back down the path. Could we take the guitarist's word for it? Had he really acted out of caution?

Constable Wright maintained his guard outside Crash's houseboat, but as Birch still hadn't spoken a word since his phone call to DCS Fletcher, now didn't feel like a good time to ask after the superintendent's whereabouts. Much as she frustrated me, I hoped they wouldn't fall out completely. Birch and I had disagreed before but he was always quick to forgive, to the point that sometimes he barely acknowledged we'd argued. But those were disagreements about things like dogs, not his late wife. As for Fletcher's perspective . . . well, Birch had said she and I were similar, and if I do say so myself, I'm pretty good at holding grudges.

'Birch,' I began, 'I'm sorry Fletcher wouldn't listen to you, but—'

'Let's do it,' he said suddenly and marched off ahead.

'Do what? Where are we going?' I asked, hurrying after him. Ace thought this sudden burst of speed was enormous fun and I struggled to keep him under control as we mounted the steps back to the road.

'Penfold Mews, of course. Time we took a look inside.'

CHAPTER THIRTY

We walked in silence; Birch's mind was obviously set on something and I was hurrying to keep up. Finally, we turned onto the cobbled street of Penfold Mews and approached the house-slash-office of Don Christopher Management Ltd.

Ace eagerly sniffed the door, keen to get inside.

'It's still a bank holiday,' I said, catching my breath. 'Even if someone does work here, they're probably not in today.'

'Good,' Birch said, and rang the doorbell. Sure enough, there was no answer. 'Good,' he said again. 'Now, look here.'

He leant in close, with an air of secrecy, and took a small metal case from his pocket. 'Picked them up before we left.' He opened the case to reveal several thin, metal tools. Like a misshapen set of Allen keys, or—

'A lockpick set,' I gasped. 'I thought you were joking.'

The former policeman and I had flouted rules before,

certainly; distracting Constable Wright to get inside Crash's houseboat wasn't even the first time we'd snuck into a crime scene together. But this was a new level of mischief.

'Thought I'd use them to help Fletcher,' he grumbled. 'But she's too damn foolish to follow the evidence under her nose. Shouldn't have taken on this case, in my opinion. Rusty. I should have listened to you,' he added sheepishly.

'Yes, you should have, and not only about Fletcher. This is no less "illegal" than what Lucy and Fox are doing, you know.' He opened his mouth to protest, but I cut him off. 'Never mind that for now. Get to work, Raffles.'

He handed Ronnie to me, then inserted the tools into the lock and began to wriggle them around. I don't pretend to know the first thing about lock picking but Birch remained calm and collected, so I trusted things were going well.

Until someone said, 'Good morning.'

Not being well versed in the art of breaking and entering, I hadn't thought to keep lookout. Now I turned to see the young hairdresser approaching, with a takeaway coffee in one hand and a paper deli bag in the other. From behind me came a startled cough and the tinkle of metal tools falling to the floor. Whether Birch had dropped them out of surprise or thrown them down deliberately, I couldn't say.

'Morning,' I replied, trying to act natural.

Unfortunately, Ronnie had other ideas. Before I could take a firmer grip he surged forward, pulling his lead from my hand and bounding over to the startled young man.

'Ronnie, *no*!' I called, running over with Ace by my side. 'Come back here!' Normally the Lab was amenable to my commands, but not when faced with a delicious-smelling sandwich. He leapt up at the hairdresser, barking loudly, trying to grab the deli bag.

'I say, ham sandwich by any chance?' Birch called out, running over to tame his dog. 'Bit keen, sorry. No harm meant.'

'That's easy for you to say!' said the hairdresser angrily, spinning in circles and holding his breakfast up out of Ronnie's reach. This made the Lab jump even higher in his efforts and I foresaw disaster if this didn't end soon.

I dropped Ace's lead and thrust a finger towards the ground in front of his nose, trusting Crash's words that he was unlikely to run off. The Collie obediently dropped to the cobbles. Then I stepped between the hairdresser and Ronnie, admonished the hungry dog with the loudest '*Ah*!' I could manage and made a grab for his lead. It was enough to draw his attention, so I held his gaze while raising a rigid index finger to the sky. He froze in place, looking from my eyes to my finger and back again, then slowly lowered his head as I brought my hand down.

I gave Ronnie's head a fuss for obeying at last and turned to apologise, but the hairdresser was already incensed.

'I told you before, you're wasting your time at that house, and you can't even keep your bloody dogs under control! Now get away or I'll call the police!'

He retreated to his shop, grumbling, and we backed up to the management company's door.

'Reckon you've got a minute, tops, before he looks out of his lounge window, sees us still here and calls the police,' I said. 'Can you do it, or shall we scarper?'

Birch was already retrieving his fallen lock-pick tools. He gave an annoyed snort. 'Not letting a nosey parker like him get the better of me.'

DCS Fletcher might have called that 'the deer mocking the rabbit's tail', but I kept schtum and let him resume work while I watched the hairdresser's house for shadows that might betray movement on his upper floor.

A *click* sounded from the door. 'Are we in?' I whispered.

'Not quite . . . almost . . .'

I thought I saw a slight change in light through the window opposite. 'Any time today, Birch . . .'

'Gotcha,' he mumbled, and I heard another, more solid *click*. 'When you're ready.' He opened the door and stood aside.

'No time like the present,' I said, refusing his chivalry, and pushed him in ahead of me.

With the dogs weaving around our legs, we all tumbled inside and I quickly slammed the door closed. Feeling like a naughty schoolchild, I peeked out through its small glass pane. The hairdresser stood at his lounge

window. Was he on the phone? Was he even looking this way? I couldn't tell.

'Don't use any lights,' I said to Birch. 'If he assumed we ran away, let's not give him reason to think otherwise.' The house interior was gloomy, but not so much we couldn't find our way.

I stepped back from the door and noticed something on the floor – or rather, the absence of something.

'How strange,' I said. 'Birch, what's wrong with this picture?'

He followed my gaze down. 'Not sure I follow. Nothing there.'

'Exactly. If this place was unused, wouldn't there be post piled up and waiting to be opened? Someone must have been here recently to pick it up.'

'Or nobody sends anything to this address?'

'I've never in my life set foot in a Domino's but they still shove a menu through my letterbox every week. I can't believe a business address five minutes' walk from Paddington doesn't receive junk mail.'

He shrugged. 'Fair. So despite what our friendly hairdresser says, someone's using the place. Perhaps coming at odd hours when everyone's asleep, like you said.'

I began climbing the stairs. 'Then let's hope our suspicions are correct and the someone in question was Crash Double, because if it turns out Don Christopher is real and decides to visit, we'll have a job explaining ourselves.'

On the first floor, in what would normally have been the living area, the theme of absence continued. The kitchen looked even less used than Crash's houseboat galley, although there was a mug drying on the sideboard and a water bowl on the floor. Ace tried to lap from it but as I had no idea what was in it, or how long it had been standing there, I snatched it up and emptied it into the sink. After refilling it with fresh water I let him drink, and Ronnie joined him.

'Not so unused after all, if there's a dog bowl,' I said.

'Only water, though,' said Birch. 'Any dog food in the cupboards?'

There wasn't, but I did find two packs of the same energy bars Crash ate. 'Why have a bolt-hole like this, but keep nothing in it?' I wondered.

The dining room and lounge were nothing more than plain walls and bare floorboards. No carpet, not even a rug. The closest thing to furniture was a blind that completely covered the window facing the street.

On the second floor, though, we finally got our answer. Like the rest of the house, the attic room wasn't furnished for creature comforts. But it did contain a desk, chair, filing cabinet . . . and a well-used dog bed in the corner. Another blind was drawn fully over the dormer window.

'Crash told me Ace suffers from separation anxiety,' I said. 'He must have brought the dog with him. No wonder Ace recognised the scent at the door.'

Besides a coaster, presumably for the mug downstairs,

the austere desk held two items: a closed laptop and a mobile phone, which was plugged in and fully charged.

'Now we know why the police didn't find Crash's mobile on his body,' I said. 'It was here all along.' Ace weaved around my legs, sniffing the desk and chair. I felt sorry for him, knowing that sooner or later he'd realise his human was never coming back again. I reached for the phone—

And jumped like a jack-in-the-box when it lit up and vibrated. Someone was calling!

I peered at the screen, hoping it would identify the caller. It did, but what I saw only further confused matters.

'Birch . . . why is Mr Patwari trying to phone Crash, when he knows perfectly well the man is dead?' Then I looked again at the phone and saw that I'd jumped too quickly to a conclusion. This wasn't the one I'd seen Crash use. It was smaller and lacked the distinctive photo case of Ace.

The phone stopped vibrating and the screen showed a missed call. Two, in fact. The one from the lawyer just now, and another from Lucy Kwok on Friday morning.

A puzzle piece clicked into place in my mind. 'It's his blackmail phone,' I said. 'Crash must have kept a separate number, so there was nothing incriminating on his regular phone. I bet that call was Mr Patwari trying to reach Don Christopher Management.'

'Explains why the phone is still here, too, rather than at the bottom of the canal. Killer never found it.'

'Let's see if the laptop can tell us anything.' I opened it, fingers poised to type *equilibrium*, but there was no demand for a password. It simply opened to the desktop.

'Curious,' said Birch, looking over my shoulder. 'Password at home, but not here?'

'Perhaps he never took this computer anywhere else? We're definitely in the right place. Look at that.'

As soon as the screen had lit up, a notification message appeared to announce a new email . . . from me. The email I'd sent to Don Christopher.

'No wonder I didn't get a reply. I was writing to a dead man.'

Unlike the computer at Crash's studio, this one was sparse and tidy. Its desktop contained four familiar folders, in alphabetical order: *Fox*, *Howard*, *Johnny*, and *Lucy*.

I opened *Lucy*. The contents were identical to what we'd seen before; a spreadsheet, a photo, and an audio file. The spreadsheet was a copy of the one we'd seen already but with one big difference: it was intact, with no missing or garbled entries.

'Copies of whatever was on the computer at his boat,' said Birch, looking over my shoulder. 'Killer damaged those, but didn't know about this computer.'

I gasped. 'Which means . . . oh, I don't want to say anything and jinx it. Let's just see.'

Like its duplicate, this folder contained two other files. I opened the photograph and was confused to see a freeze frame from the video I'd accidentally taken in

Crash's studio, showing the hooded Lucy leaping over the fence to Blomfield Road with a tartan canvas bag in hand. But then I noticed that the trees in this picture were shedding their leaves; it was the same scene, but taken at a different time.

'He saw Lucy, too,' I said. 'That's how he blackmailed her. Now, here goes nothing.'

I played the audio file. Ace's ears perked up at the sound of Crash's voice and I gave him a reassuring fuss as we listened to the undamaged recording.

Crash: '—*know you can't fool me of all people, Lucy. Rock 'n' roll lifestyle [muffled]*'

Lucy: '*So now what? [Muffled] tell the police you'd have done it already.*'

Crash: '*I still might. Unless of course we can come to a mutually beneficial arrangement, that is. I mean, buying and selling drugs is a serious offence. So five hundred a week is a small price to pay, don't you think? Sure and you must [muffled] already.*'

Lucy: '*You scheming [muffled]. If you breathe a word of this to anyone, I'll kill you.*'

Crash: '*Now why would I do that? You keep paying, and I'll keep quiet. That's how it works.*'

Birch whistled softly. 'Blackmail material, all right. Credible threat, too. What's in the other folders?'

'Let's find out,' I said, opening them all.

Ten minutes later we tumbled downstairs, barrelled out the door and ran back to Little Venice as fast as our ageing legs would allow.

We had a killer to catch.

CHAPTER THIRTY-ONE

Ace and Ronnie naturally thought our sprinting (more like breathless jogging, if I'm honest) was the most fun they'd had all day. Their incessant bouncing almost tripped us several times as we ran to the canal.

We reached the junction bridge, and I heard Lucy's amplified voice announce that she would shortly reveal the winner of the 'best boat' prize. She stood on a barge in the centre of the Pool, watched by hundreds of people in the surrounding boats and crowded on the canal-side paths. I saw Mr Choudhury the grocer among them, smiling and applauding with everyone else. It was the last day of the Carnival and a jubilant mood filled the air.

We ran on, down to the residents' area.

Clinging to Ace's lead with one hand, I scrabbled in my pocket for the key as we descended the steps. I saw Fox and Johnny approaching from the other side, walking hand in hand. The guitarist was right; there was

no need to hide their relationship any more.

Fox unlocked the gate and swung it open, then noticed me, Birch and the dogs hurrying towards it. She and Johnny leapt aside to avoid a collision.

'What the hell are you doing here?' Fox said.

'Explain . . . later . . .' I panted, hurrying through the gate.

We ran on, past Crash's houseboat.

The front door opened and DCS Fletcher stepped onto the path as we rushed past.

'Come on!' I called to her, gasping for breath. 'No time . . . to waste!'

We ran on, along the canal path.

Latesha Michaels stood by Howard's boat, looking every bit the glamorous transatlantic businesswoman with her LV luggage, oversized sunglasses propped on her head and casual chic travelling clothes.

I stopped. Ace obediently sat and looked up at me, tongue panting as he waited for the next game to begin. I envied him; if I could have stuck my own tongue out six inches to cool down, I would have.

Birch, Ronnie and DCS Fletcher all came to a halt behind me. Birch was puffing and wheezing, too, which made me feel the tiniest bit better.

'It's the Keystone Kennel Club,' said Latesha with disdain. 'Do you mind clearing a path? We have a flight to catch.'

At that moment Howard emerged from the boat, carrying a suitcase in either hand. Unlike Latesha, he

looked much the same as always in a sleeveless shirt and cargo shorts, his sole concession to travel being a multi-pocketed jacket.

'What's going on?' he said. 'We're about to leave.'

'Sorry,' I said, still trying to catch my breath, 'But no . . . you're not.'

Latesha glared at me. 'I'm gonna give you five seconds to get out of the way and then I'm calling Zabok's London lawyer. This is harassment.'

'What *is* going on, Ms Tuffel?' asked DCS Fletcher. 'I have work to do.'

'Yes, you do,' I said. 'Like arresting Crash Double's killer.'

Latesha began dialling. 'OK, that's it. You are *so* getting sued, lady.'

'I wouldn't bother if I were you,' I said. 'I doubt your lawyer will want to defend Howard in a murder trial.'

Everyone froze for a moment. Then Lucy's voice carried from the Pool, announcing that a boat called *Tadeusz* had won the boat contest, and it broke the spell.

'You silly woman,' said Howard. 'Get out of the way.'

'Steady on, sir,' said Birch, stepping up. Those old habits really did die hard.

'Ms Tuffel, this is a serious accusation,' said Fletcher. 'What evidence do you have?'

I drew myself up to my full height, which was admittedly a good deal shorter than Howard, and faced him. 'I hoped to finish my jigsaw before rehearsals resumed, but Crash's death messed everything up. Last

night I was annoyed about that and thought, If only I could turn the clocks back a couple of days . . .'

His eyes widened, and I knew he understood.

Then he shoved Latesha into us and made a run for it.

The American stumbled and fell, knocking me back into Birch, who fell into Fletcher, and we all collapsed in a heap on the path. Ace and Ronnie wagged their tails and licked our faces, united at last by the humans' highly entertaining new game.

By the time we'd untangled our limbs and got to our feet, Howard was through the gate and running under the bridge to the Pool, where the crowd stood shoulder to shoulder watching Lucy hand out the boat awards.

'He's trying to blend in,' I said, giving chase with Ace by my side. 'Don't let him get away!' I'd barely got my breath back from running down here, but if Howard escaped now we might never find him again. I hurried through the gate, about to follow him under the junction bridge when I had a better idea. Instead, I climbed the steps and ran onto the bridge, scanning the crowd from the high vantage point. I saw Howard right away, his bald head weaving between the crowd.

I was so busy watching him that I didn't pay attention to where I was going, and collided with someone standing on the bridge.

'Oh! I'm so sorry, I wasn't—' I stopped when I saw who I'd run into.

'You again!' said the bearded BuzzFeed reporter angrily, clutching his drone controller. 'If you've got a

problem with the video, take it up with my editor. Leave me alone!'

'Really, it was an accident—' I began, then saw the controller screen and had an idea. 'Your drone has a camera, right? How good are you at flying it?'

He snorted. 'Third in the Shoreditch racing league. Why?'

I resisted the temptation to ask if the league had a fourth competitor and said, 'The man who killed Crash Double just ran into that crowd to evade the police. There, with the bald head.' I pointed in Howard's direction. It was hard to pick him out now, as he was further away and moving more slowly so as not to draw attention. 'Keep him in your sights and you'll have one heck of a story.'

He hesitated, but no reporter can resist a scoop for long. He turned back to the controller and a high-pitched buzzing sounded from the sky. I watched as the tiny drone swooped over the crowd, heading for Howard's position.

'Perfect! Stay out of reach, so he can't, um . . .' I tailed off, realising what I was about to say.

'Hit it with a ball thrower?' the young man suggested acidly.

I was saved from having to respond by Birch and Ronnie, who found me on the bridge.

'Where's Fletcher?' I asked.

'Giving chase,' Birch replied, pointing down into the crowd. Sure enough, DCS Fletcher surged through the

crowd, with Constable Wright following in her wake.

I cupped my hands and called out, 'Superintendent! Look for the drone!'

Fletcher stopped and looked around, confused, then saw us standing on the bridge.

'The drone!' I shouted, pointing at the tiny flying device. 'We're following him!'

Understanding, she nodded and resumed pushing through the crowd. Several bystanders yelled at me to be quiet while they listened to Lucy. There's no accounting for taste.

But I wasn't done. 'Howard!' I called out at the top of my lungs. 'You can't get away! *Come back*! *Come back*!'

I couldn't be sure he'd heard me, but someone certainly did. Suddenly Ace leapt to his feet and bolted back across the road. 'Ace, *no*!' I called, but it was too late. I'd been so focused on watching Howard, and the Collie was normally so obedient, that I hadn't kept a firm enough grip on his lead. Now something had spooked him and he was running back to the safety of Crash's houseboat. Paralysed by indecision, I didn't know whether to give chase or trust he knew what he was doing.

Then I heard cries from below and looked down to see a ripple of people sway and move as a furry tri-colour shape weaved between them.

I laughed, remembering Ace 'dancing' with Crash. He wasn't running back to the boat. He was off to herd!

Lucy, the competition boats and most of the crowd had no idea anything was going on. The skipper of the

Tadeusz now had the mic, happily telling the crowd what an honour this was. I watched Howard slowly draw closer to the Westbourne Terrace Bridge. The drone dutifully followed, with DCS Fletcher and her policeman gaining on them both as fast as they could, but it was slow going through the mass of people.

Then, suddenly, Howard stopped moving. The skipper handed the mic back to Lucy and the crowd applauded again. Lucy motioned for quiet, and opened her mouth to deliver a speech . . .

But was drowned out by Ace barking. On the drone controller screen, I saw the Collie run in circles around Howard, clearing a space as the crowd backed away from this unknown dog. Howard tried to back away too but Ace was too fast and nipped behind him, then back around, herding him towards us, barking incessantly.

'Will someone shut that bloody dog up?!' Lucy shouted over the PA but people had stopped paying attention to her. They were all trying to see what was happening closer to home, craning their necks and standing on tiptoes.

DCS Fletcher finally caught up with Howard and he turned to shout angrily at her. The drone didn't capture sound, but it didn't take lip-reading to recognise a torrent of swear words. Then I noticed Ace sneaking up behind, the dog's body pressed close to the ground, while Howard's attention was elsewhere. He said something final to the superintendent, then turned to run – and came face to face with the Collie. Ace barked

again, something I *could* hear even from the bridge, and the guru instinctively recoiled. Unluckily for him, the movement sent him stumbling over a knot of mooring rope on the path's edge.

Arms flailing and mouth agape, Howard Zee toppled between two barges and hit the water with a mighty splash.

CHAPTER THIRTY-TWO

We gathered in Crash's saloon. It seemed appropriate.

Howard Zee was outside, being checked over by an ambulance crew after he almost drowned in the cold waters of the Pool, under the watchful gaze of Constable Wright. DCS Fletcher had agreed to open Crash's houseboat to the rest of us so I could explain.

Fox Double-Jones and Johnny Roulette took the sofa. Lucy Kwok and Latesha Michaels brought stools from the galley area. I perched on the upright piano bench, under the gold disc that hid Crash's safe. Ace lay on his corner bed, worrying at the remains of the cardboard box Mr Choudhury had given me on Friday. Was that really only three days ago?

Birch and DCS Fletcher both stood in the doorway, with an exhausted Ronnie sleeping at their feet.

'He almost got away with it,' I said when everyone had settled down. 'Especially because *everyone* involved in this was hiding their true selves behind a

façade. Nobody here is who they seem.'

Fox, Johnny, Lucy and Latesha all looked sideways at each other, but said nothing.

'Let's start at the beginning. Three years ago, Crash Double built his second floor to install a home recording studio. Whether he planned to spy on everyone, or if that was a bonus, we'll never know. But he did and that's how he first saw Lucy taking drugs to and from Fox's houseboat, climbing over the fence to avoid CCTV cameras.'

'What?!' Fletcher exploded. 'Ms Kwok, I'm afraid I'll have to—'

'Please wait, Superintendent. When you hear Lucy's tale you might be inclined to leniency.' I resumed the story. 'Crash confronted her, but not to make her stop. On the contrary, he was happy for Lucy to continue so long as she paid him hush money. That's how his blackmail operation began.'

Fox, Johnny and Howard all turned to look at Lucy. 'He was blackmailing you as well?' said Fox, incredulous.

Lucy returned the expression. 'What do you mean, "as well". . . ?'

'Crash developed a taste for easy money and expanded,' I explained. 'He discovered Fox and Johnny were having an affair and threatened to divorce her unless she paid up. Then he found out that Johnny—'

'I'm going deaf, all right?' Johnny interrupted. Lucy gasped. 'I was worried the press would find out and people would stop coming to the shows.'

Knowing what was coming next, Birch handed me

the laptop we'd found at Penfold Mews.

'You'd like us to think that's why Crash was blackmailing you, wouldn't you, Johnny?' I said. 'It's true you're losing your hearing and have been playing songs from memory for some time. But that's not a problem, because you wrote them . . . didn't you?'

I opened the *Johnny* folder on the laptop. 'Does Fox know? About the songs and the tapes?'

She clearly didn't. 'What songs? Jonathan, have you started writing again? That's wonderful.' His deadpan expression made her pause. 'Isn't it?'

The normally loquacious guitarist glowered at me in silence.

'All right,' I said, 'I'll tell her. You're right, Fox. Johnny told me he's been writing new songs for a while now. But Crash wouldn't record any of them or let him make them solo.'

'How could he stop him? I don't understand.'

I pressed Play and we all listened to Crash sing one of Bad Dice's early hits on an acoustic guitar. But this file was undamaged and included parts we hadn't heard before. Parts where Crash would play something different to the final version of the song, then stop and mutter, '*No, that doesn't work. How about this?*' before continuing with the song everyone knew. It finished and I played a second recording with similar contents.

Not knowing the songs well myself, it had taken Birch – who knew the band's discography from back to front and upside down – to understand what this meant.

It put Crash and Johnny's recorded conversation, about 'the fans finding out', in a whole new light.

Fox cottoned on quickly. 'That's Crash, from years ago. He hasn't sounded like that since their early albums. But it's like he doesn't know the songs . . .'

'Johnny told me the real money is in songwriting,' I said. 'That's where the royalties come from, how he made millions and bought the house on the Crescent; because he wrote all of the band's hits. Except it turns out that he didn't. Crash did, and they both knew it, but it couldn't be proven . . . until Crash found some old tapes in amongst all this mess.'

'They're fake,' Johnny insisted. 'You've seen his set-up, all those computers. The man could manipulate anything to sound like anything.'

I shrugged. 'Perhaps they are. I don't think so, but it doesn't really matter. What matters is that *this* is what he was really blackmailing you over, not your deafness. He threatened to release these recordings and sue for decades of royalties if you didn't pay him instead. A thousand pounds per week was quite reasonable compared to the millions you stood to lose, not to mention how your fans would react.'

Unsurprisingly, it was Lucy who zeroed in on the big question. 'I'm confused. If Crash wrote them, why did he let Johnny take credit for all these years?'

'Mr Ormond-Wiles senior was a successful banker who almost single-handedly funded the band's early days. Somehow, he convinced a young and naive Crash

to assign the songwriting to his son Johnny, presumably in return for all the financial support their family gave Bad Dice. Crash came to regret it but was powerless to change anything until he found the tapes.'

Fox had been sitting next to Johnny, holding his hand. Now she withdrew and went to stand by the French windows instead.

'We each thought he was blackmailing us alone,' she said, 'When in fact it was all three of us. So much for him being broke.'

'Actually, it was four. Blackmail is, after all, why Howard killed Crash.'

'But how, and when?' asked Fletcher. 'Howard has alibis all Thursday night and Friday morning.'

I closed the laptop. 'When I came here for the weekend, I brought a jigsaw puzzle with me. A lovely painting of the canal, which I planned to finish over the bank holiday. But I'd barely started when Crash turned up dead and after that there wasn't time. Last night I thought to myself, *If only I could turn the calendar back a couple of days*. In a way, that was the breakthrough.'

Everyone glanced sideways at one another, probably thinking I'd lost my mind.

'Let's return to Thursday afternoon,' I said. 'Crash introduced me to most of you that day. He also warned me that Howard Zee wasn't his real name, but as I'm so used to people using stage names I thought nothing of it. There were other things I should have noticed, though, such as Howard not taking clients younger than forty.

Or that when Crash said to Howard, "I'll see you later," he wasn't being polite, he meant it literally. At nine o' clock that night, in fact.'

'No, that can't be,' said Latesha. 'Howard was in session, you know that. I sent you the recording.'

'You did, and I'll explain in a moment. When I arrived on Friday morning, I met Howard returning from a jog. We came in here and the moment I opened the door Ace ran onto the path, desperate for the toilet. Then Lucy called, looking for Crash. She'd tried the night before but Crash hadn't answered the door. She was trying to make her weekly blackmail payment, which was due on Thursdays.'

Lucy huffed. 'I thought it was strange when he didn't answer. There were lights on and Ace barked when I knocked.'

'Yes,' I said, 'because there *was* someone inside, but it wasn't Crash. Luckily for them, Ace's bark is worse than his bite.' The Collie pricked up an ear at the mention of his name.

'Next, Howard gave me a key to the access gate. Crash had changed his locks after a burglary and forgot to put one on the new keyring he supplied me. That's when I first saw Howard's studio set-up, which struck me as very professional. I didn't know how significant that would be. More immediately, though, Mr Choudhury the grocer told me that Crash hadn't called in that morning as he'd planned to.'

'Why is any of this important?' said Fox. 'Didn't you

say Crash was already dead by Friday?'

I nodded. 'Long dead, in fact. Don't you see? At first, we thought Crash was killed Friday morning because he texted me about getting a car to the airport. But that text was a fake. Crash didn't answer the door to Lucy on Thursday night, or call in at Choudhury's on Friday morning because he was already at the bottom of the canal. No wonder Ace was desperate for the toilet; by the time I arrived, the poor dog had been shut up in here for almost twelve hours.'

'This is rather circumstantial,' said DCS Fletcher. 'I still don't see how it led you to Howard.'

'You will. Later on Friday, I used Crash's computer upstairs and discovered the files had been badly damaged. But they'd been fine on Thursday afternoon. Crash himself had played me some music and even recorded me talking. Now those files were damaged and the computer was open on one side. I also found four folders, all locked with a password; one for each of his blackmail victims.'

I stood up on my tiptoes and moved the gold disc aside, revealing the wall safe.

'Inside this safe, the police found a notebook, which contained lyrics for Crash's new songs. I took photos, as a keepsake for Birch.' Judging by DCS Fletcher's expression she still wasn't happy about that, but Birch couldn't resist a smile. 'It turned out to be much more than that, though. The notebook also contained the passwords to those folders. Unfortunately, the contents were so damaged it was hard to decipher them. With

Howard, for example, all we really discovered was that he was involved in a scandal with a woman called Vicki.'

'His ex-wife, right?' said Latesha.

'I'm afraid not. He fooled you, me and everyone else with that story. You were his ticket out, you see. He'd begrudgingly paid Crash to keep the real scandal a secret and then along you came, promising big money in America with Ziggy+.'

'Zabok,' she corrected me.

'Whatever. The point is, Howard couldn't afford to let this chance go. But Crash threatened to expose his scandal if Howard didn't turn down the TV deal.'

'He didn't tell me any of this,' Latesha protested.

'Of course not. He had no intention of turning you down, or of letting the blackmail follow him across the pond and risk his shot at fame. Instead, Howard came up with a plan. Everyone knew Bad Dice would be playing in Dublin over the Carnival weekend, as they do every year. So he scheduled everything around that and used you, Latesha, as bait.'

I opened the laptop again, found the *Howard* folder and played the undamaged recording of their conversation from Thursday.

Crash: '—*didn't have to come here to discuss this. You could have phoned, you know.*'

Howard: '*Not likely. Listen, we just want to talk. She knows everything, and on behalf of Zabok+ Latesha is proposing a very generous offer to*

resolve this once and for all. At least come and listen to her, will you?'

Crash: *'Don't you think you should be making your own generous offer to the likes of Vicki Richards? I tell you, if you try to leave now, I'll go to the press with the truth.'*

Howard: *'By then I'll be in the States with big money and big lawyers to fight you. So let's get serious. Nine o' clock, all right? Don't be late.'*

'None of that is true,' said Latesha, horrified. 'I don't know squat about a scandal, or paying Crash off, or anything.'

'I know,' I reassured her. 'When I mentioned it to Howard yesterday, you hadn't even heard of Vicki Richards, let alone made her a "generous offer". This conversation was a lie, designed to lure Crash to Howard's boat. He lied to us about meaning nine o'clock on Friday morning, too. I might have believed him, until I remembered that when Lucy called at the boat that morning, it was Howard himself who mentioned Crash's preference for early flights. He knew very well that he wouldn't be around at that time.'

'But Howard ran a class from nine till ten on Thursday night. I watched it myself.'

I smiled. 'Did he, though?'

'There was a live Q&A,' DCS Fletcher pointed out. 'I've seen the video in question. You can't fake that.'

'Then how do you explain his watch?' I said.

Met with a sea of blank faces, I continued, 'This wasn't a spur-of-the-moment killing. Howard had already begun making plans, and my coming here to look after Ace was the icing on the cake. Normally, Crash would hand his dog off to Fox. But not this time because she recently took in Lilith, her boat cat.' Fox turned from the French windows and I caught her eye. 'To spite Crash for the blackmail, I assume? Make him spend some of the money you were paying him on a dog sitter?'

Fox snorted. 'Stopped him coming round as often, too.'

'Yes, so you could spend more time with Johnny . . . like you did overnight on Thursday.' I turned to Lucy. 'It really was him you saw climb over the gate on Friday morning.'

'So Johnny killed Crash?!' she shrieked.

I sighed. 'No, and neither did Fox. Lilith's presence alone should have told me that earlier. If Fox planned to kill Crash, taking in a cat – which forced him to find a sitter, like me – would only have made things more difficult.'

Birch coughed. 'You could say that if not for the cat, Howard would have got away with it because Gwinny wouldn't be here.' Fletcher shot him an accusing look but he didn't apologise.

I continued, 'Two nights before, at nine o'clock on Tuesday night, Howard conducted and recorded an online session as usual – but it wasn't broadcast. Instead, for forty-five minutes Howard performed to nobody

but the camera, all the time pretending an audience was watching. He ended it, as always, by calling a five-minute break before questions and discussion. During those breaks he normally replaced the video with a countdown timer.'

As if sensing we were approaching the heart of the matter, Ace stood up from his bed and padded over to sit by me. I fussed behind his floppy ear and continued.

'At 9 p.m. on Thursday, Howard opened another online session. But instead of doing it live, he played the video he'd recorded on Tuesday. The attendees had no idea; to them it was like any other class. But while they watched a recording, the real Howard prepared a drink for Crash. What was it they found in Crash's bloodstream, Superintendent?'

'Massive amounts of Xanax,' Fletcher confirmed.

Fox perked up. 'So it wasn't poisonous plants at all!'

'No,' I reassured her, 'it was plain old pills, stolen from Crash's boat when Howard burgled it weeks ago. Crash thought nothing had been taken because he kept such a stash of Xanax that he didn't notice one missing bottle. On Thursday, Howard presumably fobbed him off about waiting for Latesha and offered him a drink full of the stuff. It would have rendered Crash unconscious very quickly. Then Howard took his keys and his phone, which he unlocked with Crash's own face. Next, he checked the coast was clear and carried him out of the boat; easy enough for a strong man like Howard. Finally, he lowered Crash into the canal. No noise, no fuss.'

'Hence water in his lungs,' Birch explained for Fletcher's benefit. 'Unconscious but not dead. Um, until he drowned, of course.'

Fletcher was confused. 'But when we analysed Howard's smoothie maker, we *did* find poisonous plants.'

'He couldn't very well get back into Crash's boat for more Xanax with you guarding the place, could he?' I said. 'Howard expected Crash to stay submerged. And if he hadn't floated to the surface on Saturday, we'd have all assumed he went missing in Dublin instead. The body turning up threw a wrench in Howard's plans, which is why he tried to throw me off with talk about Crash having a "dark side" that might have led to suicide.'

'He was blackmailing people,' said Fletcher. 'That's dark.'

'But also a reason to keep living. So when things went awry, Howard thought if he could keep us chasing our tails for another day or two, he'd be long gone on a plane to LA before anyone worked it out. Fox was easy to frame, with her poisonous plants. The display case may be locked, but everyone knows where she keeps the key.'

Fox shrugged. 'The cabinet was to prevent accidents. It never occurred to me someone would deliberately take a plant.'

'But that's exactly what Howard did. He snuck onto your boat, clipped some monk's hood, mixed it into his smoothie then drank it before Lucy was due to call, knowing she'd raise the alarm.'

Lucy looked shocked. 'He could have died!'

'No,' said Fox. 'It was a tiny amount. Even if we hadn't found him, it just would have made him ill for a while.'

'But we're getting ahead of ourselves,' I said. 'After disposing of Crash, Howard next tried to delete the incriminating blackmail material. He probably thought it would be on Crash's phone, but it wasn't – though my number was, which is how he sent me the fake text on Friday morning and later gave Latesha my number. Right?'

She shrugged. 'I didn't think it was odd. Lots of women give Howard their number.'

'More's the pity,' I grimaced. 'Anyway, there was nothing on the phone. So he came here and let himself in with Crash's keys. Ace didn't mind because he knew Howard. Then he tried to break into the safe.'

'He didn't manage it, did he?' said Johnny.

'No. Howard knows his technology but the safe was beyond him, so he left it and replaced the gold disc. When I arrived the next morning, I noticed it was askew. Next, he went upstairs to Crash's computer and resorted to brute force, wrenching open the case and . . . disconnecting wires or something. I'm not a computer person. Whatever he did, it damaged the files very badly. It was around this time that Lucy called and saw lights on inside. As I said, someone was at home. But it wasn't Crash.'

'I was inches away from a killer,' Lucy breathed. I

half-expected her to start taking notes for her next play.

'Howard waited till the next morning, sent me that fake text, then tossed the phone into the canal. With the phone gone and the computer damaged he thought that would be the end of it . . . because he didn't know Crash kept a copy of all the compromising material, as well as a separate "blackmail phone", at a secret location on Penfold Mews.'

'At a *what*?' said Fox and Johnny in unison. DCS Fletcher had the decency to look faintly embarrassed. I allowed myself a smile, pleased to know that I could still hold an audience's attention.

'Crash used the blackmail money to buy a house where he kept backups of all the files, including physical material we found in a filing cabinet. He went there on Thursday evening to update it, including the recording of his conversation with Howard. It was the last thing he did before visiting Howard's boat at nine o'clock.'

There was a commotion from the hallway and Constable Wright brought Howard into the room, wrapped and shivering in a silver-lined blanket.

'Medics say he's fit for transport,' said the constable. 'Bit chilly, that's all.'

'Sit him down, he's not going anywhere yet,' said DCS Fletcher. 'We're getting to the good bit and I want to see his face.'

Maybe the superintendent and I did have something in common after all.

'Hold on, pet,' said Johnny. 'Go back a minute. What

was that about Howard's watch? Did it track his location or something? I know they can do that now.'

'Oh, it's much simpler than that.' I opened Howard's private streaming page on the computer and began playing the session recording from Thursday evening, turning the screen around so everyone could see.

'We've already watched these,' said Fletcher. 'The recordings confirm Mr Zimmerman's alibi.'

'Do they?' I fast-forwarded to the moment when the main session ended and Howard told everyone to take a five-minute break.

'He timed this precisely. The Tuesday night recording was made at nine o' clock, and on Thursday he began playing it back at nine precisely. After forty-five minutes, as always, he tells everyone to take a break.'

On the screen Howard approached the camera to shut it off. The screen changed to a five-minute countdown clock. I fast-forwarded again until the clock ran to zero . . . but then it remained on screen.

'I haven't paused it,' I said. 'During this session the countdown sits at zero for almost two minutes. I didn't think anything of it when I first watched. But Howard's sessions are normally very punctual, so why did this Q&A session start late?'

Everyone pondered the question, but nobody could answer.

Birch came to their rescue. 'Because Lucy was standing at Crash's front door,' he explained. 'Howard had to wait until she'd gone, which delayed him.'

'Indeed,' I said. 'But here's what really seals it.'

The screen flickered to life and Howard reappeared, to chat with his class.

'I don't see anything out of place,' said Fletcher.

'Nor should you. He's wearing the same clothes, he's drinking a smoothie and he's out of breath. Not from a workout, of course, but because in the previous half-hour he murdered Crash, dumped his body in the water, broke into his boat, then ran back after being delayed by Lucy.'

I glanced at Howard to see how he was taking this. He shot daggers back at me.

'During sessions he's too far from the camera to read his watch, but as he sits here for the Q&A we can see it clearly on his wrist. Big, bright numbers.'

Everyone leant forward, peering at the image.

'It says nine-fifty-two,' said DCS Fletcher. 'Which is correct, if the break lasted seven minutes.'

'That's right. Look, you can even read the date. The eighteenth, which was Thursday.'

Everyone leant back, disappointed.

'So what are we looking for? You said this disproved his alibi.'

I smiled and rewound the video by eight minutes. 'As I said, during the workout you can't read his watch. But when he finishes, and walks to the camera to turn it off for the break . . .'

I paused the video at that moment, with Howard's watch clearly visible as he reached to turn off the camera.

It read nine-forty-five pm . . . on the sixteenth.

Two days earlier.

Fletcher grinned and clamped a hand on Howard's shoulder. 'Bang to rights, Mr Zee. I'd say you're up spit creek without a chimney.'

I wondered if she knew she was the *only* person who'd say that. 'Hold on, though, Superintendent. You still don't know why he killed Crash.'

'Yes, we do. Blackmail, like you said. Makes perfect sense.'

Lucy shook her head. 'But what was the blackmail for? You said this Vicki woman isn't his ex-wife, so why would Howard kill Crash because of her?'

'Well,' I said, 'first you have to understand that Howard Zimmerman didn't kill Crash.'

The room erupted, as I'd known it would. I was enjoying myself.

'You just spent ten minutes telling us he did!' cried Fox. 'What are you playing at?'

'Remember I said that nobody here is who they seem? That pathetic man over there, shivering in a blanket, killed Crash. But he's not Howard Zimmerman.'

CHAPTER THIRTY-THREE

I had everyone's attention, especially 'Howard' himself. Until now there'd still been a chance he could talk his way out of it; DCS Fletcher had pointed out the evidence was circumstantial, and as Johnny said, you can manipulate all sorts of things on computers these days.

But now he was cornered.

'Crash told me that "Howard Zee" wasn't his real name. I assumed he was talking about the *Zee* part, shortened to make a stage name. But he actually meant much more. You see, the only English teacher I could find called Howard Zimmerman died a few years ago.'

'Was his death suspicious?' asked Fox.

'Not in the least. He also looked nothing like the Howard we know, and there was no hint of scandal around him at all, let alone with anyone called Vicki.'

'You're saying he took the dead man's name?' Fletcher asked. 'But why?'

'To escape the real scandal, of course. When Howard

said the mysterious "Vicki" was his ex-wife, we had no reason not to believe him. In fact, I foolishly gave him the opportunity to spin that lie in the first place and took his word for it. But I kept thinking about the recorded conversation between Crash and Howard. It strongly implied Crash knew who Vicki was and why Howard was hiding from her. So I searched for that connection . . . and found a woman called Vicki Richards with whom Crash had been photographed leaving a club.'

Howard groaned. He knew the game was up.

I continued, 'Two years ago, Vicki Richards was one of several women who accused a TV director of sexual assault in the 1990s. His name was Archie Gough, and he worked on a Saturday morning children's show where Vicki and her friends were audience regulars. They weren't even teenagers. Soon after they made the accusations, though, the director vanished into thin air.'

Everyone in the room turned to look at Howard, who struggled against Constable Wright's grip.

'The professionalism of Howard's set-up should have been a red flag. What would an English teacher know about things like camera coverage and studio lighting? But, like most people, I had no idea what Archie Gough looked like. TV directing isn't as glamorous as making films so there aren't many pictures of him online. Crash found one, though.'

On the laptop, I opened the photo of the newspaper article that had been too badly damaged to read when I first saw it. Now it was crystal clear, explaining the

scandal around Archie Gough and featuring a photo of him with his big mop of dark hair and tinted glasses.

'This is why he didn't teach women under forty,' I explained. 'It ensured Vicki and her friends couldn't accidentally sign up and recognise him. His social media pictures are also cropped so you can't see his face.'

'But that picture looks nothing like him,' said Fox, peering at the screen.

'You're right. Howard is bald, has a luxuriant beard and doesn't wear glasses. But when I fell over playing with Ace in the Gardens, Howard came to see if I was OK. From that angle, looking at him upside down, it was almost like he was clean-shaven with a big bouffant of hair. I thought nothing of it, but later it made me wonder how easily he could change his appearance.' I turned to DCS Fletcher. 'Superintendent, when you found Howard unconscious in his bedroom, was there a contact lens holder on his nightstand?'

She nodded. 'There was indeed.'

'Enabling him to lose the glasses. And anyone looking closely can see he isn't naturally bald, but rather hides his hair by shaving his head. Constable, perhaps you could check his jacket for a passport?'

Fletcher nodded agreement and Constable Wright searched Howard's multi-pocketed jacket. Soon enough he found the waterlogged document and opened it carefully. 'Photo's a bit ruined.'

She took the passport and read it. 'The name's still

readable, though.' She turned it around to display the ID page. 'Wouldn't you agree, Mr Archibald Gough?'

Howard – or rather, Archie – growled. 'That silly bitch and her mates weren't angels, you know! Everyone just wanted to have fun! It was another time! People behaved differently!'

'They were underage girls, legally unable to consent,' I said. 'Their parents placed them in the care of people like you, trusting you to treat them like the children they were, not playthings for your wandering hands. And for all Crash's faults, he clearly felt the same way.'

I tapped the laptop. 'The first time I saw this spreadsheet it looked like you were paying him twice a week for some reason. But when I read the intact version, I saw that the second payments were nothing to do with you. They were payments *out*, from Crash to Vicki Richards. He gave her most of the money he took from you and refused to let you pay him off before escaping to America. So you killed Crash, hoping your secret would die with him – or that by the time it came out you'd be in Los Angeles with a team of expensive lawyers ready to defend you against any accusations.'

DCS Fletcher pulled Archie to his feet. 'Looks like your swan is fried, my son.' Oblivious to everyone's confused looks, she and Constable Wright frogmarched him outside. 'Archibald Gough, I'm arresting you on suspicion of murder . . .'

Her voice trailed away, then she suddenly poked her head back in the lounge to point at Lucy and Fox. 'Don't

think I've forgotten about you two. We'll be having words later.'

'Don't worry,' I said when she left again, 'Birch and I will put in a good word for you both. Won't we?' I looked at him with a determined expression.

He hesitated, then twitched his moustache and smiled. 'Of course, ma'am. No harm done.'

CHAPTER THIRTY-FOUR

'They did what?' asked Birch as we strolled lazily through Regent's Park a week later. Ronnie was happily wearing himself out, chasing squirrels in vain.

'I'll show you,' I said. 'Hold your phone as if you're taking a selfie.'

He did, slightly embarrassed. I doubted the former policeman had ever taken a selfie in his life. Then I showed him what people lined up outside the Sunrise Theatre's stage door had been asking me to do; look into the camera and adopt an angry expression while pretending to thump them on the chin.

When I'd called Bostin Jim to relate these bizarre requests, he explained that thanks to the video of me whacking the drone outside Crash's houseboat, for a while at least I would be known everywhere as 'the angry old drone lady'. Hardly flattering, but apparently people had also connected it to Violet's video from the Carnival where we plugged the play, and within hours

the first two weeks of *Mixed Mothers* had sold out. Jim had cannily used this leverage to demand I be paid my full original fee, and even got me bumped up the billing order to boot.

Swings and roundabouts.

Birch frowned. 'Can't say I understand it. But good that more people recognise you now. As it should be.'

I smiled at his flattery and almost pecked him on the cheek before thinking better of it.

'That reminds me, guess what else has gone viral?' he said, and played another video. It was the BuzzFeed reporter's video from his new drone, when it joined the chase at the Pool. In slow motion we watched Howard Zee, aka Archie Gough, back away from Ace and fall into the canal over and over again on a loop.

I'd already seen the clip on TV a few times, in places you'd expect, like *Graham Norton*, and places you certainly wouldn't, like *Newsnight*. But I let Birch have his moment of discovery and said, 'That'll haunt him in prison, I should think.'

I watched Ace herd the killer towards the water and smiled. I'd been concerned about handing the Border Collie off to a rescue, but at the last minute he was taken in by Johnny Roulette, of all people. The guitarist insisted he and Fox would work it out somehow. As for Fox, she and Lucy had got away with small fines over the cannabis after we defended them. The only person Lucy was 'supplying' besides herself was Fox, anyway. I don't know if my support helped, but the word of the Met's

own DCI Alan Birch, retired, certainly did.

Crash's daughter Ellie had finally arrived from Tokyo on Monday afternoon as the Carnival boats were leaving. The Pool suddenly felt very empty without them. Ellie made sure I was paid for looking after Ace, Fox grudgingly thanked me . . . then made it clear they wanted to be left alone.

I understood. It wasn't so long ago I grieved for my own father. In some ways I still did because it never really leaves you; it just becomes a smaller part of you.

Latesha Michaels had returned to America empty-handed. After I ruined their cash cow, I suspect Zabok+ won't be calling my agent any time soon.

Speaking of cash, while I now had some money, I knew it wouldn't last. I still had to replace the reporter's first drone, for one thing, and after seeing the price I was even more grateful I'd be getting my full fee for the play.

Then there was the building work. With everything else going on, I'd forgotten all about it until I woke up on Tuesday to find Darren sitting on the scaffold outside my house, chatting and laughing with the Dowager Lady Ragley. Laughing! She'd even made him a cup of tea. Apparently, he was the fourth cousin twice removed of some baronet or other, which was enough for the Dowager to decide he was a good sort. 'Much better than those foreign chaps,' she'd said and I fought the urge to roll my eyes.

Which left one matter to clear up.

'Birch,' I said, as he threw a stick for Ronnie. 'Can we speak frankly?'

'Always.'

'Do I really remind you of DCS Fletcher?'

He wisely took a minute to consider his answer, as we watched Ronnie bound into the lake to cool off.

'Have to admit, thought you'd get along. Peas in a pod, all that. Not afraid to admit I was wrong, though.'

'That's not what I asked,' I said, nudging him. 'What sort of relationship did you have with her, when you were in the Met?'

He turned to me, offended. 'How dare you! Strictly professional. Beatrice was still alive.'

Rats! I hadn't meant it like that, but now I'd offended Birch *and* inadvertently summoned the ghost of his late wife. Well played, Gwinny. At this rate we'd both be in a care home before I got so much as a kiss out of him. Damn it, we weren't getting any younger and I couldn't play second fiddle to a dead woman forever.

'Birch, I'm sorry, I didn't—'

'I'm only teasing,' he said, with a twinkle in his eye. 'I knew what you meant. For the record, you're very alike. But relationship-wise, very different . . . I hope.'

To my surprise, he took my hand. His was softer than I expected, but something felt wrong. I glanced down and saw he no longer wore his wedding ring.

'There you are!' called out a voice behind us.

We separated, embarrassed at being caught in the act like teenagers, and turned to see Tina Chapel bearing down on us with a wide grin. Her Salukis, Spera and Fede, trotted elegantly by her side. She wasn't unexpected; I'd

invited her to join us for a stroll, but we'd started without her because Tina is one of those people for whom time is an abstract concept.

From the corner of my eye I spied Ronnie leap out of the lake, shake himself off and run to greet the Salukis. Not wanting to get soaked, I quickly fussed them first then hugged Tina.

'Darling, it's so lovely to see you. You won't believe what happened last weekend in Little Venice.'

'Never mind that, you secret lovebirds,' she said with a wink. 'Now, we've got all afternoon. Tell me *everything . . .*'

ACKNOWLEDGEMENTS

The first thing I must say is that Little Venice is a real place, is quite lovely and you should visit if you're able. It's even good for you – research shows that regular use of the UK's canals and waterways for leisure saves the NHS over £1 billion per year.

However, many aspects of the Little Venice in this book have been thoroughly fictionalised for the sake of story (not least its murderous residents). And while the real Pool hosts a 'Canalway Cavalcade' festival every spring, to the best of my knowledge the celebrations have never included a dead body.

Sophomore entries in a series are always tricky, and this book was no exception. Striking the balance between recurring characters and new situations, between familiarity and novelty, was particularly difficult. As always, I'm indebted to my redoubtable beta readers for their feedback and notes.

Thanks also go to Jeremy Burge and his circle of

boating friends for help with matters on the canal; to Linda Stratmann for advice on poisons and paralysis; and to James Thomson for technical musings.

Thank you to everyone who bought, read, enjoyed, reviewed, and contacted me about *The Dog Sitter Detective*, particularly the dog lovers and rescue volunteers. The book even won the Barker Book Award for fiction, which I'm still a bit speechless about. When this series was announced I said I hoped readers would come to love Gwinny and her peculiarities as much as I do, and it seems you have. I appreciate every kind word.

I also appreciate some of the kindest people you could ever meet, namely my fellow crime authors. The crime writing community, and the Crime Writers' Association in particular, continues to be a source of great friendship and camaraderie.

The team working at and for Allison & Busby have been tremendously supportive. A hearty thank you to Fiona Paterson, Fliss Bage, Libby Haddock, Lesley Crooks, and Daniel Scott; to David Wardle for the amazing covers; Helen Richardson for her sterling PR work; and of course A&B supremo Susie Dunlop herself.

As always, my agent Sarah Such remains a voice of sanity and guidance in an ever more chaotic world.

Finally, I really couldn't do any of it without Marcia, who has the most important and difficult job of all: living with an author.

ANTONY JOHNSTON's career has spanned books, award-winning video games and graphic novels including collaborations with Anthony Horowitz and Alan Moore. He wrote the New York Times bestseller *Daredevil Season One* for Marvel Comics and is the creator of *Atomic Blonde* which grossed over $100 million at the box office. The first book featuring Gwinny Tuffel, *The Dog Sitter Detective*, was the winner of the Barker Fiction Award. Johnston can often be found writing at home in Lancashire with a snoozing hound for company.

dogsitterdetective.com
@AntonyJohnston

Rebecca Makkai is the author of the n̶ Hundred-Year House, and The Borrowe collection *Music for Wartime*. *The Great Believers* was a finalist for the Pulitzer Prize and the National Book Award, and received the ALA Carnegie Medal and the LA Times Book Prize, among other honors. Makkai is on the MFA faculties of Sierra Nevada College and Northwestern University, and she is Artistic Director of StoryStudio Chicago. She lives in Chicago and Vermont with her husband and two daughters.

Praise for *The Hundred-Year House*

**Winner of the Chicago Writers Association's
Book of the Year Award
Named a Best Book of 2014 by *BookPage*,
Chicago Reader, and POPSUGAR**

"A witty mystery set at a countryside estate . . . Makkai's humorous, expertly orchestrated storytelling will surprise you." —Oprah.com

"A juicy and moving story of art and love and the luck it takes for either to last." —*Los Angeles Times*

"Makkai guides her twisty, maximalist story with impressive command and a natural ear for satire." —*The New York Times Book Review*

"Ingenious . . . sharp and ambitious . . . [brimming] with humor and a fondness for hijinks . . . This is a book with something for pretty much everyone. . . . You will smile, guaranteed." —*The Cleveland Plain Dealer*

"[Makkai] nimbly remakes her novel at every turn. . . . It takes a special trick to remake the world without a reader noticing; it takes a tremendous talent to do it again and again." —NPR.org

"The hand that keeps giving the kaleidoscope another turn, controlling just how the pieces land, isn't fate, of course. It's the artist. Makkai is one." —*Chicago Tribune*

"A sly, funny, literary mystery, a meet-cute romantic comedy, and a metafictional meditation on fate rolled up into one."
—*The Austin Chronicle*

"Clever and acrobatic . . . Makkai is a juggler, handling the many plots, characters, and ideas with ease and humor and, at times, pathos."
—*San Francisco Chronicle*

"Makkai's screwball intrigue [is] fresh and fun." —*Good Housekeeping*

"Compelling . . . clever . . . The delight is in the details, so don't plan to consume this one between naps. . . . Revelations, increasingly delicious and devastating, come faster and more furiously as the text progresses."
—*The Denver Post*

"[An] utterly delightful work of fiction . . . infused with a respect for literature and literary culture . . . [and] starring a house with as much personality as Manderley or Hill House."
—*BookPage*

"Hilarious and heartbreaking . . . Witty and engrossing . . . Utterly absorbing . . . Deceptively light and fast-paced, the story will stay with the reader long after the satisfying conclusion." —*San Antonio Current*

"The pleasures of Makkai's novel are contagious. . . . [She] manages the rare feat of crafting a smart comedy with a satisfyingly fierce pace—this book is a true page-turner—while indulging in an unusual structure. . . . [Makkai is] a writer with an innately intelligent and assured comedic voice."
—*Toronto Star*

"Deliciously entertaining . . . Rare indeed is the novel that combines beautiful prose with ideas as robust as those on display in *The Hundred-Year House*—not to mention a story like a set of Penrose stairs, connected in the most playful, the most surprising of ways. . . . A wonderful novel, as beautifully written as it is painstakingly plotted, with the structure to please any literary critic, and a story absorbing enough to satisfy the most ravenous reader."
—*Winnipeg Free Press*

"An imaginative and lively epic."
—*Flavorwire*

"Makkai humorously turns the conventional family saga on its head, in a clever exploration of metamorphosis and secrecy."
—*HuffPost*, The Book We're Talking About

"A puzzle-box of a story that moves backward in time . . . Makkai invites the reader, more than any character, to play detective. Flipping back to earlier sections to spot . . . clues hidden in plain sight is one of the book's distinct pleasures. Makkai [is] a mainstay of contemporary literary fiction."
—*The Kansas City Star*

"A funny, engaging, time-traveling love story."   —*Tampa Bay Times*

"*The Hundred-Year House* is a puzzle, a plunge into a world of fascinating characters, and an examination of human relationships. It is not to be missed."
—*BookBrowse*

"This novel is stunning: ambitious, readable, and intriguing. Its gothic elements, complexity, and plot twists are reminiscent of Margaret Atwood's *The Blind Assassin*. Chilling and thoroughly enjoyable . . . A daring takeoff from her entertaining debut."
—*Library Journal* (starred review)

"Charmingly clever and mischievously funny . . . A dazzling plot spiked with secrets . . . [Makkai] stealthily investigates the complexities of ambition, sexism, violence, creativity, and love in this diverting yet richly dimensional novel."
—*Booklist* (starred review)

"A lively and clever story . . . Exceptionally well-constructed, with engaging characters busy reinventing themselves throughout, and delightful twists that surprise and satisfy."
—*Publishers Weekly* (starred review)

"Suspenseful [and] amusing . . . Makkai's novel will keep readers on edge until the last piece of the puzzle drops into place and the whole brilliant picture can be seen at once, sharp and clear."
—*Shelf Awareness* (starred review)

"This book is difficult to describe. So first, NB: it's good. *Really* good. . . .
To lapse into cliché, you'll laugh, you'll cry. . . . Characterization is first-
rate, the acerbic satire is clever . . . This is one impressively dimensional
book."
—Historical Novel Society

"Rebecca Makkai is the most refreshing kind of writer there is: both
genius and generous. Every masterfully crafted connection, every lov-
ingly nestled detail, is a gift to the attentive reader. Playful, poignant,
and richly rewarding, *The Hundred-Year House* is the most absorbing
book I've read in ages. Before you've finished, you'll want to read it
again."
—Eleanor Henderson, author of *Ten Thousand Saints*

"A mesmerizing story of self-reinvention that delights on every page,
told with keen wit and a perceptive eye. Like the unforgettable characters in this gripping novel, Laurelfield will draw you into its spell."
—Charlie Lovett, author of *The Bookman's Tale*

"*The Hundred-Year House* is a funny, sad, and delightful romp through
the beginning, middle, and end of an artists' colony as well as the family mansion that sheltered it and the family members who do and don't
survive it. Told backward from the viewpoints of an array of eccentric
and intertwined characters, the story's secrets are revealed with stunning acuity. An ambitious work, well-realized."
—B. A. Shapiro, author of *The Art Forger*

"Makkai fulfills the promise of her debut with this witty and darkly
acerbic novel set in the rich soils of an artists' colony. The inverted
timeline of the multigenerational narrative deepens the layered myster-
ies at its heart. As decades unfold in reverse, we find that nothing about
Laurelfield's various inhabitants is at it first appears, and neither talent
nor history sits on solid ground."
—Ru Freeman, author of *On Sal Mal Lane*

THE
HUNDRED-YEAR
HOUSE

REBECCA MAKKAI

PENGUIN BOOKS

PENGUIN BOOKS

An imprint of Penguin Random House LLC
penguinrandomhouse.com

First published in the United States of America by Viking,
an imprint of Penguin Random House LLC, 2014
Published in Penguin Books 2015

ISBN 9780143127444 (paperback)

THE LIBRARY OF CONGRESS HAS CATALOGED THE HARDCOVER EDITION AS FOLLOWS:
Makkai, Rebecca.
The hundred-year house / Rebecca Makkai.
p. cm.
ISBN 9780525426684 (hardcover)
ISBN 9780698163546 (ebook)
1. College teachers—Fiction. 2. Family secrets—Fiction. 3. Artist colonies—Fiction.
4. Eccentrics and eccentricities—Fiction. I. Title.
PS3613.A36H85 2014
813'.6—dc23   2013047855

Printed in the United States of America
5

Designed by Nancy Resnick

for
—but not about—
Ragdale and Yaddo
with boundless gratitude

Nothing of her was left, except her shining loveliness.

—Ovid's *Metamorphoses*, "The Transformation of Daphne"

CONTENTS

CONTENTS

PART I

―――――

1999

For a ghost story, the tale of Violet Saville Devohr was vague and underwhelming. She had lived, she was unhappy, and she died by her own hand somewhere in that vast house. If the house hadn't been a mansion, if the death hadn't been a suicide, if Violet Devohr's dark, refined beauty hadn't smoldered down from that massive oil portrait, it wouldn't have been a ghost story at all. Beauty and wealth, it seems, get you as far in the afterlife as they do here on earth. We can't all afford to be ghosts.

In April, as they repainted the kitchen of the coach house, Zee told Doug more than she ever had about her years in the big house: how she'd spent her entire, ignorant youth there without feeling haunted in the slightest—until one summer, home from boarding school, when her mother had looked up from her shopping list to say, "You're pale. You're not depressed, are you? There's no reason to succumb to that. You know your great-grandmother killed herself in this house. I understand she was quite self-absorbed." After that, Zee would listen all night long, like the heroine of one of the gothic novels she loved, to the house creaking on its foundation, to the knocking she'd once been assured was tree branches hitting the windows.

Doug said, "I can't imagine you superstitious."

"People change."

They were painting pale blue over the chipped yellow. They'd pulled the appliances from the wall, covered the floor in plastic.

There was a defunct light switch, and there was a place near the refrigerator where the wall had been patched with a big square board years earlier. Both were thick with previous layers of paint, so Doug just painted right on top.

He said, "You realize we're making the room smaller. Every layer just shrinks the room." His hair was splattered with blue.

It was one of the moments when Zee remembered to be happy: looking at him, considering what she had. A job and a house and a broad-shouldered man. A glass of white wine in her left hand.

It was a borrowed house, but that was fine. When Zee and Doug first moved back to town two years ago, they'd found a cramped and mildewed apartment above a gourmet deli. On three separate occasions, Zee had received a mild electric shock when she plugged in her hair dryer. And then her mother offered them the coach house last summer and Zee surprised herself by accepting.

She'd only agreed to return home because she was well beyond her irrational phase. She could measure her adulthood against the child she'd been when she lived here last. As Zee peeled the tape from the window above the sink and looked out at the lights of the big house, she could picture her mother and Bruce in there drinking rum in front of the news, and Sofia grabbing the recycling on her way out, and that horrible dog sprawled on his back. Fifteen years earlier, she'd have looked at those windows and imagined Violet Devohr jostling the curtains with a century of pent-up energy. When the oaks leaned toward the house and plastered their wet leaves to the windows, Zee used to imagine that it wasn't the rain or wind but Violet, in there still, sucking everything toward her, caught forever in her final, desperate circuit of the hallways.

They finished painting at two in the morning, and they sat in the middle of the floor and ate pizza. Doug said, "Does it feel more like it's ours now?" And Zee said, "Yes."

At a department meeting later that same week, Zee reluctantly agreed to take the helm of a popular fall seminar. English 372 (The Spirit in the House: Ghosts in the British and American Traditions) consisted of ghost stories both oral and literary. It wasn't Zee's kind of course—she preferred to examine power structures and class struggles and imperialism, not things that go bump in the night—but she wasn't in a position to say no. Doug would laugh when she told him.

On the bright side, it was the course she wished she could have taken herself, once upon a time. Because if there was a way to kill a ghost story, this was it. What the stake did to the heart of the vampire, literary analysis could surely accomplish for the legend of Violet Devohr.

Doug worked in secret whenever Zee left the house.

The folders on his desk were still optimistically full of xeroxed articles on the poet Edwin Parfitt. And he *was* still writing a book on Parfitt, in that its bones continued to exist, on forty printed pages and two separate diskettes. The wallpaper on his computer (Zee had set it up) was the famous photo of Parfitt kissing Edna St. Vincent Millay on the cheek.

But what Doug was actually sitting down to write, after a respectful silence for the death of both his career and the last shred of his manhood, was book number 118 in the *Friends for Life* series, *Melissa Calls the Shots*. He hid the document on his hard drive in a file called "Systems Operating Folder 30." This book, unlike the Parfitt monograph, even had an actual editor, a woman named Frieda who called once a week to check his progress.

Doug's stopover in the land of preteen literature was only the latest in a wretched chain of events—lack of money, paralysis on the monograph, failure to find employment, surreal indignity of moving into the coach house on Zee's mother's estate—but it would be the last. He would get this done and get paid, and then, because he'd be on a roll, he'd get other things done. He would publish the Parfitt book, he'd land a tenure-track post, and somehow along the way his hair would grow thicker.

He'd found Frieda through his friend Leland, a luckless poet who wrote wilderness adventures at the same press for "two grand a pop." Leland talked like that, and he drank whiskey because Faulkner had. "They give you the entire plot," he said, "and you just stick to the style. Really there *is* no style. It's refreshing." Leland claimed they took a week each, and Doug was enchanted with the idea of shooting out a fully formed book like some kind of owl pellet. He hadn't written fiction since grad school, when he'd published a few experimental stories (talking trees, towns overcome with love) that now mortified him, even if Zee still adored them. But these publication credentials, plus Leland's endorsement, landed him the gig. He knew nothing about wilderness adventure, but the press was suddenly short a writer for their middle-grade girls' series—and desperate enough to hire a man. And so. Here he was.

The money would be nice. The coach house was free, but not the food, the car payments, the chiropractor. And that last wasn't optional: If Dr. Morsi didn't fix Doug's back twice a week, he'd be unable to sit and work on anything at all. Frieda sent him four other books from the series, plus a green binder labeled "THE FFL BIBLE" with fact sheets on each character. "Melissa *hates* dark chocolate!" came several bullet points above "Melissa's grandfather, Boppy, died of cancer in #103."

"The first chapter," Frieda told him on the phone, "introduces the conflict, which is the Populars on the team, will Melissa ever be goalie, *et cetera*." He'd never met Frieda, but imagined she wore pastel blazers. "The second chapter is where you recap the founding of the club. Our return readers skip it, so you can plagiarize chunks from other volumes. The rest will be clear from the outline. Everything's wrapped up at the end, but there's that thread you leave hanging, 'What's wrong with Candy,' which is where 119 picks up; 119 is being written already, so—as we tell all our writers—it's important you don't make uninvited changes to the world of the series." Doug took comfort in the fact that this was clearly a memorized speech, part of the formula.

He dumped the books at the thrift store, hid the "Bible" pages among some old tax forms, then went to the library every day for a week to skim the series.

And meanwhile, the little house was strangling him, tightening its screws and hinges. There was an infestation of ladybugs that spring, a plague straight out of Exodus. Not even real ladybugs but imposter Japanese beetles with dull copper shells, ugly black underwings jutting out below. Twice a day, Doug would suck them off the window screens with the vacuum attachment, listening as each hit the inner bag with a satisfying *thwack*. The living ones smelled like singed hair—whether from landing too close to lightbulbs or from some vile secretion, no one was sure. Sometimes Doug would take a sip of water and it would taste burnt, and he would know a bug had been in that glass, swimming for its life and winning.

There was a morning in May—notable only for Zee storming around in full academic regalia, late for commencement—when Doug, still in bed, nearly blurted it all out. Wasn't it a tenet of a good marriage that you kept no secrets beyond the gastrointestinal? Hundreds of movies and one drunken stranger in a bar had told him as much. And so he almost spilled it, casual-like, as she tossed shoes from the closet. "Hey," he might have said, "I have this project on the side." But he knew the look Zee would give: concern just stopping her dark eyes from rolling to the ceiling. A long silence before she kissed his forehead. He didn't blame her. She'd married the guy with the fellowship and bright future and trail of heartbroken exes, not this schlub who needed sympathy and prodding. When she dumped her entire purse out on the bed and refilled it with just her keys and wallet, he took it as a convenient sign: *Shut the hell up, Doug.* He might have that tattooed on his arm one day.

Zee's mother, Gracie, would sometimes include the two of them in her parties, where she'd steer Doug around by the elbow: "My son-in-law Douglas Herriot, who's a fantastic *poet*, and you know, I think it's *wonderful*. They're in the coach house till he's all done writing. It's my own little NEA grant!" Doug would mutter that he wasn't a poet at all, that he was a "freelance PhD" writing *about* a poet, but no one seemed to hear.

The monograph was an attempt to turn his anemic doctoral dissertation on Edwin Parfitt into something publishable. Parfitt was coming back into style, to the extent that dead, marginal modernists can, and if Doug finished this thing soon he could get in on the first wave of what he planned, in job interviews, to call "the Parfitt renaissance." The dissertation had been straight analysis, and Doug wanted to incorporate some archival research, to be the first to assemble a timeline of the poet's turbulent life. In her less patient moments, Zee accused him of trying to write a biography—academically uncouth and unhelpful career-wise— but Doug didn't see what harm it would do to set some context. And the man's life story was intriguing: Eddie Parfitt (Doug couldn't help but use his nickname, mentally—after nine years of research he felt he knew the guy) was wealthy, ironic, gay, and unhappy, a prodigy who struggled to fulfill his own early promise. He committed suicide at thirty-seven after his lover died in the Second World War. Parfitt had left few personal records, though. Nor had he flitted about the Algonquin Round Table and cracked wise for posterity. Entire periods—the publication gap between 1929 and late 1930, for instance, after which his work became astonishingly flat—lacked any documentation whatsoever.

Not that it mattered now.

Each morning, as Doug switched off his soul and settled in to write ("*Twelve-year-old Melissa Hopper didn't take 'no' for an answer,*" the thing began), he imagined little Parfitt stuffed in the bottom desk drawer on those diskettes, biding his time between the staplers, choking with thirst. The ladybugs hurled their bodies against his desk lamp, and it sounded like knocking—like the ghost of Parfitt, frantically pounding against the wood.

In the brief window between commencement and the start of Zee's summer teaching, Gracie invited them to the big house for brunch. They ate on the back terrace overlooking the grounds—the paths, the fountain, the fish ponds. It was like the garden behind a museum, a place where art students might take picnic lunches. Bruce, Gracie's second husband, had conveniently excused himself to make his tee time when Gracie announced that she had invited Bruce's son and daughter-in-law to move into the coach house too.

"It's really a two-family house," she said, "and what was done, way back, was to keep the gardener's family there as well as the driver's, and they all shared the kitchen. Can you believe, so many servants? I couldn't manage."

Zee didn't put the butter dish down. "Mom, I've met Case *twice*. We're strangers." Bruce's children had always lived in Texas.

"Yes," Gracie said, "and it's a shame. Didn't you dance with him at our wedding, Zilla? You'd have been in college, the both of you. He's quite athletic."

"No."

"Well he's out of work. He lost five million dollars and they fired him. Miriam's a wonderful artist, but it doesn't support them, you know how *that* is, so they need the space as much as you."

Doug managed to nod, and hoped Zee wouldn't hold it against him.

"So they'll both hang around the house all day," Zee said.

"Well yes, but it shouldn't bother you, as you'll be at work. It only concerns Douglas. He could even write about them!" Gracie rubbed the coral lipstick off her mug and smoothed her hair—still blonde, still perfect. "And something will open up at the college for Douglas, I'm sure of it. Are you asking for him?"

"Really," Doug said, "I don't mind. I can get used to anything."

———

That afternoon, Doug watched his wife from the window above his desk. She stood on the lawn between the big house and the coach house. Anyone else might have paced. For Zee, stillness was the surest sign of stress. She stared at the coach house as if she might burn it down. As if it might burn *her* down.

She wouldn't let herself pitch a fit. At some point she and Gracie had come to the tacit agreement that no actual money or property would pass between them. It was the apotheosis of that old-money creed that money should never be discussed: In this family, it couldn't even be *used*. Doug had doubts whether Zee would even accept her eventual inheritance, or just give it directly to some charity Gracie wouldn't approve of. She was a Marxist literary scholar—this was how she actually introduced herself at wine and cheese receptions, leaving Doug to explain to the confused physics professor or music department secretary that this was more a theoretical distinction than a political one—and having money would not help her credibility. But she had accepted the house.

And now this.

The Texans were just *there* one Tuesday in June when Doug returned from the gym. He picked a box off the U-Haul lip and carried it up to the kitchen, which sat between the two second-floor apartments. Doug loved the feel of an upstairs kitchen, of looking out over the driveway as he flipped pancakes.

A woman with curly brown hair stood on the counter in cutoffs and a tank top, arranging plates in a high cupboard. He put the box down softly, worried that if he startled her, she'd fall. He waited, watching, which seemed somehow inappropriate, and he was about to clear his throat when she turned.

"Oh!" she said. "You're—Hey!" He offered a hand, but she shook it first, then realized what it was for and held on tight as she hopped to the floor. She was a bit younger than Doug and Zee, maybe twenty-eight. And tiny. She came to his armpit. "Miriam, obviously. I hope we're not in your way. I had to scoot some glasses over."

"Doug Herriot," he said, and wondered at his own formality. "I can clear out the lower cupboards. You'll never reach that."

"I'm not so tall, am I! But Case is. We'll be fine." She opened the box on the table, saw it contained clothes, and closed it again. "This is a hell of a place."

He looked out the window and laughed. "Yeah, it's not subtle."

"Oh, I meant *this* place!" She tapped the open cabinet door. "This is quarter sawn oak!"

Doug had no idea what she meant, but he nodded. He wasn't surprised that the kitchen should be well built; the same architect had designed both houses, and presumably the same carpenters and brick layers had constructed them. The stone wall that bordered the estate also formed the eastern wall of the coach house, or at least its ground floor. The second story rose above that, making the structure look from the road like a child's playhouse perched atop the wall. Really it was quite large. The ground floor had at first been open garage space, with two arched entrances for cars. Gracie and her first husband, Zee's father, had the arches filled in with glass panels, and stuck a sunporch on the back. Why they bothered was unclear, except that in the post-chauffeur sixties they'd wanted an attached garage on the big house and felt they ought to transform the old one into something useful and rentable.

The estate had belonged to Gracie's family all along—the Devohrs, though Gracie never used her maiden name. The Devohrs sat firmly in the second tier of the great families of the last century, not with the Rockefellers and Vanderbilts of the world but certainly shoulder-to-shoulder with the Astors, the Fricks, and were lesser known in these parts only by virtue of their Canadian roots. Toronto was hardly Tuxedo Park. Of those families, though, only the Devohrs were so continually subject to scandal and tragedy and rumor. An unkind tabloid paper of the 1920s had run a headline about the "Devohrcing Devohrs," and the name had stuck. So had the behavior that prompted it.

Before that infamy, back in 1900, Augustus Devohr (unfocused son of the self-made patriarch), wanting to oversee his grain investments more closely, had built this castle near Lake Michigan, thirty miles straight north of Chicago. By 1906, after his wife killed herself in the house—the suicide that had so bothered an adolescent Zee—he wanted nothing more to do with the Midwest or its crops. In either a fit of charity or a deft tax dodge, Augustus allowed the home to be used for many years as an artists' colony. Writers and painters and musicians would stay, expenses paid, for one to six months. And—a knife in Doug's heart—Edwin Parfitt himself had visited the colony, had worked and lived right behind one of those windows, though Doug would never know which one. It was the real reason Doug had even agreed to move into the coach house: as if the proximity would, through some magical osmosis, help his research.

Miriam climbed back on the counter, her small legs folding and then unfolding like a nimble insect's. She redid her ponytail. She wasn't exactly attractive, Doug decided (he'd been deliberating, against his will), but she had an interesting face with a jutting chin, eyes bright like a little dog's. And as soon as he thought it, he recognized it. It was the beginning of a thousand love stories. ("She wasn't beautiful, but she had an interesting face, the kind artists asked to paint.") And uninvited, the next thought bore down: He was supposed to fall in love. It wasn't true, and it wouldn't happen, but there it was, and it stuck. Anyone watching him in a movie would *expect* him to fall in love, would wait patiently through the whole bag of popcorn. He tried to push the thought away before she turned again, before she saw it on his face. He excused himself and left the room.

3

D oug was reading in bed when Zee got home. She closed the door. "Did you see them?"

"I met her—Miriam—and she's okay. She's small. But then I stayed in here working. I'm sure we don't have to whisper."

It was probably true—the two bedrooms were at opposite ends of the second floor. Each apartment had a large entry room, which would once have been the sitting area but which Doug and Zee used as a study, desks under both windows. Before the Texans came, they would use the other apartment for laundry folding or exercise or sex.

"You just hid in here? Did you meet Case?"

"I didn't want to make them feel they were invading. You know, like if I sat and watched them unpack. Right?"

She was disappointed. She'd wanted the whole story, the gruesome details. Something concrete at which to direct her anger.

She had managed to stay calm and pleasant all day. She had forced herself to smile when Sid Cole had called to her across the lawn—in front of students—that "Marxists don't drink cappuccino!" She'd even raised her coffee cup into the air. She had laughed out loud: Ha!

The irony was not lost on her that she, willfully mistaken for a Communist by her most obnoxious colleagues, should be allergic to communal living.

"Does she have a Texas accent?"

"No, actually. I don't think so. Not really, more like—I don't know."

What was wrong with him?

She said, "Did she take Case's last name?"

"I have no idea."

"That would have a horrible sound. Miriam Breen. It's too ugly."

"Yes, it's ugly."

Zee changed and found her glasses and lay on top of the covers, underlining an article in *The New York Review of Books*.

"It should give you some impetus to write," she said. "The more annoying these people are, the better."

"I'm writing every day."

She hoped it was true. The worst part of her wanted to stand over his shoulder as he wrote, to suggest commas. Once, early in grad school, she'd tidied up a paper of his when he was out for the night. He'd never noticed.

Doug flipped himself around on the bed and started rubbing her feet.

"Doug," she said. "Stop it."

"I can't hear you."

"I have stuff to do."

"I'm sorry, I'm way down here by your feet, and I can't hear you."

He peeked over the crest of her knees like a groundhog, then ducked down. He did it till she laughed. She put the journal down, and he worked his way up.

4

Case and Miriam and Zee were at the table when Doug came out the next morning, fortunately having remembered to put on pants. Case was tall, as Miriam had said, and deeply tan with big, straight teeth. Polo shirt and flip-flops. In a movie, Doug thought, he'd be the guy who beats up John Cusack. The men shook hands, and Doug found himself giving Miriam a ridiculous little salute. He began making eggs, just so he had something to do.

Zee was dressed for teaching her summer session class, silk blouse tucked into her skirt in such a tidy way that if he hadn't known better, Doug would have imagined her morning routine involved duct tape. "So," she said, "I hear you're searching for a job, Case."

Case looked up from his cereal, leaned back, and regarded Zee as if she'd ruined his beach vacation by asking where he planned to be five years from next Thursday. "I'm in no rush," he said. And then he laughed, releasing them all abruptly from whatever contempt he'd held them in. Doug decided, in that moment, that he despised Case Breen.

"He needs a few weeks to recoup," Miriam said. "We're aiming for September."

"Gonna get some exercise. Might shop for a new car."

Zee said, "What's wrong with your old one?"

Miriam put her hand on Case's shoulder and said, "I hope we

won't be in the way. I know you're making a sacrifice. I was going to set up on the sunporch to work, but only if it's okay with you."

Doug gestured to the constellation of ladybugs on the ceiling. "You won't be more trouble than our other houseguests." No one laughed.

"Or the ghost," Zee added, and smiled as if she'd just played some kind of trump card, as if Case and Miriam would now spring up and flee. "Violet mostly sticks to the big house, but you'll hear her knocking on the windows some nights. You'll get used to it."

Miriam said, "Oh, I *love* ghost stories. I do."

Zee picked up her keys. "I'm kidding, of course."

She left, and Doug ate his eggs standing up. Case asked if Doug wanted to join him for a run, and he managed to bow out, blaming his bad knees.

"Suit yourself," Case said, and (Doug could have sworn) glanced at Doug's paunch before leaving the room.

Doug started scrubbing dishes, and a minute later Case appeared down on the drive, changed and stretching his calves. Miriam came over to rinse and dry, and they talked above the sound of the water. He learned that Miriam's art was mixed-media mosaics.

"Most people would call it detritus collage," she said. "But I use classical mosaic techniques. Just using found pieces. I'm always cutting up Case's clothes." She pushed her curls from her face with a wet hand. "Tell me about your poetry."

"*No*," he said, which she didn't deserve. "Sorry. I'm not a poet. I'm writing *about* a poet. Gracie's mixed up. I didn't mean to shout at you."

She smiled, as if it were regular and amusing for people to make idiots of themselves in front of her. "What poet?"

"Oh. Edwin Parfitt? He was a modernist."

"Sure, right, that one poem! From high school! I mean, not—"

" 'Apollo on the Mississippi.' "

"Yes! 'Whose eyes' bright embers gleam.' That one!"

"He was a one-hit wonder. It's his worst poem, but it's all any-one knows. That and his suicide note. He drowned himself in a lake, and the note had instructions for his friends to burn his body on the beach just like the poet Shelley. And they *did* it." He let the soapy water out and sprayed down the basin. All because of that inane thought yesterday, he was aware of the distance between their bodies.

"I'd love to read it," she said. "Your book, not the suicide note." She dried her little red hands. "Well, both."

Zee took two aspirin, forgetting they'd just make her sicker to her stomach. The cramps might have been from dehydration, or from the hell of teaching summer school English to the seventeen-year-olds who were supposed to be experiencing college-level academics but were more interested in college-level drinking. But the headache was definitely from having her home invaded.

She gave up on grading ("Most people," began one essay on *Heart of Darkness*, "will encounter water at some point in their lives") and stacked the papers neatly on the corner of the desk, so it would look like a planned installation rather than an abandonment. On top she put the strange metal thing she'd found in the woods behind the big house that spring. It was probably some sort of machine part, but she loved the design of it, the waffled roundness, and she loved its thick and ancient rust. She thought of it as a metal daisy top: six hollow petals around a hollow center. She stuck a pencil in one of the holes, and now the stack looked complete.

She checked mail and got coffee in the English office. Chantal, the department secretary, was on the phone, so Zee lingered over a sabbatical notice on the board.

Zee was obsessive about the bulletin board, and about the campus papers and the department calendar. She figured her job had two parts: the work part and the career part. The work part right now was teaching, publishing, flying to petty conferences in depressing university towns. The career part was showing up at concerts and sitting behind the college president, keeping in touch with everyone from grad school. If she could, she'd have hosted dinner parties. It was easy enough to tell her colleagues she and Doug were renting a coach house in town, but it would be far too risky to bring them so close to the Devohr family history. She couldn't imagine the jokes Sid Cole would make if he knew she'd been to the manor born.

Thank God the "Devohr" was buried under her father's name, Grant. She'd been tempted to take Doug's name just to inter the Devohrs one layer further, but she refused to part with that last scrap of her father. She told colleagues, if they asked, that her mother had stayed home, and her father had been a journalist and a recovering alcoholic, all of which was true. Really, she felt she could say "recovered" alcoholic now, in defiance of all the careful AA jargon, because he'd never have the chance to fall off the wagon again, and never had in the twelve years she knew him, not even on the night Nixon was reelected and he was the only man in town hurling books at the TV. He had a lifelong habit of sucking coins—popping a nickel in his mouth and flipping it with his tongue while he wrote or thought—that she figured must have been some kind of crutch. A reminder not to drink, maybe.

Chantal hung up and crossed her eyes at Zee. "Are we working out?" she said.

"I need to punch someone. But working out will suffice."

Chantal had a thousand little braids, and not one was ever askew. She was the most competent person Zee knew—a filing system to rival the FBI's—and Zee liked her better than any actual department member. They did the ellipticals side by side, and Zee told Chantal about the Texans moving in. "I never get along with southern women," she said. "I'm always offending them.

What I see as debate, they see as assault. The worst part is, Doug will fall in love with her." She was whispering. There were students all around.

"Is she pretty?"

"The point is she's *there*."

Chantal was cheating, taking her hands off the grips. "But he's not like that, is he? Your husband?"

"He's so desperate not to work on the Parfitt thing, he'd fall in love with a zebra. He might not *do* anything about it, but he'll fall in love." A woman like Miriam, with the wild eyes and chewed-off fingernails, would fall for anyone who listened to her emote— especially Doug, whose half smile was a sort of magical charm. It had disarmed even Zee. But Doug wouldn't recognize the difference between love and a diversion, would think that just because he hadn't been distracted like this before, there was destiny involved. "You know what his nickname was, in school? Dough. Because he was Doug H., but also because he's just—he's malleable. He's suggestible."

Chantal pushed the button to up her speed. "Keep him on his toes. Not to tell you what to do. But a bored man is—I don't know, isn't there an expression for that?" She laughed. "A bored man is not a good thing."

Doug walked to the library, even though he was more inclined to watch morning TV and do half-hearted yoga downstairs. The Texans might not irritate him into working harder, but they would embarrass him out of doing anything else. He even stayed up in the adult section, something he hadn't done since he'd started the *Friends* book.

"I wondered if you had anything on Laurelfield," he said to the reference librarian. "The old artists' colony." He'd asked just a few months ago, but there was always the chance something new had appeared.

Laurelfield was still, technically, the name of the house. Those olden-day Devohrs had named their homes like pets. When Zee and Doug were first dating, Gracie had sent out Christmas cards with an artist's rendering of the estate on the front, the word *Laurelfield* in script beneath. "It looks like the logo of a ham company," Zee had said. "Thank you for buying Laurelfield smoked sausages." It was the first time Doug had fully stopped to think what it meant that his girlfriend's family had spawned five Canadian MPs, that they had namesake buildings and foundations all over Ontario.

The librarian led him to the glass-front cabinet and pulled out four books on local history. The only helpful one was the photo book of local estates he'd seen before, but he sat anyway in a computer chair staring again at the grainy photo dated 1929.

Designed in the English country style by Adler Ross in 1900 for the Devohrs of Toronto, Laurelfield was home to the Laurelfield Arts Colony from 1912 to 1954. Notable residents included the artists Charles Demuth, Grant Wood, and Emil Armin; composer Charles Ives; and poets Marianne Moore, Lola Ridge, and Edwin Parfitt. The home is now again a private residence.

These seven guests, while impressive, were the only seven he'd ever seen listed—and were, in other words, the only ones of note. Perhaps this was why there were no archives, no coffee table books of photographs and reminiscences.

The picture was taken from high up. It showed the north end of the big house, plus the space between the two buildings, filled by a massive, long-gone oak. Doug squinted at the windows, hoping to see lord knows what. Parfitt making out with Charles Demuth, maybe. There, in the bottom right corner, sat the coach house, two cars on the gravel drive in front, the ground floor still open to motor traffic. A man in knickers leaned against the eastern wall near the cars, his hand raised to his mouth. Smoking. By his feet, a blur of a dog. Doug knew the man wasn't Parfitt, though he couldn't say exactly why. The prosaic hat, perhaps, or some intangibly heterosexual angle to the hips, or the fact that here he stood by the cars when Parfitt would be upstairs on his bed, ankles crossed, gin in his left hand, black fountain pen in his right.

Doug had no idea when Parfitt was actually in residence at Laurelfield. He visited both Laurelfield and the MacDowell Colony in New Hampshire throughout the twenties and thirties, but the Parfitt archive at Princeton mentioned Laurelfield only once, in a letter from 1942: "I haven't been as sick since one summer at Laurelfield," he wrote to his niece, "and this time it's worse because I'm getting old, Annette, I am." When Doug had found that reference, he was already dating Zee, had already seen the

Laurelfield Christmas card. He double-checked with her, as casually as he could ("Didn't you say your house was an artists' colony?
At some point?") and when Zee confirmed, it wasn't that Doug
saw her as a ticket to Laurelfield but that he took the connection
for a sign. Here was this woman whose childhood bedroom might
have been the very room in which Parfitt had written! The stars
were aligned, and he should marry her. Zee, no Parfitt fan, was
less impressed by the coincidence. "Lots of people stayed there,"
she said. "He was probably in Grand Central Station at some
point, too. That doesn't make it hallowed ground."

Doug xeroxed the picture and started home. It was blazing
hot, the time of day when more reasonable nations took a siesta.
He felt productive, for a moment, the xerox folded in his pocket,
until it hit him that *this* was his way of "getting to work" on what
should have been hard-nosed textual analysis: copying a picture
of a house that he could see out his bedroom window anyway.

Halfway back, Case passed him running, on the opposite side
of the street. Shining in the sun. Looking like he belonged in this
town, in a way Doug never would.

Zee decided not to drink at the lunch.

The eight department members still in town were squeezed into the back room of Pasquali's with spouses. Zee did not invite Doug to these events, preferring to talk him up in his absence. She'd created, over the past year, a mythical Doug whose earth-shattering book would soon be completed, whose thesis adviser wanted him to return to teach in Madison.

The celebration of Sid Cole's twentieth year at the college (his thirty-fifth year teaching overall) had been put off for a few weeks by Sid's gall bladder surgery. But now here he was, with his caterpillar eyebrows and obsessive lip-licking, as sprightly and malevolent as ever. Old age turns the most horrible people into "characters," their misanthropy masquerading as crustiness. Sid was known to offer students a five-minute break in the middle of long afternoon classes, then mock anyone with the nerve to leave. The adoring faithful stayed and gleefully jotted "Coleisms" in their notebooks.

Cole was to blame, in Zee's mind, for Doug's joblessness. Two years ago, right after the college hired her, they offered Sid Cole's job to Doug. Cole had announced his retirement, and Doug was the perfect fit. Then, the day before Doug was to meet with the dean and talk salary, twelve of Cole's students showed up at the old man's house with a bag of letters. They quoted Milton and Frost and Thoreau. They convinced him to stay. Zee's contract was already signed, and Doug's only other leads were on the east coast. Now, even if Cole retired, Doug—two years and zero publications later—was significantly less qualified for the job than he'd been back then.

Two things were necessary: a vaguely Doug-shaped hole, and a Doug who could account, impressively, for the past two years. The latter she had some control over; he'd finish the book this summer, even if she had to write the damn thing for him. The former was harder, but there were two small colleges in this town alone and a dozen more in Chicago, any one of which might become an option. It seemed even the adjuncts had sunk in their teeth, though, and weren't budging.

And Cole announced, regularly, that now he was in for life. "They'll have to carry me out on my desk chair," he said, "exams clutched to my chest with rigor mortis."

Zee sat between Ida Hayes and Jerry Keaton, grateful at least for her free pasta. Golda Blum, the acting chair, made a toast to "Sid's illustrious decades of terrorizing students and baffling his colleagues." It was an unspoken rule that to toast Cole was to roast him, and that he in turn would grunt and curse like the village drunk. Hoffman and Grasso stood to read a poem they'd written in a fit of Chianti-induced cleverness: "Old King Cole was a Derrida soul, and a Derrida soul was he—and he called for his Yeats and he called for his Poe and he called for his lady-friends three!"

Cole stood to give a brief speech about how he planned, in his twenty-first year at the college, to scare each and every student out of his classes, until he was left with "exactly one attractive and intelligent specimen that will grade its own papers and massage my neck." When even Golda laughed, Zee pretended to as well. Cole must have felt his age protected him against rumors of impropriety, though Zee understood there were plenty of whispers about the man back in the eighties. She'd heard a senior boy claim he knew "for a fact" that the policy of leaving office doors cracked during student conferences could be traced to Cole's misbehavior some fifteen years earlier. He had been married once, briefly, but by the time he came to campus he'd long been a swinging bachelor—attractive, back then, too—so rumors were bound to follow him. The fact that the rumors *stuck*, though, spoke to his behavior, not his erstwhile good looks. Jerry Keaton, for instance, with his kind eyes and soft voice and pictures of his toddler son all over his office, would never attract such talk.

Zee got through lunch by pretending it was Cole's retirement party. And when that fantasy failed, she imagined relaying one of her own less amusing Cole anecdotes. She might tell about his sophomore advisee who came to Zee crying, after she'd shown Cole a course list including Stage Makeup for her double major in theater. "So you're learning to put on makeup?" he'd asked. The girl had shrugged and said, "Basically." He took her face in his hand, turned her head to the side, and said, "Well, it's about damn time." But even if Zee had worked up the nerve to tell this story, to say "Let's raise a glass to the most insensitive man in Illinois," the others would have chuckled, waiting with bated breath for the old man's reply.

Cole, she realized, was talking to her from down the table, pointing his empty fork at her chest. "Comrade Grant is uncharacteristically withdrawn today," he called. "I suspect she's planning her Marxist revolution!" Before the laughter died down, he continued. "This is why I'll never leave. She'll replace me with her minions and all the seniors will take 'Why Dickens Was a Stalinist.'"

She felt, as she often did around Cole, like a child outwitted by a clever uncle for the amusement of other adults. Mercifully, the conversation swelled again, and the waiter brought coffee. Zee wished he would sweep her up with the empty wine glasses and carry her back to the kitchen and plunge her into the sink, where she could remain till the lunch was over.

The other day, her mother had called her office number. "I was thinking," she said. "Why couldn't Douglas work in Admissions? Because that doesn't require you to publish, does it?"

"Admissions is bubbly twenty-four-year-olds with diverse backgrounds."

"Well he's diverse. He certainly didn't grow up here." Zee had said she had to go, and her mother said, "It's not going to fall in his lap, dear. To be perfectly frank, I don't know what good that biography will do. There are so many books nowadays! But we'll think of something."

Sitting there sober with her drunken department, Zee *did* think of something. Doug was a man who needed a job. Cole was a man who did not deserve the job he had. And here she was, passively wishing. And leaving Doug home alone all day with that woman. When Chantal had said to keep him on his toes, she'd probably meant something along the lines of meeting him at the door in lingerie. But Zee had more at her disposal than underwear. And she knew how to do more than grade papers and wait.

She turned her tiramisu slab on its side to cut it better. She had nearly forgotten who she was.

8

They were all due at the big house at six, for cocktails and dinner to welcome the Texans "officially." The Breens, Doug tried calling them in his head, but to him Bruce and Gracie were the Breens, so Texans it was. Maybe if he started calling Case "Tex," he'd like him better.

In the two weeks they'd shared the house, the couples had fallen into a routine of cooking separate dinners, perhaps overlapping in the kitchen for five or ten awkwardly sociable minutes. Doug and Zee found themselves eating takeout downstairs more and more.

Zee came into the bathroom when Doug was brushing his teeth. She said, "I have some motivation for you. I think something might be happening with Cole. This might be his last year."

Doug made a mouth-full-of-toothbrush noise. Zee wasn't often prone to wishful thinking, but Doug knew enough about Cole not to get his hopes up.

They all four walked up the drive together, Doug carrying a bottle of wine too cheap for Gracie and Bruce to drink. They passed Case's new car: a black 2000 BMW 3 Series convertible, liquid-shiny, parked beside their own weathered Subaru. Doug had gladly joined in Zee's eye rolling, wondering how Case thought he could blow through his savings, how weirdly sure he was of landing a new job the moment he started looking. How a convertible would get him through a Chicago winter. But privately, all Doug wanted to do was lick the hubcaps.

He marveled anew at the way the thick ivy turned the big house into an organic entity. The house turned brown every fall, it died every winter, and by late spring it was in full foliage.

The front door was locked, and so they stood waiting as Hidalgo, Gracie's standard poodle ("Is there something bigger than standard?" Doug had asked Zee several times now. "Because he's really not normal") flung himself at the window again and again, claws scraping the glass.

"Oh God," Miriam said, "I *hate* poodles."

"Just wait," Doug said.

Bruce answered the door himself, tossing Hidalgo peanuts to keep him at bay. "Welcome!" He gave each woman a long kiss on the wrist like a lecherous Austrian prince, pumped Doug's hand, and slapped his arm around Case. "My boy!" he shouted, as if he'd never talked to his son before in his life.

Bruce was red-faced, with big cheeks and a ring of white hair and a belly of hardened fat. Later, he would bully Doug into smoking a cigar with him out back. But he was a good man, and Doug hadn't really had a father, so the handshakes, the cigar, the talk about bumping into the Clintons on Martha's Vineyard—he found them weirdly thrilling.

Doug saw Hidalgo advancing and kneed him in the chest before the claws could make contact with his shoulders, before the beast could leave welts down his arms again. Hidalgo was not one of those poodles with the haircuts. He was shaggy, fur the color of a rotten peach, breath like hot compost. Bruce threw another peanut.

Gracie stood waiting in the library, in a long, gauzy green thing that Doug's mother would have called a Hostess Dress. Zee kissed her cheek. "So you're locking us out now?"

"Bruce," Gracie said, "did you lock the door? The ghost must've done it."

"The ghost only ever does three things," Doug whispered to Miriam. "Closes doors, knocks on things, and flushes toilets."

Miriam whispered back: "Maybe it died from getting locked out of the bathroom."

Bruce mixed everyone gin and tonics without asking, and poured himself his standard glass of Mount Gay rum. "Let me tell you something, though," he said, in a voice that wasn't at all asking permission to let it tell you something. "We're going to need new locks anyway. Y2K, December thirty-one, these fancy security systems are worthless. Crime will shoot up, credit cards won't work, and are you aware, even your *car*, your *car* has a computer. I'm buying a '57 Chevy. No computer, and I've always wanted one anyway. But I'll tell you, no one should be out celebrating that night. *Nuclear power plants*, think about that. Best we can do is hunker down with the canned goods and barricade the doors."

"How festive," Gracie said. Bruce had given the same speech at every opportunity for the past year, but this was the first time he'd mentioned the nuclear plants. "Let's change the subject, shall we? Something less apocalyptic. Case, how's your job search?"

Case, sprawling on the couch, stretched his legs out. "I got some fish in the water," he said.

Zee said, "Some lines?"

"One could say that, Zee. One could say that."

Bruce said, "I'm going to introduce him to Clarence Mahoney. Big guy in Chicago. Lots of projects, and none of this dot-com nonsense. Watch what happens to those dot-com folks, January one."

Case turned to Doug. "Tell us what your poems are about," he said. "Nature, or what?"

Doug tried to hide the ice cube under his tongue while he talked. "I'm actually writing a monograph. A book. On a poet named Edwin Parfitt. He stayed here a few times, at the arts colony."

"Just imagine," Gracie said, gesturing around the room. "This place filled with painters and musicians!"

"I've been meaning to ask," Doug went on, willing himself not to look at Zee. "What about back in Toronto? There wouldn't be anything from the colony up there, would there? Archives or photos? That got taken back?" He'd asked it before, but her answers were always so evasive that he held out hope she might blurt something different if she was in a good mood, if the weather was right, if she'd had enough to drink. (Once, after champagne, she'd volunteered the story of Zee's birth in fairly graphic detail.) Plus she never seemed to remember that she'd already turned him down.

"Oh, dear God, no. The colony was such a burden to my father, he'd have shredded all that. The woman who ran the place, you know, turned out to be a Communist. And the drinking! It was always in the papers, someone driving into a fence. He was glad to be rid of the whole mess."

Zee would bawl him out when they got home. Not just for bothering her mother, but for grasping at straws. Zee so often had to defend, to people like Sid Cole, her own interest in historicity and context, that she ought to have been sympathetic to Doug's search for something archival. But she saw no similarity.

"So that's when you moved here?" Miriam asked. "After it closed?"

"More or less."

There had been profound resentment in the artistic community back in the fifties, when her father reclaimed the house and moved Gracie in here with her new husband, George, Zee's father. When Doug was engaged to Zee, he had secretly ordered a history of the Devohr family through interlibrary loan. That was the only mention of Gracie at all—the strong implication that her father closed Laurelfield just to get the drinking, womanizing George Grant out of Canada.

"So your job is to write the story of this guy's life?" Case seemed to find this hilarious.

"It's really an analysis of the poems. How his life affected his work."

"Like a term paper," Gracie offered.

"Yes," Doug said, after he drained his glass. "Like a really long high school English paper."

Zee, to his relief, smiled sympathetically from the other couch. She was stunning in her blue sundress, and her collarbones were a work of art.

"Refills," Bruce announced. "Would anyone care to climb Mount Gay with me?"

Doug had been prepared for the line, was always prepared for it, but it was still a struggle not to lose it. And it was a struggle not to look at the flaming, shaking, red spot next to him that was Miriam's face.

Doug stayed quiet through dinner. Sofia, the housekeeper, shuttled back and forth with plates of swordfish and asparagus, lemon sorbet, pineapple cake.

Case was telling them all a story about sailing, something about his buddy getting lost in the Gulf, when he leaned the whole chair back and hit the sideboard behind him, sending a green china vase to the floor and into a million pieces. "I'll—oh, God, I'll—hey, I'll pay for that," Case said.

"With what?" Gracie muttered.

Miriam convinced Sofia to surrender the dustpan so she could sweep the shards herself.

"He gets his coordination from me!" Bruce shouted. "That's why they kicked him off the football team!"

Case looked like he didn't know what to do with his hands, or how to arrange his mouth.

Doug searched for a way to change the subject, but Zee beat him to it. "You do realize that's the ghost behind you," she said to Miriam. "The painting, I mean."

Bruce gave the ancestor a look most men reserved for center-folds. "She's a beauty, isn't she? A *natural* beauty. Nothing fake back then."

"Except the paint," Zee said.

Doug didn't know much about art, but he could recognize that it was a great picture. If he ran into this woman on the street in modern dress, he'd recognize her instantly. Gorgeous, it was true, by any standards. Black hair and dark eyes, like Zee, balanced by the shoulders of a black gown. But somehow profoundly evasive. Some paintings seemed to follow you with their eyes, but this one had the opposite effect: No matter where you stood, Violet woudn't meet your gaze. He couldn't figure out why—he just knew he didn't want to be alone in this room at night.

"Do you mind my asking how she did it?" Miriam said. "How she died?" She was still down on the floor sweeping, a disembod-ied voice.

"I always imagined hanging," Gracie said. "But my family never spoke of it."

"Maybe that's why I'm getting a vibe on the staircases! Maybe she did it from a railing."

Doug hadn't contemplated this before in detail. He'd always imagined her drinking poison quietly in bed. "She might have jumped from a window."

"She'd make a better ghost if she wore white," Case offered.

Miriam stood up with her dustpan and looked at the painting. "She's got me fully convinced."

9

They were all back in the solarium with coffee, windows open, hot night air rolling through. Hidalgo slept on his back. Zee wanted to be home and asleep, but she forced herself to smile at Miriam. "I've peeked at your new project," she said. "I hope you'll hang some of your pieces around the coach house."

"Anything that doesn't sell."

Zee wondered if Miriam had ever sold a piece in her life. The new one was an atrocious swirl of orange with blue and brown things sticking out.

"Tell me, what inspired that orange piece?"

"Oh, it's a fractal! It's basically math, so don't ask me to explain! You can just *see* they're amazing, the colors and symmetry." Zee wanted to shake her. It was her greatest fear for her female students, that they'd end up giggling and apologizing at everything.

Case grinned. "You know what I call those? The barf pictures. It's the barf series." He'd been drunk for a while.

"I'm starting a new bunch, though. Unloved dresses. I'm butchering them and doing tessellation around the forms. If you have any old prom dresses or anything . . . And I have to say, I've never worked better in my life than I have the past few days. This place must have a magic spring under it."

Gracie patted her knees and sat forward. "Miriam, we've got

the perfect little consulting job for you. There's a painting I want to rotate out of storage, and Bruce hates it. The signature is unreadable, so we have just no idea. It's raw, but I think it's sweet."

Bruce loped behind the far couch and returned with a gilt frame, the farmhouse and pasture inside all awkward angles and illogical sunlight. Like the product of an art therapy class at a nursing home. Bruce said, "We should be paying for her opinion. She's an expert, you know."

"We'll pay her with old dresses!" Gracie said. "She can take Zilla's cotillion dress. It's still up in the closet. Remember the yellow one, with the shoulder pads? Oh, it was ghastly! I told you at the time."

Something came to a boil inside Zee's head, some irrational sibling rivalry she'd never had to develop skills for dealing with. She did not need a yellow silk dress from an arcane ritual she'd been forced through at age fifteen, even if Greg Stiefler had kissed her in that same dress on the lawn of the Chippeway Club. "You can't give away my dress," she said.

Bruce said, "I thought you were for the redistribution of goods to the proletariat!"

"Where did you get this?" Miriam asked. She rested the frame on her lap, squinting down at the corner, running a finger over the paint. She pulled her curls back.

Gracie said, "I believe it's left from the colony. *There* you go, Doug! Something from the colony!"

"It *could* be . . ." Miriam said. It obviously pained her to be critical. "This person might have had some natural skill, but no training. The perspective is off."

Case squinted over her shoulder. "Isn't that what the modernists did?"

"Well, not like *this*. I'm just saying it's not likely from the colony."

Gracie flushed and took the painting off Miriam's lap. "Oh,

don't worry, dear. We value your opinion. It's funny, though. George, Zee's father, seemed awfully fond of it. And he was an art critic! He must have seen something there. I wouldn't know one way or the other. Sofia!" Sofia was clearing the sugar and cream. "Can you run to the northwest bedroom, the flowered one, and see if Zilla's old yellow formal dress is still in the closet?"

"Oh, please don't—" Miriam started, but she swallowed her words. Sofia was already gone.

10

(The white skin
Of his inner arm

The back of his neck, where
His hairline rubs his collar

His hipbones

I could drag him to me
By the beltloops)

The house had settled into a peaceful rhythm, everyone happily ignoring everyone else. (Sofia, fortunately for all, hadn't found the yellow dress that night. She'd come down with dust in her hair and sweat on her upper lip. "I even look in the old things from forty years ago, all the long gowns!" On a certain level, Doug was disappointed. He'd pay for a glimpse of this ugly dress.)

And then, on Saturday, Case had been out for a long run when Doug and Zee heard him scream so loudly from below that they'd both leapt from the table. They found him crumpled in the doorway. He'd simply missed the step into the house, landed terribly, and his Achilles tendon had snapped and "rolled up like a window blind," according to the medic.

Doug was in the kitchen one morning a few days later when Miriam came up, filled a glass with ice and whiskey, and headed downstairs again. Doug followed a minute later (victim to a potent mix of curiosity and procrastination) and found Case with his leg propped on the ottoman in its blue medical boot, the drink half-drained. Miriam sat cross-legged on the floor, and they were watching a black and white movie. Doug knew Miriam had been renting them all summer—*Sunset Boulevard* and *Top Hat* and *The Big Sleep*—but this was the first time he'd seen Case join her.

"Mind if I take a break down here?" Doug said. Case shrugged and Miriam said, "Please do." He sat on the arm of the couch, across from the Morris chair Case had claimed, the one Doug had come to think of as his own. Doug guessed the chair had been in the coach house all along. A brass bar for adjusting its hinged back; worn, cracked leather. He could picture the beleaguered chauffeur who once sat there to read the paper and dream of sailing to Siam.

Doug said, "What are we watching?"

It was *Bluebeard*, Miriam explained, the 1930 MGM version. "It was a cursed movie," she said, a few minutes later. Case didn't seem to mind when she turned the volume down. He was watching his glass, anyway, not the screen. Doug didn't mind either, as her narrative was more interesting than the film. "Absolutely everyone in it was dead within seven years. That's Renée Adorée, the French one, and she died of something normal. But the other one, playing her sister, that's Marie Prevost. She died alone in her apartment, and her dachshund started to eat her."

"Jesus."

"And John Gilbert, Bluebeard, he was married to Greta Garbo, but he drank himself to death. And then the German maid, the one giving the dirty looks?" Miriam usually moved her hands when she talked, but right now she kept them wrapped around the remote, as if the actors onscreen were doing the gesturing for her. "That's Marceline Horn. She died the day after *Bluebeard* wrapped, and they realized it was from poisoned makeup in her dressing room. Someone put arsenic in her lipstick. The sicker she got, the worse she looked, so she put on more and more makeup to cover it up."

"Seriously?"

"There's a scene—I'll show you—in one scene, you can see she's sick. She was supposed to eat the food, but she couldn't."

Case cleared his throat and said, "You done, babe?"

Miriam stood. She took a moment to tighten her body, to compose a smile. She handed Case the remote and went to the sunporch. Case switched to CNN, where the news was about people building survival shelters in Colorado, taking their millennial fears a few steps further than Bruce.

"Look," Doug said, "I had knee surgery a while back. I know it's—you feel kind of trapped. I know."

Case didn't answer.

12

I f she hadn't already decided to take action, two things would
have made up Zee's mind. The first was Sid Cole knocking
on her office door. He'd climbed all those stairs just to ask if
she'd noticed that Jerry Keaton was calling his seminar "The Gay
Canon."

"You were at that meeting," she said. "Weren't you?"

"I'm going to teach a class called 'Milton the Marginalized.'
How about 'Chaucer, the Forgotten Poet'?"

Zee knew better than to pick a fight, even on someone else's
behalf. She said, "If it makes you feel better, I think he's got some
Shakespeare sonnets on the syllabus."

"Haaa!" Cole made a great show of collapsing against her wall.
"Shakespeare, that famous queer. The Pansy of Stratford-on-Avon."

The second thing was that Doug had begun working harder
on the monograph. The very day after she told him something
might be happening with Cole, she came home to find him still
at the computer at five thirty, still in the boxers and undershirt
he'd slept in. He'd forgotten to eat lunch. It almost broke her
heart, to see him working this hard on something no one really
cared about, something no one but Zee was waiting for. (The
book wasn't for the masses, but for the fifteen people in the world
who already knew everything about Parfitt, and the hiring com-
mittees that would never read it but would care that he'd written
it.) She couldn't bear if his effort were all for nothing.

It was funny how much she'd hated Doug when she met him in grad school. He had that lingering, sideways half smile that so often presaged trouble: Here was a man who'd make you feel like the center of the universe, until, just after you'd become hopelessly attached, you realized he looked this way at all women. Besides which he had questionable taste in both shirts and poetry (Edwin Parfitt was a poet her father had once rightly called "miniscule"), and he'd somehow conned all the professors into believing he was the greatest student ever to walk through the program. She invited him to her February spaghetti party along with everyone else, but she'd been rude enough to him over the past six months that she was shocked when he showed up. He held out a bottle of sake, which he told her he'd brought precisely so she couldn't serve it with spaghetti. "You have to save it for yourself."

Much later, as the lingerers helped clean up, his wayward elbow knocked a picture frame off her end table, and although the glass was fine, the frame, made of porcelain, had cracked into quarters. The picture was the one of herself, age five, reading *Green Eggs and Ham* to her father. She didn't want him to fix it. "I *know* you have superglue," he said. "Don't lie to me." And long after everyone else had gone, he sat on the couch holding pieces together until the glue was set and the thing was whole, if spiderwebbed. "She's not quite seaworthy," he said. He put it in the middle of the coffee table, a sort of offering.

It was certainly not his macho insistence on solving her problems that won her over—she did not see herself as a fragile thing that needed fixing—but the fact that he seemed so determined to make her not hate him. It became hard not to root for him. It was another six months before they became romantically involved, but the dots weren't hard to connect. Was there much distance between rooting for someone and loving him? Was there any difference at all, even now?

13

Five weeks in (and a week overdue) Doug was still stuck on the soccer team tryout, so he was going back to chapter two, which he'd saved because it was easiest. This was the plagiarism bit, the part that necessitated the presence of the actual *Friends for Life* books. He'd borrowed several from the library, and he placed pens across the pages of each to hold them open.

The first sentence of chapter two was always something like "It seemed the club had been together forever, thought Candy [or Molly, or Melissa] gazing at the faces of her five friends." Doug started with, "They had so many memories together, these six friends, and as Melissa looked into their faces, she was transported back to that day when they first formed their club."

He moved on to his descriptions of each girl. By the time he got to Cece ("She was the crazy one of the group," the others uniformly read. "She even showed up at school once wearing her brother's army jacket as a skirt!") he was punchy and decided he'd venture into new territory. "Crazy old Cece," he wrote, "had started a business of writing poems on her friends' hands. She charged ten cents a line and had already made enough for a new pair of earrings!"

And so of course it would happen to be this particular day that Miriam knocked softly behind him. He managed to close the computer window, but not the books. He swiveled, hitting his knee on an open drawer.

"I'm on a quest," she said. She held out a small, orangish-red piece of glass. "I'm searching for absolutely anything in this color."

"Let's look." He led her quickly into the bedroom. Of course there was nothing orange, and now he was just staring at the unmade bed. Doug knelt to examine the stack of books under his nightstand. He rifled through his own laundry basket, hoping not to be faced with the dilemma of dirty boxers in just the right shade. He moved to Zee's dresser—as if she'd ever let Miriam use her jewelry—but Miriam was gone. He found her back in the study, in his desk chair.

"I used to love these!" she said. She was holding *Candy Takes the Cake*. "God, these have been around forever!"

Doug sank to the floor, where all he could do was laugh. "Don't you want to know why I have them?"

"I figured it wasn't my business. I was looking for orange covers, but I see they're library books. Is this . . . research for the monograph?"

"Oh, Christ. Yeah. So. The monograph is apparently titled *Melissa Calls the Shots*," he said. "Number 118. I've never done this before. It's just for the money."

"I'd *hope* so."

"You're the only one who knows. Zee would kill me for not working on Parfitt. There *is* an actual book I'm neglecting. A serious book."

"You don't call this serious? Listen: 'Lauren might have forgotten a lot of math that summer, but one thing she learned was this: She would never take the Terrible Triplets camping again.' That's poetry!"

He stood and swiped at the book, but she held it out of reach. "Please don't say anything."

"We'll make a deal. Get me something orange, and promise to let me read your Parfitt thing *and* this thing too. It's hard to sit on such juicy gossip."

Doug found her an orange bank-logo pencil and an orange ad page from *The New Yorker*, and he suggested she might scan the storage room downstairs for seventies-vintage upholstery.

He couldn't concentrate after that. He spent the rest of the morning vacuuming ladybug carcasses from behind the furniture.

Zee knew Sid Cole would be out to dinner with the provost. And she guessed correctly that he'd fill the time between his late class and the seven o'clock reservation with the office hours he always complained were unnecessary for summer students. He sat snacking and grading and growling at any hapless teenager who dared disturb his peace. Zee stuck her head in to ask if he had any papers she could recycle for him. The man had famously refused the college-issued bin and threw everything from root beer bottles to old issues of *PMLA* into the black can under his desk. He smiled up at her, his mouth full of pretzel.

"You are a hardboiled egg, Zsa-Zsa. A hardboiled egg." Last spring he'd started amusing himself by supplying ridiculous endings for her initial, as if he'd never seen her full name on articles and campus directories.

She made three more trips down from her office and past his second floor one, returning from the student snack bar with a newspaper, then a coffee, then a brownie. By six forty-five his was the last light on, and by six fifty he had gone, leaving his door closed but unlocked. It was lucky, but it also meant he'd be back: For years he'd done all his writing in his office at night. She had an hour though, at least.

His computer was on, as she'd hoped. The air-conditioning blasted. The rumor, according to Chantal, was that he kept the room cold so he could see the girls' nipples through their shirts.

"Has anyone reported it?" Zee had asked.

"Oh, it's just what the kids say. How would they prove something like that?"

Zee jiggled the mouse to wake the computer, and went online, relieved that his Internet was even hooked up. Cole was largely computer illiterate, using his new, department-purchased iMac for nothing more than typing.

She spent the next hour downloading the most explicit free pornography she could find. She was careful to avoid anything potentially illegal (as much as she loathed Cole, she didn't want him arrested), but focused on college-aged girls, on sites that claimed "She Just Turned 18 and She's Wet for You!" The downloading was painfully slow, but she managed to save thirty pictures in a folder labeled "Photoedit"—easy enough to find if someone was searching, but nothing Cole would notice himself.

It was funny: As she slunk out the door, she felt some feminist guilt over the pornography itself, the girls who probably weren't eighteen at all but sixteen with drug problems, but she felt no moral guilt about the act of sabotage, about advancing her husband's career by less than legitimate means. She felt less like Machiavelli than Robin Hood, taking from the rich and giving to the poor. And helping the department, too, and the students. Cole was a parasite, a toxin, a cancer cell. Zee wasn't upsetting the universe, but balancing it.

She did the same thing on Thursday, when Cole simply left his office unlocked for the night, and again the following Wednesday. It would look better if they were downloaded on more than one occasion—less like sabotage, more like porn addiction.

Meanwhile, she told the following story to her classes, to Chantal, to three different colleagues, and to all the college students she could find who'd stayed in town as lab assistants or nannies: "You won't believe this, but I've heard one of our summer kids has Cole using the Internet! He needed to buy pants, but he hates running into students in the stores, so apparently this lovely young woman showed him how to shop online at L.L.Bean. Really she did it *for* him, but he was sitting right there. He was worried about getting lost on the Internet, so she showed him the 'Home' button. He goes, 'So I just click my heels together three times?' He said he was going to look up White Sox scores. I think he might be hooked!"

Her colleagues believed it, even Chantal believed it, because despite Zee's abiding hatred for the man, she'd been careful never to say a quotable word against him, careful to throw him an acerbic line when she passed his office.

If anyone teased Cole about online shopping he'd respond that he never used the Internet—but they'd take it as another of his jokes, more crustiness on top of the crust that was Cole.

On Sheridan Road, the traffic was stopped. No way to turn her Subaru around. She waited and cursed her luck and tried to see what kind of flashing lights those were, so far ahead.

When the cars finally oozed forward, she rubbernecked with everyone else. A fire truck, and, in front of it, a little black BMW, its hood charred and smoldering. No collision, no dents. Just one of those burst-into-flame scenarios.

She wouldn't have recognized the man who sat folded on the curb, head in his hands, if it weren't for the blue medical boot on his foot, the crutches stacked neatly at his side.

Doug turned in *Melissa Calls the Shots* just twelve days overdue, and after he'd finished some quick revisions for Frieda he received an actual two thousand dollar check in the mail, followed by the contract to complete two more books before the end of summer. One was another Melissa book, this time about her work backstage at the school play, and one was a Cece book. "I loved the detail about her poetry business!" Frieda said. "I think you'll have a great ear for her."

The whole week had been hot, but Doug made himself exercise anyway, circling the grounds and stretching. Behind the big house, he stopped to do the back releases Dr. Morsi taught him, then stepped on the fountain lip to stretch his hamstrings.

Miriam had been digging at the back of the fountain, and he nearly stepped in the hole. Apparently she'd been out here breaking old plates when she noticed a different shard, a red and white one, sticking out of the dirt. She'd pulled it out and dug around and found more—not just that one pattern but dozens of other colors of porcelain and glass and terra cotta. She'd excavated about two cubic feet back there. Her own archeological dig. "It's like the house is giving me pieces," she said. "Like they're growing from the ground." ("Or like someone had a really bad temper tantrum once," Zee said. "And broke all the china in the house.")

He'd remembered to bring bread crumbs, and he dropped them in the three koi ponds. How long did koi live? Eighty years?

These ones were enormous and mottled and drowsy, and he liked to imagine Edwin Parfitt feeding them his leftover breakfast.

At the south end of the property, he toed helplessly at the foundations of the studios Gracie tore down in the seventies, when they were past repair—the long one that must have housed several artists, and the small one behind that. Both lay far enough back that the remains weren't eyesores, and Gracie seemed content to wait for erosion and vegetation to swallow them. Even farther in the woods stood a granite statue of a squatting bear, about three feet high, moss covering its right flank. Doug sometimes rubbed its head for good luck. What else were statues for? The one surviving studio, on the other end of the property behind the vegetable gardens, had long ago been converted to a groundskeeper's shed, but Zee remembered her father referring to it as the composer's cottage—which was the only reason Doug hadn't cut through the padlock and scoured the walls for Parfitt-era graffiti.

As he rounded the big house, he saw Sofia heaving paper grocery bags from the back of her van to the garage floor. The driveway was eerily empty: Gracie and Bruce off on separate golf dates, the Subaru with Zee in the city, Case's BMW zapped by the Greek gods. Doug offered to help, but Sofia shook her head. Then she said, "This is ridiculous that Mr. Breen wants."

There must have been twenty bags, from several different stores—Jewel, Dominick's, Sunset, Don's. He righted a Jewel bag that had fallen and saw it was full of blue cylinders of Morton's table salt. So was the next bag over, and the next.

"He is for the end of the world," Sofia said. "On the New Years."

"He's . . . stockpiling salt for the end of the world?"

"Is for take the water out of the food."

"Wow."

"Yes, is wow."

Doug held up his hands as if to say, Hey, he's your employer, not mine. Although Sofia probably saw them all as family, saw Doug as part of this entitled clan as much as anybody. And really, he was. Who was he kidding? Yet as he headed back to the coach house, he felt the urge to call over his shoulder that he'd gone to a crappy public school, that he never had a decent bike, that he was raised on off-brand TV dinners.

Up in the kitchen, he opened a beer and watched Sofia out the window. He could hear her grunting from all the way up here. No, that wasn't right. She was too far, and it was coming from downstairs.

He went back down and found Miriam sobbing on the sun-porch, her face folded into her arms on her card table. He tried hard to walk away.

"Hey," he said, "hey."

"I'm sorry, this is so embarrassing." Miriam sat up, still sobbing, and wiped her face with the bottom of her T-shirt. He was surprised she didn't leave makeup on it—he'd been told women from Texas wore makeup at all times. "This is so stupid."

"I can leave," he said.

"It's—did you hear what happened?"

"Case's car? Yeah, we all heard."

"Oh. No, not that. John F. Kennedy Jr. He was flying his own plane last night, with his wife, and it crashed in the ocean."

"They died?"

"This is the silliest thing to be crying about. I guess I was just a little bit in love with him. Like everybody else, right? I mean, I just always thought someday I'd at least get to *meet* him, and we'd have a really great conversation."

Doug was thinking, on one level, about the Kennedys, about little John-John saluting his father's coffin. On another, much louder level, he was realizing: Miriam is crazy. Miriam is absolutely bat-shit crazy.

He should have seen it before, in the bizarre, clashing mosaics covering the sunporch floor, in her cutting scraps from cracker boxes, her smashing empty wine bottles and saving grape stems. He looked closely now at the two big pieces on the floor. The one that was nearly finished centered around a blue sundress covered almost entirely by other, tiny things—paper, wood, broken plastic toys, beads, a clock hand, pen caps, dried flower petals, paper clips—so that they constituted another dress, a beautiful one, with swimming lines and arcs of light. But there was something insane about it, something that screamed "outsider art," the kind of work made by someone who lived in a cabin and produced her best pieces when she went off her meds.

"You must think I'm crazy," she said.

"No, no, not at all! It's a sad event. That's horrible, that whole family. There was the one who just died on the skis, right? And now this. And he was the best one."

She sniffed wetly. He wanted to leave, but she'd be hurt. So he said, "Did you see what Bruce is making Sofia do?" and told her about the salt for the end of the world.

"Oh, he asked us to store the canned goods! Did you know that? He goes, 'You have all that room on the ground floor, how about we fill you up?' He's worried about mice in the basement at the big house."

"Mice that bite through cans?"

She smiled a little, which was a relief. "Apparently. I mean, I guess there's pasta boxes and stuff. And their pantries are packed already, and he said the attic is full of old furniture and file cabinets Gracie won't throw out."

He laughed, trying to make her laugh. "What *files* could Gracie need? I've never seen that woman touch a piece of paper that wasn't a note to the staff."

"Maybe they're from that arts camp. He said the furniture was. He said there were at least twenty mattresses up there, and headboards and dressers."

"*Really.*" He'd been leaning against the door frame, but now he sat on the floor among the heaps of cloth and shredded magazines.

The vague promise of some artifact of Edwin Parfitt's had hit Doug in the solar plexus, and he felt like a man meeting his former lover on the street, someone he believed he'd forgotten but whose overwhelming effect indicated otherwise.

"Christ," he said. "That old bitch! Listen, you know first of all it wasn't an arts *camp*, it was a major arts colony. Okay, so, no, a minor one, but extremely important, at least in the twenties. I mean, you're an artist: Charles Demuth? Grant Wood? There could be—think what could be *up* there!"

"What do you mean, Charles Demuth? He stayed here? I adore him!"

"I mean his stuff's in the attic."

She looked as if he'd told her JFK Jr. had just swum to shore, shaken but still dreamy.

"Potentially," he added. "But didn't artists do that, sometimes? They'd leave paintings as payment?"

She sunk her head again. "I don't know, Doug, this isn't what it sounded like, with Bruce. He just said there were disgusting file cabinets and the furniture. If there were anything valuable, he'd know."

"But if someone like Demuth just doodled on an envelope! Bruce would have no idea what that even was!" Doug wasn't sure why he was trying to get Miriam interested, since he didn't want her messing this up for him. Maybe he was just irrationally insulted that she wasn't as excited as he was.

He refrained from mentioning Parfitt. If she'd been paying any attention that night at the big house, she'd have heard him say Parfitt stayed there. But then she hadn't even seemed to register that it was a real arts colony. In her short time here, she hadn't struck him as someone terribly curious about much outside her jungle of beads and scraps. She hadn't been out to explore the town, and she never talked on the phone. It had all seemed vaguely charming before, but now, for some reason, it upset him.

He left her to her collages and her weeping, and asked her not to say anything about the files.

"More secrets!" she said. He couldn't read her tone. "What fun."

(There was a man
I wanted to kiss
On the eyes
And there was a man
I needed to pin down.
There was a man
I wanted to smash
Into my breasts and there was a man
Whose lips were pillows. Here
Is what I want to do
To you: throw you to the floor and lick
The crease behind your ear.
It is a part of yourself
You have never seen.
I see it every day.
I want to leave you
Diminished.)

17

Zee needed to get off campus for her own sanity, which was the only reason she'd agreed to meet Gracie at the Chippeway Club. It was one of those places she'd rather not be seen, on principle, by some faculty member who'd wrangled an invitation.

Gracie reclined by the pool in a pink one-piece, her limbs tan and slim. Zee joined her and watched the lunchtime calm at the kiddie end as children sat by their nannies to digest their grilled cheeses. Between the pool and the golf course stretched a field of browning grass decorated with three white teepees, some kind of sick and inaccurate homage to the Chippewa, who hadn't really lived here anyway. Zee herself hadn't set foot at the club till after her father died, when her mother shocked her by saying they'd been members all along, and now that her father couldn't object they were free to go there, and wouldn't Zee like to learn golf? As a teenager she knew that the other kids, the fun ones, would sneak out to the teepees during weddings and graduation parties to deflower each other and finish the wine they'd stolen.

Zee ordered a Long Island iced tea. The club served them notoriously strong.

"Mom, we need Case and Miriam out of that house. It's distracting Doug." Her mother's expression behind the big sunglasses was unclear, but she kept talking. "The whole point of moving in was the peace and quiet." She hadn't planned on bringing this up today, but then this morning at breakfast, Doug had asked Miriam if she wanted the used coffee filter for her "art," and she'd folded it in fourths and tucked it in her shorts pocket.

"Are they loud? I suppose it's cultural."

"Miriam has that whole porch covered with the trash for her collages. I mean literally, *garbage*."

Gracie shook her head. "Bruce is convinced of this Y2K fiasco, and he won't throw his son on the street with the world about to end. And the poor thing. His tendon! And now they have no car. How would they even leave? On horseback?"

The waiter handed Zee her drink in a frosted glass. She hated how good it felt to be taken care of. Zee drank like someone was timing her and then lay back to feel the sun tighten her skin. She remembered her father's objection to the club name: "Chippeway," he said, every time they passed the sign, "in that context, suggests nothing so much as poorly played golf."

Zee kept her eyes closed and said, "I'll make a deal with you. After the New Year, if the world doesn't end, Case and Miriam need to leave. His ankle will be better. If you get them out, I promise Doug's book will be done and he'll be at the college by next fall. If they stay . . . I don't know."

"I can work on Bruce, but I don't see how you can guarantee anything about poor Doug."

"I've always been lucky."

18

All the cars were gone, and Doug let himself into the big house through the garage with the emergency key.

As often as he'd been on the ground floor, he hadn't ventured upstairs since the days when he was dating Zee and she'd bring him home for Thanksgiving and set him up in a guest room with a set of fluffy towels. He dragged his hand up the railing. This must be what people meant by *patina*, this buttery softness. The house seemed as much alive on the inside as on the leafy outside—the way the wood of the door frames contracted in winter and expanded in summer, the way the glass on these staircase windows was thicker at the bottom than the top, from the slow, liquid pull of a century.

Hidalgo hadn't met him at the door, and Doug assumed the beast was in his crate. There were clicks, though, and creaks, all around him in the hall, and he reminded himself about houses settling. He tried to recall which was the door to the attic stairs. It must be this one, at the north end: next to a closet, but not a closet, the brass keyhole made for one of those toothy old keys with a loop handle. He tried the elliptical little knob, but it just clinked tightly back and forth. He knelt, his eye to the inch of gap at the bottom of the door. It wasn't dark—he remembered the dormers running along both the back and front of the house—but all he could see was tan. The riser of the bottom step.

Something crackled behind him. Doug's back had been turned on the hallway for a long time, as if he'd never watched a spy movie in his life. He rose and turned, certain he'd see an angry Bruce or a frightened Sofia. But there was just afternoon light from a high window, magnifying a million specks of floating dust. Now that he'd become aware of his back, of the fact that he couldn't turn his head like an owl, he was uncomfortable whichever way he faced. He wanted to flatten himself against a wall. Instead he walked calmly down the stairs and out the garage door.

After one more Long Island iced tea, Zee left her car at the club and Gracie drove her home, a Bobby Darin CD playing and the windows down.

"Aren't we living it up?" Gracie said.

Sofia was unloading the dry cleaning from her van. Miriam, barefoot, sat on the bench by the coach house with a book in her lap. And, bizarrely, Doug was emerging from the big house's garage, staring at everyone. As Gracie got out, Miriam rose and hopped across the hot gravel. They formed a little group of four on the driveway, which Zee watched from the car for a long, blurry second. Something was off. The pieces of the world were not where she'd left them.

Her mother waved her out of the car, and by the time Zee stuck her head into the heat Sofia was backing toward the big house. "You see! I get, I get!" Zee wanted to form a question, but she couldn't decide which one, and her lips were asleep.

"Thought I heard Hidalgo freaking out in there," Doug was saying, and "wanted to be sure he was okay," but Gracie wasn't listening.

Sofia returned, butter-yellow fabric in her plump arms.

"This is the one? I find it on the floor of the flower bedroom, behind the bed. This is whose?"

Zee blinked at the thing. It was her cotillion dress, shoulder pads and ruched waist, but wadded and wrinkled.

"I haven't seen that in nineteen years," Zee managed to say. And yet she felt she somehow had—but no, it was just that they'd talked about it so recently.

Gracie clapped her hands, as if chunks weren't falling out of the universe and onto guest room floors. "Well, that's just the luck of Laurelfield! Miriam, you need to know that this is the distinctive legacy of the house: ridiculous luck, whether good or bad. We've had tragedies here too, but then magic things like this happen! Now you have to make a *wonderful* mosaic out of it."

Sofia held the dress out, but Miriam looked at the thing like it was tainted. "I don't understand," she said.

Sofia shrugged. "Maybe was the ghost."

Zee took it from Sofia herself. It wasn't dirty, just creased in a thousand places. The sun was too hot, and even the dress was hot, and she felt she might melt into it. "Maybe it was Doug," Zee said, not looking at him. "Maybe he was trying to help Miriam find it."

Doug made a startled, choked noise, a refutation and a laugh at once.

Gracie said, "Why on earth would he do that? And leave it on the floor? He's not a raccoon, dear."

Zee draped the dress over Miriam's arm. "Here," she said. "Clearly it was meant to be."

She wondered if this would all make sense once she sobered up, but she doubted that. She wanted to stomp, to scream, to ask why things would rearrange themselves just when she'd got them straightened out. Instead she walked back to the coach house, trying not to sway. Doug caught up and whispered: "What the hell was that? Was that a joke?"

"Covering for Sofia. She probably went back to look, and it was on the closet floor. My mom would pitch a fit about the wrong hangers or something." She wasn't certain she'd made sense, but she hadn't slurred. Doug stalked past and turned on the TV.

Could that have been it? Or could Doug really have snuck into the house days ago to find the thing, to present it to Miriam like a dog with a bone? And then, when he heard footsteps, stuffed the dress behind the bed. Then he'd gone back to retrieve it today, only it wasn't where he'd thought it would be.

When Zee saw from the upstairs window that Miriam had gone back to her bench, the dress folded neatly beside her, she went down to Doug on the couch. She straddled him and unbuttoned her blouse and yanked his head back by the hair. She knew he wanted to be mad at her, and she knew he wanted to fall in love with Miriam, but for the next ten minutes he'd be unable to do either.

20

On the hottest day of August, Doug met up with the friend who'd gotten him started on *Friends for Life* and the lucrative but soul-sapping Melissa Hopper in the first place. Doug and Leland had taught high school together in Ohio, in the hazy few years between college and grad school—the same years when Zee was off on her Fulbright, saving the world. Leland had recently begun wearing black button-downs with the collars wide open, so now Doug was a little worried, meeting him in a Highwood bar, that they'd be mistaken for a gay couple. Leland taught poetry classes all over the suburbs, living not off the paychecks but off the wealthy women who preferred him to their CEO husbands.

"It's on me today," Doug said. "You saved my ass. You saved my pocketbook."

"And they're fun, right? You get to be the adolescent girl you never were."

"I will never admit to that."

There was a bowl of nuts on the bar. It was good to be out of the house, and it was good to be eating nuts and drinking and watching the Cubs. When they started tanking in the fourth, Doug filled him in on Case and Miriam. He described the scooter Case was now using to get around town—how he'd prop his bad leg up on a little shelf and push off with the other. He'd had a few job interviews set up in the city, but he'd canceled those, worried how he'd look showing up sweaty from the train and cab, on top of wounded.

"Tex and the crazy lady," Leland said. "Tex and the Wreck. That's a country song, right there. This woman, is she of the attractive persuasion?"

"Fortunately no. I mean, maybe a six. The craziness doesn't help. Six point five."

"This kid's an asshole." He was talking about the Cubs. "But then, your wife makes everyone look like shit, right? Tell me something: The Victoria's Secret catalogue gets to your house, you even bother to look? Or is it like, hey, I got better stuff upstairs?"

Doug was glad there seemed no obligation to answer. Leland had met Zee only once or twice, and he hadn't looked at her with any more interest than most men did. Doug knew what he was really saying, what everyone was really saying when they commented on her beauty: They weren't sure how she'd ended up with Doug. He wasn't shorter than her, or bad looking. He'd always gotten plenty of girls. It was more what people presumed about women as intense as Zee, about what they were after and what they could get. Women like Zee did not pick nice guys with average golf games who occasionally forgot to brush their teeth. They picked jackass publishing executives with famous ex-wives and ski houses.

"And can we get the bullpen up?" Leland said.

Partly to keep him from talking about baseball when Doug knew relatively little about the Cubs, and partly because this was why he'd called Leland in the first place, Doug told him about the files in the attic. He told him too about the past month of unsuccessful fishing. In the days after he tried the attic door himself, Doug tried wheedling a key out of Sofia, who apparently didn't have one, and out of Bruce, who'd laughed and said, "You want Gracie to kill me? I been up there *once*, to trap a squirrel. Look, I don't even open the crisper drawer without her say-so. You know? This is called marital peace."

"Do you *have* a key?" Doug had asked, and Bruce had clapped him on the back.

"It's not really my house, right? And—Doug, my friend—it's definitely not yours." Bruce turned to go, then came back. "Hey. Don't let me hear you bothering Gracie with this. She's had enough stress with the landscapers."

And before all that he'd asked Zee—as she lay there with her head on his lap, in those lovely, sleepy minutes after she came down and fucked him on the TV room couch—if her mother might ever let him explore the attic and basement for colony artifacts. She'd given him the look the question deserved. "I've hardly been in that attic," she said. "And I can tell you exactly what's in the basement, and right now it's supplies for Armageddon."

Leland had turned on his bar stool so his back was to the TV. "Marianne *Moore*," he said finally. "Christ. I know you're gay for Parfitt and all, but do you realize what someone could do with unpublished Moore documents? Jesus God, I'm *drooling* here. Fuck. I mean, if she stayed there, it'd be late in life. She never went anywhere without her mother while the mother was alive. So this isn't early shit. This isn't *juvenilia*. This is, like. *Fuck*." He slid his empty glass to the bartender. "I mean, just a draft. A photo!"

It was sublimely gratifying to see Leland's reaction, after Miriam's calm pessimism. "I know. It's gotta be *something*. Otherwise why the evasion, you know? That's what I'm saying."

"So you gotta get it out of there."

"Sure. I know. It's keeping me awake."

"You tell Zee?"

Doug shook his head. With each day he knew he was less likely to. He wasn't sure if she would laugh and tell him he needed real source material, not old phone bills, or if she'd storm the attic herself and take over the whole enterprise, but something in his bones rebelled against what should have been spousal transparency.

Maybe the secret of the *Friends* books had indeed been a tiny wedge.

"So you're going to help me."

"I'm—okay, what, we're breaking in? I wear a ski mask?"

"You pretend to be a photographer."

Leland laughed and shook his head. "No, no, this is sounding like a sitcom."

"Listen: Any Moore documents, any correspondence, you can have it. You can publish it, sell it, it's yours."

"Huh. Christ."

"I just want the Parfitt stuff."

What he asked Leland to do was call Gracie pretending to be with the Adler Ross Foundation. Adler Ross was the architect of the place, just famous enough for someone to care about his attics. Leland was going to be sad and sweet and claim this was the last attic he needed to photograph to complete the records. He'd take pictures of the windows, throw around some jargon, get out of there. "It's reconnaissance," Doug said. "You just see if there are file cabinets. And if everything's going well, maybe ask if you can move one to get a better picture, then you say, 'God, these are heavy, what's in these things,' right? And meanwhile you're watching what key she uses on the attic door, where she puts it when she's done."

"This is insane, Doug. I'm not a good liar."

"Marianne Moore. Marianne Moore's undiscovered poem about her secret affair with Mickey Mantle."

"Well, yeah. Okay. True."

21

Z ee had waited patiently through the whole summer session, through one sweltering reception on the president's lawn, and the first two weeks of class. She finally let herself go to the science building computer lab to type up the letter. She sat with her back to the windows and typed in eight-point font, then blew it up only for proofreading.

Dear Dean Shaumber and Prof. Blum,

I write on behalf of myself and two other female students who feel disturbed by the photos on Dr. Cole's computer. We are sure you are familiar with the photos, as they are common knowledge. Although he closes that file when we enter the office, it is unnerving to know he has been looking at the photos, and that he is in a state of mind to degrade women.

We simply wish him to consider the effect this behavior has on those women who visit his office. We are also upset about his continual use of the word "coed," but this is old news and we understand nothing is going to be done about it, and furthermore we and the other students we have spoken to are far more disturbed about the pornography.

Respectfully submitted by three women who wish to remain anonymous.

Zee went back and forth on the spelling of *effect*, but figured the three imaginary girls would be imaginary English majors, and would get it right. She left two copies in the printer trays where they could be found by students, then stuck one copy in Shaumber's mailbox and one in Blum's.

This last she did right in front of Chantal, but there were plenty of other papers in there already. She turned calmly and asked Chantal to make some copies. Her mother had always maintained, back in the days when Zee and her father had played hide-and-seek around the house, her father as gleeful as any eight-year-old, that plain sight was the best place to hide. They'd talk Gracie into hiding, and when they found her she'd been sitting in the kitchen right where they'd left her, smoking a Virginia Slim. "But it took you five minutes!" she'd say when they complained. That was in the days before her mother put on airs, back when the estate was just a ramshackle shell for a regular, sloppy family, entire guest rooms given over to Zee's Lego configurations. Friends from the art world—George's reviews eventually went beyond the local scene, and the house became a pit stop for artists passing through Chicago—would play Mastermind with Zee at the table while Gracie cooked eggs. The only formality was her father's predilection for folding the dinner napkins into sailboats on special occasions. Things hardened after his death. It was later that year—Zee was still twelve—when her mother saw her take a spoonful of chocolate frosting from the container and said, "That's how girls get fat." Her mother had gotten a manicure, had wallpapered the bathrooms, had joined the Presbyterian church, all new things Zee didn't understand except to know that everything was different now, that without her father's laugh dismissing the rest of the world, there were appearances to be maintained.

On her way out of the building she ran into Cole, who held the door open. Those eyebrows: long white hairs among the dark short ones. Someone had planted them in the wrong garden. "Smile!" he shouted, and because her every interaction with the man was a charade anyway, she did just that. He didn't let her past, though. He poked a bony finger into her sternum, right above her blouse. "Do you know why I like it when you smile?"

"I do not," she said, still grinning, though her ears were hot now, and her neck.

"You resemble someone I used to know. It's uncanny. The ears and chin."

"Why, thank you," Zee said, and leaned back so she could get around his finger without it grazing her breast.

"A man, mind you!" he called after her. "It was a man!"

Doug had been much more confident about the soccer chapters in the previous book—he'd played varsity in high school, three lifetimes ago—than about the theater business here. He was flummoxed by the parts of Frieda's outline where the Populars and the Friends shared a dressing room. In the back of an old notebook, he'd begun listing things he needed to research:

Would have bra?
Purse? Backpack?
Stage makeup?
Undress in front of each other or hide in stalls?
Chairs backstage? Benches?

They read like a pedophilic stalker's notes, and he wanted them scratched out as soon as possible. He could maybe use the Internet for the theater parts, but he shuddered to think where an AltaVista search for "twelve-year-old, brassiere" would lead.

He started down to look for Miriam, but she was on the landing of the stairs, cross-legged, sorting through an ice cube tray of colored beads. She said "Oh!" and some of the glassy blue ones splashed out and rolled down the steps. Doug bounded down, picked them up with the sweat of his fingertips, then shook them into Miriam's outstretched palm.

"I'll tell you why I'm here," she said, as Doug sat on the step above her. He regretted his choice of seat immediately. She wasn't wearing a bra, and he could see too far down her green tank top. He leaned back and looked instead at the ceiling. Miriam said, "I wasn't sleeping well, so I thought I'd spend time in the ghostliest part of the coach house. Just to dare something to happen. If it does, I'll know. And if it doesn't, I'll sleep better."

"Why is this the ghostliest part?" He hoped she didn't have a good answer.

"Oh, you know. Doorways, staircases, attics, windows. You never see a ghost in the middle of the room."

"I've never seen a ghost at all."

"Well, yes. That."

"But Doug," she said. "I found out. How she died."

"What, Violet?" He sat back up despite himself.

"I went to the library and they got me set with microfiche. There was an obituary with no information at all—But did you know she was born in England? I love it! English ghosts are scarier, right?—so I was about to give up. But then there was this weird article a few days later that was like, 'Husbands, pray for your wives!' You know, very 1906. And then it talks about 'to perish by starvation, in this land of plenty.' And it was clearly about her. *Starvation.*"

"Seriously. Wow. Wait, I thought she killed herself."

"Exactly. Something doesn't add up."

"Was anorexia a thing back then?"

Miriam tilted her head. "That's the boring version. I think Augustus killed her. I think he starved her."

Doug let out a low, slow whistle and laughed. "So I need your help on something less serious," he said. "Since you're already in on my secret." He decided not to ask the bra question, in light of current circumstances. "Do twelve-year-olds carry purses?"

She put the bead tray down. "Oh, fun! Well, the Populars

would have *chic* purses. The Friends should have backpacks. Cece probably has an army surplus bag, something cool that she stenciled on." Doug scribbled in the notebook as she talked, and twenty minutes later most of his problems were solved.

She said, "Just pay me back when you find that original Demuth painting."

And then, before he could fathom why he was doing it, he told her about the plan with Leland, who had conceded to go undercover next week. Maybe it was for the same reason he hadn't shared the news with Zee: One secret, whether shared or kept, begot more.

"I want to help!" she said. "I won't get in the way. It's just that nothing exciting has happened to me for such a long time."

"You'd be handy for identifying art," he said. "Not that my hopes are up. I'm skeptical. But just a list of who stayed here and when, if Parfitt were on the list—it would be huge. You know, who was with him, that kind of thing."

Miriam rubbed her bare arms. "See, don't you feel the ghosts around you when you say things like that? All those people, all that creative energy—it had to go *somewhere*. And Parfitt was another suicide. People like that are the most probable ghosts."

He stretched his legs, which had fallen asleep.

"Oh!" Miriam said. "You have scars!" She was eye level with his knees and the thick white scars below each kneecap, and to Doug's surprise she reached out her finger and traced down the length of the left one, as if it concerned her greatly.

Doug knew he ought to run for his life, but he did the next best thing. He said, pointedly, "How did you and Case meet?"

"Oh, he bought one of my pieces. And I thought he was so *old*, because he was twenty-eight! Can you believe that? I was still in college."

"He's had a rough go here." He laughed in what he hoped was a friendly way.

She said, "I wonder about this house. This whole place. Gracie said it's lucky and it's unlucky. It's been lucky for me. I've never done so much good work in my life."

"Don't take philosophical advice from Gracie."

Miriam picked a red bead out of the container. "I've seen an astrologer do a birth chart for a house, just like a person." She saw the look on his face. "I know, *stars*, but it's no weirder than genetics or pheromones telling us what to do, right? It's just the genome of a place."

"But *you* like it here."

"It's like—did you ever play with magnets as a kid? You know how if you have them turned to the wrong pole it pushes away, but you flip the same magnet around and it clicks together? I feel like Case is the wrong pole, the one that gets pushed. And I'm the right one."

It wasn't till he was back in his room, silently mouthing her words just to feel their strangeness on his lips, that he felt they almost made a kind of sense.

One Twix and two beers later, he was on fire. He found the bra information in the *FFL Bible*. He was stupid not to have looked there first. Candy got a bra in book 60, apparently, then Molly, but not Melissa. He spun his chair to celebrate, and got back to work. With Violet's unexplained starvation fresh on his mind, he decided (why the hell not? The books could use some edge) to give one of the Populars an eating disorder. He showed Amelia Wynn, the sixth-grade dictator, eating a glass of salted ice. He showed her counting her ribs in the dressing-room mirror. Her arms were as thin as tapers.

(I wrap my ankles around chair rungs
So I don't spring out and bite your shoulder.

Your thumb and finger
On the edges of a CD

Your tongue
Makes its way between your teeth
In time with music

I want to be
That music

The hair just below
Your navel
Curls to the left.
Let me untwist it)

By October, there were rumors. Cole was rarely in his office, and one afternoon Zee saw Jerry Keaton pull Bob Grasso into the seminar room and close the door. She asked Chantal if she knew what was going on, and Chantal shook her head—but she did not ask what Zee was referring to. And that was confirmation enough.

Her seminar kids were already calling themselves The Ghostbusters and had written wonderful essays on *The Turn of the Screw* and *The Haunting of Hill House*. They'd been quick to point out that these stories weren't so much about ghosts as madness, and our slippery hold on reality. Good kids. She was surprised to find she was having more fun with them than with her Fictions of Empire students.

After class, Fran Leffler followed Zee to her office to talk about grad school. Fran was a major, a sorority girl with dimples. Zee told her to sign up for Literary Theory, then leaned across her desk: "Listen, Fran, this is under wraps, but I'm sure you've heard about Professor Cole?"

Fran looked concerned, like Zee was about to tell her the man had cancer.

"I'm just asking because I believe this sort of thing is important to talk about, and you seem like someone who might hear if—Well, I just want to make sure people feel comfortable coming forward."

"Coming *forward*? Did he, like—"

"Oh, no! No, not that. It's just his computer. I guess—I shouldn't say this, but I've probably said too much already, and I don't want your imagination getting the best of you. Apparently some students, some female students, have been made uncomfortable by the images on his computer. They were, you know . . . explicit."

Fran shook her head in horror, but her eyes were lit with gossip. "Is he in trouble?"

"He'll be in trouble if he *needs* to be. Who knows if it's even true. But, as a senior—if you heard anything from younger women, anyone in your sorority—I hope you'd let someone know. At this point they're just gathering information. And you didn't hear it from me, please."

As Fran left, Zee took her shoes off and stretched her feet. Later that same day, she watched Golda Blum and some man she'd never seen before, a dumpy guy in a communist-green polo shirt who could only work for IT, go into Cole's office without him.

"It's marvelous," Gracie said. They were at the breakfast table in the big house late that afternoon. Zee had just told her she could stop worrying about Doug, that there *would* be openings by the fall, as long as he could finish his book in an unshared house. (The debate would take months, of course, and they'd let Cole finish the year. But they'd start the head hunt soon to replace him.) Hidalgo, under the table, breathed hot air on Zee's legs. "Do you think the school will really remain open, though, after this whole computer thing?" It took Zee a few terrifying seconds to realize she meant the Y2K bug. "Bruce reads absolutely all the news, and the smartest people are saying it's just the end of everything."

Sofia was cleaning out the refrigerator, tossing old containers of deli salads Gracie and Bruce had never gotten around to eating. Zee wanted to ask her more about that dress, that yellow dress that had no reason to be on the floor, but now was not the time. It had been bothering her for weeks now, and the more she thought about it, the more she felt that somehow she'd seen it very recently, and remembered touching it. She'd started to consider that she might have done something in her sleep, walked to the big house and found the dress, crumpled it and hidden it from Miriam.

But this was ridiculous, and she'd long ago trained herself not to second-guess things to the point where she lost the reality of them. She used to worry all the time about losing her mind. In the library at boarding school she'd found a book, *The New World Barons*, published in the 1960s, with sections on the Palmers and Carnegies and Devohrs, among others. "The Devohr history is not one of summer estates and long lineage held taut by familial love; it is one of scandal, Diaspora, insanity." She spent hours on the floor between shelves, reading about the Devohrs who killed themselves, the ones who vanished into Mexico, the one they found buried under old newspapers. She returned to the book many times, to trace the lines of the small, gray jaws with her pinky. Great-aunts and distant cousins. Her grandfather, Gamaliel, as a long-haired boy in a dress. (His mother, Violet, not a Devohr by birth and not a Devohr for long, merited mention only as "another suicide.") Zee had never met any of them. Gracie's parents died before Zee was born, and Gracie's brothers were all "degenerates" to whom she no longer spoke. No cousins ever visited, no aunts. The Devohrs weren't people so much as sea turtles that laid their eggs and then crawled back to the ocean, not particularly invested in meeting their progeny ever again. That she and Gracie were relatively close was a miracle.

Gracie said, "Do you think the college might find a job for Case as well? Something in the business office?"

Zee was still contemplating what kind of response this merited when Gracie's phone rang. She answered it and handed it to Zee. It was Doug.

"Hey!" he said. "You're at your mom's!" He was a terrible actor.

"What's wrong?"

"Nothing, no, I just wondered. So you won't be back for a while?"

"Maybe an hour."

"Okay. Like, a whole hour? Okay!"

She hung up and told her mother she needed to get going right away.

"It's just as well. Some poor fellow's coming over to take pictures. The architects are sending him. I don't know what on earth he wants."

Zee put her teacup in the sink, kissed her mother's cheek, and ran out the side door. A car was pulling up to the front, the beat-up black Saturn of the architectural lackey, who had no idea what Gracie would put him through.

In the coach house, it seemed eerily like a normal Thursday afternoon. Miriam on the sunporch, fully clothed, working on her unloved dress collages. Case sulking at the kitchen table. Doug sprawled on the bed with *Sports Illustrated*, smiling, as if he'd been expecting her.

On the phone, Leland had said the pictures turned out but he wasn't sure what the hell he was looking for. Doug didn't know why this was disappointing. He hadn't really believed Leland would find a cardboard box labeled "Parfitt's Memoirs." But somewhere between getting Leland into the attic, and getting Zee out of the house in time, and arranging this meeting down at the beach, Doug had come to assume there would be a major payoff. He'd stopped considering the possibility that Bruce was wrong about the file cabinets. That there might be nothing there but a pile of dusty bed frames. He'd forgotten that even if there *were* colony files, they might have just been heating bills.

It was a cool, sunny day, and Lake Michigan was Caribbean blue. Doug found Leland and Miriam at separate picnic benches on the grass between the sand and the cars. He introduced them, and Leland poured out an envelope of snapshots: windows, bureaus with missing drawers, piles of headboards and desk chairs, and yes, four black metal file cabinets, each two drawers high, with no visible locks.

"They were old enough. You see the script on the logo?" He'd managed to sneak a close-up of the manufacturer's plaque on one cabinet. "Looks like what, forties? Fifties? That fits, right?" Leland attempted to lay the photos into the general shape of the attic. "It wasn't easy," he said. He was taking up one whole bench, his legs spread wide, looking at Miriam in her yellow shirt in a way that implied Doug had sold her short. "I didn't tell her it was the attic I wanted till I'd thanked her a million times, told her what a jackass my boss was, how I was afraid I'd get fired. So by the time I said 'attic,' she'd feel bad saying no. Oh, and I told her my girl-friend was from Toronto. That helped. I don't have a girlfriend, but hey. So she *did* say no, she told me there were bats and she hadn't been up there in years. So I go, 'Oh, well if it's hard for you to climb, I can go by myself.'"

"Oooh, brilliant!" Gurgle of southern laughter, toss of curls.

"So twenty seconds later she's marching up the stairs. And here." He shuffled through the photos and found two of the attic door—one from outside, one from inside. "It's a simple old lock. The key was just two prongs."

"But she had the key *on* her?"

"No. I mean, I was exaggerating about the twenty seconds. Really she disappeared for five minutes and came back with the key. So sue me. I'm a poet. I'm prone to exaggeration." He grinned at Miriam, who was too absorbed in the photos to notice.

"Here's what I think," she said. "I doubt there's anything valuable there. No one would put a rolled up painting in a file cabinet."

"But a poem!" Leland said. "A poem that was part of some-one's application!"

"Slides," Doug said. "Letters of recommendation. Project pro-posals. Listen: Just this summer? The New York Public Library bought the archives from the Yaddo colony for some huge amount, and they're saying there's unpublished Carson McCullers in there. We're not in the same league, but still."

"So how do we convince her to let us look?"

Doug sighed and watched the joggers going past. He wasn't sure if Gracie's persistent and decisive evasion of Laurelfield his-tory had to do with her guilt at having displaced the colony, or her shame at being associated with so many unwashed artists, but she hadn't budged. At Bruce's birthday dinner last week, when Doug had asked if historians had ever shown interest in documenting Laurelfield, Gracie had said, "Douglas, isn't there something more productive you ought to focus on? Perhaps you could publish a novel." ("What is her *problem?*" Miriam had whispered later. "Her energy is so off.")

"What if we talk her into donating it to a library?" Leland said. "Or the college?"

Doug said, "I think she'd sooner donate her kidneys."

"It doesn't seem that Gracie's the right person to make the judgment call," Miriam said. "She's not a writer, she's not an artist, she's not a historian. And didn't you say"—she turned to Leland—"it's an easy lock to pick?"

When a man sat down at the next bench with his laptop they began whispering, but what they came up with over the next hour was a hypothetical scenario so risky that Doug knew he'd never pull the trigger on it. They were having fun though, and so he let Leland and Miriam plot.

They agreed that the best time to break into the attic would *not* be on one of the rare occasions when both Gracie and Bruce were gone. Sofia was usually around, as were Bruce's personal secretary and the guy who came to walk Hidalgo. If someone met them on their way out, they'd have a hard time explaining the armloads of files. Miriam was the one who remembered the Democratic fund-raiser Gracie and Bruce were hosting in early December, which Doug and Zee and the younger Breens would be expected to attend. They could easily smuggle Leland in. Sofia would be working downstairs with the caterers. It would be loud. No one would hear if they had to bust down the attic door.

"It'll be like *Notorious!*" Miriam said. "Only we won't get caught like Ingrid Bergman." Seeing how her hands flew around her hair and her nose flared out, how her whole face was pink and bright, Doug wondered if she'd actually been depressed all summer. Those other times she'd seemed happy, like standing on the counter that first day with those plates, it must have been something fake. It was nothing like this.

Doug finally shook his head. "Zee would never forgive me," he said. "Not for going after the files, but—I mean, Gracie would kick us out." He could imagine his mother-in-law smiling thinly, saying that now that he'd found a new career in espionage, he could surely afford his own home.

"It's five weeks away," Miriam said. "You have time to decide. Don't say no just yet."

When they finally disbanded, Doug felt they should all put their hands in a heap and chant something, like a field hockey team. But he let it end with Miriam heading down the beach for pebbles and he and Leland trudging all the way back to town for coffee.

"You jackass," Leland said as they crossed the train tracks. "I can't fucking believe you."

"What?"

He shook his head in a rueful way that he must have stood in front of the mirror and practiced, a poet's astonishment at the varied and exasperating world. "You rate a woman a six point five and go off about how crazy she is."

"Oh, she has her moments. I probably didn't do her justice."

"That's not what I meant. You're in love with her."

Doug almost ran into the guardrail. So they were starting, the inevitable assumptions. He decided to wait long enough that his answer wouldn't seem defensive, because it wasn't, and he needed Leland to understand that.

They were all the way across the street by the time he said, "I am sincerely not."

"I'm just saying, the only reason I can think to sell a lovely person like that so short is that maybe you're fighting something."

"Or maybe she's really crazy. You walk in when she's working, and she looks like a homeless person. She's got pencils behind both ears, and pins sticking from her mouth, hair frizzed out. Her pupils are fully dilated."

"Okay, sure. Sure. But let me ask you this: Why do you keep walking in when she's working?"

Doug considered punching Leland in the face, but decided against it.

26

As Zee sorted handouts before class, the talk grew shrill in the corner. "It was right there on the screen," Meghan Dwyer said. A smart, sweet girl who could actually write. Everyone was turned toward her. "And I wouldn't say it was underage stuff. But it was graphic. I know some people are picturing just, like, a topless woman leaning on a car. But this was, like—" she looked around, saw Zee immersed in her papers, and mouthed the words "—butt-fucking."

Zee wondered, in brief amazement, if it *had* all been true, if she'd simply set things in motion. But no, this was her own creation, her own monster. She had willed this into being.

Near the end of class, Dev Kapoor raised his hand, a look on his face like he was trying to fend off a headache. He said, "How come ghosts are always from the past? I mean, why are they never from the future?" The class snickered. Zee suspected his peers had a different impression of Dev than she'd gotten from his workmanlike papers.

"Go on," she said.

"A ghost from the future would have a lot more at stake. Ghosts from the past are always in the Hamlet model, right? Like, remember me and avenge my death. But a ghost from the future is going to be desperate. If things don't go right he won't be born."

"Time doesn't work that way," Fran Leffler said, and then they all started in, telling him he'd watched too many movies.

"Maybe I don't mean a ghost. More like a spirit or a force. But anyway, my point is, a ghost from the future *wouldn't* be scary, right?"

Zee said, "So we're afraid of the undead, but not the unborn."

Sarah Bonheur thrust her hand definitively into the air and didn't wait to be called on. "*A Christmas Carol*," she said. "By Charles Dickens. The ghost of Christmas Future is the scariest of all."

Dev said, "Oh. Right," and collapsed back in his chair.

But Antwon Haynes picked up the ball. "That's an exception. Maybe it's like what we're afraid of isn't death, but the *past*. No one walks by a crime scene the very next day and feels a ghost. It takes twenty years, right?"

They were on to something, Zee thought. We aren't haunted by the dead, but by the impossible reach of history. By how unknowable these others are to us, how unfathomable we'd be to them.

She started writing on the board.

Cole had been making himself scarce outside of class, so Zee was caught off guard when, as she passed his office, he stuck his head out and motioned her in. It was the first time she'd set foot there since the sabotage, but here were the same books stacked on the floor, same Post-its covering the Indiana University diploma.

"Zenobia, my dear, I need your advice," he said. He sat on the front edge of his desk, which left Zee choosing between the student chair, three inches from Sid Cole's crotch, and his own desk chair, inappropriate in a different way. She opted for leaning against a bookcase. "As a communist, you're interested in intellectual freedom, no?"

"I'm not a communist, I'm a Marxist scholar."

"Here's my point: The administration should not be able to access the computers of tenured faculty. Let's imagine you were looking at some Web site of a communist politician, and then you're hauled in front of a committee. When the whole point of tenure is the freedom."

"I'm not tenured."

"You've heard what's happening, I'm sure."

Zee attempted to look bewildered, but he shook his head.

"You hear everything. You know what the deans ate for breakfast. You know when Blum takes a crap. And what I want to know is, when did we become afraid of sex? We ask them to read *Lolita* and Chaucer, but a nude picture is going to warp their minds? They're *adults*!"

Zee genuinely *was* bewildered now, by what seemed a confession, but she reminded herself that this was just Cole, that he was the kind of man who would argue against the Dalai Lama, simply for the thrill of battle. So she said, "I think if you believe strongly in this, you should fight it, whether you did the thing or not."

"Ha! I'm not asking your permission. What I'm wondering is this: You always have your finger on the pulse, so to speak. How many faculty do you suppose would back me?"

"It depends what you're planning to do."

"If I say, either you stay out of my computer or I quit my job and take this very public. How many people would support me on that?"

"You're not asking them to quit *with* you."

"No. Write letters, shave their heads."

She picked up a little jade monkey from the shelf and felt its smooth back with her thumb. A strangely delicate object for Cole to possess. "I imagine you'd have some support. Just don't count on all the feminists."

"Isn't everyone a feminist now? I thought that was the point of Women's Studies."

"I can probably help with the feminists."

Despite everything, when he winked at her right then, she could see why he charmed the kids. It was so hard to get on his good side that once you got there, even under false pretenses, it felt validating, like the hard-won respect of a difficult father.

Doug looked much younger asleep. It was comforting, in a way. A reminder that she was the one with the plans, that she was the one keeping things together.

You could only lose control if you let go. You could only lose *anything* if you let it go. She said to herself.

From the shoulder of Doug's T-shirt she pulled a long, curly brown hair.

The ivy on the big house had yellowed, to disturbing effect. The vines seemed somehow malevolent now, a strangling, draining force, all roots and tendrils, fused with the stone. Doug thought all through the rest of October about the risk involved in going behind Gracie's back once and for all. He considered, too, that a political fund-raiser might involve Secret Service in some way. He asked Zee, casually, if there would be guards. She said, "It's more like a Tupperware party."

But the real threat wasn't Gracie or even men with earpieces. It was Zee, who had surely already noticed how antsy he was lately. If they went through with it, he wouldn't be able to look her in the eye for weeks.

He knew Zee wanted, more than anything, for him to finish the monograph—but she'd see this as more procrastination, as chasing fingerprints when he ought to be engaged in hard-nosed analysis. He could imagine her forehead creased, her hands on his shoulders. "You thought," she'd say, "that you could finish your book by breaking into my mother's attic? *That* was your plan? Show me how much you've written."

He felt, bizarrely, that he was choosing between Edwin Parfitt and his wife—and not for the first time. The night he met Zee, at a welcome cocktail party at the graduate dean's house, and she'd learned he was planning to write about Parfitt, she'd said, "*Parfitt.* Wow. Oh dear. I put him in a category with Joyce Kilmer."

Doug had been blinded by the shine of her black hair, by the thin straps of her dress, but he'd managed to call her out. "That's because you know exactly one poem by each. You know Kilmer's 'Trees,' and you know Parfitt's 'Apollo on the Mississippi,' and they're both sappy. They were completely different poets in every way. They weren't even writing at the same time!"

"Yes, they *are* different. They're both trite, but Parfitt is also opaque. And my God, you could march to his rhythms, right?"

Doug was holding a bacon-wrapped scallop that he had no idea what to do with. "He just had this one cheesy period: 1930 to '32. Everything got all happy and rhymey. I mean, happiness is bad for poetry. And 'Apollo' was from that time. But that's the stuff that got famous. You need to read his early sonnets. The Persephone series, and the Aeneas ones. And his last poems are devastating. Have you read 'Proteus Wept'? Or 'Pond's Edge, Forgotten Girl'? It's so different from what you think."

"I've read it. He loved to eroticize those drowned women, didn't he?"

Doug had decided by this point that he hated this bitch, this sharp-chinned bitch who was looking over his shoulder for someone better to talk to. "Well, he was gay," he said. "If drowning turns you on, that's *your* issue." He'd stalked away.

Over the next year, as hatred melted into repartee and then to lust and sex and dating and engagement, he'd managed to convince her that Parfitt was someone she *ought* to like, though she never did become a fan. "You have a similar worldview," he told her.

"What worldview is that?"

He couldn't answer, but he wanted to say: Both of you—you feel so small that you'll never realize the volume of your own voice.

28

Miriam stood at the counter, prying a small pumpkin open with a kitchen knife. She was making soup to go with the lasagna Doug had prepped that afternoon, or so she had announced, but Zee had yet to see so much as a pot. It was already six thirty, with the older Breens due at the coach house in half an hour.

Doug was in a suspiciously good mood, bouncing around and inviting Case to join him for a beer on the tiny, precarious balcony off the kitchen. Zee almost stopped them, almost said that if Case stepped on the balcony, it was sure to be hit by lightning and break clean off the house. His ankle should have healed twice over by now, but he'd strained the tendon again leaping from his flaming car. So here he was, four months after the initial injury, still in the boot, still in pain. If things continued this way, one day Case would just combust like his car had. Miriam would wander back to Texas alone with her garbage. Problem solved.

Now that things were going so well with Cole, Zee was meditating, that night, on the one issue remaining: how to guarantee that Doug finished saying whatever he had to say about Edwin Parfitt so the monograph could be under contract by spring. Despite his improved work ethic, whenever she asked how much he'd written it was never more than a hundred words, and he was never ready to show her.

With everyone occupied, Zee walked quietly back into the apartment.

Getting into Doug's computer was so easy, compared with the risk of hacking Cole, that her pulse hardly rose. She looked first, optimistically, in the "Recent Documents" menu. The list included "In the last months of," "To Whom It May Concern," "Budget 99" and "Systems Work Folder 30, B." She checked the first, the only one with any promise, hoping the document would refer to the last months of Edwin Parfitt's life. It did. It read, in its entirety, "In the last months of Parfitt's short life, these five poems comprised not only the (don't repeat w/ thesis, but + PATHOS of Apollo on Miss. and Peonies)."

She knew he saved chapters individually, and he claimed he'd completed at least four, but this fragment was not encouraging. And if he hadn't been writing, what had he been doing every day? Zee's head began throbbing. The anger was there, strongly—the urge to throw the computer through the window and watch it shatter on the gravel—but more overwhelming was the sensation of the entire universe backfiring. Here was the precise opposite of everything she'd fought for. No: It was as if some malevolent genie had twisted her wishes into realities she couldn't handle. Cole was imploding—confessing, even!—but Doug wouldn't be ready to take the job. The job would open up just in time to go to some wunderkind who'd hold it for fifty years.

She should look at the other documents to make sure, and she should look at everything saved in his "Diss." folder, no matter how old, and she should look on all the disks she could find, just in case he'd been an idiot and neglected to save his work on the hard drive. With twenty minutes before her aggressively punctual mother and stepfather would arrive, she began searching in earnest.

29

Miriam's soup, she announced, wouldn't be ready for another hour, but it was worth the wait. Doug served Bruce from the bottle of Mount Gay purchased specially for the occasion. The rest of them got to work on a Pinot Noir. Zee was still hiding in the bedroom, sleeping or seething or grading papers, and nobody proposed calling her into the kitchen.

Gracie wandered, inspecting the cabinet hinges and the chipped tiles by the oven. She paused by the old panel right next to the refrigerator, about three feet square, that they'd painted over that spring with the same light blue as the rest of the kitchen.

"This was cheaply patched," she said, "wasn't it? Long before my time. I believe it's where they cut to install the electricity. My grandfather had the big house all wired up just as early as it was ever done, but he left the colony director living here with no lights until, I don't know, the thirties. He was never one to think of his employees."

It was the first time Doug heard Gracie refer to the colony with anything other than complete disregard. Apparently her disregard for her father was stronger. Gamaliel—a name Doug found suitably villainous for the man who'd shuttered the colony. When he'd mentioned him to Miriam, she'd said, "Oh, let's call him Gargamel! Like the bad guy from *The Smurfs*!" And ever since, Doug had pictured a man skulking around in a black robe, plotting the demise of the little artists. The real Gamaliel had suffered a nervous breakdown following the 1929 stock market crash, and although his fortunes had recovered, his mind never did. At least this was what Doug had gathered from *The Devohrs of Toronto: A Family Portrait*, back in graduate school.

"Miriam, *there's* a commission for you!" Gracie said. She was still examining the panel. "You might as well make yourself useful. Couldn't you paint it or something? A landscape?"

Miriam had perched on the counter, bare feet swinging, wine glass in hand. "I don't paint much. How about a traditional mosaic? In glass and little tiles?"

Case said, "Hey, see?" He turned to Bruce with a sharp, unfriendly grin. "That's how it's supposed to work. Hooking people up with gigs. What are you doing for *me*?" Joking, but of course he wasn't.

Bruce looked at his son with what Doug took for deep irritation. "My friend Clarence Mahoney will be at the fund-raiser. That's what I'm doing for you."

The art project, at least, was quickly settled, and Bruce told Gracie she was "a regular Medici." Miriam was already eyeing the piece of wood like something she planned to ravish.

There was a small crash from Doug and Zee's rooms, and a grunt of what sounded like frustration. They ignored it.

"Oh, just think!" Gracie said. "This might turn out to be your best artwork ever, and I thought of it just by happensack!"

Case let out a quick burst of laughter, and Miriam quickly stuck her head into the oven under the pretense of checking the pumpkin. Bruce beamed like Gracie was the cutest thing.

"Just by happensack," Doug repeated, and managed to keep a straight face. "And of course you'll pay Miriam for the tiles," he said, because he knew Miriam wouldn't say it, and he knew Gracie wouldn't think of it. "Unless you want it made of snipped up shirts and compost." He looked at Miriam to see if he'd offended her, but when she emerged from the oven she was smiling appreciatively.

"Oh, of course. And something extra for the labor. Shall we see what's keeping Zilla?" There was a horrible scraping sound just then, though, and no one volunteered.

By the time the soup was blended, the orange mess sopped from the counter, the remains served, and the lasagna finishing in the oven, they were all in high spirits. Maybe not Case, but certainly the rest of them. Gracie was more and more talkative with the wine, and Doug and Miriam couldn't stop giggling. The soup was delicious.

Gracie said, "I'll have you know we hung that farmhouse painting in the solarium regardless. I realize it's a bit naïve, Miriam, but it's *innocent*, and I like that. I don't like *violent* art. And my late husband, as I mentioned, adored it."

"Good King George," Bruce said. He was sloshed. "George the Late. George the Infallible."

Miriam took a big breath and glanced—apologetically, it seemed—at Doug, and then said, "Speaking of things I could be doing with my days. Bruce mentioned there were old filing cabinets—up in the attic? Those must be a burden. Wouldn't you like help cleaning those out?" Doug's first inclination was to panic, to kick Miriam under the table, but he supposed it was all right. Zee wasn't there to hear, and Case didn't care, and Bruce's presence might force Gracie's hand. "I mean, I want to earn my keep."

Gracie didn't look at Bruce at all, just blinked at Miriam. She said, "I can't help but think it's a shame you never had braces, Miriam. It really does mark a person. I always say, if you want to know someone's lot in life, look at the teeth."

Zee returned to the kitchen as the main course was served, and there was something about her smile, her slow pace, that made her look like a drunk trying to walk a straight line. She kissed her mother's cheek, and Miriam scrambled for another place setting.

Gracie was going off about the Internet, and Zee joined the group of baffled, nodding heads. "What's so horrifying is they can just put your name on there, and there's nothing you can do about it," Gracie said. "Even for the phone book they have to have your permission! And correct me if I'm wrong, but I have the impression they can even show photographs. I don't know if you need a special computer to get them, but just think! Miriam, have you seen this? In your work with the computers?"

Miriam protested that she was a technophobe in disguise, and Doug could practically hear the creak of Zee's eyes rolling beside him. "Some of my *planning* is on the computer," Miriam said, "but then it's all hand work."

"Tell them about the secrets!" Bruce said. "All her secrets are under there!"

Miriam's neck turned red. "Oh. Behind the materials," she said. "After I've outlined my shapes, and before the mortar, I write a secret in paint. People like knowing it's there, I think. If a buyer asks, I'll sometimes tell what it said."

Case said, "Secrets about me, right babe?"

"I didn't know it myself, till we read that article last year," Bruce said. "Miriam, have they seen the article?"

Zee said, "It's amazing the secrets people can keep. Isn't it." There was something wrong with her. Doug put his hand on her knee and she jerked away. "I used to think I could tell when someone had a secret. I really did. And it turns out—"

But Gracie shrieked and they all turned to her. "There was a ladybug!" she said. "Right on my plate."

Zee rose from bed like a heavy animal, her legs slow and numb.

Out at the table, the two of them giggling over breakfast. "Happensack—the luckiest town in New Jersey!" Miriam could hardly get her breath.

Doug: "It's the karma that gets you stuck on the turnpike!"

Zee couldn't look at them.

Miriam: "It's a sack full of four-leaf clovers!"

"It's when someone accidentally kicks you in the nuts!"

Doug's book bag lay on the floor. He was headed to the library, he said. She wanted to tear the zipper off, to see what was really inside. Books about adolescent girls, love letters to Miriam, a hundred bags of cocaine. The possibilities were endless.

Instead she said, "Miriam, why don't you meet me for coffee this morning? We haven't had a chance to talk much lately." They'd had nothing *but* chances to talk: right now, for instance, and the million times Zee swept past the sunporch pretending to be absorbed in the mail.

Miriam said, "Oh, lovely," and Zee said, "There's a chance I'll be waylaid by the dean."

And at ten o'clock, with Miriam waiting at Starbucks, with Case off at the doctor, chauffeured by Sofia, Zee drove back to the house and slammed her way into the silent, cold porch. Finished canvases leaned three deep against the walls, but the piece centered

on Zee's yellow cotillion dress was still in progress, laid out on the
floor like a corpse. The black swirls around it were finished—river
stones and coffee beans and checkers and an old Escape key and
barrettes. The dress was only half covered, in yellow but also orange
and little spots of brown and green. The green: It took a minute to
realize why the green looked so familiar. Here were the shards of her
mother's celadon vase, the one Case had knocked to pieces. Had
Miriam even asked to keep these? Had she stolen them that night?
Zee wiggled her thumb under the bottom of the hemline and
yanked up. Stones and scraps flew off, skittered across the floor.
Some of the fabric tore. It was only half a dress, really, as Miriam
had cut the back entirely away. But here were the words, the secrets,
just as Bruce had said. Zee left the dress attached by the left shoulder and read what she could of the black painted script below, ob-
scured by glue, bitten around the edges by the mortar and stones.

> *The hair just below*
> *Your navel*
> *Curls to the left*
> *Let me untwist it*

That was near the top. Farther down, below an unreadable swath:

> *Lick the scars*
> *Up your knees*
> *Taste what*
> *You drank*

And down by the hemline:

> *I forget to look*
> *In mirrors*

My guts have all
Sprung loose

She slapped the dress back down. There was an ugly satisfaction in finding what she'd known she would, despite the sudden light show behind her eyelids that was like the beginning of a migraine, but with a drumbeat.

Zee dragged Hidalgo from the big house. She got saltines from upstairs and sprinkled them all around, behind Miriam's trays of beads, under her papers. Then she shut him in. He might get free, but not before doing a lot more damage and clawing up the windows. He watched her leave, his eyes black and questioning. "Be bad," she said.

Her face, her smile, her breathing, would be fine at the coffee shop. If she could smile at Sid Cole, she could smile at Miriam. As she sped to town she developed the leaden sensation, though, that she hadn't just been right in her fears, but had actually caused something, yet again, to happen. That she'd willed this into being as surely as she'd brought about Cole's implicit confessions. She was getting everything she wanted, but also—like in a nightmare, where you're the author and also the victim—she was getting everything she feared: Miriam's crush, Doug's ineptitude, even the appearance of that stupid dress. She thought, *I need to be careful what I fear next.* And then she thought: *What I fear next is madness. What I fear next is madness. What I fear next is madness.*

31

I'm so glad we can chat," Frieda said, though she didn't sound glad at all. Doug had gone on an absolute tear the past few weeks and finished the two new books, FedExing the diskettes and riding his bike triumphantly home from the post office.

"Something tells me I messed up." He sat down with the phone base in his lap.

"Well, we can fix it. It's not unusual that our writers find their voice and start embellishing a bit, and please take that as a compliment. You're a real writer."

"It was the eating disorder thing."

"The problem, in this case, is that it's the topic of the next book in the series, *What's Eating Molly*, which has already been written. And then—the Cece book is wonderful, you really have an ear for her, but we meant for the character of the neighbor to be peripheral. As it is, you've fleshed him out so much that I think readers would expect him to return."

"Right. Okay."

"What it boils down to, really, is that you've made uninvited changes to the world of the story. And you know, a little thing can have huge repercussions down the line. Someone discovers they're allergic to peanuts, for example, and then five books later—"

"I get it. How long do I have to fix this?"

Frieda sighed—an actual sigh, a rope around Doug's neck. "At this point, you know, you've been fabulous, but we have faster writers, ones who can do this in their sleep. I'm going to bring one of them in, and they'll split the payment."

Doug was surprised how upset he was. There was the money issue, to be sure, the four thousand dollars he'd counted on cut down to two or less, and there was the ignominy of being, essentially, fired. But moreover he felt a sense of failure, of stupidity. He'd messed up something that should have been a piece of cake. And for what? For trying too hard. When here sat his other project, the *real* project, for which he'd accomplished nothing at all beyond breaking and entering.

He poured yesterday's tepid coffee into his thermos. He was searching for milk when he heard Miriam sobbing again, this time from inside the rooms she shared with Case. He was about to make a silent joke about another dead Kennedy when he realized Case was in there with her, that the sobs were covering the rumble of an angry male voice. Doug heard the word *disaster*, and he heard *actually* and *Texas* and *forget it*. He waited longer than he was comfortable, listened for any reason to break down the door: slaps or crashes or sudden screams. But it was just this torrent of words and crying.

Doug started humming loudly as he dumped in a scoop of sugar and shook the thermos up. He gave words to the humming: *This is my cue to leave. This is my cue to leave.* Okay, then. He dug in his desk and found the diskettes that were Edwin Parfitt's prison, and he found the bound copy of his dissertation, and he found last year's research—Xeroxes and notes and outlines. He stuck them in his bag with the thermos. It had taken a punch in the balls from Frieda and Melissa Hopper, it had taken hysterical Texans spooking him from the house, but he would finally get to work.

And what was more: He was done being a baby. If there were files twenty yards away from him, he was going to help himself.

The fund-raiser was a week away, but that was enough time to plan the details. He'd have knocked on Miriam's door right then to tell her so, if she hadn't been indisposed. Instead, he headed out the door and into the rain.

In front of a library computer, he spread things out. He borrowed a stapler and some markers from the front desk. By the end of two hours, he had a plan for a new shape to the book, given that something, anything, could be found in the files. Parfitt was famous (if he was famous for anything, which he wasn't) for periods of hyperproductivity followed by long fallow stretches. This was often attributed to his depression, though Doug had never found any signs of the man's mood swings other than his offing himself—and Doug wondered if he could piece together some other theory, based on the poet's time at MacDowell and Laurelfield and his publication schedule. The MacDowell archives were at the Library of Congress, and maybe he'd be allowed access. Those librarians couldn't be harder to get past than Gracie. And the sickness Parfitt had mentioned in that letter to his niece—there might be something about that in the Laurelfield files. That he'd had to leave early, that he was depressed, that he had some condition like lupus that would have immobilized him for months or years. Perhaps he'd had, like Doug, an invisible troll sitting on his shoulders keeping him from his work—until, one day, the troll hopped off.

As the days grew short, as the ghost stories of the semester piled up in her dreams and (as fifteen-page papers) in her inbox, as she lay awake half the night and walked sleeping through the day, Zee began to wonder if her sanity, her residency in the rational world, wasn't a thin veneer. Something ready, all along, to crack.

She'd always believed she could read Doug like a book, but apparently this wasn't true. She hadn't even known what he was writing. She looked at him in the mornings and wondered who he was.

So what was real? And who was running the show? She used to think she was the one in charge. Now she began to fear this same thing.

She found herself pressing on the kitchen counter to see if it would give way, if it would turn to a liquid or a vapor.

The last weeks of November passed in a dull and angry blur. Chantal asked if she was feeling all right. "No," she said, and walked away.

In the bathroom of the English building, she noticed her arms had grown thin. There she was in the glass above the sink, still visible, fluorescently lit. What had once been a nice, symmetrical face had grown bony and shiny, like a cartoon of an unfortunate stepsister. As she stood at the hand dryer, the tiles on the floor began rearranging themselves, jumping to new spots. No. It was scraps of toilet paper, blown by the hot air.

Doug didn't seem to notice that she'd spoken maybe twelve sentences in the past week. She'd climb into bed and pretend to fall asleep immediately. He'd keep reading for an hour, his face glowing in the lamp and from some deeper contentment too. She found five hundred dollars in his sock drawer and figured he'd gotten it from those horrible books. She wondered if he was spending it on Miriam. She took a fifty from the stack, and used it to buy the bottle of vodka that lived in her office desk for the next week till it was empty.

She walked in to find her ghost seminar in deep debate. Sarah Bonheur was red in the face, practically shouting. "It would be a statement on how this school feels about women," she said. "Like, look at their date rape policy. Oh, excuse me, their *lack* of policy."

Chad Crosley, polo shirt and ratty cap, shorts despite the freezing weather, leaned back and said, with authority, "You know why they'll never fire him? He's an alum."

"*Exactly!* It's the old boys' network. The alum thing is a *male* thing."

Zee, setting down her papers, shook her head. "He's not, Chad. He went to Indiana." Fran was agreeing loudly with Sarah. "Look how long it took them to build sorority houses! Like we're some afterthought. If Dr. Cole is still here after Christmas, I'm transferring."

Zee—maybe it was the swig of vodka before class—snapped. "Look, Fran, you don't know the whole story. We're trying to teach you to think like adults, and you're jumping to conclusions like children." Fran stared, cowed. Zee wondered why she'd just defended Cole, without ever deciding to. "Professor Cole has *nothing* to do with your sorority house, Fran."

Chad, sullen under his cap: "I'm sure that dude's an alum."

Zee had no fondness for Case Breen, but she wanted to cry when she saw him. He lay on the downstairs couch, covered in ice packs, his neck swollen so his chin had nearly vanished. Miriam knelt by his side, and when Zee asked what had happened she lifted the ice packs to show how his face had swallowed his eyes, reduced them to slits.

"He was out walking," Miriam said. "Which he shouldn't have been. You know that bear statue, back in the woods?" Apparently Case, in an effort to avoid the trucks out front, the florists and caterers setting up for tonight's fund-raiser, had circled the rear of the property and taken a rest on the pedestal of the statue. (Zee, in her childhood, had named the bear Theo. She hadn't been back there in ages.) Bees began swarming out from under the thing, and Case, leaving his crutches behind, didn't get far enough fast enough. "He isn't allergic at least, but they took out forty-three stingers. And of course he hurt his ankle again."

"Good God. Really? Bees in November?"

Case made a noise from the couch, low and guttural. His arms were covered with white cream. Zee wondered if he could still talk, but then he said, "Leave me alone. Both of you. Go away."

33

There were two complications at the beginning of the fund-raiser, even after Miriam managed to prop the puffed-up shell of Case in the corner, a scotch in his hand, and leave him to his own devices. The first was that Gracie had recognized Leland, despite his Clark Kent act (shaved face, glasses). But Doug and Miriam had been standing far away, after sneaking him in through the garage, and Leland had preempted her question by saying, "I hope you remember me. I'm Jack Spence, whose life you so kindly saved by letting me photograph your attic. And I'm also a big Gore supporter. When I learned the event would be at your house, I couldn't resist!" Gracie had smiled warmly and introduced him to the lanky state senator holding court by the cheese table. Zee recognized Leland too, but only vaguely. "We've met before," he said, and before he could give her the second speech he'd practiced, she nodded and wandered away.

The second snag was when Zee pulled Doug into the closed-off hallway to Bruce's study, pushed him up against the wall, and unzipped his pants. In seconds he was growing full in her hand, and his brain had turned almost completely off. It was seven fifty-five, and he was supposed to meet Leland and Miriam outside the kitchen at eight o'clock, in the moments right before the speeches started. With every reserve of physical willpower, he peeled his mouth from hers and slid down the wall and zipped back up. "Not here," he said.

By the time he turned back, she'd been replaced by a blade of ice. She wrapped her arms around her stomach and glared so deeply into him that it seemed a serious accusation, an indictment. But he didn't have mental space left to decipher the look. She walked away, and he sat on the couch to wait out his erection.

At a minute past eight, Doug scooted past a scurrying caterer and planted a hand on Leland's shoulder. Bruce was clanking a glass already in the library. The quartet had stopped playing.

Miriam grinned up at Doug, all teeth. This was the happiest he'd seen her since before Hidalgo tore up her work. She had chosen a silver cocktail dress so she could be the one to handle anything dusty, afraid streaks would show on the men's black dress pants. She'd straightened her hair and pulled it back. Leland, meanwhile, was bouncing out of his skin. His pockets were full of the needles and keys he'd cadged from the same friend who'd been tutoring him all week on picking old locks. The three passed through the kitchen to climb the back stairs. The caterers paid no attention. No one was there as they made their way down the silent hall to the attic door. And no one heard as Miriam said, "We're like the Bloodhound Gang!"

And really, that was exactly what it felt like to Doug—that for the first time since maybe college, he had a cohort, and a pack mentality. Earlier, as the room had filled, Doug felt connected to them both by invisible strings. Their eye contact was loaded with a thousand reminders and encouragements.

Doug stood guard at the top of the stairs, and Leland told Miriam she should try the lock first. "I'm sure you have the steadiest hands," he said. There was no time for such gallantry, and Doug saw from the way Leland was rocking on his heels that he couldn't wait to take over, to show off his new skills. "Give me some light," Miriam said, and Leland produced his little pocket flashlight and held it right over her ear. Doug wondered if his heart might actually stop, if the sustained thumping he hadn't endured since his last real soccer game (twelve years ago? thirteen?) might simply kill him, if he might become the next ghost of Laurelfield: *The man who died for no reason in the middle of a party. They found his crumpled body at the foot of the stairs.*

But then he heard a click and a gasp, and he turned to find them both staring at the door, an inch-thick crack of darkness at its open edge. "Jesus!" Leland said. "God, that was impressive! I think I'm in love!"

Doug pulled out his own flashlight, and they passed the switch on the wall without flipping it. They closed the door, careful to test that it would reopen on the way out. "Oh, wow," Miriam said, climbing first, "don't you guys feel that? On the stairs? Don't you feel that presence?"

Leland said, "I can't believe that worked. I can't fucking believe it."

Doug climbed behind the other two, overcome by the unhelpful realization that he wanted out, that it was too much, that he'd rather be down on Bruce's couch getting screwed by his wife, or at the party listening to fund-raising news, or, better yet, in bed with a magazine and a beer. But no: The new Doug *did* things. For instance, the new Doug held the flashlight steady even when Miriam announced brightly, "Hey, there are micies! Don't worry, little guy! Oh, he ran away." And the new Doug was the one who navigated the maze of bed frames and dressers until he came, with awe and recognition, to the four file cabinets forming a crooked little quad by one of the moonlit dormers.

"Okay," Leland said, "say a prayer." And he pulled the top drawer of one cabinet. With a musical creak, it opened. He said, "Give me the light. Okay. Okay. Tisdale, Robin. Tollman, Harold. Tower, Rosamund."

Miriam squealed and threw her arms around Doug's neck, then hugged Leland from behind and tried to peer over his shoulder. They shushed one another and opened more drawers, announced the contents and shushed again. Two entire cabinets held the alphabetized colonist files, and the other two were a jumble of year-by-year records and correspondence. Miriam dove into those, instructed to search specifically through the twenties and thirties, and the men focused on the drawer that would contain both M and P. Because M came first, Leland dug through first. Doug restrained himself from shouting that the Parfitt research was the reason they were up here to begin with. He held the flashlight for Leland. Miriam pulled out files to read their labels by the moonlight.

"Moor, no E," Leland said. "Another Moor, no E. Christ. Oh, Christ. Marlon Moore? *Marlon Moore?* This is what they're going by?" He hefted an enormous file from the cabinet and sat with it on the floor. "Some douchebag named Marlon Moore. There's half a book here. No, literally. There's half a novel. And some idiot thought this was Marianne Fucking Moore."

"Can you scoot over?" Doug said. "We don't have time." He stepped across Leland and pulled the drawer as far as it would go. There it was: Parfitt, Edwin, a hanging file with a white label. It was alarmingly thin, though, and as he pulled it out he feared there would be a single piece of paper inside, an unpaid fifty-cent phone bill.

When he did open the folder there was, indeed, a single sheet, but that sheet was so bizarre he didn't have time to gape at its thinness, its singularity. He didn't say anything at all as he shone his flashlight around the edges. It was a photograph, taken outside. The more he looked at the background, the more he became convinced this was the back corner of the big house, the largest koi pond off to the right, and a bench. But the background was hard to focus on, because the subject of the photo was two men, both stark naked, both dripping wet. One was laughing, head lolled back. The other stared straight at the camera, his grin urgent and almost malevolent. Each man had a hand around the other's penis. And neither man was Edwin Parfitt.

Doug struggled for something to announce, but his brain had short-circuited entirely, and Leland was reading aloud from Marlon Moore's manuscript. "*Rose was mad with grief,*" he said. "Yeah, I'm mad with grief. Listen to this: *One who has not wandered under those titanic pines will scarce comprehend the weight of time that settles on the solitary philosopher seeking shelter 'neath their dripping arms.* The pages are out of order, too. Not that it matters."

"It's eight thirty," Doug said. "We need to load up."

"Did you find Parfitt stuff?" Miriam turned to him, eyes alarmingly bright in the moonlight.

"I'll show you later."

"I've got 1920 through '39, but each year is three inches of stuff. You have to pick."

"Pick for me. No, 1933."

She pulled two files from the drawer. Leland handed Miriam his suit jacket, then loosened the belt of his too-large slacks, and Doug and Miriam worked together to tuck the two thick 1933 folders and the flat Parfitt one into the waistband. Miriam secured the last and tightened the belt, and Leland wiggled his brows over her head at Doug. When he was retucked, jacket covering the bulges, he took a few trial steps.

"What about this, though?" Miriam grabbed a small green lockbox off the top of one cabinet. "This has to be interesting, right?"

Doug had noticed it in Leland's photographs, but he'd been so focused on the promise of Parfitt files he hadn't thought much of it. Now, though, he was willing to try anything.

"Just carry it out," Doug said. It looked natural in Leland's hand, like something he was supposed to be taking from a political fund-raiser. "Walk with authority."

The music started far below. Leland swore and Doug scooped

the Marlon Moore file back into its drawer. Miriam used the dust cloth from Doug's pocket to wipe any sign of activity from the cabinet tops.

Back at the party, with Leland gone right out the front door, Doug and Miriam filtered into the living room, each grabbing coffee and then talking loudly to each other about Bill Bradley. There stood Case, alone next to the grandfather clock. He'd been meant to find Clarence Mahoney, Bruce's friend with all the connections—he'd been banking on it, in fact, on schmoozing his way into a job tonight—but his drained glass and the fact that he didn't seem to have moved were not auspicious. Doug wondered if he could even see the room, with his eyes swollen like that. There was Bruce, cheeks and nose bright red, throwing his arm around someone. There was Zee, keeping a narrow balance as she crossed the room. She put her hand on Doug's tie and slid it down to his navel. Her voice was flat, her face centimeters from his own. "Where were you?"

"I stepped outside for a breather," he said, as planned. But it was freezing out, he realized, and he was drenched with sweat.

Zee just smiled, and slowly turned to Miriam. "Miriam, what did you think of the state senator? The one from the South Side?"

"Oh, the—wasn't he? He was great."

"And the one after him. What was his name again?"

"Oh, you're asking the wrong person!"

Zee said, "Yes. I am."

34

*Z*ee was composing her final exam when Cole knocked on her office door. "Zelda, my one true friend!" he said. "I had to see for myself!" Every wall of her office was covered with pictures of nude men, which she'd had color printed at Kinko's. Some lounged on motorcycles, some touched themselves, some coyly pulled their jeans down to their knees. Cole stood in the middle of the room, turned a slow circle, emitted a long whistle. "They're not for the ladies, are they?" he said. "These pictures are for the fancy boys." Zee had taped them up on Monday, and by Tuesday Jerry Keaton had gone as far as he dared, sticking a postcard of a lingerie-clad Betty Paige on his office door. Ida Hayes, playing it safe but perhaps saying something more profound about the principles at stake, had copied Adrienne Rich's explicit "floating sonnet" for her classes. Golda Blum had come by to advise Zee that if she was being more flagrant than Cole she might expect starker consequences as well. But Golda was only exasperated and stressed. Zee knew when Golda was furious, and this wasn't it.

What Zee had realized, the day she snapped at Fran, was that her support of Cole had shifted from ironic and undermining to genuine. The first letters she wrote on his behalf were designed to make things worse. ("His jokes about wishing to date certain students have been largely misconstrued.") But around the time she realized what Doug was really writing, around the time he began mooning over Miriam, disappearing with her at the fund-raiser, she'd lost all interest in getting him Cole's job. The thought of Doug, undeserving, unambitious, sitting lovestruck in an office he didn't deserve—in Cole's office, the good little corner one, where that man had written real articles, had graded and conferred for twenty years—made her sick. And without Doug to root for, she found it harder and harder to root against Cole, especially when she saw the tenacity with which he fought his case, never once, never *once*, claiming the pornography wasn't his. She regretted, now, what she'd done, but it was a strange brand of remorse—more tactical than moral.

"And why, pray tell, do you possess a pistol cylinder?"

She tried hard to understand, and finally realized Cole was looking down at her desk. The metal flower, from the woods.

She picked it up and looked through the six perfect holes. She felt stupid—hadn't she seen them in a thousand movies?—but Cole didn't need to know that. "Souvenir," she said. "From my last shootout."

And there was Chad Crosley walking in to ask about his C-minus paper, beet red, hands around his eyes like blinders. He'd been warned.

35

Leland's apartment in Evanston smelled pleasantly of cigar smoke. The walls were lined with bookshelves, and an inordinate number of small, dim lamps lit the living room. The three of them sat on the floor, around the neat stack of files and the lockbox. It had been two days since the fund-raiser, but this was the first time they'd been able to meet. Doug had said he was going to the Northwestern library, and Miriam had invented a yoga class.

"Did you read the files?" Doug asked.

"I did better." Leland flicked the lockbox open, and Miriam applauded. "Well, my locksmith buddy did better."

"What's in it?" Doug lifted out the stack of papers and envelopes.

"Nothing good, sorry to say. It's just Gracie's stuff. We can't be this lucky with locks and get lucky with the content too. But you have your Parfitt file, right?"

"You really didn't look? That's amazing restraint." Doug ceremoniously opened the file to reveal the photograph: wet bodies, laughter, penises.

"Jesus God," Leland said. "Is that Parfitt?"

"Not even."

Miriam had gone bug-eyed, and some old rule flitted through Doug's mind, something about not being vulgar in front of southern women. But what she finally said was, "You know what's weird? They don't even have hard-ons. I mean, it's not *sexy*, you know?"

Leland turned it over. "Crap. Did you see this?" He pointed to the spidery handwriting on the back, the single slanted word and question mark: *Father?* "Someone thinks that's their father? It can't be Parfitt's father, right? The photo quality looks like twenties or thirties, at least."

As Leland and Miriam passed the photo, Doug flipped through the lockbox papers. The 1954 deed to a car. A 1955 marriage license for George Robert Grant and Grace Saville Devohr. A copy of Gracie's birth certificate.

"Hey, guys," he said. "How old did you think Gracie was?"

"Sixty," said Leland. "Maybe fifty-eight."

"Sixty-two," Miriam said. "Bruce is sixty-four, and she's two years younger."

"Look." He put the certificate on the floor. "1925. She's seventy-four."

They both squinted at it, with as much voyeuristic glee as they'd ogled the photo.

"So she had Zee when she was forty," Doug said. "But does Bruce really think she's younger than him?"

"Maybe that's why she didn't want you in the attic," Leland said.

Miriam said, "That's why she's afraid of getting put on the Internet! She doesn't want anyone doing the math."

They spent the next hour poring over the 1933 files, and the one major validation for Doug was the fact that at the end of the file lay a document with the heading "Confirmed Guests, Winter 1934," in which "E. Parfitt" was listed, alongside the note "(4th visit)." Although there was nothing he could immediately use, there was the promise of more. And the fact that the records were so detailed boded well for lists of who was there with Parfitt on his other stays, even minus anything meaningful in his own file.

The other artists might even have mentioned him in their own diaries and correspondence. It would be enough for a clever writer to build some analysis around, some stuff about influence—provided he could get back up to the rest of the files. They'd left the attic door unlocked, but they were sure Sofia, ever thorough, would have discovered it by now and said something to Gracie.

They ordered pizza and Leland dialed up his Internet. Their intent was to find Gracie, to see what was already out there about her. Leland had some vague idea that Doug could use her real birth date to his advantage, either by threatening to expose her or promising to protect her, though Doug doubted he had the guts to pull off either. They found a photo of Gracie as a toddler, blonde curls and a white dress; and another of her at eleven or twelve with her three younger brothers, all a bit petulant next to their dour grandfather, Augustus. It was, indeed, dated 1936. ("My God," Miriam said, "see, he's terrifying! Don't you think he murdered Violet?" "No, but I can see why she wanted out," Doug said. And Miriam said, "I'm glad it's her ghost and not *his*.") And then, following Leland's hunch, they looked up Gracie's father, Gamaliel, and studied his face.

"That *could* be him," Leland said. He was holding the photo of the two naked men next to the computer, comparing the stern businessman on the screen with the naked man on the right, the one throwing his head back in laughter. "It's a funny angle."

Miriam said, "And we don't have Gargamel's penis online, for comparison."

"I can't imagine the chain of events, though," Doug said. "Gracie finds this picture, recognizes her father, writes on the back, and then of all things she puts it in Edwin Parfitt's empty file folder?"

"*Or*," Miriam said, "she emptied the folder because she knew you'd get up there. And she put this there instead."

"Does she hate me that much?"

"Why else would this be the only file that's different? Like, where's his confirmation letter? Where's his application?"

They stared a bit longer at the online photo of Gamaliel. He was older, but the chin was right, the ears were feasible. Doug remembered that game from the senior yearbook, match the baby with the eighteen-year-old, and how it had been impossible, except for the one Asian kid. Impossible to identify the people who had been your whole world for four years.

It was getting late, but there was more to discuss: How to return the lockbox to the attic, for instance, before Gracie discovered it was gone. How to get the rest of the files.

Leland said, "Look, you don't need to sneak around anymore. You don't need to pretend you did nothing wrong. You can play your hand."

"I didn't know I had a hand."

"You have—you have some *tools* at least. You know Gracie's real age. You know her father might or might not have gone skinny dipping with a male companion."

Miriam said, "We know she either hates Doug or doesn't want him writing about Laurelfield."

"That's not really a tool," Leland said.

"*You're* a tool."

He pelted her with a pizza crust.

Doug added, "And we know her biggest fears. That civilization ends on the thirty-first, or that it doesn't and the Internet survives."

Miriam nodded slowly. "That's all you need, isn't it? That's all it takes to run the world. Knowing people's fears."

36

(The air between
our bodies

The miles between
intention
and act

The windows, eclipses, forgettings, doorways,
misses and losses and half-slept dreams

The shrinking space between now
And century's end

Here
Under stone
Overboard

I'll tell
the secret I have seen:
The ghosts live in
the space between)

37

On December 31 Zee and Doug walked to the big house, arms full of belated gifts. They'd spent Christmas itself at Doug's mother's house in Pennsylvania, and there, amid the hoarded statuettes and smoke-stained walls, Zee had felt almost normal again. They ate casserole for four days straight, and helped put in storm windows. It didn't feel like a return to stability or even a vacation, though, so much as a stay of execution. They had to come back to Laurelfield to face their lives and their marriage and the end of the millennium. Any number of explosive things.

Gracie had decreed that the millennium would go out with a late Noel, and that all presents must be wrapped in silver and blue to make Miriam more comfortable. ("I don't get it," Doug had said, and Zee had said, "Just because she's Jewish. My mother's an idiot." "Miriam's Jewish?" And when she'd stared at him in disbelief, he'd added, "I guess I just thought of her as Texan." "What, they don't have Jews in Texas?" "No, like 'Don't Mess with Texas.' Like that sort of overrides everything. I don't know." And she'd looked at him hard, trying to figure out if he was really this clueless, or if he thought he needed to pretend, this late in the game, that he hardly knew Miriam. She wanted to tell him he needn't bother.)

They gathered in the living room around the tree, Case and Miriam underdressed in jeans. Case still wore his boot, but at least his face had resumed its normal shape. The golden tan he'd shown up with that summer was long gone, replaced by a sickly gray. Sofia was off, the food she prepared yesterday already reheating in the oven.

There were flashlights and oil lamps lined up on the sideboard, waiting for midnight, and boxes in the kitchen full of food and aspirin and matches and batteries and vitamin C and toilet paper, alongside office-sized bottles of water and a kerosene stove. Bruce kept checking his watch. It was only six thirty, but every hour he turned on the TV to check the march of time and potential disaster. City after city survived. Electricity had stayed on in Beijing and New Delhi and Moscow and Paris. Bruce was convinced now that the real trouble wouldn't start until midnight hit the U.S. east coast, and so that's what they were waiting for: eleven o'clock central, when the Times Square ball would fall and so, presumably, would humanity.

Miriam scooted around the floor like a lithe elf to distribute the packages. For Bruce, a book on subsistence farming. For Gracie, an antique toast rack. When Miriam opened her present from Doug, Zee nearly gagged: a Ziploc bag of sea glass, blue and green and copper. It would have taken him weeks on the frigid beach to collect so much. Miriam said, "I know how I can work them in!" She meant the monstrous thing on the board in the kitchen, the vertiginous patterns she was laying down inch by inch in wet mortar, better than her other work only in that the pieces were tile and glass instead of garbage. Case gave everyone chocolate. Miriam began opening Zee's gift, which was truly awful. Three days ago, Zee had gone back to her office and grabbed the pistol cylinder. It was an antique, of sorts. It was interesting. It was also a nongift. It was, quite literally, an empty threat of violence.

But Miriam didn't seem alarmed. "This is amazing!" she said.

"I thought you could stick pencils in it."

"It has to be ancient. I *love* it."

Zee was chagrined that no one had to ask what it was. Even her mother, after a moment of silence, said, "Zilla, where on earth did you find such a thing?"

And Zee said, "Boston."

There were survival kits from Bruce, sweaters from Gracie, a collection of Marianne Moore poems from Miriam to Doug, with a bizarre inscription: *for walks under those titanic pines*. Doug turned pink. He smiled at his shoes.

And then—as if Zee had done it herself, as if her rage had flown across the room—the window behind the tree shattered into a million raining shards. They kept falling, with a sound like a xylophone, until nothing was left, just a rectangle of night and frigid wind. Gracie stopped shrieking and they all took shelter on the far side of the room. Miriam's arm was cut, and Doug's eyebrow, but not badly. Bruce checked his watch (only seven fifteen, not nearly time for the apocalypse), grabbed a poker, and headed out to make sure it wasn't a thrown rock—but they knew it wasn't, the way the glass had just disintegrated so gracefully, from everywhere at once. Gracie scampered to silence the burglar alarm.

They all moved gingerly for the rest of the night, in case another window shattered. After dinner, Zee cleared the table and snuck back to the living room. Bruce had duct taped a blanket over the window, but the frozen air still crept through. She poured straight vodka into her teacup, and let the tea bag diffuse and turn the liquid golden. She didn't care how it tasted. Bruce retreated to his study to watch the New Year hit whatever Atlantic islands were three hours ahead. Gracie stood in the kitchen, sorting absently through yesterday's mail, throwing away a late Christmas card from distant family in Toronto. "I don't know why they persist in sending these," she said. Back in the dining room, Miriam hovered over Doug's chair, inspecting his eyebrow. Her small breasts were inches from his mouth. "I'm worried there's a sliver still," she said.

Zee pretended to read Bruce's *Tribune* and then circled back to the dark living room again, her teacup empty. She'd already started to pour when she noticed Case standing silent with his crutches by the blown-out window. If she hadn't been numbed from the alcohol, she'd have screamed.

"Would you like a drink?" she said.

Case's face was ravaged, sunken, nothing but eye sockets and cheekbones. It was hard to remember the way he used to smirk at everything.

She tried again. "Case, I'm sorry about all of it. You've had terrible luck. No one deserves that."

"You know what's funny?"

She shook her head.

"As soon as someone says *luck*, you know we're not really talking about luck anymore. If it were luck, the coin would come up heads half the time. Right? It would balance."

"But it never does."

"I just think *luck*'s the wrong word. When we bother talking about it, we mean there's been a whole string of good things or a string of bad things. Like the coin keeps coming up tails."

"So maybe what we mean is fate."

"You know about her, don't you? You know about her."

"Oh. Oh, Case." It was terrible: She honestly hadn't given him much thought in all this. He had it worse than her, home all day to see it, no job. "I *do* know. Case, I'm sorry. I—everyone's going to get through this." She brought him a glass of vodka, which he took and held like he didn't know what it was for.

Case said, "She put her finger on my lips." He reached out one finger and actually pressed it right to Zee's mouth before she could move, before she could even register his words. His eyes were wild and green, fixed on hers. Zee took his hand as gently as she could and removed it from her face. "And you've seen her too, I know you have. She comes to you too."

Zee regretted the alcohol fog that wasn't quite allowing her to shift paradigms. He couldn't be talking about Miriam, could he? He looked like he might cry, actually cry. "Are you talking about Violet?"

He shrugged, humiliated, and didn't answer.

"Case, I think you need to see a doctor. This house can get to people, but no, I haven't seen—not *literally*. Not like that."

He was devastated, she could tell. However difficult it was for him to say all this, he'd been counting on her understanding, on some kind of validation.

"This place doesn't want me," he said. "It's rejecting me. Like a transplanted organ."

"You shouldn't be here. You should go back to Texas." She said it purely out of concern, and only afterward remembered that this was what she'd wanted all along.

He blinked down at the vodka. "Miriam won't leave. This is the happiest she's ever been. This is the best work she's ever done."

She wished she could tell him that it wasn't the house, that Miriam was only happy because she was in love with Doug, and it was the wrong kind of happiness. But she couldn't do that to him right now. "Tomorrow, if the world doesn't end. Bruce will loan you guys money, right? Go home and get healthy."

But now Gracie was in the doorway saying "*There* you are," and asking who would join Bruce for a spin in the '57 Chevy "before the streets get dangerous."

Case said he would, and he handed Zee the vodka and walked from the room like a broken marionette. Zee went back to the dining room, where Miriam and Doug both still sat. Their whispering stopped the moment she appeared. But she wasn't there for *them*, she wished they knew. She walked around to the back wall, to the portrait of Violet. If the artist had been less skilled, her great-grandmother might have remained as flat and uninteresting as any other ancestor. Instead, her skin glowed and her mouth hovered before some small movement, as if she were just now about to say something she'd held in these past hundred years. Zee tried to look at Violet straight on, but Violet was always looking somewhere else.

It was frustrating. Because (and maybe it was just the vodka) Zee needed that moment of silent communication. She had a question for Violet today, a hypothesis she wanted confirmed in this most unscientific of manners. *You aren't even the ghost,* she wanted to ask, *are you? Something drove you crazy in this house, and it's the same thing killing Case, and it's the same thing driving me mad. Everyone in this house is crazy. And look at the blown-out window, the strangling ivy. It isn't you. This is why I felt fine in Pennsylvania. Something's wrong with this house. Something's broken. Things don't work normally here.* (If the semester weren't over, she'd float the idea by her seminar: not a haunted house, a haunting house.)

But Violet avoided her eyes.

38

At ten thirty, fortified by bourbon, Doug asked Gracie if he could speak to her in the solarium. Gracie had been drinking champagne since six, and Miriam had made sure to refill her glass every time it was even halfway empty, till she was wobbly and glassy-eyed. Miriam ran interference now on everyone else, making sure they stayed in the den, where the TV replayed the celebrations from the International Dateline and points west. Doug and Gracie sat on the long white couch and he said, "I have an offer for you. A good one."

She looked skeptical. She said, "If this is about your employment situation, I can't do more than I already am."

"No. It's—I think you know that I've been in the attic."

Her hand fluttered to her forehead.

"I shouldn't have, I know, but please understand how important this is for me. Those archives are the whole meat of the book. But I'll get back to that." He pushed his fists into his knees. "While I was up there, quite by accident, I also found some personal papers of yours."

"Oh, Douglas." She started looking for her champagne glass. Doug found it on the floor and handed it to her.

"And I did figure some things out. I want to help you. In exchange—I mean, I know you're nervous about the Internet. I checked, and it's already out there. It says you're seventy-four. We can't change what's already there. But if it's important to you, there are ways to create alternate timelines, to get those circulated as well, to confuse things. I have a friend who does Internet stuff. I want to help you. I do."

Gracie leaned back, her eyes closed. She looked pale—fine wrinkles on top of tissue-paper skin on top of a sudden gray bloodlessness—and he felt he should be taking care of her, getting her a blanket, rather than tormenting her like this. But then she sat up and leaned toward him. She tapped his leg.

"Douglas, you're clever. And I'm smarter than I seem. I want you to know that."

"I'm sure we can strike a reasonable bargain." He was glad Miriam and Leland weren't there to hear how ridiculous he sounded.

"Those papers are just a joke. People with our kind of wealth, we need other documents sometimes. *Alternate* documents."

"But that would be illegal."

"Not at all. Bruce is smart with these things, and he has lawyer friends."

"Gracie, I'm talking about *old* documents. Long before you knew Bruce."

Miriam had told him just to stare Gracie down if he was at a loss. He pressed his thumbs together and looked right at her. She gave a high laugh, a sound like a teacup hitting the floor.

"Well. Are you trying to ask for money, Douglas? You've never been direct."

"I just want the colony files."

"What files?"

He said, with as much conviction as he could summon, with an edge of threat that surprised him when he heard it: "The Parfitt files. You know exactly what I mean, because you're the one who replaced them."

Gracie looked furious now, which was at least a development, if not an admission. She said, "I don't know what on earth you're talking about. *Replaced* them!"

"I went searching, and instead of what I should have found—"

"Douglas, I've been good to you."

"And that's why I know we can help each other."

"What precisely did you find?" The downside of her champagne consumption, he realized, was that she'd become difficult to read. He didn't want to anger her further by implying that her father was gay, so he tried to word things carefully.

"I found—I mean, you must know. It was those two people who—I don't know who they were, exactly. Two people, here at this house. Doing something very strange, very unorthodox. You *do* know what I mean. And please don't lie to me."

Gracie took a breath so deep that Doug worried about her ribs. "The world's about to end, isn't it? One way or the other." She was so small on the other end of the couch. She said nothing for a long time, and Doug wondered if the question wasn't rhetorical after all. Then she said, "But you have to understand that there was *no* point calling the police. Douglas, there was a lipstick mark halfway down the top of her dress. That's how far her neck had snapped. The car was like an accordion."

Doug had the horrible feeling that he'd jumped down the wrong rabbit hole, that the prospect of Edwin Parfitt was growing dimmer and dimmer as he fell. All he could think to say was "Oh."

"It was the worst thing I'd seen in my life." She was crying, he saw with horror. Her eyes were pink. He felt like hyperventilating himself, and it was only his utter confusion that kept him pinned to the couch, that kept him from breaking down over lipstick and accordions himself. "But you *do* know it was an accident. I'd die if you thought otherwise. Max would never have let him take the car if he knew Grace was in it. He didn't answer the phone—he wouldn't answer the phone—but he didn't know it was *her*."

There was a paper napkin in Doug's pocket, and he unfolded it and handed it to her and tried to rewind those last sentences, tried to guess whether speaking of herself in the third person was a rhetorical flourish or a sign of mental breakdown.

He said, idiotically, or perhaps brilliantly, "Max wouldn't have let him. If he knew Gracie was in it. The car."

"She was always *Grace*. Oh, she was a fool. No one got divorced in 1955, but still, I remember thinking there was something wrong with her that she didn't leave him. He was terrible. A *terrible* person."

Doug wished he had Leland on an earpiece, telling him what to say. He managed: "How so?"

"Oh, you know, a drunkard." She was still crying, but there was a gossipy edge to her voice now, a mean one. She spoke quickly. "That's why the family left them alone out here. They *never* came to check on her. Not *once*. They died not long after— the father, and then the mother a few years later—and the brothers didn't care for her a fig. But Douglas, that family! They made it easy for us, by not caring. Half the time she was hiding a black eye. He tried me, but I could handle him. I knew about drunks. My father was in *jail*, Douglas. Can you believe that? George never dared mess with me."

George was Zee's father, the gentle man who had taken Zee on the train to the Art Institute once a month. Doug knew he'd once had a drinking problem, but he'd never heard of any violence. And Gracie's father might indeed have been jailed once or twice—the Devohrs were never long out of the gossip columns in those days—but none of it, together, made sense. Hidalgo trotted in and stuck his nose in Doug's crotch.

"And what would we have done, if we hadn't stayed? The family would have come and covered the furniture with white sheets. They'd have been in no hurry to sell. We'd have been out on our ears. And Max would have died. It would have *killed* him to leave, I really believe that. He was a true gentleman. You should have seen how he turned the pages of the newspaper: He picked up the corner with his finger and thumb, and just lifted it over. Everyone I'd ever known turned pages with their whole palm, like something they were wiping away. It wasn't a *romantic* relationship we had. But it was better than most, and Zilla is something. We wanted her so badly. She was born ten years later, exactly. I always took it for a sign. Ten years."

Doug tried to think if he'd ever heard of someone named Max. He managed to push Hidalgo away and lock his knees against further attack. He said, "Who else knows all this?" As if he himself knew it, or understood it, or had any idea how much of it was a joke.

Gracie shook her head. She was looking at some spot near Doug's face, but not at Doug. "Max, until he died. I suppose the gardener knew. I always guessed Max bribed him, but I said I wanted no part of it. The hole for the greenhouse was already dug, but the cement wasn't poured yet. So it was all done the next day, just Max and the gardener. I hid upstairs, but I could hear the wheelbarrows crunching along the drive to the big house. *Wheelbarrows.*" She covered her nose and mouth with her hands and closed her eyes. The sound of wheelbarrows was apparently the worst part, to her. "And he fired the rest of the staff. *Big* tips, of course. More money than they'd ever seen. And hired new people."

Miriam poked her head in the door just then. If she'd overheard anything, it was only that last sentence. "Ten fifty-five. Five minutes till doomsday, east."

"We're just finishing up," Doug said, though he didn't know if that was true.

Miriam raised an eyebrow—Doug's face must have looked as ashen as it felt—and ducked out.

"I need you to know it hasn't been *easy*, Douglas. Especially at first. The research we had to do, the places we had to avoid. It helped that she'd *never* shown her face in town, and they'd only been here a few months. Those ridiculous sunglasses. And he was always off in Highwood, drinking. They looked nothing alike. George and Max. But it didn't matter a bit, in the end. People see what they expect to. And the rest can be handled with money. Still, if you think I haven't had a thousand heart attacks along the way. And the close calls, the parties where someone was from Toronto and I'd have to get sick and leave. It's stolen *years* from my life."

Doug took a risk. "So it's—under the greenhouse." He wasn't sure at all what he was referring to, but the remote possibility remained that it was something to do with Parfitt. Or else why the missing file? He looked over his shoulder, at the sliding glass doors that separated the solarium from the greenhouse. He could see a few geraniums out there, borrowing some of the indoor light.

"Yes. Both of them. Good lord. If you want the real ghosts of the house, it's those two, not poor old Violet."

"Those two, meaning—"

"They made that window shatter, you know. They've done it before."

And there was Bruce at the door, waving urgently. "Come on!" he shouted. "This is the big one!"

As they hurried down the hall after him, Doug realized he hadn't gotten a single answer about Parfitt. He didn't understand what she was saying, but he believed her. He just had no idea what it was he was supposed to believe. What ingredients he'd just swallowed. He wanted to march Gracie back to the solarium and lock the door, to ask her fifty more questions, but first he needed to see if the world was ending. He was less certain of its survival than he'd been an hour ago.

Zee and Miriam and Case sat on the leather couch, staring at Dick Clark and the drunken masses in Times Square. No one on the screen seemed particularly panicked. They jumped around in the cold, kissing strangers.

Doug and Bruce and Gracie stood with their hands on the couch back, braced for some kind of impact.

The ball came down, and the world did not end.

President Clinton addressed the nation. Bands played, proposals abounded, and after a soothing update about the absence of nuclear meltdowns, the station switched over to the Chicago team and the depressingly anticlimactic forty minutes they had to fill until midnight Central from the floor of a balloon-filled ballroom.

Case said, "We're still here." Something odd about his voice, as if he wasn't entirely sure of the fact. Or as if he was disappointed to find himself still alive, still on the couch, the lights still on.

Bruce turned down the volume and spoke for the first time. "Well, you never know," he said. There was phlegm in his voice. "You never know what could still happen. But it looks like a lot of bullshit, doesn't it? It looks like a great deal of human folly here this evening."

"It never hurts to be prepared," Gracie said.

"And the things we bought—the car, the food, the water— they're not useless. I'd always wanted that Chevy, all my life."

They nodded. Doug was afraid Bruce would start weeping. He couldn't handle any more of that tonight.

"You know what else? We've lost sight of something, with all this millennium bullshit, with all the computer nightmare. We're forgetting that this is the end of a *century*. The worst century, I believe, in all of human history. Hitler, Stalin, genocide, the worst warfare in what, a million years of human life on this planet."

"But a lot of good, too," Miriam said.

Zee turned to face her. "Oh? Like what?"

"Penicillin? And all the art. Think of, you know, Georgia O'Keeffe. And jazz, and movies! And airplanes. All of it."

Gracie said, "It's the house's birthday. Did you know that? This house is a hundred years old now."

"I don't think they built it on New Year's, Mom."

"They started building in nineteen hundred!"

"What do you think, Doug?" Bruce's voice was a little off, a little too loud. He put down his rum with a clatter and undid his collar. "You're the writer here. Was the twentieth century a comedy, or a tragedy?"

"Or a tragicomedy," said Zee.

Doug said, "I don't know." He was still thinking about Gracie, and didn't trust himself to form a coherent sentence.

"Well, I think it was a tragedy," Bruce said. "An absolute and gruesome tragedy. The whole damn century would've made more sense backward. Where we've ended is worse than where we began."

Miriam said, "Maybe it was a love story."

Doug was so busy watching Zee sneer at Miriam that he didn't see Bruce collapse on the floor beside him. He heard Gracie scream, and there was Bruce, his right arm flapping, his face pale and wet.

Case ran to the phone, and for the five minutes it took the ambulance to get there, Gracie kept shrieking that someone should do CPR, and Zee kept calmly explaining that you could only perform CPR on a dead person and Bruce wasn't dead.

Doug monitored Bruce's pulse, which was weak but consistent, and tried to remember what other medical skills he'd been taught in his 1985 training for YMCA camp counselor. Hidalgo ran in circles and barked.

Miriam managed to let the paramedics in through the triple-locked doors, and as they carried the stretcher through the house Hidalgo lunged at it again and again with his front paws, until one of the men sent him flying with a knee to the sternum. Bruce was stable as they carried him out, conscious and wheezing and trying to lift his head.

Gracie rode in the ambulance. Once she was out the door, Doug suggested that Zee drive with Case in Gracie's car, and he and Miriam follow in the Subaru. "Someone needs to put Hidalgo in his cage," he said. The job would take twenty minutes of bribery and wrestling, and required at least two people. "We'll come right behind." Zee shot him a withering look he couldn't quite interpret, but she grabbed Case's elbow and steered him out the door.

Miriam held up her hand to show it shaking. If she'd been closer to her father-in-law he would have waited, but he couldn't hold it in. "You won't believe this," he said.

As they turned off the TV (seven minutes to midnight) and the lights, and constructed a trail of Milkbones to Hidalgo's kennel in the mudroom, he repeated what he could. He knew he was leaving things out, and he told her at least three times about the man named Max and the way he turned the newspaper pages.

"I was totally drawn in," he said. "I couldn't think straight. You'd have done a better job. Anyone would've."

Miriam spun in circles, trying to catch Hidalgo's red leather collar. "So basically her story is she can't be seventy-four because she's really some other person?"

"I believe that was the gist of it. She kept talking about 'Grace' like that wasn't her. So allegedly Grace *died*, I think? In the car crash. And someone else died too. I don't know if she said it was George, but that was what I got. She said 1955."

"Hmm. Those are the principles of a good lie. Tell a big one, and throw in details. Hidalgo! Sit! Hidalgo!"

"Right. So you—you think she was lying."

"She gave you one excuse for the papers, and when you didn't believe it she gave you another, complete with tears and melodrama. She told you *nothing* about the files?"

Doug felt like an utter idiot. He'd become a dimwitted television viewer, sucked into a soap opera and too distracted by the amnesia and stolen identity and ghosts to realize he'd just watched five ads for laundry detergent. Gracie had warned him, hadn't she? That she was smarter than she looked. But no, it had been real. It had *felt* real.

"She was crying," he said. "I can't explain—it wasn't like she was making something up. She was letting something out." He got Hidalgo straddled for one second, but in the next Doug was falling into the wall and Hidalgo was again circling frantically.

"It's insane. I mean, for many reasons. Not one person in the whole town saw they weren't the real Grants? Not one family member suspected something funny?"

"I didn't tell that part right. The woman, Grace, she always had a black eye, because the husband hit her, and he was always out drinking. So they didn't go into town. And the family didn't visit." He wasn't sure if he was defending Gracie's story, or only his own credulity, however fragile.

"I'm not buying it. Hidalgo! Biscuit!"

If Miriam didn't believe it, *Miriam*, who believed houses had souls, who wouldn't write anyone a letter when Mercury was retrograde, then was he the most gullible man in the world? But his narration was flawed. Nothing new there. He had made uninvited changes to the world of the story.

In one ninja-fast move, Miriam wrapped her fingers through Hidalgo's collar and pushed his backside until he stood, stunned and whimpering, in his kennel.

"Impressive," Doug said. He checked his watch. "In fact, that was officially the best dog-wrangling of the twenty-first century."

"Of the millennium!" Miriam said. "Happy New Year."

They sat with Zee a long time in the ER waiting room, watching Ricky Martin gyrate soundlessly on the overhead TV. Case came out at two-thirty to lead them to the ICU, where chairs lined the end of the hallway. Places for people to get bad news. Gracie was in one, her legs crossed at the ankle, her pocketbook clutched on her lap.

"He's still stable," she said. "It was a massive coronary. Doesn't that sound dramatic? But they've got the best doctors in there. Bruce and I are big supporters of this hospital, and not for nothing. Douglas is going to help me get some coffee now, because in my nervous state I can't pour a thing."

She held his arm all the way down the corridor and around the corner. She stopped and clenched both his shoulders in her hands. She was sharply sober. "It should go without saying," she said, "that what passed between us was privileged information." He feared for a moment that she'd guessed what he told Miriam. But no, it was just a warning. "You do know which side your bread is buttered on. If this information were to get out at all—*at all*—there would be Devohr cousins descending on us in an instant. Like locusts. *You'd* be homeless, among other things. Not to mention, it would kill Zilla."

He said, "I wouldn't dream of repeating—"

"Good. And I want you to know that while I wouldn't cheapen our relationship by paying you off, I do guarantee that if you hold your tongue, I'll make it worth your while in the long run."

He wanted to ask if there was some medication she'd been neglecting, and he wanted to ask if she thought he was a moron, and at the same time he wanted to tell her he believed every word. But here was his opportunity. "All I need is the colony files in the attic. Just the key to the attic, really." Doug saw dimly, through the fog, that he was demanding things from a woman whose husband was in Intensive Care. He was a bad person.

"Oh, for Pete's sake. Of course. Run and get me coffee, though. Cream and sugar."

Doug practically floated to the cafeteria, and although he told himself several times that he should be worried about Bruce, all he could think of was that key, and those files, and of how he'd relate Gracie's vehemence to Miriam later.

He returned with a thin cup of scalding coffee. Back in the ICU corridor, they were all standing: Zee with her hands on her hips; Miriam clinging to Case; Case pale and thin; Gracie with her hand to her forehead; two doctors, one tall, one short. As Doug approached the group, Zee turned and glared. "He's dead," she said. As if it were Doug's fault. As if Doug, in those five minutes, had betrayed them all.

39

That ridiculous cup of coffee, that flimsy prop. When it was obvious to everyone—humiliatingly, glaringly—that even in the midst of her crisis, her husband *dying*, Gracie had felt the need to drag Doug aside and upbraid him for his brazenness, for staying behind with Miriam to wait for midnight, to kiss her at midnight, to be with her alone in case the world ended, to leave Zee an abandoned fool at the end of the world. When Zee and Case had met her in the ER, Gracie had grabbed her arm so frantically, asking where was Doug, and Zee saw that she *knew*. No one could hide anything from her mother.

They went into the room, first Gracie and then Case and then all of them, and there was Bruce, still so pink, so sweaty, the hairs in his nostrils still wet, his fat hands resting so lightly on the sheet, that he couldn't possibly be dead. They should have waited an hour, till he was bluer and smaller.

The nurse said, "There's been a whole lot of heart attacks, the last few days. A lot of stress right now." As if it were all the rage.

Case, behind Zee, said quietly: "This is my fault." Zee turned and saw that Miriam was over near Doug—of course—and he must have been saying it just to her, to Zee.

She whispered back: "That's not true, Case."

"You know it is. I'm a lightning rod. I *told* you."

She pulled him away from the bed. The others were talking to the nurse. She said, "Case, I used to hate you, I really did, with your little car and your haircut, but—you didn't do it. It's not your fault." She should have stopped there. She didn't. "You just need to get away from that house. I mean, especially now. Why stay?"

Zee was asking herself as much as she was asking him, but he was the one who turned and crutched his way out of the room. She didn't follow.

Gracie leaned over the bedrail, gazed at Bruce's face with her blue eyes huge and dull, but she didn't make any noise. When Zee's father died, Gracie had folded up like a clever piece of ori-gami, right in a hallway of this same hospital, and Zee stood there, twelve years old, stroking her mother's hair and waiting to feel something more violent, more physical, herself.

She marveled at the difference in Gracie's reactions, at her stolidity now, her asking the nurses what she needed to sign and how soon the body would be moved. But of course Zee's father had been her first love, and they'd been so *deeply* in love. And his illness had been drawn out—*protracted* was the word—and he'd been in pain for months, his body weakened by those early years of heavy drinking, his liver and spleen finally both giving way.

Her father was a good man, maybe the only good man she ever knew. He was gentle and quiet, and in third grade when her friend Ellen said he was just like Mr. Rogers, only smaller, Zee said, "You're totally right!" and wasn't offended at all.

He took her to the Art Institute and showed her the hidden woman behind Picasso's blue guitarist. He taught her to handle books like precious objects, never to dog-ear. He told her long, fantastic stories, and if she sat in his lap she could sometimes hear a coin clinking against his teeth.

What would he make of her life? He'd be proud of her work, she was certain, proud of her commitment to dissecting power structures and money and class. He who had vetoed the Chip-peway Club. The grounds crew and maids he hired (of necessity, or the house would fall apart) were always starving artists who did a terrible job for which he overpaid them. He'd be sad at the spiral she was in. And he'd be disappointed that she'd abandoned her name. By twelve, the burden of the nickname Godzilla became too much, and so after his death she reduced herself to the sound of a single letter. He had named her, and she had lost her name, and for some reason this made her sadder than anything else. He had loved that house, and she had tried to come home, but it was destroying her. She began sobbing. She went for a walk through the halls.

When she came back, there were Doug and Miriam and Case in a little triangle. Miriam was saying, "You need to lie down. Why don't I drive you home?"

"Just dizzy," Case said. "I'm not tired." He looked up and saw Zee. His eyes were flat little plates that reflected no light at all.

Doug said, "Case, sit down. You're going to pass out."

He didn't move.

"You look terrible," Doug said.

Case didn't even look at him, just kept staring at Zee. She ought to have said something reassuring about the laws of the universe, about cause and effect. (The things she wasn't sure she believed in anymore.) But Doug kept talking.

He said, "I'll drive you."

Case said, "No, man, I'm good." Then he looked at Miriam, a terrible look, and said, "You can have it, Mir."

Miriam sat on the floor and put her head in her hands. Her shoulders started moving up and down.

Doug said, "What? She can have what?"

Case walked right past Doug, right past Zee, and out of the hospital.

In the big window at the end of the corridor, the sun was coming up on the twenty-first century. New nurses were starting the morning shift.

40

Though Case came back to town for the funeral and posted himself next to Miriam in the church, he wasn't staying in the coach house. Doug was reminded of Hamlet, skulking back to the graveside before heading into more tragedy. Doug didn't understand what had happened that night at the hospital, or the next day, when Miriam shut herself in the sunporch and Case packed things into duffel bags and headed off in a cab. He worried it was his fault, that something he'd said in the hospital hallway—what had he even said?—had broken their marriage in two.

Zee implied there was more to it, that she'd seen this coming. But Zee was always seeing things he wasn't.

Miriam moved slowly in the next weeks, fragile and unfocused—but she didn't have that wild look of someone who's reliving a shock again and again. Whatever it was that had gone bad, she'd already figured it out ages back. There were purple circles under her eyes, but Doug never heard her crying.

She worked only occasionally on the kitchen mosaic they'd come to call the Happensack, and spent most of her time on a series of Gothic mansions, cross-sectioned like dollhouses. She used bigger scraps and tiles, creating flaps that lifted to show secret rooms beneath. Sometimes there would be a second, smaller door behind the first. One piece was based on *Jane Eyre*: a mad face painted on a button, peering from an attic window. Another was *The Secret Garden*, another was *Rebecca*, and a fourth was Laurelfield itself, the big house and coach house, built from symbols of luck both good and bad: clovers, acorns, rabbit's foot keychains, broken mirrors, pennies, toy ladders, and—most disturbingly to Doug—hundreds of ladybugs she'd swept from the floor, their faded bodies forming the borders between the rooms.

Doug cooked dinner for all three of them every night, and Zee would take her pasta or soup back to her desk. She wasn't comfortable with grief. Doug ate with Miriam at the kitchen table, and when they talked it was about music or celebrities or *Seinfeld*.

They watched *Bluebeard* again together, and she pointed out the scenes where Marceline Horn looked sick. They paused the movie to study her face, then fast-forwarded. At double speed, the two sisters ran to the tower to lock themselves away from Bluebeard. At double speed, Bluebeard beat down the door.

Both Gracie's story and the subject of the colony files had been put on ice for now. Nor could Doug claim the attic key yet. Gracie was barraged with a stream of visitors and fruit baskets and hadn't emerged much from the big house. And to bring up the story with Miriam would be to bring up New Year's Eve, the night that her world did, after all, come to a halt, even as the rest of the planet kept spinning. Doug promised Leland he'd fill him in when things settled, when he had time to digest the bizarre changes of fortune that had befallen everyone in the house. Everyone but Zee, really. She was the only one whose life wasn't massively altered for better or worse. But Zee had always been above the sways of fortune.

And so it was three weeks later that Leland finally came for dinner, and the Bloodhound Gang reunited. Zee was at a conference in New York, and Doug made flatbreads. As they opened the second bottle of wine, Miriam brought her materials up to work on the Happensack, and the men sat watching her and discussing Gracie's story. Doug had made sure this time to tell it slowly and accurately, hoping he could get Miriam to understand what it was he'd heard that was so persuasive. But when he finished, it was Leland who spoke. "What an amazing load of bullshit! Did Scooby-Doo pop out and rip off her mask?"

"I'm just saying it was convincing, the way she told it. At least she *thinks* it's true."

Leland took a long sip of wine. "She hears the wheelbarrows 'going off' to the big house, right? Meaning she was *here*, in the coach house. So she's what, a maid or something?" He hit the table. "Can you imagine Gracie in a maid outfit? Can you imagine her *cleaning*? Okay, and we have this Max, and we have a gardener. And Max has something to do with the car. And the phone. If it's 1955, how old is Gracie? If she's really sixty-two right now."

Doug calculated. "Eighteen."

Leland was having fun, it was clear. And possibly showing off for Miriam. She was inscrutable, though, focused on her tessellations. "And then there's Grace Devohr and George Grant. They're married, they've just moved here, right?"

"The colony closed at the end of '54," Doug said. "So it fits."

"And no one in the entire town knows them. And they get in a car crash."

"Somewhere close, I think," Doug said. "Like, on the property."

"So Max and the gardener roll their bodies away in wheelbarrows, and bury them under the greenhouse."

"Oh, *God*," Miriam said. "Can we not?"

"I'm just sorting the bullshit from the baloney here. And then follows the most brilliant identity theft of all time. Max and Gracie—whatever her real name is, Molly the Maid—become the Grants. So Zee's parents—Zee's the daughter of some maid and butler. Not a Devohr at all. I love it! And no one suspects anything for *forty-four years*. Eleven presidential terms."

Doug said, "Well, yeah. Yeah. But honestly, why *would* they suspect? Look, it doesn't have to be *likely*. It just has to be *possible*. I mean, we think it's hard to get away with crimes because we only ever know the stories where someone gets caught. So we think everyone gets caught. But we have no idea how much never comes to light."

"*Maybe*," Leland said, pointing a finger at him, and for a moment Doug thought he was serious, "maybe Gracie is really Marianne Moore. She'd only be about a hundred ten."

Doug said, "Look. Look around this town. You think *all* the millionaires in this town came by their money honestly? You think there were no Cayman accounts, no fraud? I'm just saying weirder things happen every day. And why would she make up a lie that's self-incriminating? When you lie, you make yourself sound *good*. Not like a felon."

"God," Leland said. "Suddenly you're a Baptist preacher."

They looked to Miriam for a verdict. She turned from the Happensack to face them, balanced in a squat. "I've been thinking about it. A lot. And no, I don't believe her. Because people don't reveal everything the first time you push them. If you think you're caught, you only tell *half* the story. Right? But that means whatever she's covering is *worse*, or more embarrassing. Something about the colony, maybe. Because that's the one thing she won't even talk about."

Leland said, "Who wants to bet the colony was a front for a sex club!"

"Sex club, arts colony," Doug said. "What's the difference."

But Miriam didn't laugh. She went back to her mosaic, and they watched in silence as she arranged a two-inch square section on a cookie sheet, using tweezers, and pressed a sheet of sticky contact paper to the top. She spread the mortar quickly on a new patch of board, then pushed the sheet of tiles into it, holding it in place a minute. When she peeled the contact paper away, the pieces were embedded. It was hypnotic: both the way she worked and the Happensack itself. Doug grew dizzy if he stared too long at the unending pathways, the shapes that were clear one second and dissolved the next into chaos. She had incorporated Zee's pistol cylinder into the bottom right corner, sticking a piece of glass in each compartment. It looked like a flower.

Miriam finally said, "For instance. Let's say the real Grants truly died. How do we know their deaths were accidents? It's much more likely the servants killed them."

Leland said, "Don't eat any food she cooks."

Miriam told him to stop.

Down on the sunporch, they turned on Miriam's computer. They were hoping for a wedding photo of Grace Devohr and George Grant, or any adult photo at all, really, but they had no luck. Doug had brought down the photo from Zee's dresser, the one of her reading with her father, its frame still showing the cracks he'd fixed back in grad school. But there was nothing to compare this picture with. She was about five, so George Grant (based on the marriage license) should have been forty-seven. This man looked closer to sixty—his hair gray, his face well carved. Even Leland and Miriam had to admit it. But then he had those puckish features that can make a man look either older or younger than he is.

Doug had always been drawn to his face, this father-in-law he'd never met. It was his wife's face, sharp and quick. Small eyes, round ears. He'd always felt he could picture George Grant moving, could hear his voice. Now, Doug tried to imagine this man starting life as someone named Max, someone in charge of the cars. The same driver he'd pictured so many times as he sat in the old Morris chair, the man dreaming of faraway lands. So perhaps Max had reached those lands, ending his days as master of the mansion, critic of the arts, father of a golden child. Doug wanted to believe that life could be like that.

Something had occurred to him: Zee's middle name was Devohr. It might have been a way to cement Zee's inheritance, if any questions arose later. It might have been a joke or homage or apology. But Leland and Miriam would only have used this information as proof of Gracie's lying—and he surprised himself by saying nothing, protecting the story as if it were his own.

"So what's next?" Leland said as he left. It was funny how they all assumed they'd reunite immediately. But it felt as natural as if these had been Doug's college roommates, back when "Where are we going tonight?" was not a presumptuous question.

Miriam rubbed her hands together. "Tomorrow's the day Doug gets the rest of the files," she said. "It's time."

With Leland gone, with the kitchen quiet, Doug was antsy. The little house was a boat in icy water. As he helped Miriam put away her tiles, she said, "I have to admit I'm a little freaked out."

"Don't let Leland get to you."

"It's not—it's just everything." She looked a little shaky. "Would it be weird if we camped here, in the kitchen? I've got sleeping bags. You could leave once I'm asleep. I mean, like, far apart sleeping bags, not—"

"It wouldn't be weird."

Miriam brought out the two shiny blue mummy bags she and Case used for camping back in Texas. They put one on each side of the kitchen table, separated by a little forest of chair legs. Lying there, the finished bits of the Happensack glowing in the light from the window, they talked for another hour.

"I think part of my skepticism," Miriam said, "a *small* part, is Gracie's sense of entitlement. Some of the things she *says*! Remember what she said about my teeth?"

"I don't know. Sometimes the people who think they deserve stuff are the ones who started life deprived. And then when they're lucky they feel they earned it."

"And all the things she'd have to have gotten away with! I just can't wrap my mind around someone having *that much* good luck."

"But can you imagine the same amount of bad luck?"

It was a mistake. He shouldn't have said it.

"Yes," she said.

"You look like a caterpillar in there."

"Good night, caterpillar."

"Good night, caterpillar."

41

Zee was a fraction of herself, a vertical fraction, and another sliver of her was still back in New York at the interviews, and another was in the mirror that spat her decaying face back at her, and another had curled up and died.

There was no one home in the coach house, and she left the door open to the wind. The bed, yes, she checked twice, was still short-sheeted. The jackass hadn't even made an effort to rumple the covers. Two wine bottles in the recycling.

All she'd needed, in the end, was physical proof. There had always been the possibility, however remote, that those words on Miriam's work had been about some other man with scarred knees. That they'd been wishful thinking. That nothing had happened yet, as thick as the air was with inevitability.

In the last weeks, their private jokes had grown more flagrant. "This is the greatest soup of the millennium!" Miriam had said, and Zee could only assume it had to do with the night they stayed back at the house, the night of the heart attack, when Doug would have stooped to kiss her at midnight, and Miriam would have tucked her head under his arm and said, "That was the greatest kiss of the millennium."

She threw things into two suitcases. Clothes and jewelry and shoes, medicine and family photos. Sofia could pack the books up later, could send them to New York.

She'd felt clearheaded in New York, but back here she was underwater again. She had to leave. Obviously, she had to leave. The only question had been whether to take Doug with her. They could have waited till summer. If she'd come home and found no evidence, that's what she'd have done. Broken the news slowly, convinced him he wanted to live in New York, and they'd be away from her mother and Miriam and Laurelfield, horrible Laurelfield, by July. But here was the evidence, and there was a spare room waiting for her in New York, and Doug was a stranger.

Or maybe it was as simple as this: She'd never been a hardboiled egg but a raw one—and Doug, Doug's solid devotion, had been the shell keeping her in. When that shell cracked, what else could a raw egg do but run?

Down on Miriam's sunporch, she found red acrylic paint and a firm, narrow brush. She took them back through the TV room—there were mountains of file folders there, probably something to do with Miriam's next ridiculous series—and up to the bedroom, and covered the wall with words.

Doug, you idiot.

You left a trail.

But I already knew, and I took a job in NY.

I never saw how ugly I was till you reflected it back
at me.

If Case comes home, tell him I'm sorry.

Tell him to run far away.

Tell Miriam that thing in the kitchen is the only
pretty thing she ever made.

She stood in the woods behind the big house, and she looked at it, at all the windows. She closed her eyes, but when she opened them the house was still there.

She stuck a brief resignation in Golda's box, ignoring Chantal. She might have said in the letter that the porn was her fault, but Cole wouldn't even have wanted that. He'd adopted this battle wholeheartedly.

She'd brought with her the photo of herself reading *Green Eggs and Ham*, the one where she looked so much like her listening father. She had another copy in her album, and she wanted to leave this part of herself, this sharp and innocent part of herself, here. But more importantly, she didn't want to keep the frame that Doug had fixed so long ago. She leaned it against Cole's closed office door, with a note. *Dear old bastard*, it said. *For you to remember me. Portrait of the Communist Heretic Zilla Devohr Grant, circa 1970. You're laughing at "Devohr," aren't you? That's my real gift to you.* Back in her office, she filled boxes with books and syllabi and handouts. Her diplomas, journals with her articles. She saved everything from the computer to disk. She wouldn't teach many of the same courses in New York—the school was so nontraditional that the intros and surveys didn't even exist—but she wanted all her files nonetheless. Gretchen, her roommate for one year of college, was hard-skulled and ironic, as perfect a department head as Zee could imagine, and her phone call had been a sudden shaft of light. Yes, Zee had said, she was very much interested in a job like that. Zee had told both Gretchen and the hiring dean the story of Cole (the official one, minus her interferences) over dinner, and—she knew it would be all right after the dean told about hanging Robert Bork in effigy on the Oberlin quad—she also told them what she was planning to do. It wouldn't affect her new contract, they assured her.

She'd been thinking a lot lately about the myths her father used to read her at night: Daphne, Philomela, Actaeon. She realized years later they were all stories of metamorphosis, and she wondered how much he needed these myths to affirm his own reinvention from alcoholic slouch to responsible father and art critic. She'd tried so hard to transform herself—Zee the earnest academic was not the same person as Zilla the privileged child—but she'd slipped. She'd ended up living at home, and sure enough her entire adult life had crumbled away.

She would do it properly this time, in a town where she knew exactly one person. As her father had done, leaving Toronto with his new wife, remaking himself in the grandest American fashion. Some things she could not escape: that gene for mental illness. The sharp and unattractive edges of her own personality. But in New York she'd be away from Doug, and from the self who'd been played for a fool. She'd be away from that house.

She marveled at the lucidity of her thoughts, then realized this was not a good sign. When did people do that, except when they were drunk? And she wasn't, she was fairly sure.

She took the boxes to her car, and she bought, for the last time, a grilled cheese sandwich from the co-op. It was the only thing they did well, and they did it exquisitely. It was half butter, and the toasted bread broke in your mouth and then melted like the thinnest sheet of ice. In an hour she'd be free. She needed to finish just this one thing first—to undo her damage, outscandal the scandal.

At two fifteen, as a class period ended, she stood in the middle of her office and took off her clothes, all of them, and folded them into her purse. Her flesh was pale from the winter, her arms and legs unrecognizably thin. She stuck another muscle relaxer on her tongue. She walked, with just her purse, into the hallway and down the stairs, past students she knew and ones she didn't, past

Chad Crosley, past Fran Leffler. If sound came from their open mouths, she couldn't hear. She walked past Jerry Keaton, who tried to grab her arm and then thought better of it. She heard Chantal calling out: "Zee! Dr. Grant! Can you—Oh, someone get her a—Zee, come *in* here!" Out onto the lawn, the icy lawn, her feet in the slush. She didn't care if she fell, but she didn't fall. Past the administrative building, through parting clusters of students in parkas. She heard one say, "Where's my camera?" And another, "Oh, dude, it's about Cole! I get it, it's about Cole." And another, "Hey it's that math prof! Shane, wasn't that your math prof?"

Past the library, past the co-op.

All the way to her car. She couldn't feel her feet.

She drove off campus with the conviction, the finality, of someone driving off the entire planet.

42

D oug had started to see the world as reticulated. The way the colored pieces of any view fit together: windowsill, wall, sky, driveway, tree, roof. Shoe, carpet, book. If you looked long enough, the three-dimensional world flattened to a plane where every block of color was a tile, so tightly clicked together that no mortar showed at the cracks.

He stared at the Happensack for hours a day, whether Miriam was in front of it smoothing mortar over the top and scrubbing it off with a hard sponge, or whether he was alone at two a.m. as Miriam, similarly insomniac, worked downstairs on other things. They continued to sleep in the kitchen. The first night, he hadn't gone to bed at all. He'd been at the police station, and then slumped at Gracie's table. ("What did you *do?*" Gracie kept saying, until Doug worried the officers would think he'd strangled his wife.) The police traipsed through the coach house. "Talk about the writing on the wall," one said, unhelpfully, and even his partner didn't laugh. The second night, he'd been downtown meeting a private detective, and afterward he made it only back up to Leland's place, where he lay on the couch for five hours but didn't sleep. The third night, Miriam told him he needed to lie down. She zipped him in and brought him a pill and put a washcloth on his forehead, and then it was morning. And for fifty nights since then, he'd crawled in four feet away from her.

He worried the hard kitchen floor would ruin his back, but it didn't. Dr. Morsi agreed: Regardless of the disintegration of his heart and brain, his back had never been better.

Gracie had accused him, in those first weeks, of telling Zee what he knew. She said, "It would have pushed her over the edge. She *worshipped* her father." Doug might have asked *which* father, and who Zee's father even was, if her father was a chauffeur named Max, if her father had perhaps posed nude by the koi ponds. But his jaw was full of lead, and Gracie was in a dull and constant rage. He only encountered her now on the driveway, roaring past in the Mercedes. It was a miracle of good timing that Doug had gotten the files out of the attic the day before Zee left, or Gracie might never have handed over the key at all.

Although the Parfitt file was still conspicuously missing—he and Miriam wondered if it was actually Zee who'd replaced it with the photo, falling apart long before he knew it but one step ahead as always—the rest was a treasure trove. If he could have crawled into the files to live, and never had to worry about food or detectives or showering, he'd have done it. There were sheaths of correspondence between the longtime director, Samantha Mays, and the artists and writers and composers who saw her as their guardian angel. There were slides of paintings. Miriam pored over the Demuth ones, comparing them to prints in library books and calling a friend at the School of the Art Institute who drove up to borrow them, along with the Grant Wood slides and the files of artists Doug hadn't heard of. There were project proposals and sample work. There were letters of recommendation.

Miriam was most excited about the files of two female sculptors, Fannie Cadfael and Josephine Lizer. "I *knew* it," she said. "I knew it, I knew it, I knew it! The bear statue, in the woods! I *knew* that was a Lizer. I should've said so! White rabbits!" Even Doug registered, through his haze, that this made no sense. Miriam explained, her hands flying, that the White Rabbits were the women who had assisted the sculptor Lorado Taft before the Columbian Exposition in 1893. Taft begged special permission to use women, until the man in charge snapped that he could use white rabbits if they'd get the job done. Those women proudly clung to the name as they launched their own careers as some of the first successful female sculptors. A Josephine Lizer piece, even one covered with moss, was a big enough deal that it sent Miriam running for the phone.

Less valuable but more personally intriguing were the references, in the forties and fifties, to a colony caretaker named Maxwell Perry. "That has to be Max!" Doug said. "And he stayed after they kicked the artists out."

Miriam said, "Well, sure, that was probably really the driver's name, and he'd probably really been the caretaker. When people lie, they don't make up *all* the details."

Leland just said, "Any caretakers named Marianne Moore?"

Parfitt, it seemed, had stayed at least six times, and as late as 1941, just four years before his suicide. Some rosters listed his apartment on Rush Street in Chicago, and the earliest—in 1929—had a Philadelphia address that was news to Doug. The most useful detail was the fact that for every stay but the last, his lover, the artist Armand Cox, had been there at the same time. ("*Armand Cox?*" Miriam said. "That's his real name?") It meant their relationship started earlier than was thought. Doug imagined Parfitt writing at a Laurelfield desk, his partner down in a studio designing stage sets and drawing his magazine covers, his fadeaway girls. The two reuniting at the dinner table, discussing the day's work.

Even so, it wasn't enough. Doug tried his best, in the blur of weeks after Zee left, to imagine what a project centered around these scraps of information might look like. And then, the punch in the gut: In late March, a professor from Yale published a long article on Parfitt in *The New Yorker*, a rediscovery piece. The professor, said his bio, was about to publish a book on the lost modernists. It wasn't that his work entirely supplanted Doug's. It was that ten other people were now going to get the same idea, and do it better, and do it faster, and be more qualified to tell the story.

But Doug imagined he might write a nonacademic article about Laurelfield itself, or about artists' residencies in the 1920s. He could drive to other colonies, the places that still kept their records in dusty attics. He had a hell of a story for the introduction, at least: the first-person narrative of recovering the lost Laurelfield archive.

He spoke to the historical society about taking the files off his hands once he'd copied the parts he wanted.

These papers were the trails of the artists—and, in the cases of the most obscure visitors, these might have been the only remnants of their art. But what trail he himself had left, what had prompted Zee to choose that word, *trail*, for the wall, he still wasn't sure. Something told him it wasn't a trail up the attic stairs, but something that had led her to Melissa Hopper and her soccer tryouts, her babysitting gigs, her crushes—yet the trailhead was missing. He'd hidden every scrap of paper, scoured his desk every day before Zee came home. He felt stupid, or at least outsmarted. He had a thousand imaginary conversations with her. The speech evolved and mutated. It went through angry cycles, conciliatory ones, and there was a pleading phase. It grew shorter and more concise. Eventually it became a single and blanketing word, a one-breath mantra: "*No.*" With every step around the fish ponds, every thrash in his sleep. No to it all. No, this didn't happen. No, you couldn't have been in your right mind. No, I'm not the pathetic slug you think I am. No, I didn't want this. No, I don't take it back. No. No. No. No. No.

A package arrived in the mail: *Melissa Calls the Shots, Melissa Takes a Bow, Cece Makes the Grade.* He dumped them in a desk drawer. He spent the day wishing he could call Zee and tell her that the changes she'd made just weren't working for him. "You altered the universe," he'd say. "We're going to ask you to start over."

In April, a call from the detective: Zee was in rural New York. Here was her address. Here was her number. "Look, man," the guy said, "you could try and get her committed, but I haven't seen that work out so well. Seemed fine to me."

This was the afternoon of the same day Miriam filed for divorce from Case. Doug might have driven straight to New York that very night, but he couldn't leave Miriam alone right then. And moreover: If he was still sure of anything about Zee, it was that contacting her against her will would make things worse. He wanted to believe this was all that kept him back, that fear wasn't part of it. That a modicum of relief wasn't part of it.

Miriam wanted sushi, so they went out and Doug let her order for him. She told him, only after he'd swallowed and liked it, that unagi was eel. She told him that when she met Case she'd been so young that she'd taken the regular trappings of his adult life—his job, his car, his drawer full of polo shirts—as signs of maturity and stability. Here was someone who could support her while she made art, a steady rock on which to build her life. Really he'd been anything but. Every year had been worse, every day had been worse—and then they came here, and things got unbearable.

"I think I feel happy tonight," Miriam said. "Is that awful to say?"

Doug looked at the sushi on his plate. It, too, was tessellated: the wet pink rhombus of salmon, the grains of the rice, the thin edge of seaweed. He thought, *I am a different person now. I am someone who eats eel, and this small artist is my best friend. I am someone who has turned the TV room into a file-sorting station, someone who believes fantastical tales of identity theft.*

If everything else were still the same, he'd have felt Zee's absence like a gaping hole. But if he could continue to reconfigure his entire life, there would be no missing place where Zee had been. He thought of Parfitt's last published poem, "Proteus Wept." In Greek mythology, the sea god Proteus changed shape to avoid telling mortals the future. Parfitt had twisted it, though: Parfitt's Proteus changed to avoid remembering the past. It ended with a litany of the forms he took: A *lark, a crow, a spoonbill! / This seafoam, rank and green*. Yet Parfitt himself ultimately chose death over reinvention. It was as if he wrote the poem to convince himself of future possibility, and failed. But Doug could do better.

He didn't drive to New York the next day, or the day after. He didn't call, and then he continued not calling.

What he did instead was ask Sofia to make him an appointment with Gracie. She had written Zee a letter once they had her address, and Zee had written a short note back that, by not expressing anger over car crashes and wheelbarrows, had put Gracie's mind at ease.

Hidalgo greeted him at the door, relatively sedate. Doug scratched him, just to steal a moment to fortify himself. It had occurred to him that the reason Gracie let him continue to stay in the coach house was that she thought he had far more information than he did. He had to choose his questions well, lest they betray his ignorance. He wasn't sure how to begin.

But, at the kitchen table, Gracie spoke first.

"Douglas, I've come to a place of peace," she said. "Either my daughter is crazy, or I raised her wrong, but I don't believe this was your fault."

He said, "I really didn't do anything, Gracie. Honest to God, I didn't."

They talked about the detective, and about leaving Zee alone awhile.

Then Doug said, "I hope you can help with something." He showed her the photograph, careful to keep a hand over the men's naked torsos. "Because I've appreciated your honesty. What I still need to know are these men's full names."

She put on her reading glasses and squinted down. "I haven't a clue. Is there a correct answer?"

"Theoretically."

"That's out back of the house, isn't it? It's the kind of thing Zilla's father would have known. Every few years, someone would call up asking about the colony. He'd rattle off who stayed here."

"But you don't know these men?"

"I've never seen them in my life. What are you hiding under there?"

He slid the photo back in its envelope and asked her blessing to transfer the files to the historical society. "They should be preserved," he said. "With acid-free folders. And there's nothing in there that would, you know, incriminate you. I've been through every inch."

Gracie folded her glasses. "Douglas, I've been a bit of a fool. When you cornered me on New Year's Eve—that's really what you did, you *cornered* me—I was in quite a state. Bruce had me convinced of the end of the world, for one thing. I can't quite remember all I told you. But I realize I might have said more than I needed."

Doug said, "I'd already been in the attic, remember. There were a lot of papers up there."

"I see." It didn't seem to bother her particularly, though. "The papers you want to donate—it's *just* the colony papers, correct?"

"I have no desire to get you in trouble."

She was quiet, and he worried he'd said the wrong thing. Finally she said, "There's actually something I need from you. I've made a decision, Douglas. With Zilla away, with Bruce gone, I think the time has come for me to move on. Did you know I have a sister? A half sister named Elizabeth, and I never stopped writing to her. She doesn't know quite where I am, just that I've had a good life. She writes me back at the post office. We got together in Colorado a few times, after Zilla's father passed, and before I met Bruce. She's moved to Sedona. It's beautiful out there. You know, it was the saddest part of leaving Florida, not knowing what would happen to my sister. She was only four, and leaving her was the worst thing I ever did, the worst thing in my life. But she got out too, and she was a teacher, and now she's divorced. I've been sending her money every month since she was old enough to cash a check. And I think it's time to be Amy Hall again, to go out and join her. Grace can't live much longer, and there's the matter of the Internet. The last thing I want is to become famous for being the oldest living person. Where would I be then? Max made sure from the start that we kept paying ourselves salaries. Every month I'd write a check from Grace Grant to Amy Hall, and I'd cash it at the bank in Libertyville. And Max did the same. I have quite a bit saved up, and that's all I need."

Doug tried to look skeptical, but found himself nodding instead. "Sedona is beautiful."

"Douglas." She put her hand on his. Veins like mountain ranges. "I want you and Miriam to take care of everything here. I've talked to my lawyers, and there can be a transfer of property and funds. To the two of you. Lord knows Zilla doesn't want it. Maybe she'll come back, and maybe she won't. But the house will be yours. We'll keep Grace alive a few years, and then she'll die. These things can be arranged, with money to grease the wheels. It'll be my worry."

"You want us to take the *house*?" The squeak of his voice woke Hidalgo, who stood and hit his head on the table.

"I want you to reopen the colony."

He wasn't entirely sure what his face was doing. It was the most outrageous thing anyone had ever said to him.

"Don't answer yet. It's the right thing. The colony was shut down for bad reasons, for greed and spite. Max would tell me stories—artists by the ponds, writers under the trees. When I first showed up there were still cabins, you know, artist's studios, with skylights and sinks. I know I always spoke poorly of it, but that was—I felt I had to. He said it was quiet all day, everyone working, and then at night they all came together and made a racket and had dinner in the dining room. Can you imagine? And the work they made! We never could have reopened it ourselves, even though Max wanted to, he wanted to desperately. It would have brought too much attention. The Devohrs would have descended. But you and Miriam, you're so many layers removed. It would set the universe right."

"Wouldn't the right thing, technically, be to give it back to the Devohrs?"

"The Devohrs left Grace out here with an alcoholic husband, and they never once came to see her. Never once." She pointed a finger right at him, as if he were trying to argue otherwise. "We had a plan in case they did, a whole elaborate plan. But it never happened. They made it easy for me. It was easy because they never showed up, and it was easy because I never felt bad. And they don't need it, do they? Zilla's the one always talking about Marxism, and look! Here I am, little old me, redistributing the wealth!"

"Oh. God." There was still the possibility this was all a bribe, Gracie's chance to cover up something gruesome, to get out of town before Doug turned her in. That's what Miriam would have said.

"There's money to get it started. I know how much these things cost, I'm not naïve, and there's plenty. Of course it's mostly Bruce's money at this point, so he's the one to thank. I was nearly broke before he came along. And poor sweet Miriam can help you. She knows the art world. She'd know how to build a studio.

Why she married that pompous ass is beyond me, but otherwise she's a smart girl."

Doug realized that in the time she'd been talking, every color in the kitchen had grown brighter. His mind was listing reasons why this wasn't a tenable plan, but it was thinking twice as fast of what would need to be done, planning where people would sleep, what grants could be applied for, what Leland could bring to the table. Doug would have a job. He'd have a life. He felt as if he'd stepped into the Happensack, into its vertiginous abundance.

Leland would tell him he was a sucker, and Miriam would worry Gracie was leaving them with a basement full of dead bodies or worse, but when you're drowning in the ocean and someone throws you a rope, you don't ask what it's made of.

He said, "I have to talk to Miriam. I'd have to tell her— I mean, what could I tell her?"

"Don't worry about it." She smiled, and he knew it must have been painfully obvious that he'd already told Miriam everything. "Go talk to her now."

And he got his things, and he walked back to the coach house.

No, look: He was running.

43

S ummer and fall swept through with a cleansing, scorching heat, and when the students returned to campus, they eagerly told the few seniors returning from a year abroad the story of Professor Grant walking off campus nude.

There was Old King Cole. His Melville class applauded him the first day. For still being there, for still being Cole, for waggling those eyebrows and saying, "You don't kill an old virus *that* easy."

When students came to his office, he pointed to the little framed photo on the wall, the girl and her father. She was reading and she was happy. Each time he'd say, "That's a picture of the bravest woman in the world."

44

On June 10, 2001, a poet named Sara Calovelli pulled into the Laurelfield driveway in a dying Honda Civic with Ohio plates. Though eight more artists and writers and composers would arrive later that afternoon, she was officially the first resident of the Laurelfield Arts Colony in forty-seven years.

Doug and Miriam ran out from the office to meet her, and introduced her to Ben, who'd get her settled in the main house. Dinner was at six, they told her, and then there would be a bonfire out back. When Sara had disappeared through the front door with her suitcase, Miriam did a little jump and clapped her hands.

The chef had the grill going, Sofia and her crew were putting out soaps and towels, and Denise and Chantal worked frantically from the office that used to be the coach house TV room, dealing with all the last-minute things like medical forms.

Everything had fallen into place—money, staffing, town approval—with such ease and speed that Doug and Miriam kept waiting in vain for something to go terribly wrong. That winter, they'd received a donation from some Miss Abbaticchio, an elderly woman in town, that surpassed even the money Gracie had left. The desks from the attic were all still usable. The Illinois Arts Council came through nicely.

The buzz they'd built in the year of frantic work created a deep applicant pool, and Miriam and Leland knew the right people to rope into admissions panels and a board. An article in the *Tribune*,

"Refounding a Haven," came out the same day Doug learned that Zee was living with a sixty-year-old physics professor.

And it was the strangest thing: That night, as he lay in bed, he had to remind himself to feel sad.

His bed was downtown now, in an apartment above the bagel shop. Miriam stayed in the coach house, and Doug and Zee's old quarters had become a guest room and studio.

Gracie had sent them congratulatory flowers, delivered that morning. She wrote them occasional notes from Sedona, which Doug took to be some kind of proof. ("Her going where she said she'd go proves exactly nothing," Miriam said.)

They sat next to the driveway, and Miriam picked up a handful of its smooth gravel: white and tan and black. She arranged the stones in a trail down her shin.

Doug said, "Are you tessellating yourself?"

She said, "I've had a funny thought all day. It seems like this is the only way things could have turned out. You know? Like all the bizarre and horrible things that happened, they pushed us both here. The colony was taken away, the house went back to the Devohrs, and after everything here we are, two people who aren't even Devohrs, opening it back up."

Doug laughed and said, "You think the house just really wanted to be a colony again? It missed all the artists, so it smashed that car and waited half a century?"

"I wasn't going to say the house," Miriam said. "I was going to say ghosts."

At some point they'd agreed that if he could believe Gracie's story, she could believe in her ghosts, and he wasn't allowed to laugh.

Doug said, "Last chance to dig up the greenhouse. Before that writer gets here."

"Ha."

"Just to prove I'm not a gullible ass."

"We'll never do it. It's such a great studio. If I were a writer, it's the studio I'd want." She cleared the gravel from her leg and it fell on the driveway with a sound like rain. "Even if we did," she said, "even if we found bones. What would it prove? You'll never know the whole story. You realize that, right? That you'll never know."

Doug looked at her, speechless. She was right. Like so much she said, it was a revelation. It was also an absolution.

Before dinner, there were cocktails in the library. The travel-weary artists revived, chattering and checking out the displays. Doug had filled the shelves with copies of all the books and musical scores he could find by the earlier generation of residents, and books of art prints as well. He'd even hunted down Marlon Moore's only published work, which seemed to have predated the attic manuscript. Moore turned out to have been a local writer, a professor in Zee's old department in the late twenties. The novel, *Jack of the Woods*, was truly awful, but Moore's spot on the shelf was one of Doug's favorites.

Doug had finally convinced Miriam that what would make the room complete was to put the Happensack above the fire-place, where Gracie's farmhouse painting had once hung. They'd wanted to install it before the guests arrived, but they ran out of time. There were so many little crises in those final days of preparation. For now, the spot was empty.

After dinner, the artists toured the grounds—the recon-structed cabin studios, the wood-chip path to the bear statue—and gathered at the bonfire, which Leland had roaring. Beside him on the ground was a stack of things to be burned.

Miriam explained it to the group. "There's been a lot of good and a lot of bad at Laurelfield since artists last gathered here. Those of us who've been working to make this all happen—we wanted to clear away the past to make room for the new, and the amazing, and the good. And so tonight we're going to burn some bad art."

The crowd laughed, and Doug held up the farmhouse painting, removed from its frame, and tossed it on the fire. It cracked and hissed and then it blazed away.

Leland personally threw in, with great relish, some horrendous poems he'd written after a breakup five years back. Miriam contributed what was left of the yellow dress piece—clawed to scraps by Hidalgo, never really salvageable. Doug threw in three slim paperbacks: *Melissa Calls the Shots, Melissa takes a Bow, Cece Makes the Grade.*

"Oh, I used to love those!" said someone across the fire. "They were terrible!"

As the night grew cool the artists gathered closer to the blaze for a minute, and then they headed off. They had work to do: canvases to prime, desks to arrange, poems to start.

Doug turned to Miriam and said, "Let's get the Happensack right now. We'll be too busy tomorrow."

"We don't have anything to patch the wall with. We'll have a gaping hole for days."

He shook his head. "I want it in the library when they come down to breakfast."

Up in the coach house, they took turns hammering a chisel to break the thick paint seal around the edge, then going at it with the pry bar, getting behind each of the four nailed corners in turn, a bit at a time.

Doug took a shift as Miriam held the edges of the board, ready to catch its full weight if it came loose. He felt utterly happy. It was a happiness beyond the colony, beyond the triumph of the day. He didn't know, after all the disastrous things that had happened, why he should be so profoundly, overwhelmingly satisfied with life. But he was.

The board gave a thrilling crack and Miriam wrested it backward, the nails sliding out, and Doug wasn't sure if he should grab the board or catch her from behind. But moreover—in that exact moment, as he watched her stepping back, finding her balance, panting—he felt as if something had dislodged inside him as well. He said, "Put it down." He let the pry bar fall to the floor.

"No, I've got it."

"Please put it down."

"Why?"

"Put it down."

She did, she leaned it against the wall, and he stood and hooked two fingers into the collar of her shirt and pulled her, stumbling, toward him. In front of the gaping mouth of the wall, he kissed her. There would be time later to move the board, and time to shine flashlights into the wall, and time to replace the small orange tile that had clattered to the floor. He'd been waiting only three seconds for her, but he felt he'd been waiting a century, as if there were nothing more obvious, more necessary, in the world.

PART II

———

1955

After all, Grace had grown up with stories about attics. *A Little Princess*, and *Jane Eyre*, and a hundred campfire ghost stories. The one, for instance, about the bride trapped in the trunk on her wedding night. And that spring on the honeymoon she'd picked up Anne Frank's diary at the English bookshop in Paris. When George disappeared on the third day, she sat in La Rotonde with her open book, a glass of Chablis and a bowl of mussels. She'd brought the book as a shield, hoping she could pass for a young art student, a girl who dined alone once a week when she tired of the French boys in her sculpture class. She still looked twenty, it was true. The waiter called her *Mademoiselle*.

Her water refilled as if from an underground spring. The sun turned to twilight and then streetlamps, the crowd thickened around her, but the waiter never brought the *addition*, just more bread and then, with a wink, more wine. By then the book had plunged her into a world so vivid that the Paris around her seemed the fiction. She was Anne Frank, and this Paris street was a dream after death. She returned to the hotel around midnight to finish the book in bed. When George banged on the door twenty minutes later, his key lost forever, it was too easy to pretend he was a Nazi ripping the bookcase from the Annex door. She lay in bed and tried not to breathe. He shouted and kicked and tried to force the handle. Only when he went silent, presumably starting down the hall to wake the night manager, did she jump up and turn the knob.

"I was asleep," she said.

He steadied himself, his eyes swimming so fast that she knew he saw three of her. He smelled sweet and complicated—like whiskey and cigars and fifty women—and she unbuttoned his shirt. He knocked the door closed with his elbow.

She lay back across the bed. She'd bought a pale green nightgown that afternoon on the Rue de Rivoli. She pressed her white foot to his thigh. She said, "And I was alone all day thinking about you. You'll have to make it up to me."

So was it such a surprise back here, in this vast and disconsolate brick trap, when the smell of Paris had faded from her palate, when George's disappearances left her not ensconced in a café of strangers but humiliated in front of the staff, that she'd claim the attic for her haven? She figured she loved it for the reason we always love attics, for the reason they figure in our dreams: because they are the hidden rooms where we store our pasts. Where we stick the things we can't bear to throw away but hope we never have to see again.

And more practically—it had cooled with the fall air, and here she could sit, invisible, and see everything. The people below were tiny and featureless, dolls around a dollhouse: Max the driver, who claimed he'd been at Laurelfield twenty-five years, more than half his life. Mrs. Carmichael the housekeeper. Beatrice and Ludo in the garden. Rosamund, the cook. The mailman, coming and going. The dairy man, coming and going. Peculiar little Amy, Max's niece, who showed up one day in July startled as a deer and just stayed and stayed. George, taking off in the Capri with Max or in the Darrin without him, or just lurking the grounds, leering at Beatrice as she bent over the squash bed, leering at Amy as she carried linens from the big house to the coach house.

Grace imagined bringing darts up here, perfecting her aim, and launching them at the unsuspecting dolls. One in Max's tire. One in Amy's round posterior. One right in the muscle of George's beautiful arm. One in the koi pond, one in the milk truck. Pop.

What she brought up instead was food, just a bit, and stored it on the windowsill. A loaf of sliced bread, a pot of strawberry jam, five long and knobby carrots. She liked to calculate how long it would last her, if she decided to go missing. One week, she decided. And then down she would climb, skinny as a wraith.

On the tenth of October two strange things happened, and so she knew there would be a third.

The first was that a witch walked into the coach house. Not a real witch, this being the modern day and the rational world. Still, in October, to dress in flowing black like that, hunched at the waist against the wind, the woman was rather asking to be burned at the stake. She'd arrived by taxi from lord knew where, Salem perhaps, and darted into the coach house as if she belonged. Grace's first thought was that the witch was Amy's mother, Max's sister, come to claim her renegade daughter at last, but when Amy walked out toward the garden ten minutes later, untroubled and unhurried, she knew it couldn't be. Grace pulled her bird-watchers off the filing cabinet and trained them on the coach house's second story, above the two open garage doors. She could see them through the windows of the balcony door. The witch sat at the kitchen table, her hair in a low, gray chignon. Max sat across—there was his dark hair—his hands going up and down from the table to his mouth, eating or smoking or drinking. But that was all she could tell.

The scene brought to mind the only card she remembered from her tarot reading with George in the Marais. The others had all looked like playing cards, silly queens and princes, but then the old woman had flipped up the five of pentacles, and Grace had felt she'd seen the picture before, or maybe lived it: two beggars in the cold, outside the warm church. Locked out. She couldn't remember the woman's explanation for the card, but she knew she'd felt it in her bones. And she felt the same thing right now, watching Max. She was only a visitor at Laurelfield.

She remembered George's tarot better, only because it had seemed to trouble the old woman. As if it had revealed his problematic soul. She'd muttered her way through most of it, while Grace did her best to translate. George had wanted to know about the tower card, which looked terrifying: a turret struck by lightning, two naked figures jumping from the windows. The woman said, "C'est pas si grave. C'est la change, seulement, la change soudaine." And then, as if this were just as important, the woman had explained that in the old Belgian decks, the tower had been a tree. "What's she saying?" George demanded. And Grace said, "It means don't go outside when it's raining."

Now she chose one of the tart green apples from her sill, one of the five she'd picked that morning from the trees behind the Longhouse (three adjoined artists' studios, inhabited now by raccoons), and ate slowly around the core. All the windows were open, no screens. She'd pulled those out so birds could fly through, though her only guests had been some skittish barn swallows who hadn't even made nests under the gable eaves as she'd hoped. She started to throw the core onto the driveway, but changed her mind and crossed the broad, loud floor to the back of the house. There were George and little Amy, near the yellowing catalpa tree. There was something odd in the way they stood—the very fact of their standing together, to begin with, but moreover the way he curved above her like a cobra—so that it wasn't even a surprise when George grabbed one of Amy's wrists and pinned it above her head, against the bark of the tree. Grace grabbed her birdwatchers. She held the last bite of apple in her mouth like Snow White, not chewing or spitting or choking, just watching as George undid the top buttons of Amy's dress and yanked it down below her left breast, and her brassiere with it, so that Grace could see the pink nipple even from here. Amy's leg rose as if she were trying to kick him away but didn't know to aim for the groin. George lowered his head to Amy's breast and, since he was in profile to her, Grace could see even his tongue, circling the breast and then climbing slowly up Amy's neck. Amy pushed him away and tugged her dress back up, but she didn't run or scream, and that was what counted, wasn't it?

Well.

Well.

Grace, good literature major that she was, told herself this apple was a symbol of lost innocence, and that now, with the sweet pulp in her mouth still undissolved, would be the perfect time to feel shock and repulsion. And was it a failure on her part that she felt neither? Not shock, because she wasn't an idiot. And not true repulsion, either, not in the way she ought. This was the man she'd chosen. This was the reason she'd broken things off with Gunning Burke and Stanley Langhoff and Lionel: because they weren't the kinds of men to do anything surprising or awful or awakening. They smothered her with their patience, and she'd felt locked in a windowless, velvety room with the smell of peppermint and nowhere to vomit.

Well.

This was not the second strange thing. Because really it was not so strange.

The figures below had parted, Amy trotting across the lawn to the kitchen door. Grace supposed she was heading in there just to burn the soup. Ever since she'd shown up the food was markedly worse, and Grace suspected Rosamund was trying to teach her things, letting her chop and make salad dressings. Poor, stupid Amy, probably in love with George and not able to understand that a year from now he wouldn't recall her name.

Grace was the only kind of woman George could ever have married, just as George was the man she'd waited twenty-eight years for, through parties and debutante balls and engagements and what everyone saw as spinsterhood. And then at the Governor's Ball in '53, up had walked George Grant, a pimentoed olive in his teeth, eyes like the Big Bad Wolf. He bit down so the olive split, half in his mouth, half tumbling to his palm. He walked a step closer and, right in front of Grace's father, jammed the olive half between her lips. "It's good for you," he'd said, and walked on to scoop his arm around the slim waist of the mayor's daughter.

Her mother, scurrying up: "Who was *that*?"

And Grace, quite drunk and melodramatic already that evening, had swallowed the olive and turned away.

A pleasant paralysis set over Grace as the afternoon wore on, and she watched the coach house as Max and the witch continued to talk. Amy reappeared at one point, walked to the big house, returned to the coach house with a pillow and blankets—and yes, there she appeared in the east rooms, opening the window and preparing a bed for the witch. Grace ought to have cared that yet another guest was being welcomed on her property without her consent. Her mother never would have allowed it, would have been horrified at Grace just sitting here, watching Max build a harem in that little house. Some harem: a witch and his niece. Only she wasn't really his niece. Grace knew.

After a long while, Max and the witch strolled together out of the coach house, behind the big house, and straight into the garden shed. They emerged twenty minutes later, and so did Ludo and Beatrice, the gardeners. Max and the witch walked them to their car and kissed their cheeks before the gardeners drove off, done for the day. The witch took Max's arm, quite formally, and they disappeared back into the coach house.

The sun was setting, and she ought to head down for dinner before they sent a search party.

Amy reappeared. She was a figurine from a cuckoo clock, circling forever in and out: coach house, big house, coach house, big house. But this time, as she crossed the lawn toward the kitchen door, the earth seemed to move behind her. No, it was rabbits. Grace counted at least seven of them, hopping along behind Amy as if out of Hamelin. She didn't seem aware in the slightest. And what irony! Seven cottontails, and not a bit of good luck for Amy—sad little, odd little, hungry-eyed Amy, who thought she was desired because George pinned her to a tree. The kind of girl to whom misfortune clung like moss. Grace stood and brushed the attic dust from her lap.

So it was two strange things now, two omens. If she only kept watching, tomorrow and the next day and the next, the third thing would come. And the third was always biggest.

She felt the house waking around her in the morning before she herself was fully awake. Windows opening, Ludo's rhythmic clippers outside, feet in the hall, wheels on the gravel drive. It was the same everywhere she'd ever lived: at home at Bealey Hall, with so many more servants than here, and her brothers shouting, and later her brothers' children shouting; in the college dormitory, where some girls were always up and running baths at the crack of dawn; in hotels, where someone had been up all night at the desk, where the maids arrived at four in the morning. She wondered what it was like to awaken alone in a little cottage on a quiet street, where nothing would stir until she did. Maybe a sleeping cat at the foot of the bed, and that would be all. But here

at Laurelfield, there was something more in the mornings, a buzzing sensation about the whole house, as if it weren't the servants
keeping it running but some other energy. As if the house had
roots and leaves and was busy photosynthesizing and sending sap
up and down, and the people running through were as insignifi-
cant as burrowing beetles.

She sat at the breakfast table with a book. George wasn't there
yet. He'd begun sleeping in the small bedroom with the four-
poster on nights when he returned home closer to dawn than
sunset. He was either up there asleep or he wasn't, but wondering
wouldn't accomplish much. She asked for eggs and toast, no meat,
and opened her book to the middle. A romance. A college friend
had sent six of them as a joke wedding gift—the whole *Ancient
Passions* set, tied with pink ribbon, a calligraphed note: *For when
that flame flickers!*—and Grace had ripped through two just since
Paris. This one was set in an English manor house in the reign of
Henry VIII. The poor servant girl and the second son were madly
in love with little hope of marriage. She'd have imagined it finished badly for all, were this not the type of book that guaranteed
a happy ending. How funny it would have been, what a great trick
on the poor lonelyheart readers, if one of these stories ended terribly. Abandonment, shame, an accidental baby with six fingers
on each hand. The heroine taking to the streets.

George arrived, unshaven. His hair a mat of black curls, his
eyebrows mirrored by the dark circles beneath. He was even more
beautiful like this than neatly groomed. She closed the book, but
didn't bother hiding it under her napkin. He snorted at the cover
and asked where the cook was. Grace forked some eggs onto her
saucer and slid it across the table to him, and she poured half her
coffee into his cup.

She said, "Do you know anything about Max's new guest, in
the coach house?" She'd been going to ask him last night at

dinner, but he'd taken a phone call and she ended up eating alone. "A woman."

He scratched behind his ears. "It's your house, Duck. Tell me what you want. You want me to bark at him?"

She considered. "No. I can handle it, certainly. I just wondered if he'd cleared it with you."

George laughed and tried to catch the cook's attention through the open kitchen door. "I think the fellow's smart enough to know I'm not the one to clear it."

"Well. In any case, there's a guest. A distinguished sort of witch, all dressed in black. Just so long as you don't go mangling her bosom."

George lifted a thick eyebrow, but the look on his face was all amusement. No denial, and certainly no apology. If he'd already been drunk for the day, he might have thrown his coffee cup at her face. As it was, he seemed on the verge of saying something slick and snide, but just then Rosamund, strapping, gray-eyed Rosamund, strode through the door with the coffee and a heaping plate of eggs.

Grace said, "I'll manage it all." Though she had no idea how to speak to Max, no desire to put her authority to the test.

George paused his bite in front of his mouth and said, "Your dear departed grandmother is staring me down. Can't we move her?"

She glanced over her shoulder at the portrait. "She's beautiful, I think."

"She makes my skin crawl."

"We can change seats."

"I'd rather have a ghost look me in the eye than look down the back of my neck."

"We can't take it down. Father would be mortified."

"You think he's going to see? You think he's going to visit us?

Grace. They're never going to visit. Don't you understand that yet?"

Back in the attic, she considered how to spend her day. Her favorite corner, the northwest one, was a most comfortable nest. She had covered an old, splitting Morris chair with a green blanket, and pushed it over to the file cabinets that formed a little cove by the dormer. She'd found a half-finished painting on a piece of rolled linen, and she'd carefully unrolled it and cleaned it of dust, and tacked it to the wall below the window. It was maybe meant to be an oak leaf, in intense close-up. She put a board across the arms of the Morris chair, and this became her desk for drawing and writing letters. It was exactly like an artist's garret in Paris in the nineties, she decided, somewhere on Île Saint-Louis, and when Amy crunched by on the path Grace pretended it was a fishmonger.

Today she would plan her greenhouse. Ludo was thrilled at the idea, and he'd promised to learn orchids. She sketched it out on the back of an empty folder from the cabinets—not the architecture of it, which was already determined, but the placement of the plants—and she used a second folder as a ruler. She penciled in the neat little shelves and pots. Here, along the eastern windows, tomatoes and lettuces. How heavenly, in January, to eat a soft, ripe tomato. There should be spinach, as well. She thought of a hot vegetable pie. African violets along the inner wall by the house, unless there wasn't shade enough. Phalaenopsis along the west, framing the view of the back lawn: white, purple, pink. Yellow lady's slipper, the small ones. Ferns all over the middle, a jungle of ferns, and a little copper mister. Ferns hanging from the ceiling, as well, and other things that would lilt down with soft tendrils and green threads of hair.

In another life, she'd have been a botanist, or a painter of plants. In college she took a whole course on the plant kingdom.

The professor, an ancient British woman, had cut an apple in half the wrong way—down its equator—and turned the halves out to face the girls, to show them the stars that had been hiding there, the carpels, the seeds cut through and leaking arsenic. Stars! In the apples she'd been eating for twenty years! Suddenly, that year, every tree had a name. When boys sent her flowers, she'd sit at her dormitory desk dissecting each one, pulling daisies apart into disc flowers and ray flowers, splitting the bases of lilies with her thumbnail to find the rows of neat, white ovules.

And what was she to do with all that information now? The French literature, too, and the appreciation for Dutch art, and the ability to write a theme on Chaucer. What were those skills but silent companions in the attic, ways to keep her mind from digesting itself over the next fifty years? She imagined her classmates amusing their husbands with their intelligence. When she'd tried talking to George in Paris about the architecture of the bridges on the Seine, he'd accused her of humiliating him.

Her boredom wasn't his fault. What had she done with herself from college to the age of twenty-eight? Precisely nothing. She'd traveled to Italy with her mother (educational, but none of the Italian stuck), she'd answered telephones in her father's office, she'd been engaged, or pretended to be, to two boys, which took a great deal of time and energy but little creativity. She'd been sick for an entire winter with pneumonia. She'd organized blood drives for the Canadian Red Cross. Never, in that time, had she impressed anyone with her knowledge of Chaucer.

Here came Amy, crossing the drive, arms empty for once. She walked with her nose down, as if someone had forbidden her from seeing anything beautiful in the world. Grace was not ready yet to confront Max, but she could talk to Amy. She could get her bearings.

By the time Grace got downstairs, Amy had disappeared. She looked for her in the kitchen (no Amy, but Rosamund had a question about what vegetables Mr. Grant would accept in his stew) and down by the linen closets. She finally looked out the dining room windows and spotted her standing under the catalpa tree, the same one where George had manhandled her. But she was facing the tree, staring at its bark, and George was nowhere around. So Grace walked outside despite the cold, and came up slowly beside her.

"It's a northern catalpa," she said, and Amy jumped and gave a rough little shriek.

"Mrs. Grant," she said. "I'm sorry. I thought—maybe you were an animal or something."

"Well, I suppose I am. And that's a northern catalpa. It can't be as impressive to you, coming from the south. But up here, it's got the largest leaves of any tree, by quite a lot. It isn't always so ugly." In early summer, it had been sublime in its inflorescence: white flowers hanging like bridal trains, foot-long seed pods, leaves as big as dinner plates. But now the leaves were sickly yellow, the pods brown and distressingly phallic.

"No, it's very pretty," Amy said. "It is."

"Don't lie."

"Oh."

Amy looked as if she might cry. Grace was tempted to push her further, to see if she would, but instead she said, "Come sit with me a minute." She led her to the bench by the koi pond. She'd have to ask Max soon what was to be done with the fish once the weather fully turned. She didn't know if they'd be brought indoors, or if they continued to live here, sealed beneath a sheet of ice. They sat, and Amy immediately buried the toes of her saddle shoes in the leaves. She was a child, Grace reminded herself. Max said she was eighteen, and she looked it, but there was something much younger about her, something stuck at seven. Grace said, "Your uncle has a visitor."

There was just the shortest flicker of confusion before Amy

said "Yes." Of course. Because Max, Grace had figured out weeks ago, was not Amy's uncle. Max had been flawless in his story, introducing Amy back in July with a proud hand on her shoulder, including just the right number of details: "the daughter of my sister Ellen," and "took the train all the way from Florida by herself," and "planned to stay with friends but it's all fallen through." Grace had bought it completely. Why wouldn't she? She'd said Amy could stay as long as she needed. And in August, when he'd come to her again and said that Amy would really love to work, that she could use the experience, Grace had thought of what her own mother would do, the manners and generosity she'd seen modeled for years before she learned, in history class, to call it *noblesse oblige*. The housekeeper, Mrs. Carmichael, was ancient and nearsighted and gouty, and Grace had been sure she wouldn't mind the help. Amy could fill in wherever needed, Grace had said, and Amy had broken her own outpouring of gratitude only to say that she didn't have a green thumb at all, that she could clean and help in the kitchen, but the gardeners would be better off without her.

Then certain details started to needle Grace. There was something so raw and low about Amy, a harshness to her vowels that was separate from her southern accent. Her teeth were crooked, she didn't know what a sideboard was, she bit her nails. In asking Mrs. Carmichael how to reshelve the records in the library, she pronounced "Mozart" with a soft Z. Whereas Max was a true Brahmin. Grace had no idea of his background, besides his long attachment to the colony, but the man spoke fluent French and subscribed to *Harper's*. It didn't fit that his sister would be Amy's mother. And so Grace had devised a test. She found Max in the garage one day in September, and said, "I'm thinking already about Christmas. I know, here we are roasting to death—but it's my first Christmas as a married woman. How did you celebrate, Max? When you were growing up? I need inspiration." And he'd told her about sticking cloves into oranges, about opening gifts by candlelight on the Eve, church service at nine in the morning, duck for dinner, carols and eggnog after. And then, the next day, Grace had come into the kitchen and asked the same thing of both Amy and the cook. Amy had swallowed hard and said, "Well, we always had bowls of nuts on the coffee table. That was a real treat." Grace pressed further and heard about turkey the night before, leftovers for Christmas dinner itself, a mad rush for gifts at dawn.

Grace was certain, then: There was no way a woman who'd grown up in the house Max had described would invent Amy's Christmas for her own children. It answered her question, but it raised many more: Who in heaven was this Amy Hall, and why did Max want her here, and what did she want from Laurelfield? There was something about her weakness that made Grace want to hurt her, to test how long she could hold herself together. Perhaps it was the same instinct that had led George to pin Amy to the tree. She and George were so similar, after all.

Grace said, "Who is she?"

Amy seemed relieved that the question was this easy. "Miss Silverman. From New York City."

"*Silverman.* And she—Miss Silverman is a friend? Of your uncle's?"

"I think so."

"Jewish. A name like that."

"Oh. I wouldn't know, ma'am."

"Had you met her before?"

"No, not before."

"She seems quite odd. Don't you think?" She leaned toward Amy and whispered, twelve-year-olds in the schoolyard. "She dresses like a witch."

Amy let out a short giggle.

"Is she still here today?"

"She went down to the Art Institute," Amy said. "On the train. I worried about her, going all alone, but I guess if she's from New York City she can find her way around."

"Certainly. And is she—*attached* to your uncle? In a romantic sense?" Even though the witch seemed older than Max. She was gray, and he was not.

"Oh, no! I mean, she hasn't seen him in years. That's what I gathered."

"Amy," she said, "one thing I admire about you is your power of observation. No one could have learned this place faster than you. I'm still learning it myself."

"Thank you, ma'am."

"I'm just trying to find out what I can, because I don't want to make your uncle uncomfortable. The truth is that he never asked to invite a guest."

"Oh, but he didn't know she was coming!"

"Are you sure?"

"You've never seen anyone so surprised. He—well, I don't know. He was upset that she'd come. It's really not his fault, I think."

Grace decided to be quiet until Amy said something else. This was one of her father's negotiation tactics, and she rarely had reason to use it. Perhaps she was still improving her mind after all. She stared at Amy, and Amy kicked the leaves and looked generally terrified. It only took a few seconds.

"I'll tell you what she said, though. It was after he got over his shock, and they'd sat down at the table, but I was still on the stairs. She said, 'I had to see for myself. You have no idea what I went through to get away.' And then they were quiet a long time, and I thought they were either laughing or crying."

Grace was impressed, despite herself, with the old-fashioned Yankee accent Amy had put on for Miss Silverman's voice. She was a good mimic. Why, then, did she so doggedly keep her wretched twang when she was capable of speaking properly? Grace would like to write out the ways Amy might elevate herself.

"I imagine she was referring to the colony," Grace said. "To the colony closing. Do you suppose it's an artist rushing here to see the damage?"

"She said—she said no one in New York knew where she was. I left that out. She said she'd told them all she was visiting her brother in Wisconsin."

"And where does she sleep?"

"Oh, not—not with—he asked if I wouldn't mind sleeping down on the couch in the mechanical room. And I don't. So she's got my quarters, and I don't mind at all."

"You're very helpful, Amy. You truly are." She hated the sound of Amy's name in her mouth. Such horrible vowels, such an egregious mangling of the French Aimée—*loved*, but who loved little Amy? Not her. Not George. Probably not Max.

"Thank you, ma'am."

Part of what bothered her about this girl was how much the two of them resembled each other. Both blonde, both with long eyebrows, strong chins. Though Amy was at least twelve years younger. And prettier, even discounting age. Grace, at eighteen, had not been as pretty as Amy at eighteen. It was only fair. Amy had been luckier in looks, and Grace had been far, far luckier in breeding. If she were Amy, though, she might find it odd that this woman, this sad and tired Mrs. Grace Grant, should be elevated so far above her, in defiance of the hierarchy biology itself had bestowed. In the court of femininity, looks trump all. The gorgeous lady-in-waiting can always smirk pityingly at the plain-faced princess. And *this* was what enraged Grace. She'd finally pinpointed it. That Amy pitied her. Their similarities invited comparison, and Amy must be measuring herself against Grace all the time. And pitying, and gloating, and letting George claw her by the tree.

Grace stood. She didn't want to talk to Amy anymore, even if she had more information.

Amy stood too. "Ma'am, if I might ask something."

"Certainly."

"Your eye." And she reddened as soon as she'd said it. She might have no manners, no sense of propriety, but she must have seen that Grace wanted to slap her.

Grace restrained herself, though, and touched her own cheekbone with two fingers. She was about to say that she'd slipped in the bathroom. But she felt like wounding Amy, and so she told the truth. She said, "George hit me with a large salt shaker. Thank you for your assistance, Amy."

She needed her coat before she walked all the way to see Max. Her mother had sent her an alpaca coat, and this was the first day it was cold enough to wear it. She walked back in through the kitchen, and was nearly to the hall closet when George (a whole herd of Georges) thundered down the front stairs and saw her and said, "You're coming with me. We're playing golf."

"Now?"

"We've been here five months. I want to get in one round before Christmas."

He could have gone without her, but the membership at the Chippeway Club was in her father's name, and she knew George was secretly terrified of being turned away at the door. Grace was his human shield. She'd been making excuses for weeks.

"I'm wearing slacks. I'm not sure of the dress code—"

"Well, change."

"I'll freeze."

He didn't answer, though. He was headed for the basement to scare up the golf bags.

In the end she kept her slacks on, half hoping it would get

them kicked out, though she could already imagine George screaming that she'd embarrassed him. She put on a cardigan and the alpaca coat, and she wore cat-eye sunglasses that didn't quite cover the bruising. By the time she came down, George was already in the back of the Capri, which Max had pulled up to the front door for loading the golf bags.

"Why don't we take the Darrin?" she said to both of them. "Max shouldn't have to come. He has a guest, after all."

Max looked startled, as if he'd hoped this fact had escaped her notice. He rested her bag on the lip of the trunk.

"I'm happy to drive," he said.

"What are we paying this guy for, if he never drives us anywhere? Come on, hop in."

Grace wanted to protest that this wasn't done, that people didn't need drivers to transport them one mile across town, that it wasn't 1920, but George would think she was lecturing him on cultured behavior. And perhaps it was safer to have Max along.

She leaned her head on the window as they rode. So many pretty houses. The maple trees were still red.

George was worrying his trouser knee. Someone had once told her that if a man sees the line of a woman's suntan—the strip of white peeking out beneath the strap of her bathing suit or the collar of her dress—he'll fall in love with her. Because he will believe he's seen her truest self, raw and pale, something no other man knows. And this was the reason she'd fallen in love with George: She could see the desperate nerves beneath the bluster. He came from nothing, and nobody, and nowhere. His parents were middle class, but they died when he was three, and he was shuttled between orphanages and aunts, and everyone robbed him till he was grown and lethally charming with no money at all. He'd survived childhood only by ingratiating himself to women, and as an adult it remained his leading skill. He showed up in Windsor at the age of twenty, and his only lie was an aristocratic British accent. Everything he said was technically true: orphan, penniless, et cetera. Once people heard that bit, they never pressed him on his background. He met a rich girl and seduced her and followed her to Toronto, where she introduced him to everyone and he dropped the accent. He went to a different party every night, spiraling up the social world, and he ended with everyone considering him a sort of relative, a crazy cousin to be endured. He'd pay a girl a lot of attention, get her father to give him a job, get her brother to loan him a bed, and then before they knew it he was on to another place. None of the girls loved him, though, so he didn't break many hearts. To his credit, he was always careful to pick out the adventuresses. He told Grace all these things, tearful and drunk, a few nights after they met. She should have been horrified by his crying, but instead it did her in, and she put his head in her lap and ran her fingers through his hair.

A Negro in uniform nodded them through the gates of the Chippeway Club, and another opened Grace's door at the front entrance.

She spoke before George could, before he could even get out of the car. "We're guests of a member," she said. "But he isn't with us. Could you direct us, please?"

He led them to the golf office while Max gave the bags to a caddy. She watched him out the office window, standing there by the car, waiting to see if they'd be turned away, and she wanted to tell him to leave, to stop caring about them and go back home to his witch. The man in the office gave them a tee time and welcomed them cordially. He asked if they'd like a drink on the back porch. Grace nodded, figuring at least on a porch it wouldn't be ridiculous to keep her sunglasses on. They followed the man. Max would have to figure out on his own that they were settled, that he was dismissed.

Everyone on the glassed-in porch was ancient, hunched over

bowls of soup and snifters of brandy. On the weekends it must be
different, businessmen and their bouncy wives. In summer, it
would be full of children. She knew there were women her age in
town—she'd seen them at the pharmacy and the hairdresser,
even if she did turn down the invitation from the Newcomers'
Society—but they all had children, and nothing in common
with her. She'd counted on neighbors, but the house to the south
was vacant and the older couple to the north spent all their time
in Virginia. Grace had no idea how to insinuate herself into a
new town, and no pressing desire to. She was unaccustomed.
Toronto society had simply flowed through her parlor, and
her friends and beaux had appeared as naturally as wildflowers.
George knew how to do it, but now that he had the house and the
wife and no need for a job, he had no motivation to meet and
charm anyone but the regulars at the Highwood bars, the men
with loose and shady business ventures who could use an investor
like George. Besides which, he wasn't interested now in social
climbing so much as in having a good time. One Sunday, in an
aborted effort to be sociable, Grace had gone to the Presbyterian
Church, but she only wound up sitting alone in the back and trying to delineate the families, putting mental dividers in the pews.
Four blond children, bookended by blond parents. Two teenage
girls with pageboy cuts, and their graying mother. Grace hadn't
been back. The last thing she wanted was someone who knew her
name, who looked for her every Sunday, and then worried when
she showed up with a purple jaw.

She looked out across the eighteenth hole to where three teepees stood in a row. It was simultaneously 1955 and 1800 out there.

George ordered them both gin and tonics, and the waiter already knew his name: "Yes, sir, Mr. Grant."

At the next table, an old man sliced into a cylinder of pinkish
aspic.

She whispered to George: "We've checked into the geriatric ward."

"Your father picked a hell of a club."

"Oh, he hardly came. It was only a way to keep friendly with the locals when the colony was open. The artists were always making such a ruckus. He'd golf with the mayor, that sort of thing. I think his parents were members, way back."

George laughed too loudly. "That's why Madame Violet offed herself. Too boring at the old country club."

Their drinks arrived, with small wedges of lime.

After the waiter had gone, Grace said, "We can't very well charge these to my father."

"Are you going to take those ridiculous glasses off?"

"It depends if you'd like people to call the police."

"What you need is to be better with makeup. Makeup would cover that, if you did it right."

"Miss Georgia, the cosmetician."

George reached a finger across the table toward Grace's stemmed glass of ice water. He touched it as if he were about to say something about it, something important, but then he kept pushing, and the whole glass tipped slowly toward Grace, until gravity sped it up and the ice cubes and water tumbled into her lap.

She made a noise but managed to keep her lips closed. She stood and shook the ice to the floor, and the aspic-slicing man handed her a napkin and his wife rushed around the table to see if she could help. George stayed calmly in his seat, and Grace refused to look at him.

She said, to the older couple, "I'm sorry, I'm sorry," and she said it to the waiter, who had run over with a broom and dustpan to collect the ice: "I'm so sorry." She ran through the dining room and toward what she thought was the front door, but it was an empty banquet hall. She ran back around a corner and another corner, and yanked off her sunglasses to see better, and finally she found the door. She had no plan except to walk home, or maybe into town—but there, just a bit farther around the drive than where he'd dropped them, was Max, leaning against the Capri. He dropped his cigarette and squashed it with his toe. He opened the back door as if he'd expected her at precisely this moment.

"Mr. Grant won't be joining us till later," she said. Max put on his driving gloves and handed back a handkerchief.

He said, "I'll return for him. I assume he'll play the full eighteen?"

She couldn't very well question him about the witch now, even though she had him alone. That could wait till she was breathing evenly, till she wasn't riding in a vehicle he controlled.

When her father had made all the arrangements, he'd said Max would look after her. At first she worried he was meant to report back to Toronto about George's behavior, but Max was far too tight-lipped for that, besides which he and her father didn't seem fond of each other in the slightest. "I *can't* fire the fellow," is what her father had said, as if he wanted nothing more in the world. "He's been there longer than the trees." But Max seemed to be following some deeper imperative than just driving and overseeing the grounds. He acted, at times such as these, like Grace's appointed protector. Perhaps he was fond of her. But that made little sense, seeing as she and George had usurped the estate. This wasn't really the way it happened, but it was the narrative she knew the colony people had told one another: Old Gamby Devohr is shutting us down so he can hide his daughter and her drunken husband while her brother runs for Parliament. When really it was just a convenient confluence. The colony's death knells had been sounding for years, and yes, they wanted George far from Ontario, and they wanted Grace to live with her mistake, here in the suburban wilderness, till she recognized the error of her ways and came crying back, divorced and wiser. And her idiot brother had as much chance of winning that seat as he had of winning the Nobel Prize in physics.

Her mother's parting words: "You'll see, when you can't run him around Toronto shocking everybody. You'll see what he's like to live with. And you'll see how it is when no one cares that you're Grace Devohr."

That last bit was true: At both the beauty parlor and the florist, she'd slipped and given her maiden name, and there wasn't the slightest recognition. Of course, that same hairdresser, when she learned Grace was Canadian, asked, "Do you have a president up there now, or do you still believe in the queen?" This town was a vacuum. Well, she'd live with it. She'd have to live with it. And perhaps invisibility could be her great adventure.

Max dropped her at the front door, and she took the mail off the hall table and climbed immediately to the attic. A letter, in her mother's elegant hand: Father was a little better, but still coping with the gout, and short of breath with the autumn air. Wallace was growing discouraged in his infant run for Parliament, and it seemed the public saw him as a lazy gadabout (true, Grace thought), but he had a year and a half to change their minds. Uncle Linus had run off again, and no one was doing much about it. The maids dusted Grace's bedroom every day, and she'd be welcomed home on a moment's notice. Deer had eaten all the mums.

The rest of the mail was bills and a catalogue. It was odd that she never got mail intended for the colony, from far-flung artists who hadn't heard of its demise. But she supposed Mrs. Carmichael must sift that out. She ought to ask.

And now, again, she was facing a blank day. She couldn't plan the greenhouse much further without Ludo. Her brother Morton, or rather his personal secretary, had sent a Paint-by-Number kit for her birthday in July, and it seemed the most tedious and point-less exercise in the world—but then today was a tedious and pointless day. She laid out all the packaged supplies. Pots and pots of little oil paints, five brushes, turpentine, a cup. Three poster boards: Big Ben, the Eiffel Tower, the Leaning Tower of Pisa. She picked Pisa: Imminent gravitational tragedy suited her mood. There were several old easels with the colony furniture, crammed along with the beds and desks and bureaus into the two front wings, and she hauled one back to her northwest corner and set the little poster board up. The unpainted picture was fascinating, an unfathomable mess of pale blue lines, shapes that weren't shapes, full abutment, no spaces between.

She opened a pot of alluring gray-blue, and painted, with the smallest brush, a wedge of sky, until the number 8 was covered and the edges looked crisp. It was tremendously satisfying. The oak leaf painting was still tacked under the window, and Grace resisted the urge to reach down and daub some paint in the cor-ners, to finish the job. It was perfect as it was, though, even if clearly incomplete: the frilled, fleshy edges of the leaf blade, pink-ish brown, as if it were blushing, as if the artist had discovered, deep in the forest, a fallen leaf that was more vibrant after death. It ought to make her sad, to paint something segmented and pre-scribed so close to this delicate blurring, this confident restraint, but really she felt lovely just to be painting *near* it.

She worked for quite a long time, then set the brushes to soak in the turpentine. The afternoon was getting on, and she hadn't eaten lunch, but she wasn't ready to go down yet. She stretched, then leafed a bit through the colony files. She loved the names, and the old penmanship, and she loved the woman who, to compensate for a broken typewriter hammer, had written in all her *D*s with purple ink. There was even a novel manuscript in there that she'd once tried to read, until she found it was unrewardingly dense. Today she pulled out the chunk behind that, N through P. Earl Napp would not attend for the summer of 1939 after all. Alma Nellis wondered if she had left her valise. Samantha Mays, the director, wrote back: No, she hadn't, and they'd even checked at the train station for her, and they dearly hoped there was nothing of value inside.

A name she recognized, though she couldn't place it: Viktor Osin, a "maître de ballet," had stayed five times in the twenties and thirties. A recommendation glowed about his "kinetic vivacity." Then it clicked in place like a jigsaw piece. That spring, right after they'd moved in, that strange article in the *Tribune*. A choreographer who'd gone missing and turned up in Grant Park, a common wino. One of his own male dancers had found him, had recognized him through the grime and the beard. The dancer had washed him off and sobered him up. There'd been a photo of him, Mr. Viktor Osin, on the front of the Arts section, attending a performance of his own work, a version of *The Winter's Tale* he'd choreographed some twenty-five years earlier. But something was off about it all, and this is why Grace remembered, why she'd even read the accompanying article in the first place. Despite his suit, his shaved chin, his combed white hair, there was still something deeply wrong with the man and his hollow eyes—as if they'd reanimated his corpse just for the occasion. She remembered how she'd felt at her wedding. Everyone so falsely happy for her, congratulating her for—what?—for showing up, for existing. She wanted to climb into the newspaper, to tell Viktor Osin that she understood him, that she forgave him. And here in the letter: "kinetic vivacity"? She wondered what had gone wrong, what broke him.

A creak traveled across the attic floor, and shook her awake. She didn't know how long she'd been staring at that file, and she became disgusted that she'd spent her afternoon painting in someone else's version of the sky and dwelling on the minutiae of twenty years ago, when she might deal with Max. George was out of the way, and even the witch was off at the museum.

She rested the files on one of the cabinets, and got her coat from the hook at the top of the stairs. But here was Max, after all, coming to find her, knocking at the door below. Or at least someone was, and she assumed it was Max, not Mrs. Carmichael, from the quick confidence of the raps. She trotted down, but when she opened the door the whole hall was empty. She looked in the flowered bedroom on the right, and in the guest suite to the left, but there was no one. Ridiculous child, to get goose bumps on her arms. It was the acorns, of course. They'd been falling all week, pelting the windows and roof.

Without thinking she started back up, as if that had been her mission all along, and it wasn't till she got to the top that she remembered Max. But meanwhile the files had all spilled down from the top of the cabinet, onto the Morris chair and floor. She sorted what she could: the letters, some slides, a postcard from poor, luggageless Alma Nellis. Sticking halfway out from the top of a folder that read *Parfitt, Edwin*, was a photograph. She pulled it out. A *revolting* photograph, the kind she knew existed, the kind she'd glimpsed in boxes of postcards at the *bouquinistes* by the Seine, but it was never *men*, and never so *anatomical*. She dangled it upside down between her thumb and finger. There was nothing else in the Edwin Parfitt file, and nothing else that seemed to belong there. She turned the photo right side up so she could properly read the expressions on the two men's faces. The one on the left was grinning like the devil. The one on the right: Oh, oh, oh. The man on the right was her father.

Down in the library, she poured herself a glass of George's scotch. She preferred to taste something harsh and stinging just then. She didn't know what to do with herself, besides crawl out of her own skin.

She moved the little jade monkey from a bookshelf to the top of the bar, as if it were contemplating what to drink next. It was one of the few items she remembered from her childhood visits to Laurelfield, and she'd been delighted to find it still in the library. What she remembered was a plump, friendly woman pressing it into her hand, saying, "We haven't many toys here, but this might do."

She drank one more glass of scotch and waited till she could feel it in her cheekbones, and then she marched off to the coach house, the photograph in her coat pocket.

She found Max in the garage, washing the windshield of the Darrin. It was a ridiculous car, two seats only, pale yellow with a puckered grille in front, sliding doors and a sliding roof that always got stuck halfway open. And George had been one of the only saps in the world to buy the thing.

"Max," she said. "I want to inquire about your guest."

He stopped and folded the rag. "I do apologize. That's Miss Silverman. An old friend of the colony." But he wasn't apologizing at all, really, and his brazenness brought her up short. For such a tiny, quiet man, he was awfully sure of himself. "Are you feeling all right, Mrs. Grant? Perhaps you'll take a seat." He indicated the passenger side of the Darrin, but she knew she'd have to remain standing if she wanted to show any authority at all.

"So she's an artist."

"Just a friend of the colony."

"Then she must hate me."

He smiled far too kindly. "None of us bears you ill will, Mrs. Grant. You needed a place to live."

"Do you know the irony?" she said. "I'm the only one of my family who ever loved this place. I came here several times as a child. I remember the dog. Miss Mays, the director, had a wonderful sort of walrusy dog."

"Alfie."

"Yes! It was Alfie!"

"He's buried back in the woods."

"Oh, he's—Oh, now I'm sad and I don't even know why. You'll have to show me, sometime, where he is. You must have been here then yourself, but I don't remember."

"I was lower on the totem pole, at the time. Lawn care and such." He gestured, again, to the seat, and she wondered if she'd really gone that pale, or if maybe she'd smeared blue paint on her face without realizing. She gave in this time, and slid the little door, and sat. Max came around so he wasn't looking at her through the glass.

"And do you know, I always thought that when I was grown I'd come stay here. That I'd be an artist, and I'd show up with an assumed name, and no one would know. Sometimes I think it was a horrible mistake to tell my father so. What if he closed it all down just to spite me? And then sent me here to babysit the corpse. But I had to live somewhere. And I knew if I didn't come take it, he'd put it up for sale."

"There were offers," Max said.

"Max, do you suppose there's something wrong with him? With my father? I think I've just realized that I don't know him at all."

He said, "I can't speak ill of my employer."

"But how well do you know him? How *long* have you known him?"

"We were never great friends."

She put her head down on the dashboard. "Do you know what I want? I want to start all over again with a different name. I want amnesia, I think. I'd like to wake up in some city like San Francisco with no idea who I am."

He was quiet a moment and then quickly, as if he'd been working up the courage to ask it: "Have you heard of the poet Edwin Parfitt?"

Her blood reversed direction in her limbs. Yes, she'd heard of him not twenty minutes ago, and he was now committing an act of sodomy in her coat pocket. "Just recently," she said.

Max made a little cluck. "I'm surprised. He's horribly out-of-date. I have something for you. Please don't leave." And he scurried around the corner and up the stairs to the living quarters.

She worked out what she'd ask him when he came down, and the way she might hand the picture to him. But he was gone quite a long time, and when he finally returned the witch was behind him. When had she returned? Grace was upset with herself for missing it.

She climbed out of the car and struggled for balance.

Max said, "Allow me a belated introduction. My dear friend Zilla Silverman."

She extended a hand. "Miss Silverman," she said. "I do hope you enjoyed the museum."

And she immediately took it all back about this woman looking like a witch. Her eyes were kind and pale blue, a liquid blue, and there was something noble about her, the way she held her shoulders, the way she clasped Grace's hand. She said, "I'm absolutely taken with this little car behind you. It looks made of butter, doesn't it?"

Grace stepped aside so Miss Silverman could view it better. "It's pretty from the side, but from the front it has a pushed-in pig face. My husband paid far too much. It's made of fiberglass. Doesn't that sound like it would shatter from just a pebble?"

"What's it called? No, don't tell me. The Elegant Swine. The Zippy Creampuff!"

"The Gilded Lily," Grace said, and she was thrilled when Miss Silverman laughed. She found that she very much wanted this woman to like her.

"It does have the funniest face on the front. The Pucker-Up-and-Kiss-Me-Quick. What *is* it called?"

"The Kaiser-Darrin."

"Oh, it's German!"

"No, no, George would never." She knew what she was implying, what she'd often implied back in Toronto—that George had
served—when really he'd spent the war years scooping up young
widows like candy from a piñata. But she found that the implication excused his behavior somewhat. And if this Zilla Silverman
planned on staying for any length of time, she was sure, sooner or
later, to see George at his worst. It was true though that he'd
never buy a German car.

And then, because she wanted to change the subject, and
because the scotch was getting to her, she said, "You have the
loveliest teeth. Like pearls. It shows you were well raised. I've always said, if you want to know someone's lot in life, look at his
teeth." In fact there was a small space between Miss Silverman's
incisors, one of which was chipped, but the effect was all the
more charming.

"Well, that's a new idea. Fortune-telling by the teeth. Dento-
mancy!"

"Orthomancy," Max offered.

"Yes! I was just thinking it about poor Amy, the other day,
looking at her teeth. They're horrid, and you can tell she just
hasn't had a fair chance in life. I do wish she could get them
fixed." She'd forgotten about the ruse that Amy was Max's
niece—it was clumsy of her—but she could see now by the look
on Max's face that there was something far worse wrong
than that. He was looking past her shoulder, back toward the
door of the mechanical room. Grace just barely avoided turning
to see if Amy was standing right there in the doorway. It was
where Amy had said she was sleeping, and it was surely where she
was right now. Well, *now* there was another reason for Amy to
despise her, to glare. Grace was only glad she hadn't brought up

the photograph, with Amy hiding the whole time and listening like a little rabbit. "Well," she said. "Hadn't you better fetch George soon from the club?"

Max handed her a small, red book. *Edwin Parfitt: His Selected Verse.* He said, "I've marked the right poem with a paper."

She turned back, halfway to the door. "I meant to ask about the fish," she said. "What are we to do with them in winter? Do they just freeze solid?"

"I bring them in," Max said. His voice stayed as quiet as ever, though she was all the way across the garage. "They'll outlive us both." She was nearly out the door when he said, "Do you know what they like better than anything?"

"No."

"A root beer float."

"I don't understand." She thought over the words. It was like a riddle, but it made no sense.

"You don't?" He looked almost sad.

"Oh, don't worry, dear," Miss Silverman said. "I've never understood him myself!"

Grace stuck both the book and photo in the attic so George wouldn't come across them. Miss Silverman walked the grounds when Max took off to retrieve George, and Ludo raked leaves. Nothing else of note happened the rest of the day.

She was quite taken with the poem, which was about Proteus, and she was pleased that her recall of mythology and meter and rhyme were finally being tested. She appreciated certain lines, the "thickening, quickening night," and "Daphne's branches, sleeved in moss." She also understood the inversion Parfitt had accomplished: In his telling, everyone wanted to pin Proteus down to make him remember the past, not to tell the future. Though what he was so loath to remember she couldn't quite glean. Something about a lightning crash, and the bit about "paying to Charon his tongue-lidded coin," which she took to mean a death.

Most fascinating, though, was the short introduction written in 1950 by Edna St. Vincent Millay. *"Edwin Parfitt was not so much a giant of the poetic world,"* it read, *"as one of its forest elves, whose song lures us deeper into the wood—though we may neither recognize the tune nor ever find the piper."* It went on to claim that his classicism of theme and form had been horribly misread by the critics. At the end came an astonishing paragraph:

> It has been five years now since Eddie Parfitt, after an insurmountable personal loss, took his own life at Lake Glinow, Wisconsin. In accordance with his wishes, he was not buried but wrapped in white cloth and burned, his ashes set loose to the wind. Those of us in attendance took some small delight in knowing those ashes would find rest on far and unsuspecting plots of earth, that they would bless and fertilize their landing places. As, too, will these poems.

Grace wondered if this paragraph was the true reason Max had given her the book: if, after her outburst, he assumed she knew more than she did, and wanted her to learn what had become of her father's partner in sodomy. That didn't seem right, though. She scanned it again, wishing she'd find the words *fish* or *root beer*, wishing the paragraph would tell her where Amy had come from or when Zilla Silverman would leave. Perhaps this book could read her tarot.

Really she supposed Max had only given it to her because she'd spoken of starting over, and he had recalled the poem about Proteus shifting shape. But he must have misunderstood her, then. What Grace wanted to run from wasn't the past, or even the future as the original Proteus had, but rather the present. Here she was, crystallized in time, in a place where nothing ever really happened, at least not to her, while the world marched on without her back in Toronto. It wasn't so much the house that she wanted to escape, or George, even as his charm faded like a sun-tan, but the feel of every moment being precisely *now*, with no cause and no consequence. She supposed a Buddhist might appreciate it. But it wasn't for her.

On Friday morning (nothing around but sunlight and some distant sounds traveling out the kitchen windows and back in through the dormers), she sat in the attic in her robe and slippers and read the introduction for the fifth time. It struck her only then that Millay referred to Parfitt's "small dark eyes, and dark hair, slickly parted." She crossed the floor and pulled out the file she'd sworn she'd never open again. The grinning man on the left had pale, wavy hair. Golden or light brown. No one would call his eyes small. It couldn't be Parfitt. But neither could the man on the right, who, she was more certain than ever, was her father. His uneven shoulders, his chin. She turned it over, to see if some perverse and helpful archivist had recorded their names for posterity, but there was nothing. Well. She'd do it herself, then. She snatched up the pencil from her greenhouse sketch and, holding the photo up to the window so she could see the image through its paper, wrote "*Father*" right across his backside. It felt like nailing him down, accusing him. On the reverse of the other man's buttocks, she drew a question mark. Then she stuffed it back in the folder, and the folder back in the cabinet.

Miss Silverman was gone, had been gone since yesterday, and Grace was unduly bereft. A spectator with no spectacle. George had disappeared for a day and then returned. The leaves were gone, except on a few stubborn oaks, and the catalpa was all pods. They made music in the wind, like maracas. It was freezing now in the attic, and so she walked its perimeter, closing each of the twelve dormers, and came to the northeast one last, the one closest to the coach house. Sometimes she thought this was where her grandmother had done it. Her father would never talk about Violet, so most of the very little that Grace knew she'd learned from her mother. Violet had killed herself at Laurelfield in 1906, when Grace's father was only two. For this, she was never to be forgiven by anyone in the family. Her name was never used for babies, her grave (they'd taken the body by train all the way back to Toronto) wasn't visited. When Grace and George first arrived, back in May, Grace had asked Mrs. Carmichael which part of the house was supposed to be the haunted bit. "Oh, the attic!" Mrs. Carmichael had said, and then Grace had to endure fifteen minutes of ridiculous stories about flickering lights and doors that shut themselves. "So that's where she did it, then?" Grace had asked. "Violet, I mean. It was the attic?" Mrs. Carmichael had laughed. "I wasn't here myself, ma'am. I couldn't tell you beyond what I've heard. But the artists used to say so."

"And did she hang herself?"

Mrs. Carmichael put down her silver polish and looked puzzled. "It's funny. I don't know why, but I always assumed she jumped."

Grace watched George take the Darrin out of the garage. Max waved after him, and George backed out toward the big house, then took off like a French racer through the gate. When he drove like that, when he took the Darrin, it was a sure sign he wouldn't be home the same day. Maybe he was headed to Chicago. To a whorehouse. She wondered what it would be like to start life over as a whore, to show up on the step of a *house of ill repute*, to live there entertaining the men, the handsome ones only, until, one day, George would stumble in. And either recognize her, or not.

Max closed the garage door and disappeared inside, and then there was absolutely no one left in the world but Grace. She wasn't serious about it in the slightest, but before she closed this last window for the winter, she wanted to see what it felt like, if it was even possible. She stepped out of her slippers and up onto the sill, bracing her feet against the outer edges, clinging with both hands to the bottom of the glass. She had to crouch to fit inside the small, open square, and the wind rushed straight through her dressing gown. It didn't look far enough, really. You'd land on the grass, if you didn't hit the pine tree on your way down. You'd at least end up in a wheelchair, but you might or might not die, and someone wanting to do herself in would undoubtedly choose something more certain. Maybe she'd poisoned herself, after all.

Below, Max came out of the coach house, out the mechanical room door right next to the stone wall. It wasn't his usual way out, and there was something odd about the way he walked too: slowly at first, as if he were scoping things out, then very quickly, all the way along the wall to the gate. He had a leather satchel over his shoulder.

Perhaps this was the third strange thing, the one she'd been waiting for after the rabbits and the witch.

She ought to follow him. It was better than hanging out a window, and better than sitting here waiting for some five-act drama to unfold right on the lawn. She hopped inside and dressed quickly and retrieved her bicycle from the tree it had been leaning against, untouched, since July. She assumed Max must have walked toward town, and she was right: After a few blocks she saw him hurrying along the opposite sidewalk. He turned left, toward the college, and she hung back and followed as obliquely as possible.

He walked past the main gates, across a quadrangle, and through the side door of a Gothic building. Grace parked at a stand of student bikes and walked toward the same door, trying to look purposeful and collegiate. Inside, students milled and sat on hallway benches, and in all directions the classrooms were filling. The signs on the bulletin boards seemed history related. Max had vanished. She peeked tentatively through an open door, then another, and finally she spied the back of his head in a lecture hall. He took a notebook from his satchel, just as his neighbors were doing, and set it on the table in front of him. He turned and whispered something to the thin-shouldered blond boy on his right. A few more students brushed past Grace, and finally a professor strode to the front, with a ripped shopping bag instead of a briefcase.

"Have we spent every waking moment reading about the Bolsheviks?" he asked, and a laughing groan rose from the room. "Fantastic."

She shouldn't hang around, even though she might have liked to audit a class herself. An art class, perhaps. She'd adore a good course on the Dutch masters. She knew what would happen, though. George would find out, and then one day he'd storm in and drag her out of the class by the arm. And she couldn't abide the looks, the gawking undergraduates, and she'd never be able to return. So that was the end of that particular fantasy. She walked out of the building, smiling at the students: the girls in their sweater sets, the boys leaning and smoking and glancing with curiosity at Grace.

Back through town. She aimed her bicycle wheels at individual dead leaves, loving the crunch. She didn't particularly want to go home just yet. There was a beauty parlor with a bicycle stand in front, Matilda's House of Style, and she might as well follow her impulse inside. She had put ten dollars in her pocket, and this would at least be a place to sit down. The cycling had tired her quite a bit.

The woman at the desk told her there was a spot open in twenty minutes, and asked her name. "Amy Hall," Grace said.

And she smiled and tucked her hair behind her ears, and sat to read a copy of *Vogue*.

When they called Amy, she was ready—she'd prepared herself to respond to the name—and she had a shampoo and then sat in the chair while Matilda cleaned her scissors.

"I want it just below the ears," she said. "I need a new look." Matilda began combing, and told her she had lovely hair, just like Grace Kelly. "Oh, you're too sweet." She was trying out just a bit of southern accent, not a harsh one like Amy's but a refined version. "You know, I've just moved here from Florida. My husband Max and I. I thought I'd like a new cut to go with the new house."

"Oh, congratulations!"

"It's just a little one. You know, a starter home. It used to be the coach house of an old estate, but they've converted it. I'll tell you, though, I'm not used to this cold. And to think, it's only October! I don't know what I'll do with myself this winter."

"Long underwear!" Matilda said. "That's my advice." She raked Grace's hair out in a straight line and chopped an inch from the end. "And maybe you'll start a family. Some meat on the bones will keep you warm."

To her surprise, Grace actually blushed. She'd sooner give herself a lobotomy than have a baby with George right now, but the newlywed Amy and her husband Max might indeed love to have a daughter, a little girl with soft cheeks and smocked dresses. She marveled at how readily she could feel the emotions of this invented self.

She was on her way through the front door when she saw rabbits. Just three this time, moving quickly along the front of the house. Not so much fleeing her footsteps as running toward a secret party. Grace wondered why on earth God or nature would put that puff of white on their rear ends, when everything else about the rabbit seemed designed for maximum camouflage. Their silence, their speed, their fur like dried grass. But then, at the back, this white target, this flash of light. And they'd never know, would they? Had any rabbit ever seen its own backside, seen the way it was trailed by its own demise?

She followed them around the house.

Outside the solarium, Ludo had marked the lines for the greenhouse with little flags. He'd made arrangements for a crew to come dig out the foundation before the ground got hard. He'd ordered the glass and cement, too, and was working with a friend who'd built greenhouses up and down the North Shore.

She couldn't see where the rabbits had gone. The ivy on the house had shrunk back a bit for fall, as slowly as a balding man's hair. Beneath, the bricks showed through. She found their regularity troubling, their strict overlapping. Something about the lockstep rigidity sickened her, and she thought she'd rather have the tangles of ivy back.

Back inside, she walked through the living room—she wasn't at all sure what to do with it, but maybe paint it over in coral— and the dining room, which, when empty, was so overwhelmed by her grandmother's portrait as to seem a shrine. Violet always looked a little surprised, as if Grace had caught her in the middle of some wildly inappropriate thought and she'd just managed to compose herself.

Grace heard someone across in the library, but when she got there it was empty. She loved this room best if only because there were still small relics of the artists who'd gathered every night for predinner drinks just a year before. Scribbled in the endpapers of an old copy of *Dombey and Son*, she'd found a ridiculous "List of Demands," added to over the years in different hands: head massages, a bugle corps, Chinese footmen, better weather, lullabies, resident astrologer. She'd hidden that book deep in the shelf to protect it, and she checked now that it was safe. The jade monkey was gone from the bar, though, and she wondered where it could have gone. She checked all the shelves, and she checked under the leather couches. She'd have thought George took it, but he hated the library even more than he hated the portrait of Violet— he'd seen strange shadows there the week they moved in, and hadn't set foot in it since. At first he had Mrs. Carmichael bring him out his drinks, but then he just began stocking his bureau as a bar. Grace would have, as a result, spent all her time in this room for the privacy, were it not for the windows between each set of shelves, on three sides of the room. It was an observation tank, and anyone walking from the driveway to the kitchen door would see right in. And perhaps that was what happened. Amy had looked in, on her walks from the coach house, envying the little monkey till she had to have it. But to make sure, Grace went first to Mrs. Carmichael, watering in the solarium, and to Rosamund in the kitchen, and even to Ludo and Beatrice, and none of them even knew what she was talking about, except Mrs. Carmichael, who was sure she had dusted it Friday.

It *must* be, then. Amy was a child, a greedy child. Grace had known this all along. She walked straight to the coach house, and up the stairs to the living quarters. The stairs came out in the small kitchen, and she had to orient herself to think which was Max's apartment and which must be Amy's. She knocked on Max's door first, to be sure he wasn't back, then walked into Amy's side without knocking. The outer room had a sitting area. Well-thumbed fashion magazines on a little table. Fashion! All Amy ever wore were those three cotton dresses, in rotation.

She moved silently to the next doorway. Amy lay on her bed, on her stomach. Grace said, "Amy, I do hope you plan to return everything you've borrowed."

The girl bolted up and straightened her blanket. "I'm—hello. Mrs. Grant."

"I expect my things returned before dinner."

"Only, I—which things?"

"Anything borrowed from the estate, including the jade monkey from the library. I don't think you'll be staying much longer, but you might yet salvage a letter of reference from me if you're forthcoming."

Amy stood and looked around the room frantically, as if checking that she'd hidden everything properly. "Ma'am, I truly don't understand. If I've done something wrong it was a pure mistake."

"Amy," she said. "I don't know who you are, except that you are not Max's niece. Maybe you're his lover, only I don't think so. That's not it, is it? You're a child, but you sit in judgment and you think you know how you'd act if you were me. You think George wouldn't hit you, that you'd tame him. Well, you couldn't."

"Ma'am, you're mistaken." There were fat tears collecting on her chin. "I'm sorry, but you're mistaken."

Grace felt Amy's pain in her own stomach, she did. It was a convulsion, like holding back a sob. But all she could think to do was make it worse, as if that would solve everything. She imagined this was how a killer felt, halfway through the job. Finish stabbing the fellow, so there was no one left to feel it. She said, "Here's what you don't know yet: So often in life, you get exactly what you look for. If you want a George, you'll get a George. The worst thing I could wish you is everything you want."

She meant to leave Amy standing there silenced and shamed, but as she turned Amy said, quietly, "Speak for yourself."

And Grace might have slapped her, she really might have, if she hadn't heard Max come up to the kitchen just then. She walked out and told Max she'd been wondering where he was.

"A quick trip to the doctor," he said, and smiled. "My old knee problem from the war. Can I drive you somewhere?"

"Oh!" she said. "No, but—what time did George take the Darrin out?"

"Around ten."

Grace glanced around the kitchen, and tried to find something to say. "We should get that fixed," she said, pointing at the big board patching up the wall. It was the wall shared with Amy's bathroom and closet, and it was painted yellow, like the rest of the kitchen. "What is it?"

"It's—I believe there was an electrical problem once. It doesn't bother me a bit."

"But you shouldn't have to live someplace all stitched together."

He set his satchel on the table. It looked so soft.

"I know there to be at least five layers of paint over that thing. Another five, and it will all come even. Really, it's not worth the disruption."

His ears were round, like little handles. Grace liked that about him, and she liked the way he sometimes looked almost in love with her. Perhaps he was. She felt wonderfully visible just then, as if something might happen to her, and not just in front of her.

She said, "All right, Max," and smiled in a way she normally wouldn't have, a way her mother never would have smiled at a servant. She trotted downstairs and waved to Ludo, who was pushing a wheelbarrow full of sticks back to the fire pile.

George was shaking her by the hip. He was saying, "What's that smell? What is it?"

Grace rolled over and tried to feel where the blanket had gone. "Is something burning?"

"No, it's you." He turned the light on, and when Grace managed to open her eyes she saw that he hadn't shaved all day, that the cleft in his chin was filled in with black stubble. He had a long red string tied around his neck, like an opera-length neck-lace, and she couldn't think why that would be. "Why do you smell that way?" He came back to the bed, though it took him a few tries to propel himself in the right direction. Grace sat up, and George stood over her and put his fingers in her hair. "Why did you cut your hair off?"

"The hairdresser did. I needed a trim."

"You think I want you looking like a boy?"

"George, I want to sleep." She slid down under the blanket. "What time is it?"

He pulled the covers completely off the bed and stood over her. "You smell like sex."

"That's ridiculous. I smell like the outdoors. I went for a bike ride."

He yanked her nightgown up to her stomach, and stuck his face between her legs and sniffed loudly. "You smell like you were fucking some fungus-covered hustler."

"*George.*"

She meant to pull him on top of her and turn it into sex before things got worse, but he had rolled her, with one push, to the edge of the bed, and he rolled her again till she fell. Her forehead hit something on the way down. It was hard and sharp, and it must have been the corner of the nightstand. Her whole head and neck throbbed, but especially above her left eyebrow, and when she put her hand there it came away covered in blood.

"George, *look!*"

"Oh, shit," he said. "Oh, Grace, come on. Don't—I'll get a towel."

And he did, one of the GGG monogrammed set from her Saville cousins, and it turned from powder blue to reddish brown in seconds.

"Please ring Max," she said. "I want to go for stitches."

His mouth was open, and he looked like a fish. He said, "I'll take you."

"The hell you will. Either ring Max or bring me the phone."

"What will you say?"

"That I fell off the bed."

"Grace, I love you."

"I know that."

"And you love me."

"Yes. Yes."

He sat on the ground and put his head between his knees, and started rocking like a little boy. Grace stood gingerly and went for the telephone herself.

Max took her in the Capri. There was Amy, owl-eyed at the coach house window as they crunched down the drive.

A hat with a little veil, combined with the sunglasses, hid the stitches and bandage quite well when she ventured out, even if she did look like an escapee from Hollywood. George disappeared for five straight days after that—he was gone by the time Grace and Max returned in the morning—and Grace passed the time by following Max on her bicycle. Now that she knew where he was headed she could hang behind quite a bit, and after he left the property he never seemed to look back.

Might she be in love with him? It was one explanation for this compulsion to follow his every move, but she doubted that was it. He wasn't the type she'd enjoy making love to—he'd be too polite, too quiet, which had been the problem with all the boys back in Toronto. She thought of Lionel, who had kissed her wrist and wouldn't stop asking what she wanted. "Do you like this? Tell me what to do. What do you want me to do?" The problem with George was that she could never be happy with a man who *wasn't* George. She searched herself to see if she held any sort of physical longing for Max, and really she didn't think so. But he was a nut she wanted to crack.

He was taking two classes: the one with the Bolsheviks (Grace thought for a while that it was Russian history, but one day as she listened at the door the professor talked about the Balkans, and she became less sure) and one on the novels of Thackeray and Dickens. She heard enough of that one that she became curious about *Vanity Fair*, which she'd never read, and scared up a copy from the Laurelfield library. Becky Sharp was a wicked heroine, and Grace loved her immediately. Becky was doomed, that was clear. No vice went unpunished in the nineteenth-century novel.

She never stayed more than ten minutes outside the classroom doors, afraid Max might one day head out to use the restroom and discover her. She found, though, that when she biked directly home, Max often didn't return for two or three hours. Certainly the classes weren't that long. In the English building was a smaller hallway off the main one, and she realized she could stand by the corner examining the framed map of Literary England without arousing much suspicion. She did that one Tuesday as the class let out. She was ready to run, but Max lingered by the door with the same blond boy he'd whispered to that first day in the history lecture. They walked together, shoulder to shoulder, down the stairs. Grace stayed and looked down from the window, and saw which way they walked: to the large building with ivy, talking together the whole time. After they'd passed through the double doors, she followed.

It was the library. She picked a direction and walked briskly past the front desk, only to find herself in a reference room with no one in it. She found a larger room with card catalogues, and a study area where the students sat smoking, but she didn't see Max. Upstairs were study carrels and shelves packed thickly together. She supposed if Max saw her she could always pretend she'd been looking for some book. It wasn't any odder for her to be here, after all, than for him to be.

A girl raced past and nearly knocked Grace over with her poodle skirt. Peering down a long aisle, Grace saw, on the far end, the blond boy, walking alone now. She went as far down the aisle as she dared, and managed to watch him through the last bit of shelf. He walked through a door and shut it. There were several such doors along the far wall, and through the open ones she could see very small rooms with desks. Her own college library had offered similar setups: for the girls who wanted no distractions, the ones with ambitious senior projects.

Not two feet in front of her, Max passed by, eyes down. He didn't notice her. She watched as he entered the same room, and as the door once again clicked shut.

If it hadn't been for that photograph, so fresh in her mind, it might have taken her quite a bit longer to figure it all out.

She stood there at the end of the aisle, just stood there, a long time, feeling like an all-around nitwit. She was humiliated that she'd been so fascinated by Max, that she'd liked how he looked at her. She wondered if the world were full of degenerates, Max and this boy and her father and the other man in the photograph, and who knew how many others, all around her, and she in the middle of it, blind and oblivious. Or maybe there was something connecting it all. Her father had told her that Max wasn't to be dismissed under any circumstance. And maybe it was only because Max and her father frequented the same dark bars, the same alleys and closets. Max and her father, her father and Max. Yet they didn't seem to care for each other a bit. Perhaps that wasn't a requisite, in these types of relations. Or maybe he was simply afraid of what Max knew about him.

She knew she ought to leave. If Max found her there *now*, her face would betray her. She thought about that boy, no more than twenty, and how maybe she oughtn't leave him alone there with a man twice his age, how the boy's mother would have preferred Grace to break down the door and send him home at once, his luggage following after.

She went back to the ground floor and sat on one of the smoking couches where she could see the stairs. She held the *Tribune* open in front of her face. Max came down alone, twenty minutes later, and though she expected the boy would follow a few casual paces behind, he didn't. Grace waited another twenty minutes, and then she walked upstairs and back through the aisles. She found the boy at a regular small study carrel, hunched over a textbook. There were other students, but not terribly near. She walked around the carrel, pretending to look for something, and she glanced at his face, at his prodigious eyebrows. He didn't seem distressed, or even guilty—just wholly immersed in his studies.

"Excuse me," she said, and he looked up. "I'm afraid I'm lost."

He gave a sly smile and gestured around the room. "It's the library," he whispered.

"Yes." She laughed. "And I—My husband is a trustee of the college, and he's left me to fend for myself while he meets the dean. I got here, and I don't even know what floor this is. All I'm looking for is the powder room."

The boy stood and nodded. "Pleased to help a damsel in distress." If she hadn't known better, she'd have thought he was flirting.

She followed as slowly as she could, so she'd have time to think what to ask. "You look like a senior," she said.

"Sophomore." He stopped and extended his hand. "Sidney Cole of Indianapolis. Sid."

"Amy Hall," she said. "Of New York." They continued walking. "And do you like it here?"

"Oh yes." But she doubted he did at all. How could he, the poor thing? Boys like that never lasted anywhere long.

"People are friendly?"

"Enough are."

She wanted to say something useful, but what? She had nothing to tell this boy about how to live his life. Besides, they had reached the ladies' room door. "Well," was all she could think of. "Thank you. Do take care of yourself, Sid."

The Darrin was back, parked in the middle of the driveway and waiting for Max to store it. Grace picked up the mail and went directly to the attic, and hoped George at least wasn't drunk enough to destroy things down below.

A letter from her college friend Harriet, tentative, curious if Grace would come home soon. Harriet had been one of the very few at the wedding, and—of those—one of the only ones not to pull Grace aside, to ask if she was *sure*.

She wouldn't write back. What was there to say?

By dinnertime, the Darrin was gone again, and a hard knot that she hadn't realized was in her stomach melted away. She'd have dinner alone, and she was getting rather used to it. She brought down *Vanity Fair*—Captain Osborne had just asked Becky to run away with him—and sat at the table.

After a long time, she heard a wail from the kitchen, a cry that wasn't sudden or surprised, more like part of an ongoing tantrum. There was talking—several voices, all female—and then a low, constant sob. Grace considered heading back there, but it was on principle that she didn't. Dinner was fourteen minutes late. The cook could apologize when she emerged.

The crying got louder before it stopped altogether. When Rosamund walked out, she didn't have a single dish in her hands. Her face was red, but Grace could tell immediately she hadn't been the one crying. She'd known all along, really, that it was Amy. Rosamund stood inside the door, her arms folded across her waist, and she said, "I can't do it any longer. I'd gladly stay on for you, but I won't work for *him*. I refuse."

"He's not even here tonight," Grace said. "He took the Darrin out again. And you haven't served him a meal in five days."

"Listen." She had lowered her voice, though she didn't come any closer to Grace. Why didn't she talk like a servant? None of these American ones did. "I apologize for my language. But, ma'am—he's raped her." Her nostrils flared and she put her hand to her earlobe, but she kept her eyes straight on Grace. All Grace could think of was throwing a plate right at Rosamund's mouth until she stopped talking, until she vanished from the earth. "She's been in there two hours, and she won't stop to breathe. Beatrice is giving her tea. He took her into the Longhouse and he forced himself on her."

"Well," Grace said. And she spoke on instinct, or at least she said what she imagined her mother might say, even though she didn't know what that would be till she heard it come out of her mouth. "I very much doubt that's true. If you must know, Amy lies and steals, and she's quite in love with George. He's had his way with her, I do know that, I'm not blind. But I've *seen* her. She was quite willing. I'm afraid she's played you for a fool."

"Now why would she do that?"

Grace stood from the table and left her chair out, and pushed past the cook into the kitchen. Amy was perfectly well clothed, her dress not even ripped or stained, except that someone had draped a kitchen towel around her shoulders. She and Beatrice sat side by side on chairs, Beatrice still in her gardening boots. Grace wanted to stick all three women into the Frigidaire and lock the door.

"Amy," she said. "Are you with child?"

Amy looked up with red, swollen little eyes. She choked out a whisper: "No, ma'am. I don't think the timing—no."

"Then I don't understand the change. It's all been fine with you up till now. Or perhaps it's because I caught you stealing. The thing of it, Amy, is that you aren't going to wedge us apart. If I leave George, or if George leaves me, it won't be because of some thieving girl."

Amy screamed into her hands and rocked forward, and Beatrice bent over her and rubbed her back. Beatrice said, "I found her outside the Longhouse."

"But you didn't hear her when she was *in* the Longhouse, did you? She must not have screamed very loudly. Beatrice, I haven't invited you into my kitchen."

Beatrice looked shocked, but then, as Grace had known she would, she nodded and walked slowly to the back door. She said, "Amy, I'll be in the garden cottage."

There was soup boiling on the stove, getting too thick, probably.

Grace said, "Amy, are you quitting your job?"

"No, ma'am."

"*I'm* the one quitting," Rosamund said. "And, forgive me, you ought to quit too, ma'am. You ought to leave this house and get back to Canada before he slices you to bits. And Amy ought to leave, and Beatrice ought to leave, and anyone with any sense should get out of here. But as it seems I'm the only one with a backbone, I'll be leaving alone tonight." She whipped her apron off, as if more drama were necessary, and left it behind her on the counter.

She was gone, and it was just Grace and Amy, alone in the kitchen.

Grace said, "You'll have to serve the soup then."

"Yes."

She didn't know what to think. How could she possibly know what to think? But she did have one clear and horrible realization, as she sat back at the dining table. The drama she had sought in George, the lust and fire, would never involve her anymore, because she was the one married to him. He might gash her face, but he wouldn't ravish her, wouldn't focus his whole being on her seduction. The drama would always be, from now on, about other women.

Amy brought her the soup, clattering the bowl on the saucer and hyperventilating the whole way. Cream of squash, cooked to a gelatinous mess.

Grace wanted to sob until she flowed to the floor and out of the house and into Lake Michigan.

She said, "Amy, I'll want more water."

And when Amy brought her more water, she sent her back for another roll.

And when she brought the roll, she told her to take the soup away because it wasn't any good.

The next day there was a telegram from Toronto: FATHER GRAVELY ILL. TWO OR THREE WEEKS LEFT PLEASE COME HOME.

She wouldn't do it. She couldn't face him now. He'd see right through everything, he'd see that she knew about his degeneracy, and he'd see that he'd been right about George, and she'd break down screaming and she'd tear her clothes and move back to Toronto forever. And do what? And live how? And George would follow her there, and ruin everything for everyone, for her brother and her mother, and the whole city would see her as the girl who came home broken, rather than the girl who ran off for love.

And then she sat and cried all afternoon. Because if it was true that her father was dying, and if George was right that no one would ever visit her here, and if she was too stubborn to go home, then she'd never see any of them again.

Three days later, she went to the coach house when Amy was busy in the kitchen. Amy was cooking everything now, though Grace knew Beatrice snuck in there, whenever she could, to help. The food was dreadful: browned meat covered in sour cream and baked for an eternity; chopped celery covered in cheese and baked; sliced apples for dessert, smothered in a mash of cream cheese and powdered sugar. Grace wanted her gone, wanted her back wherever she'd come from, but she couldn't bring herself to do it, not least because Amy might go to the police then, might say enough that word would spread, as word always spreads, and word could reach Canada. It could reach her father on his deathbed.

But she did have a plan, and having one made her feel better. It came together just when the greenhouse plans came together, as if she were turning out, after all, to be the architect of her own life.

She found Max in the garage and asked him to walk with her to see the digging. "I want your opinion," she said, though it made no sense why someone would have any particular opinion about a hole in the ground. They walked to the far end of the house and stared into the rectangular hollow for the greenhouse foundation. Ludo and two Negroes and a red-haired man all stood in it, poking around the edges of the steps that currently led down from the door of the solarium. They'd have to pull out those steps like decayed teeth, and the concrete floor of the greenhouse would come even with the door. Max greeted the men and looked without great interest at their progress, and when she asked if she might speak to him on the terrace, he nodded and followed her around the corner. They sat looking out at the fountain and the paths that spread from it like rays, and the fire pile growing tall back by the woods, and the Longhouse, and the little studio behind that and, on the far side, the cottage studio that used to house composers and was now the shed for Ludo and Beatrice. Next to the cottage, Beatrice's vegetable garden was finished and brown.

Grace said, "Max, I'm going to ask a favor of you. Amy's been here quite a while now, and it's time for her to move on. You know

she's become a terrible distraction to everyone. I think she's begun stealing things, as well."

"You'd be out a cook."

"She's no cook. And you've seen how unhappy she's been,
these past few days." Max looked puzzled, and she wondered if
Amy and Beatrice had managed to keep all the hysterics from
him. "Don't you think you can send her home now?"

He rested his hands on his legs as if he were keeping them still
only through great effort. "It would be difficult."

Grace reached into her coat pocket and brought out a key ring
with four small keys. "I thought I'd offer you my keys to the artists'
studios. You could use them however you'd like. You know—" and
she was glad he was gazing out at the grounds in confusion, and
not at her "—sometimes I think about those boys at the college.
I worry about them, so far from home. If you meet any who are in
need of a good meal, or a place to rest, you could invite them to
visit you here, and they might even use the daybeds in the studios. Surely there's someone who wants a quiet space."

She hadn't been sure, when she'd rehearsed this, what his reaction might be. Shame, perhaps, and a grateful exchanging of fa-
vors. Or he might be angry and take it as blackmail, which would
work as well. She wasn't prepared for him to turn and grin at her.
She'd never even seen such an expression on his face. All the
composure, all the reserve she'd come to know as Max, fell away
in that moment, and she was looking at someone she'd never met.

"I already have keys," he said. "You should hold on to those."

"She's not your niece," Grace said.

"Not technically."

"But she'll listen to you. I don't imagine she's in *love* with you."

He laughed softly. "No. She's quite naïve, I think. She's not
like you, she doesn't realize how I am, but she's fond of me. And
Grace, I'll say quite plainly that I won't send her home." Only a

moment later did she realize that he'd not only defied her, he'd called her Grace. And what could she do about any of it? Threaten to tell her father, when she had no idea what history lay between them? If she couldn't dismiss him, and he wouldn't do what she said, then it was quite obvious that he was really the one in charge. He said, "Some fellow brought her to Chicago, is what happened. He convinced her to leave Florida with him, which, from what I understand, likely saved her life. But it turned disastrous. As those things tend to. She's only eighteen. Do you know how she came to us? Beatrice found her outside the gate, peering in. She'd been knocking on every door down the street, looking for work. She's remarkably resourceful. In Chicago, before she left the man, she asked around where the nicest houses were, and someone said she ought to come up here. She told me she figured that even if she failed, no one in a small town would let her sleep on the street. Whereas in the city . . . She'd been to a hundred houses before she met Beatrice."

"How lucky that she found us." She was amazed, really, at how sharp her voice was, how mean. It was exactly like her mother's.

"This has always been a place for strays. The people who need to find Laurelfield always find it. Listen, Grace, she's got nothing back home. A horrible family. A whole family of Georges. I can't send her."

"Why don't you just marry her, then? If you care more about Amy than your employment here. Are you capable of being with a woman? It would be a happier marriage than some, even if it were a farce. And then you could keep her out of everyone else's business, and maybe you could leave alone poor Sid Cole of Indianapolis."

Max did look startled now, and perhaps Grace shouldn't have let on that she had Sid's name. He'd been impressed with her intuition, her worldliness, and now he knew she was just a snoop.

He stood, and at first she thought he was stalking off, but he came instead and knelt down in front of her chair, right on the stone floor, right in the dead leaves.

He said, "You don't look good."

It ought to have insulted her greatly, but it didn't. Maybe it was a relief to have someone in charge, someone who cared if she lived or died. He was trying to get her to look at him, right at him. That was why he'd gotten down so low. And she couldn't do it. She looked over his shoulder, out at the dry fountain.

"Grace," he said. "Aren't you the one who needs to get out of here?"

She kept staring until the fountain became a gray blur, no closer or farther than the trees beyond.

"Grace. We're similar, you know. Maybe it's something I shouldn't say, but it's true. Did you read that poem?"

"It didn't apply."

"The point is to reinvent yourself."

She felt like reaching out to touch Max's dark hair. She might push a small dent into it with her finger, and it might stay that way. Instead she stood to leave, while she still had some small remnant of dignity.

He said, "I'd marry you myself."

"That's very kind."

Saturday was Guy Fawkes Day. No one in the States seemed to celebrate it, but when George showed up at breakfast—Grace was mildly surprised to see him, as he hadn't slept in their bed—she suggested they do a bonfire that night. The burn pile was so tall.

George said, "That's a fine plan."

He was lit by the sun, black curls in every direction, eyes bright green and unclouded. She loved him at breakfast. If she kissed him she would taste like Listerine, and when he stretched his arms and back she could hear the cracks. In the morning he was like a small, clean snowball—one that would roll downhill all day, picking up rocks and darkness and growing enormous and sharp.

A shaking Amy brought coffee without looking at either of them. It smelled terrible, acrid and offensive, and Grace thought she might retch. She said, "Amy, can you take this away? There's something wrong with it."

George tasted his. "It's perfectly fine."

But Grace handed her cup to Amy, who hurried it back to the kitchen.

"If you drop dead from poison, I'll know who did it," Grace said.

Grace asked Ludo to plan the bonfire, and she thought she and George might even have dinner on the inner terrace, after the blaze was going. But by three in the afternoon George was roaring drunk, and he found her sitting on the bed with the telegram that had just arrived from Toronto. All it said was FATHER WORSENING, PLEASE ADVISE IF COMING, but she couldn't keep from staring at it, as if it would update itself every time there was a change, every time her father sat up to eat a bite of soup. George yanked it from her and she told him what was happening, but that she didn't think she'd go.

"They're lying to you," he said. "He's not sick. They want to get you up there and lock you in a closet."

"That's not fair."

"No. Exactly."

"That isn't—George, what are you doing?"

Because now George was shredding the telegram, pouring the shreds into the ashtray on his bureau, and lighting them with a match. She thought of yelling or grabbing it, but then he might throw the whole thing, still on fire. So she waited till it had smoldered to nothing. Then she said, "That wasn't necessary."

"*Ha!* What do you do, all day long? You sit in that attic, mooning over your grandfather's precious files, then you sit at dinner staring at your lunatic grandmother."

"They aren't my grandfather's files."

"And where the hell are we? We're in a—we're on an *altar*. This place is an altar to your family. How is this supposed to be my house when it's the Devohr International Museum?"

She hooked her finger through his belt and pulled him toward the bed. "I'll make it up to you," she said.

But he pushed her onto the mattress and left her there, and then she listened for quite a long time as he stormed through the house opening and shutting doors, until it turned from storming to crashing. He must have drunk more in the meantime. And the sun was already going down.

She stood in the bedroom doorway and watched him come up the stairs, then stumble all the way down the hall to the open door of the attic steps. He disappeared, and came back a minute later with his arms full of file folders. The Parfitt book was balanced on top.

He saw her, but he didn't stop except to call out "*Remember, remember the fifth of November!*" And then, from halfway down: "What do you say, Duck? Fall cleaning!"

Grace ran to the attic door and thought of locking it, but the key was all the way down in the kitchen. She might have gone in and locked it from the inside, only George would just kick the door in, and what would that accomplish? She went into the flowered bedroom and watched from the window as he strode across the lawn, papers flying from the files. He rolled up the folders and stuck each into a space between sticks. Ludo stood by the cottage, keeping quite a distance. Beatrice, she assumed, was in the kitchen helping Amy.

He was coming back, and she ran, while she still could, up the stairs to think what she might hide. He hadn't gotten to the middle of the alphabet yet, and so she scooped out the whole section that would contain the Edwin Parfitt file and its photographic contents and stuffed it all far back in the jungle of office furniture, between the mimeograph machine and the postage meter. She might have liked that photo burned, but she couldn't run the risk of George seeing it. He would do something horrible, she was sure, something that would finish off her father. Besides which she hadn't solved its mystery yet. She wasn't *done* with it yet.

George was back, before she could get more files. She considered hiding, but when he appeared she was just standing by the cabinets, unable to move.

He saw her and said, "*What.*"

"I was curious."

She ducked before he could push her aside, and he snatched the oak leaf painting from under the window, the tacks flying from its corners and skittering across the floor. He said, "Whose vagina is this?"

"It's—first of all it's an oak leaf."

He held it at arm's length. "That is a vagina."

"It might be valuable."

"Sure. What you need, Grace Devohr, is more money. All your problems will be solved." He rolled it and tucked it under his arm and scooped more files out. His hands were massive—it was the first thing she loved about him, that his hands were like bear paws—and he grabbed up six inches of folders in each hand. He stacked them against his chest, held them down with his chin, and Grace thought they might all fall, but only a few did.

She said, "Here, I'll carry the painting."

"The hell you will."

He went past her, and down the stairs, and this time she followed him all the way out, watched him strip to his undershirt to stuff things into the pile. Ludo, when he saw her, retreated into the cottage. Max stood on the path by the catalpa, watching, hands in his pockets. She wondered if he recognized what was being burned today, if he cared as much as she did about these last relics of the colony. There were two faces as well in the kitchen window: Beatrice, Amy. Three gas cans near the pile, but it didn't smell like he'd used them yet.

She knew something right then. She saw George pushing those files into the sticks, saw him bent on destroying something. And not because he loved it but because he *didn't*. Because he didn't care at all. And she knew then that Amy had told the truth, that she hadn't offered herself to him.

George said, "I'm not leaving you out here alone," and he pulled her by the arm back to the house. They passed not five feet from Max, and she looked straight at him and tried to send him a message to rescue the painting, at least the painting, but he looked like a man trapped in stone.

In through the terrace to the living room, up the stairs, down the hall, letting go of her at last, and up the attic stairs.

And when he was halfway up, when she was still on the bottom step, he fell. He seemed to fall forward and then, mid-pitch, his body jackknifed and it turned to a headfirst backward dive. The stairs were steep. He landed above her and slid down and came to rest with his head, face up, at her feet.

Grace surprised herself by not screaming. She just stood there looking down, her heart a kettle drum, and a thousand different futures flashed in front of her.

But no: He was still breathing. Great, deep breaths, like a child asleep.

Even so. What if she just left him here? What would be the effect of staying at this downward angle after a blow to the head? What were the odds of his drowning in his own vomit?

All the tension had gone from his face, and all the anger. His forehead was smooth and unfurrowed. Grace crouched and ran a finger from his eyebrow to his hairline. It was an odd moment to think it, but what she found herself contemplating was how the forehead is one of the more sexual parts of the body, the texture of smooth skin over hard bone. She kissed his eye, his closed and upside-down eye. And then she ran to get Max.

Max, surprisingly strong for his size, got George splayed out on the bed in the flowered room. He asked if Grace wanted him to call an ambulance, but by now George was stirring, moaning a bit and reaching for his head. Max fetched an ice pack from the kitchen instead. Then he whispered, "What can we do?"

If she hadn't guessed already that he was talking about the files, she'd have known by the way he faced the window, ready to dive right through it and reclaim everything.

"He'll remember," she said. "He rarely forgets what he was doing."

"Can we restuff them? Can we put other things in the files?"

Grace scanned the room: the pretty old washbasin, the glass-shaded lamp. "There are the two phone books in the hall," she said, "but it won't be enough." Then she remembered the unreadable novel, still hidden with its neighboring files upstairs. She told Max to wait, and she ran to get it. "This isn't important, is it?"

Max looked at the name on the two files, and at the six hundred pages crammed inside. "Good lord. No, this is nothing. It's perfect."

Grace stayed with George, stroking his hand and making sure he stayed put, while Max ran to the burn pile. She craned to watch from the window as he worked first alone and then with Ludo, collecting the folders, yanking out the contents into one huge stack, and systematically restuffing each with a few pages of phone book or failed novel.

He put the rescued papers into Ludo's wheelbarrow, and Ludo wheeled it all into the gardener's cottage. Max met her in the hallway with just the painting and a bit of the novel ("I couldn't bear burning it *all*," he said). He told her Ludo would shelter the other papers in the cottage till Max had time to sort it. He said, "I remember most of these people. It shouldn't be hard to refile. He'll miss the painting, though."

Grace ran the novel remnants back to the attic, and stowed the painting behind a pile of colony mattresses. There was nothing to replace it. She looked at her poster board with the Leaning Tower of Pisa, and laughed. It would never roll. And it was the wrong size.

George rested till dinner, groaning and stirring and eventually sitting up to ask for food. Grace intended for Amy to bring him his dinner on a tray while she ate in peace downstairs, but she stopped just short. She wouldn't send the girl to be alone with him in that room. She wouldn't send the lamb to the lion. So Grace brought him a tray herself, bread and butter, whiskey and water. Then she sat alone at the dining table. Amy smiled so kindly at Grace as she put the baked carrots and cheese in front of her that Grace wanted to scream. She wanted to gouge the girl's eyes out for knowing what she knew, for seeing Grace dragged back to the house like a child. And at the same time she wanted to fold Amy up in her sweater, to rock her to sleep.

Soon after, George went out to the pile himself and came raging back to where Grace sat in the solarium. "Where did the painting go?" he said.

"I don't know what you mean."

He seemed to be summoning the strength to fly across the room at her, but Max and Ludo had followed him, and here they came through the terrace doors.

"The painting!" he said. "*Your* painting. You think I don't know what you're doing up there?"

"I didn't paint it."

"Mr. Grant," Ludo said. "The painting is blown away. I am sorry. It—puff!—across the lawn while you sleep. I see it go."

"Ha!"

"Let's start the fire," Max said. "While the night is young."

Before he followed the men back out, George pointed at her. "If I see that painting again. If I find that you—I don't like to be lied to."

"I wouldn't, George."

"If I see that painting again, I'll burn the whole place down. The whole house."

She watched as Ludo poured gasoline on the pile. George threw the match, and everything went up in a glorious blaze.

The next morning, as soon as George took off, Max came into the dining room where Grace still sat at breakfast. The oak leaf painting was in his hands, rolled. "Can't you give it to the college?" she said. "I'd put it in the bank vault, but George has a key."

Without waiting for an invitation, Max sat in George's seat. He unrolled the linen and touched his finger to the paint. "This ought to stay at Laurelfield," he finally said.

"We can't afford that."

"The artist would want this to stay at Laurelfield. There are simply some things that you don't remove from their natural habitats." Amy opened the door from the kitchen, saw Max, and turned back. Now she'd be eavesdropping, but Grace didn't have the energy to care.

"Even if we hid it in your personal effects—it's just that George—"

Max said, "I know what George is capable of."

"I imagine it's valuable."

"Yes. This is a very good artist."

"I do love it. I love the edges of the leaves."

"We could *reconfigure* it," Max said. "It would be a great joke."

"I don't follow."

"We could paint over it. And hide it in plain view."

"I couldn't destroy it!"

"You'd be preserving it, really." The idea seemed to tickle him tremendously.

Really, the thought of George seeing it every day, walking past it, having no idea—it was appealing. It was a modicum of revenge. And when they were both seventy, and she needed to trump him in some battle, she'd point to the thing and say, *It's been there the whole time. You've been taking your coffee beneath the vagina for forty years.*

"Would oil paint work?"

"It's all that would do."

That afternoon, using an advertisement for another kit from the back of the Paint-by-Numbers box as a guide, Grace painted it over with a farmhouse scene. It ended up not terrible for a rank amateur, and there was quite enough paint in the combined pots of Paint-by-Number oils that it covered the canvas thoroughly. She and Max carried it from the big house to the coach house together, each holding two corners of canvas.

Max knew where to get it framed, as soon as it was dry enough. Six days later, it was hanging in the library.

In the next week, Grace found herself struggling to rise from bed. The room would spin, and she'd lie back to sleep for another half hour, and eventually her hunger would bring her downstairs, if the smell of Amy's horrible coffee didn't keep her from the dining room.

Then she'd walk down by the little hill of ash where the fire pile had stood. She'd follow the paths in the woods.

George was sweet for a few days, until he wasn't.

She realized she ought to move the portrait of Violet, just to be safe. Max stored it in his own room. When George saw it was gone, he wasn't happy at all. He asked if she sold it, and even though she said she hadn't, he asked how much she'd gotten for it, and what she'd done with the money. He threw his glass past her head, and it shattered on the spot where the painting had hung, and for a moment water streamed in a thousand little rivers down the wallpaper. Beatrice served the rest of the meal, and said that Amy had gone to bed with a sudden bug.

She saw Max enter the Longhouse, and two minutes later Sid Cole of Indianapolis followed. They stayed in there an hour. It happened again the next day, and then three days after that.

She didn't want to sit in the attic now that it had been defiled, and so she tried perching herself on the huge, decaying tree stump between the coach house and the big house, her legs crossed. But she felt so strange and dizzy there. It might turn to a sinkhole and swallow her. She thought of the studios, but she couldn't go into the Longhouse. She walked to the little one behind that. It had been a darkroom, Max said. And indeed there were both blinds and shutters inside the windows, and when she closed them it was dark as death. She sat on the daybed and tried not to feel her limbs. She opened the shutters and stared at the floor. Five dead bees. A dead ladybug, its body bleached pink by the sun. A 1939 penny. Someone was happy here once. Someone sang to herself and made her prints and didn't notice when she dropped a penny.

A telegram from home: COME IMMEDIATELY OR NOT AT ALL.

That afternoon, Grace walked right up into Max's apartment and sat at the table and called his name. He appeared in his doorway, his shirt unbuttoned and untucked. He put himself together and joined her. She said, "Max, if anything happens to me, if I go missing, if I turn up drowned in the fish ponds, I need you to know that George did it."

"That—yes, I'm afraid that would be my assumption."

"And if that's the case, I want you to do to him whatever you must so that he doesn't get the house and all the money. Finger him, frame him, poison him, I don't care." She'd said it, and there it was, and once she heard the words out in the air, outside her own mouth, she was sure she meant them.

"You might get out of here before that happens."

"Well. Max, my father is very ill."

"Yes."

She shouldn't have been surprised that he knew.

"When George was lying there, at the bottom of the stairs, I thought for a moment he was dead. And I thought, if George is dead and my father dies, I might do what I like. And I felt a tremendous lightness. It was only the tiniest moment, though."

Max leaned across the table with an intensity she'd have been offended at a few weeks ago, before they became complicit together in the replacement of the files and painting, and in turning the Longhouse into a refuge for fairies. He said, "What is it you'd do?"

"I didn't think it through. Maybe I'd reopen the colony. I could, you know. If I poured my trust fund into it."

"You'd be starting from scratch." He looked glassy and sad. His cheeks had turned pink.

"Yes, well. But you'd help, wouldn't you? You've been here longer than anyone."

He said, "I suppose I'm the memory of the place."

"But it's all just fantasy, and I shouldn't let myself get ahead of my feet. Because what am I going to do? I'm not going to murder George."

Max laughed, a harsh little laugh. "All you'd really have to do is nothing. Not rescue him. Next time, you leave him lying there. Next time will be different. But there will be equivalents."

"Well. And divorce is the real option. I've not wanted to let myself consider it. But he—" She stopped herself a moment, so she wouldn't cry. "Max, do you know what he did to Amy?"

Max shook his head slowly, but she saw that she didn't need to explain it. Just as well, because now she was sobbing, a big heap on the table. "I hadn't believed it was true, or I *couldn't* believe, but then when I saw him with those files, when I saw him hurting something that wasn't me—Max, I've been a perfect *monster.* I want to do something for her. Will you find out what she needs? To get set up comfortably somewhere?"

"You need to leave him," he said.

"I think I might. I'm at least going back to Toronto to see my father. I've telephoned the travel agency to see if I might fly home. I'll know in the morning. I might be able to go in the morning, for that matter. Just to visit."

It was true. She wasn't lying. It just hadn't felt real until she'd said it.

"And then you'll leave him."

"I—yes. I think so."

"But you mustn't tell him."

"I do think he'd figure it out *eventually.*"

Max chuckled—when was the last time someone had laughed at her joke?—and said, "Promise you won't get carried away and tell him so. You'll need lawyers first."

She nodded, but she imagined that part would really have to wait till her father was gone. If he was truly dying, the family lawyers would be tied up with the inheritances a while.

He said, "We'll figure it all out. We will. Grace, I don't want you alone with him."

"I promise."

That same night, George got dressed to go out. He put on his sport coat and shaved. He'd made some friends, he said, at a bar in Highwood, and they had a business opportunity for him, a solid investment. He'd said the same thing back in July about a fellow he met down in the city. George wrote him a check for two thousand dollars and never saw him again. These new friends knew someone who would take the money to Brazil and double it. George had stayed sober for the occasion, and he danced around the bedroom as he gathered his wallet and hat. Grace lay on the bed in her yellow cotton dress, a wool cardigan on top. This was what she'd pictured, when she first settled on George: the two of them together in the bedroom before the dinner hour, George happy and energized, Grace with bare feet and a book. Only she hadn't imagined feeling like a ball of lead.

She put her forehead to the window and watched as he trotted to the coach house. Max backed up the Darrin and climbed out, holding the driver's door open for George himself.

Max disappeared into the garage, and George backed partway out, but then two things happened: He circled the car around to the big house door and ran inside—for his warmer hat, probably, as it was quite cold and the Darrin was a poor choice even with the roof up. And, at that same moment, down by the maple trees and all along the inside of the stone wall, the earth began to move again just as it had that day a month ago: rabbits and rabbits and rabbits. A swarm of rabbits, a plague of rabbits. Grace slid on her shoes and ran down the stairs and past George, who was rifling through the coat closet. She had to see if they were real, and if they were, she wanted to know what it was they were all doing here, surrounding the property like a hex or a blessing.

She was out the front door, and George was still inside, when

Sid Cole of Indianapolis walked right through the front gate. Grace ought to have told Max to have him come in the side gate at least, but here he was, hands in his pockets, shoulders hunched against the cold, heading straight down the drive toward the big house. The grass was wet and cold, and he probably wanted to stay off it until he reached the path to the Longhouse, but it made it look, Grace realized with horror, as if he were here to see her in George's absence. Her young date for the evening. She didn't have time to warn him without yelling out, and George was coming out the door behind her just now. So what she did instead was to turn and catch George by the waist and turn him toward her and the coach house at once—away from Sid, who seemed oblivious in his stride. She said, "Take me with you tonight. Let me come with you." She pulled him hard against her.

He put his hand on her posterior and said, "I'm meeting these fellows."

"I'll charm them."

He stepped back and looked her up and down, judging her presentability. It was true that for once she wasn't hiding a bruise. The bandage was off her forehead and the stitches were out, just a clean pink mark now.

She said, "It'll be fun."

"All right, Duck."

He opened the passenger door with an exaggerated bow, and as she stepped in she managed to catch Sid's attention. He was only ten yards away, but when he saw the warning on her face he darted back among the maple trees before George came around the car. He wasn't well hidden, but it didn't matter.

They shot down the drive, pebbles flying up and hitting the bottom of the frame like a mortar attack. Sid was a blur out Grace's window, his face calm and curious. He couldn't have understood that Grace had just saved his life as well as her own.

———

They took the back corner table at Pasquali's, and George nodded in passing to two swarthy men at the bar. "They'll join us when their partner's here," he said. Grace realized she'd have to sit quietly through whatever ridiculous scam they wanted his money for—she'd watch mutely as he wrote a check from their joint account—or else the night could go unpleasantly wrong.

There was a record on: Frank Sinatra sang "Ain'tcha Ever Comin' Back?" Everything smelled good, and Grace was ravenous. Amy would be getting dinner ready at home and wondering where Grace had gone.

Grace steeled herself to smile at George, but he wasn't paying a bit of attention. He looked at the two men, and the door, and the bartender, and the menu, and the next table. He ordered a scotch, plus a bottle of Chianti for Grace's benefit. The wine went right to her head, though, in a way it usually didn't. It had been a while—since Paris, really—that she'd had any regular amount of wine. But one glass in, she felt dopey and dizzy, and her mouth felt full of cotton.

She ordered lasagna.

"You're getting stout," George said, when the waiter had walked away.

"It's Amy's cooking," she said, though she wanted to argue, to tell him it wasn't true at all, it was only her bust that was suddenly a bit larger. And then, wall of ice: It was November 16. She'd bled in September, back when it was warm enough to walk to the pharmacy in her blue cotton dress. And that must have been the last time. She was an idiot. A dizzy idiot, with blackness closing around her head. She'd been so distracted. Right when the witch showed up, right when George pinned Amy to the tree—that should have been the next time. She'd spent the next month watching everyone and everything but herself, and meanwhile she grew slow and slept late, and the smell of Amy's coffee made her gag, and she began crying at the drop of a hat.

The waiter set her plate in front of her. A heap of lasagna, clots of red leaking out the frilled edges. George was talking about Quebec, about taking a motor trip in the spring.

She wanted to think to herself that she'd never go on that trip because she'd be a free woman by then, but she knew it would be the opposite. She'd be at home with a watermelon stomach or a squalling baby, and maybe he'd be there too, or maybe he'd be off without her, but she'd never get free of him now.

The room blurred, and fell to little stars, and came back together in flashing colors and shapes. The shapes locked back to reality with a sickening little click. Just like the bricks of the house—everything cemented together, everything in order. Her entire life was like those bricks, she saw it now. And every attempt at escape just locked her further in. She'd tried to marry someone wild, and ended up in a prison. She'd tried to leave him, and ended up tethered to his child, growing inside her.

George was saying, "The man eats coins. Did you know that? I saw him put a nickel in his mouth, when he thought I wasn't looking."

"Oh. Who?"

"Max. The driver. I said."

"That can't be true. Did he swallow it?"

"No idea."

She managed to get a bite in. George was waving to the third man, who'd just entered.

Grace dropped her napkin on the floor and ran to the bathroom, and the vomit barely made it in the toilet. Look at the tiles on the floor. Look: a graph-paper grid. Her own, private, tessellated map to her appointment in Samarkand.

Why should she be so surprised by it all? By getting exactly what she'd signed on for, no more and no less? Except that we become so used to the twists of chance and fortune. Sometimes the greatest shock is getting exactly what we've been promised.

Back at the table, George and the men were laughing. One scooted over and patted the bench next to him. But she stayed standing and said, "George, I'm ill. I'll call Max to bring me home in the Capri."

George nodded. "Sure, Duck."

She called the coach house line from the pay phone by the bar. It rang and rang and rang, and no one picked up. It was six thirty now, and they'd left the house at five. Soon Amy would give up on her for dinner, and Max would be finished with Sid Cole. She sat back at the table. The men talked about soccer. She couldn't imagine why.

She might have slept a bit, but now she felt worse. She tried the coach house again, and the main line too, and no one picked up. She came back and waited for a pause and said, "George, why don't I drive the Darrin home and tell Max to pick *you* up in the Capri?"

"We'll be done soon," he said to her. But she could tell that they wouldn't, and that it would not be wise to press the issue. He wouldn't let her drive the Darrin even under the best circumstances, and he'd never hand over the keys in front of these men. He was quite drunk now. There was another full scotch in front of him. She made her hands into a pillow on the placemat.

Finally they finished. There were papers on the table, and George took some of them, and one of the men took the rest. George said, "Okay, Duck, let's go." But when he stood, he caught his ankle on the table and nearly pulled the whole thing over with him. He righted the table but fell himself, and Grace propped him up by the elbow.

"He okay?" one of the men said, and another of them laughed.

"We're calling someone to drive," Grace told them, and

George didn't object. She led him to the pay phone and used the same dime, the same unlucky dime, to call the coach house. It was now nine o'clock, and either Amy or Max had to be home. The men, seeing she had the receiver to her ear, nodded and left the restaurant. George leaned against the wall.

The phone rang and rang and rang. Max should be home—Sid never stayed this late—but then he might be down in the garage. It might take him a while to hear the phone and get upstairs to the kitchen. And where was Amy? George grabbed her arm. "This is ridiculous. Let's go."

She didn't hang up. "I'll drive," she said. "Or we'll call a taxi." She shouldn't have raised the issue earlier—he might have remained malleable. Now he'd never give in.

"Grace, let's go." His voice was louder than last time, and the bartender glanced in their direction. Next time would be louder, she knew, and all these people would look up from their spaghetti in dismay.

She listened for one more ring, and one more ring, and one more ring. The rings lined themselves up like bathroom tiles. One more, one more, one more. George took the phone and hung it in its cradle.

Outside, Grace tried to catch the valet's eye, hoping he'd figure out everything wrong, call the police or a cab, but he just sent a boy out to bring the car, and the boy opened Grace's door for her, then struggled to slide it back. Everyone stared at the car, the strange and shiny car, and no one noticed the problem. George took off like they were being chased.

Down Sheridan Road, down the middle of it, really, with a sharp jerk to the right whenever another pair of headlights appeared. Grace hadn't been out at night since all the leaves had fallen, and she realized with wonder that for the first time since they'd moved here in the spring, she could see the houses—see into them, even, as George tried to light a cigarette and compensated by suddenly driving too slowly. Those homes always seemed so hidden and empty, no life but for someone out on the sidewalk. Now, every illuminated room was a perfect frame of yellow. Each frame both a revelation and a further mystery. She'd forgotten that November was such a strange, unveiling time of year—not a deadening but a quickening. In the smaller houses, closer to the road, she could make out a clock, a shelf of plants, an old woman, a refrigerator. In the bigger ones, behind stone walls, just an occasional upstairs hall light. She wanted to climb into each frame, to live in each for a year. But then George picked up speed again.

She might say something about it, might see if George understood even a little bit. And if he did, she might tell him, tomorrow, about the baby too. The baby might change him. Perhaps change was possible even while staying put, staying with him, staying in the house.

They turned, and the right-side wheels went up on the curb and down with a horrible jolt. Her nausea returned, from the floor of her stomach upward in a wave, and she grabbed the door handle. She was too dizzy, too tired, to work up the appropriate anger at herself for getting into this situation, when she might have wrested the key from him or passed a note of distress to the bartender. Surely there was *something* she might have done. Wasn't there always something to be done?

They turned again, and now he was going so fast that the lights in the houses were just blurs. She knew that if she asked him to slow down, he'd only speed up.

There was Laurelfield, dark and still, the gate open. George took the entry wide and fast and nearly clipped the gate. He turned toward the coach house without slowing. The gravel hitting up again, a thousand little bullets. "Look at that," George said, meaning she should look up before they went through the open garage door, look at the bright windows of the coach house kitchen and Max's rooms. "He's home after all. The bastard is home."

And she would have looked, she would have looked, but the gravel was still hitting too fast. The trees were coming too fast.

PART III

1929

IN THE FIELD: THE TRIBE

Zilla was a moving statue in the torchlight. If Eddie could, he would love her: her hair a black puddle, her teeth a broken necklace. Her white throat, thrust forward when she laughed. Viktor, though—Viktor Osin *did* love her, or else what was this filament between them, across the night?

There were only the eight: Samantha had stayed back.

Marlon Moore led them all to the teepees, which were just as he'd described: cloth cones in the field, big enough for all to squeeze inside just one. They passed the flask again. Vital to maintain the drunken state in which the plan was hatched, lest they sober up and discover themselves ridiculous. It was only a few drinks into the evening that Marlon had volunteered his story—dragged by a colleague's wife to last year's Chippeway Ball—and several drinks later that the joke had started: A true Chippeway Ball should feature more scalping and war whoops and nudity. The sun had set, additional bottles brought to the terrace, when it became a plan, when Viktor and Marlon and Eddie drove to the college where Marlon taught, and broke into the theater's costume shop and returned with headdresses and face paint.

Across the lawn, windows full of elegant locals. Long tables, candles.

The eight undressed in the open teepee by torchlight, laughing and shushing, leaving clothes in distinct piles to speed escape.

Zilla, muscled, flat as a board. Viktor—with his impossible limbs, his dancer's limbs—staring at her like a drugged man. Ludo, pale for an Italian, a thatch of dark fur on his chest. Fannie and Josephine, the White Rabbits: one doughy, one thin as rope. Armand Cox (preposterous name!), his whole being covered in golden hairs. Marlon with his little potbelly, stretching his legs to run. Two weeks ago, Eddie hadn't been able to keep them all straight. And now he imagined he'd know their voices to his dying day.

Another adjustment: All day long, in front of his pen or typewriter, he was as alone as he'd ever been. But at night, he was a "we." Something he hadn't felt since childhood, since he'd climbed in bed with his sister in the afternoons, since she'd let him wear her shoes. He was part of a first-person plural.

Some of them wore the headdresses, and the others stuck loose feathers in their hair. Their faces: red and black stripes, yellow down the nose.

Armand and Ludo, leading the parade, each grabbed one lawn torch to hold aloft.

Zilla started the war cry, hand pulsing on her open mouth, and the others joined and rode the wave of noise onto the club porch and through the open glass doors to the dining room.

The first thing Eddie saw, he told the others later, was the fat woman in the green dress, the way her fork flew from her hand, lettuce still speared on the tines.

The tribe whooped and screeched and circled the sea of tables three times. A great deal of anatomical flapping: some high, some low, all uncomfortable, all ridiculous in the electric lights, but wasn't this the point? As the rest of them flailed and beat their chests, Viktor did actual pirouettes. He leapt over the carving table, his legs straight out like wings. The evening-gowned ladies dove into their husbands' laps. Half the men laughed and clapped and the others stood to do *something* but then weren't sure what to do.

Someone screamed, "*Stop* them!"

Ludo shouted, "We come for squaws!"

Two white-haired men tried to block the path, but moved away quickly when Armand and Ludo didn't stop, as Armand even turned and shimmied backward toward them, posterior muscles twitching. The youths, boys and girls both, watched with poorly contained glee. Viktor planted a kiss on a squealing girl's forehead and left a perfect black lip mark. On the final circuit, Eddie grabbed a dinner roll and stuffed it in his mouth.

Back into the night: some of the tuxedoed men giving chase, but only halfway across the lawn, then posting themselves cross-armed between teepees and building, shouting, guarding against further invasion.

A loud voice thinned by distance: "This is a *private estab-lishment!*"

Zilla wheezing with laughter. Armand, torch abandoned, turning a cartwheel.

The artists carried clothes in armloads and ran, some back to the waiting auto, some, with Eddie, into the woods where they dressed, and then found the path to the road, and then walked the road back to Laurelfield.

ZILLA IN HER STUDIO

She has assembled seven things on the table in the Longhouse: a potted geranium, a pile of gray rocks, a hair pin, a square of yellow cotton, a Mason jar, a feather, a dead bee. She has stapled a linen to the wall.

The choosing, the starting: It's a cliff to jump off.

She examines the feather, the way invisible hooks link each barb to the next. The way, when she pulls one strand from its neighbor, it leaves a clean gap that will not smooth together again. She doubts this cleaving can be conveyed in paint: the hooks that grip us, that tie us to each other. To place, to time. The ways we might come unhinged.

She walks to the wall and begins.

WESTERN UNION

AUG. 29-29.

SAMANTHA MAYS
CARE LAURELFIELD ARTS COLONY

HEARD OF DISTURBANCE STOP IN NY CITY
ON BUSINESS STOP ARRIVE LAURELFIELD
TOMORROW AFTERNOON STOP DO MAKE
PREPARATIONS=

    G W DEVOHR

SAMANTHA IN THE KITCHEN

It was raining all morning, dusk all morning.

From the windows of the director's house, the main house looked reflective, all windows and wet.

Samantha laid the telegram on the middle of her kitchen table so they all could read it: Armand over her shoulder, Viktor and Zilla leaning across. "He sounds furious."

Zilla said, "Everyone sounds furious in a wire."

They kept their voices low. Beatrice, Samantha's brand new office girl, was typing in the next room and needn't be alarmed. Samantha warned her the day she started that Laurelfield was hanging by a thread, that Gamby Devohr, newly in charge of his family's affairs, would take any excuse to oust them all.

Armand said, "We don't even know what disturbance he means. *Heard of disturbance.* He could think there are real Indians in the woods."

Viktor was playing with a spoon, spinning it on the oilcloth. "He's not the world's leading intellectual."

Samantha read it again, aloud. They turned on the floor lamp, the one with no shade, and dragged it to the table. As if more light would possibly help.

Zilla said, "What can he prove? No one took our photograph. I'm sure they weren't looking at our *faces.*" Zilla's voice was calming even when there was no cause for calm. Samantha had once thought of it as a liquid voice, but lately she'd refined the image:

Zilla's voice was mercury, a bubble of mercury in a phial. Liquid but metallic too.

"He can't expect me," Samantha said, "to keep everyone quiet in their rooms all night. We're not *bankers*. I think he'd like to run a banking colony."

Zilla said, "At least I'll meet the infamous Gamaliel Devohr."

"Gamby the Great," Viktor said.

Armand: "We'll meet Mr. Devohr as he's kicking us to the curb. We'll meet the bottom of his foot."

Viktor: "He can do that?"

Samantha: "It's his house, still. As far as the colony, he's just a member of the board. But he owns the property. If he kicks us out, we cease to exist."

"How nice for the Devohr family taxes," Armand said. "To turn your spare mansion into an artists' shelter."

"It's the only charitable thing they've ever done. Lord knows they aren't patrons of the ballet. And now they'd rather get the house back and sell it. I don't believe they've done well since the war."

"Oh, it's nothing," Zilla said. "I'm sure it's nothing."

Viktor stood and stretched—the man was a tree, his hands on the ceiling, pressing it away—and announced he was heading back to the Longhouse to work, and Zilla announced she would follow him. Armand and Samantha watched them go.

"Oh, Armand," she said. He sat at the table, and she put her head on his shoulder.

"They're in love, aren't they? Viktor and Zilla?"

"I should think so. She's married, though, and he's got all those dancers, and she hates that he's got his dancers. They always come here the same time, just to torture each other. I believe it's an excruciatingly chaste affair. They'd never moon around like that if they'd *had* each other." She folded the telegram up, as small as it would fold.

"We ought to lock them in her studio together and see what happens."

"It's fascinating to watch, except when it's painful."

"Mr. Devohr will love your new hair."

"Ha!" She touched what was left of the blonde curls. "He might run screaming. And end our problem."

"He'll take you for Amelia Earhart's younger brother. Tell me," he said, "now we're alone, about Eddie Parfitt."

"He's tremendously talented. Vachel Lindsay wrote his reference."

"I mean—he's been here two weeks. I'm late to the game. Is he, you know, *my sort of gentleman?*"

"Oh. Yes, I imagine. Ask Marlon. He'd know."

Armand laughed. "If Marlon knows, I'm far too late."

"He could use some bringing out of his shell, at any rate. I'll put you in charge of it. Only don't fall in love with him."

Armand looked hurt, as if she'd misread him completely. But she knew him better than he thought. It was only his first visit, but Armand had been her friend for years, since the days when he was sleeping on the floor of someone's studio in the Fine Arts Building. He'd been *so* young. Well, so had she. Later, when he finally had a bit of money, he'd bought her blue ladder painting. They'd worked together on the No-Jury show. And she knew, if nothing else, that he was quite similar to her. He believed that drawing the world would keep him at an ironic distance from it, keep him safe from caring deeply about things. When in fact it had the opposite effect. And she knew how Laurelfield had affected *her*, on her first stay—as an artist, long before she dug in her nails and managed to get hired. She'd felt exhilarated and confused, and she couldn't eat, and she couldn't sleep, and she mistook it all as love for an older poet, a man with a pipe and a wife. She'd thrown herself at him, and they were together awhile, until—later, back in the city—she realized she had no interest in the man at all. What she'd been in love with was Laurelfield, and everyone there, and her own work, and maybe even with *herself*, for the first time.

She saw that same wild look in Armand's eyes. He was looking for someone to love. He was a transitive verb with no direct object.

She said, "Just watch your heart."

Down at the bottom of the stairs, Alfie started barking. He ran all the way up and then all the way down, and Samantha followed him.

A woman struggled at the door, propping it open with her foot and hefting a wet valise through the frame. Behind her, a man unloaded trunks from a taxi straight into a puddle. The screenwriter wasn't due to arrive till tomorrow, but this was obviously her. She bore that distinct look of the arriving artist: disoriented, exhausted, profoundly relieved to be there. "I've arrived too early!" the woman said, only she said "arrifed," her voice thick with dignified German. Samantha scrambled to remember the name—Marcelina von Hornig, there it was, and she'd wondered if it would be a "Marcy" type or a "Lina," but clearly this woman was above shortening—and then, as the door closed behind her and Alfie was subdued and the woman looked up into Samantha's face, Samantha reeled. This was *Marceline Horn*, the film star Marceline Horn, in color, in three dimensions. The same high-bridged nose, the enormous eyes, eyelashes like window valances. She'd played Juliet and Charlotte Corday. She'd kissed Valentino. Samantha had gotten used, over the years, to speaking with artists and writers whose talent intimidated her. This was different, though, more like meeting Cinderella than the Brothers Grimm.

Samantha managed to say, "It's not a problem. The maid was already making up the room for you. You might have to work in the—in the library. Until it's done."

"Oh, of *course*. I need a few hours to screw my head back on."

"You've had a long trip."

"Vell, I vas in Chicago a veek."

"Yes." The address on this woman's papers—Beverly Hills, California—hadn't seemed odd, since she was coming to write two movie scripts. A letter of recommendation from L. B. Mayer, himself, of MGM. Samantha had convinced the rest of the file readers that this would be a novelty, that they'd be embracing a new form of storytelling. Mayer's letter said he'd worked with the woman in the past, but it said nothing of directing her in films, of their affair—wasn't there an affair? She remembered something, an item in *Picture Play*—just that she showed great talent and needed a quiet place. And for all Samantha could tell from the script sample, she was a natural writer.

Stupidly, her lips numb: "This is Alfie. A wirehaired pointing griffon. He's harmless."

Marceline bent to look him in the eye. "I'm a great friend of the dogs."

Samantha took in the woman's outfit: the green cloche hat, the slim black frock with pearls at the hip—all regular enough, if a bit formal for mid-morning—but below that, and above her black one-straps, she wore silk stockings appliquéd with green velvet snakes that appeared to climb her legs.

Behind her, Armand crouched on the landing, peering down. He was silent—which, Samantha knew, was his particular form of shrieking. Beatrice stood behind him, her fingers to her little chin.

"Armand," Samantha said, and he didn't answer. "Will you be a dear and see if Maisie has finished the yellow room? And the kitchen needs to know, as well, that there will be one more for dinner. You could help with the trunks. And Beatrice, the packet. For Miss von Hornig."

Beatrice vanished. Armand rushed past them both and out the door with no umbrella. It occurred to her that Armand might bang on everyone's door with the news before he bothered finding Maisie, that eight noses might be pressed to the wet window within minutes, but meanwhile she had her list of things to say, her regular and memorized orientation to Laurelfield—the quiet hours, and keys, and meals—and this woman looked as thirsty and tired as any new arrival. She invited Marceline to follow her up to the kitchen. She dropped the folded telegram into the dustbin and put the kettle on for tea.

Marceline stopped her, as she crossed the kitchen, and clasped one of Samantha's hands in her soft, strangely large ones. "I tell you, I feel like Shakespeare's Viola, vashed up on the shore of Illyria. And I can tell this is a blessed place. A *generous* place. I feel it in my feet."

"You haven't even seen it all yet!"

"It is not something von *sees*."

LUDO AND JOSEPHINE ON THE LAWN

They look at the roof, the way the sun just now, at eleven, shoots a tentative ray over the top, the last rain turning to mist. In a minute, it will be too bright to look east.

Ludo says, "No, I don't believe. Back in Napoli, one time, I go to a séance. Is all tricks. All click-click and knocking sound and guess what someone wants to hear." He laughs. "Is same with my music, no? Knock knock, tell you what you want to hear. I used to write symphonies. Now I make rhymings and bouncings."

"No ghost appeared? At the séance?"

"The ghost is in our ears."

"Marlon *swears* he heard something in the night."

"I tell you what I learn: At a colony, there always come noises in the night. Howling, thumping, door slam, moaning, bang bang bang, you know. You know what is? Is not ghosts."

"What?"

"Is people making sex."

In Residence

UPDATED 29 AUG '29

Abbaticchio, Ludo (M)
Composer
*
St: Comp. Cottage
R: Southwest
*

Cadfael, Fannie (F)
Sculptor
Cleveland Hts, Ohio
St: Solarium
R: Blue
through 9/2

Cox, Armand (M)
Illustrator
Chicago
St/R: Longhouse E
through 10/4

Lizer, Josephine (F)
Sculptor
Cleveland Hts, Ohio
St: Solarium
R: Green
through 9/2

Moore, Marlon (M)
Writer
Lake Bluff, Ill.
St/R: Northeast
through 9/5

Osin, Viktor (M)
Maître de ballet
Chicago
St/R: Longhouse Cent.
through 9/16 (extended)

Parfitt, Edwin (M)
Poet
Phil, Pa.
St/R: Flower
through 9/27

Silverman, Zilla (F)
Painter
Madison, Wis.
St/R: Longhouse W
through 10/12

Von Hornig (Horn), Marcelina (Marceline) (F)
Screenwriter
Beverly Hills, Calif.
St/R: Yellow
through 9/20

Beatrice, please note:

Miss Silverman has asked use of attic
in addition to Longhouse W.

Miss Lizer and Miss Cadfael are in fact
sharing Green bedroom; trunks of both
are stored in Blue; Miss Cadfael has
that key.

Garden studio is empty if Miss Horn
prefers it to working in her room.

Please remember Mr. Abbaticchio not to
be listed on public documents.

WHAT WE'VE GLEANED FROM MARLON

Marlon Moore claims to know a woman who knows the Devohrs. It's impossible, Samantha insists, because *no one* "knows the Devohrs." You might know one Devohr, or another Devohr, but they aren't an entity. It's like saying you know all the feral cats in the woods. You've probably just seen the same one five times. Marlon counters that his friend knows the *important* Devohrs, the ones who've stayed sane, the ones with the houses.

Marlon has heard testimony, from some of the greatest living writers, that the best way to induce strange and inspiring dreams is to eat very strong cheese before bed. He himself keeps a crock of Roquefort on the windowsill in his room. He doesn't see the problem. It has a lid! "Yes," Josephine mutters, "but your mouth does not."

Marlon knows with great certainty that back home, Ludo, our own Italian fixture, became unnecessarily political for a composer. It seems Ludo was a great friend of the Communist leader Bordiga, and wrote a song lampooning Bordiga's rival, Gramsci, and (worse) Mussolini himself. Marlon believes he rhymed "Benito" with "finito." ("Let's ask if it's true!" says Armand. "I wouldn't," says Viktor.) And so (Marlon fingers his moustache, adopts a tone of epic narration), by 1926, both Bordiga and Gramsci were in jail, and Ludo was on a boat to New York under an assumed name, quotas and papers be damned. How he landed at Laurelfield, where he's stayed the past three years, is no great mystery. Bordiga probably phoned Samantha himself. Is Ludo sleeping with Samantha? Oh, everyone assumes so. Certainly. But that's beside the point. And now Ludo has a bit of a career stateside as well, writing show tunes. "Our gain," Fannie adds emphatically. Fannie is our greatest optimist.

Marlon can tell astrological signs with great accuracy. He pegs Zilla as an Aquarius, and she nods. We are duly impressed.

Late one night, Marlon starts giggling about Viktor Osin and his ballerinas. "They're all French," he says, "or Russian. Nineteen years old, eighty pounds each. Let me tell you: a line of twelve swans? He's been under every tutu." His giggling turns shrill. "Not a single bosom between them, but can you imagine the ways they stretch?" Zilla leaves the room.

Marlon wears a silk burgundy smoking jacket over his clothes. He is poised for great things.

Marlon has heard a rumor: Mr. Devohr is already on his way.

Civic Opera Company
Mary Garden, Director
430 South Michigan Avenue
Chicago

Aug. 28

Dearest Samantha—

Dashing this off to say Gamby Devohr
has written to all the board. Received
my letter this a.m.

Samantha, what's happened? Wishing I
could zip up but all is chaos here,
moving to the new space, Aida, etc.
Tell me if I should come, though. Do.

Devohr is requesting ad hoc meeting
Sept. 3rd for what I fear are
apocalyptic purposes.

Do advise if I can help, but as you
know I haven't much clout with the
other boardsters, I'm the artistic quack
not the purse strings.

I'm worried, Sam. Tell me you're fine.
Tell me Laurelfield's fine.

  Oh dear lord,
  Mary

EDDIE IN THE LIBRARY

The hour before dinner, normally restrained—stretching writers, artists just scrubbed up, a shared bottle of gin—turned into an all-out soirée in everyone's effort to meet and impress Marceline Horn. The party continued after the meal, the artists reconvening to the library where Viktor mixed an enormous vat of orange blossoms and Ludo played the piano. It was fortunate Ludo was kept busy. Having seen Marceline as Scheherezade ("Just scarves! No other clothings!"), he couldn't speak to her without leering.

Viktor ladled a drink into a smudged glass for Eddie, slopping some down the side. Viktor was all arms and legs. A dancer and dance maker with hair of the most rebellious kind, each strand hating its neighbors with such static ferocity that his head achieved a perfect geometry of divergence.

Eddie sipped and tried to listen to the music, but it didn't help. He felt sick again: a chill that had vanished a few hours the night of the Indian raid, that the August sun baked away whenever he took lunch outdoors, but that returned the moment he reentered the house. Now the dizziness was back, the feeling that he needed to leave the house soon, or else he would fall into his bed and freeze to the mattress and never rise again. Fannie and Josephine had told him, his first night, to watch for the ghost, for the long white nightgown in the upstairs hall. They had giggled and shivered, and expected him to do likewise. But the chill, he knew, was not something he'd encounter in the corridor. It had already gotten deep in his bloodstream.

There was something wrong with the house. The windows gazed in on you instead of out at the world.

And now the White Rabbits had cornered Marceline on the davenport behind Eddie, and leaned in eagerly to tell the story of Violet Devohr. "She locked herself in the attic," Fannie said. "It's unclear why."

"Well, she was mad!" Josephine cried. "Why else does a woman lock herself in an attic?"

"And the old man, Augustus, the one who built the place for her, begged her to let him in, but he didn't go so far as to kick down the door. He was too genteel. And he didn't want the servants hearing."

"Scandal, you know."

"He figured she'd come out eventually. Every day he knocked, three times a day, and she told him to go away. And then he realized—"

"No, you forgot to say, it was five days! Five days she was up there. She had taken in the key. Did you say that part?"

"Yes, five days. And only then did he realize that she had no food or water."

"And so he broke down the door. Or he called a locksmith, I'm not sure. But it was too late. She wasn't dead yet, but she couldn't survive."

Zilla rejoined them in time to hear the end. "Are you trying to make her *leave*? She'll run off in the night!" But her voice was so soft and rolling that it was only a joke.

"Anyway," Fannie said, "that was Gamby's mother. Gamby is Gamaliel, the one who's coming to get us all in trouble. The poor dear, he was just two years old. It's no wonder he's always begrudged Laurelfield."

Over at the piano, Ludo had started one of his new songs, a

bouncy thing with a chorus designed to be joined by the flappers who, under more urban circumstances, would no doubt surround his piano. It had become a great joke to all of them in the past weeks that Ludo's English could be so tortured in conversation but so smooth in lyric. He sang with tremendous verve:

> Columbus spied the ocean shore
> He counted natives by the score
> He cried, "Exploring's such a bore
> When all of it's been found before!"

> Ohhhh—I tell you, gentle philosophers,
> In these modernest of times
> That history doesn't repeat . . .
> It merely rhymes!

There were so many layers of insulation to this one room. The leather-bound books, and then their shelves, and the walls themselves, and the outer bricks, and then the blanket of ivy that could swallow your whole hand, up to your wrist. And then the thick summer air, and the groves of mismatched trees—the legacy, apparently, of Violet Devohr's insistence on horticultural diversity—and then the stone wall, and then the woods. It should have felt safe, but instead it was smothering and cold at once.

Marlon leaned against a standing Eddie and settled his rear on the back of the davenport, just inches from Marceline's head. He wore, as usual, his smoking jacket, tied at the waist. He smelled of pomade. He said, "Do you believe in fate?"

"Sure."

"The moment I saw you, I felt certain I'd seen you before."

"I'm not sure that's fate so much as déjà vu."

"Ah. The French have no imagination."

Eddie found himself smiling back but ignoring whatever else

Marlon said. He watched Armand take a drink to Marceline. Armand dressed like a college boy, argyle sweater and bright argyle socks, knickers. The rumor of the afternoon had it that Marceline had been demoted from a lead actress at MGM, and sent here at the mercy of Mr. Mayer to try her hand at writing, to rework two old silent scripts into talkies. Her exquisite looks were fading, the sharp bob doing nothing for her nose, and that accent, it was true, would not go over now. Everyone was dying to ask about films, to ask if she knew Gary Cooper. Eddie heard her say to Armand, "You should go right now to Berlin. There are in Berlin the most vonderful pansy clubs."

In the corner, Zilla and Viktor, ignoring each other.

Samantha in tweed knickers and green broadcloth blouse, rubbing Ludo's shoulders, singing along.

Everyone coupling and recoupling around the room in laughter, like a formal dance.

Armand, hands on the White Rabbits' shoulders, swaying by the piano. His sleeves rolled up, his arms covered in dark golden hairs. The White Rabbits sang the chorus of a new song:

> *Give me back my kiss,*
> *It wasn't for you to keep.*

Eddie had languished in confusion for a full week before finally asking Zilla why the women were called White Rabbits. But he couldn't get it out of his head yet that there was some connection to their noses, both small and pink, or to their silvering hair, or to plump Josephine's buck teeth or wiry Fannie's quick little eyes.

He realized that behind him, below him, on the davenport, Samantha Mays was crying quietly, and Zilla was comforting her. He had thought of Samantha as the type of woman who didn't cry. There was something about her that was like a fourteen-year-old boy, all elbows and knees and a broad chin, and he'd always imagined she could fall off a horse and bounce. She said, softly, "But I didn't imagine he'd written to the *board*. Oh, I just don't know. He's been looking for the slightest justification."

Zilla's voice, low: "But we have a room here full of tremendously creative people. I'm sure we can think of something."

Marlon must have heard it too. He said, "Tell him we have a film star here! That'll grab his attention!"

Samantha looked up and laughed. "Oh. Oh, Marlon, don't listen to me. I'll just worry you. But no, it wouldn't help. If anything, he'll use it as proof we're a bunch of hedonists. We'll have to clean up. We'll have to hide Ludo. If anyone asks, Ludo's been gone two years."

At midnight, it was just Marceline and Armand and Zilla and Eddie. Eddie wanted to be in bed, asleep, but he didn't want to be alone yet in his little room at the top of the stairs.

Marceline was explaining that Los Angeles was a city without attics. "Vhy vould you need them? Nothing is old there, not a single antique, except the vons brought in for display. And I am myself an antique, of course."

A clamor of protest.

Eddie had worried she'd be haughty, but he found he enjoyed this woman, the tenacity with which she was determined to move on past the end of her particular, silent art.

"How is the life in Chicago?" she said to Armand. Another thing to admire: the instinct to steer the conversation away from herself.

Though Marceline had asked the question, Armand seemed to address his answer to Eddie. "It's swell. I'm in Towertown, and really I think it's better than New York. Everyone interesting in New York is actually in Paris, anyway. But Chicago's copacetic. And there's a lot doing for artists. Poets, too. Eddie, do you know Harriet Monroe? I could introduce you. If you were ever in the city. And you ought to be! What does Philadelphia have? You're out of the loop there. And what life is there, even? For people like us? You ought to be in Towertown or on a boat to Florence."

Zilla said, "Oh Armie, you made him blush!"

It was true. He was blushing at how easily Armand had read him. At Armand's ready implications. *People like us.* But the heat in his face had started before that, at Armand remembering Philadelphia—at his remembering Eddie's name at all. Eddie had grown used to assuming he was the only one in the room taking note of everything, of everyone's habits and gestures, squirreling away the details they let fall about their lives. He'd learned long ago to reintroduce himself at least three times to people whose names and drinks and life stories he'd long since memorized. He wondered if the rest of the Chicago crowd was like Armand, like himself—not in the way Armand had meant, but wide-eyed, absorbent.

Eddie struggled for something quick to say, but just then the lamp on the piano crackled, and the room was dunked in blackness. Marceline screamed, and Zilla laughed. "There," Zilla said. "I don't know why the Rabbits had to go frightening you about the attic. When clearly the ghost is right here."

FRIDAY, 10:16 A.M.

Marlon stands on the wall by the road and aims his Leica at the director's house, what used to be the coach house back when this was poor, doomed Violet's estate. Armand Cox leans there, smoking. Alfie sniffs in quick circles nearby. The wall is narrower than Marlon expected, and it takes great effort to balance. He can't quite focus the lens on Armand, and so he trains it on the giant oak between the houses instead. After the photo but before he can hop down, a voice from out on the sidewalk: "What *is* that place, anyhow?"

Marlon looks down at the speaker, a young boy with a stick. He says, "It's an asylum for people who think they're artists."

Uncaptured by the lens:

Samantha staring from her bedroom window, listening to the calming clatter of Beatrice's typewriter. Behind her, the smell of something burning. She wonders what on earth could be burning.

Ludo in the composer's cottage, hitting his head on the piano keys in frustration.

Fannie and Josephine, lying like quotation marks in bed, the afternoon sun on their feet. Fannie tracing the lines of the room from one corner all around to Josephine's shoulder, thinking about shape as sound, about silence as negative space.

Viktor in the hallway, picking Zilla's blue earring off the rug and clipping it back to her ear, letting his wrist touch her neck, watching her eyes close. Zilla scrambling like an egg.

The bootlegger, driving slowly up the road, knowing he'll recognize Laurelfield by the number of autos out front.

Eddie Parfitt, on the second floor, trying to remember what he's writing and why he's writing it, wondering what cold and congealed substance his blood has become.

John and Ralph, the two brothers who work the grounds, oiling the old wheelbarrow.

Marceline, settled now in the yellow room, swearing in German at a script never meant for words.

Gamby on the train, his daughter curled against his lap, her yellow hair spilling down his leg, her whole body expanding with every breath.

SAMANTHA IN HER ROOMS

Eddie, not knowing to let himself in, had knocked patiently at the downstairs door till Alfie barked and found Samantha. She led him up through the kitchen, and into her own rooms rather than the office, so they'd have privacy from Beatrice. She gave him the Morris chair and took the rocker herself. Poor thing, so awkward and formal. He was particularly nervous now, sucking in the lips on his little face until he resembled a gargoyle. He looked around the room, at her desk, her file cabinets, the Chinese lantern, the row of green apples ripening on the windowsill.

He took a great breath and said, "I wasn't leaving till the end of September. But I think I might go tomorrow morning." His palms flat on the arms of the chair. It dwarfed him.

"Oh," she said. "Oh dear." But she wasn't surprised at all. He'd stayed in bed so much, was so silent at breakfast, and talked at dinner only in a rushed, anxious way. (Zilla, who noticed everything, had told Samantha to keep an eye on him. "He's twenty-one," she said. "Can you imagine, coming here right from school and expecting yourself to be brilliant?" "He's already brilliant," Samantha had protested. "He published two collections at Princeton, and everyone's talking about him." "Well, regardless, he's raw. And he's afraid of the house.")

Samantha looked at him now, the way his face had thinned

in the two weeks he'd been here. She said, "You can leave whenever you need. But I hope there's nothing wrong."

"I've been doing good work here," he said. "Really good work. I've finished twelve poems, and they're different from anything I've made before. They're darker, actually. I *never* work this fast. No one does! But that gets at the problem. I'm not—something's wrong with me. I feel this place is going to swallow me whole."

"The house can have an effect."

"It's nothing at all about the way things are run."

"Eddie, why don't you see how you feel in the morning? Just enjoy yourself tonight, relax a bit, and let me know tomorrow."

He dropped his shoulders and smiled. "I will."

"You'll be getting out just in time, too. Mr. Devohr arrives tonight. Lord knows what'll happen to us all in the morning. We'll be walking the plank, I fear." She said it lightly, but really she'd spent the past day calculating frantically: the new artists due next Tuesday, the impossibility of sending Ludo back to Mussolini, the number of trustees who might eventually support a reconfigured Laurelfield, maybe on a farm up in Wisconsin. The finished canvases she was still storing in the basement for a painter who'd left in June. The prospect of having no home. Gamby might give her a month to clear out. Or maybe it was nothing. Maybe she was panicking over nothing.

They stood and walked back through the kitchen.

"May I inquire what happened to your wall?" he said.

She'd already forgotten the ugly black hole beside the icebox, the size of a large fist. And around it a larger circle of blackened wall, a foot in diameter. "I'll have to cover it before Mr. Devohr arrives. I had a lamp with no shade, and it fell against the wall this morning. When I smelled it, I thought I must have burned my lunch—and then I remembered I wasn't cooking anything."

Beatrice's voice, from the office: "We ought to dig all the way through and install the world's shortest pneumatic tube!"

Eddie laughed. "The ghost has been at the lamps lately. She snuffed ours out in the library last night."

"That lets me off the hook, doesn't it?"

THE DISH ON MARCELINE

She gets up early to work. Some of us saw her notes on the first script, when she left them by the coffee pot. *The Aspern Papers*, from a Henry James story, a failure in its first filming and sure to fail as a talkie. Because the only real characters are the old woman, her plain spinster niece, and the man obsessed with obtaining the old woman's love letters. No part here for Clara Bow, no room for a WAMPAS Baby Star. Only, if Marceline is smart, and we think she is, she'll show the audience some scenes from the past, when old Juliana was young and in love with the writer Aspern. But no, some of us argue: The whole point is the burning of the papers at the end, the fact that our man will *never* know the truth about the love affair. It would ruin it all, to show the past!

The other script, the one Marceline hasn't yet begun, is *Bluebeard*. She told us at breakfast. No, not the pirate. His beard was black. Bluebeard was the killer. The one with all the wives. Remember, the key she can't get the blood off? That one has potential.

Someone has heard that Marceline Horn once lived in sin with Ronald Coleman. Only it's not a sin in Hollywood, is it? They have different gods out there.

Someone heard she spent two thousand dollars on a Chinese rug. We are disinclined to believe this.

ZILLA IN THE ATTIC

Up here, she could concentrate. It wasn't so much that she had heard Viktor's feet through the Longhouse wall, and his humming, and occasionally the phonograph, but that she could *feel* him there, and it made her cold and it made her blood vibrate and every day she shrank. Every noise might have been his door closing, or opening, or him tapping on her window, or a woman—one of his dancing girls, or that waifish poet who left last Tuesday—coming to see him, to untuck his shirt, to lead him to the bed in the corner. So Zilla asked Samantha for the attic key, and Samantha gave it without comment, though she knew, they all knew, who wouldn't have known? And so for the fourth day now she was working on a piece of linen that she'd tacked right to the floor, for lack of properly lit wall space. And also for the difference it made. To stand *above* it, to feel she was peering straight through the linen and into the rest of the house, Fannie's bedroom below, and what was below that? The dining room. It was a hundred degrees up here, but still she was freezing from the inside out.

She wasn't sure what this painting wanted to be. She'd tried for petallate, frilled, wet, but ultimately she found she couldn't, in her state, create something verdant and expectant. She found five fallen oak leaves outside, early jumpers, stuck together with rain, not brown so much as opally pink, blushing at their early demise. And this was what she wanted to express now: a stack of soft, lovely suicides.

She'd had a letter that morning from Lemuel, holed up in Madison, "drowning in silver baths and sulphite," trying to finish the prints for his show. He wanted her home. He wanted her to keep him safe from nightmares. He said he might go up in an airplane with Kneller, which she knew was meant as a threat, as he believed all planes crashed, and believed that he, in particular, was due a fiery death. If she could, she'd stay here forever. She'd be like Ludo, minus the marooning via political unrest. She'd beg Samantha to let her stay, and then stay longer, and stay longer, until she'd become a part of the furniture. Her room, like Ludo's, would be permanently blocked off on Samantha's color-coded chart. Except that Lemuel would die, he truly would. He'd stop eating, like Violet Devohr.

The leaves were working out nicely. There was something new, a depth she could normally achieve only with many layers of oil, but that somehow came through now with just the thinnest washes. Now that she was this far from him, she was painting, in a sense, for Viktor. Though she'd never admit it aloud. And if he visited her studio along with everyone else at the end of her stay, why would he assume this particular pile of oak leaves had to do with him?

When she'd walked, travel-weary, into the library three weeks ago and seen him there, sitting as always, cigar and drink, legs halfway across the rug, she'd been shaken to the core, but only in the most familiar of ways. This time, she'd have been more surprised if he'd *not* been there. This was the third stay for both, and the third time their visits had coincided. He didn't need to tell her he hadn't arranged it this way: The blanching of his face was enough. It wasn't Samantha's doing, either—Samantha, who, in '27, asked them in all earnestness if they'd overlapped before. Zilla had come to feel the house itself was responsible, a magnetic field drawing them both back at regular intervals.

In March of '25, right after her first solo show, she'd come here to recover, to try to make something she didn't loathe as much as the work she'd just stared at till she wished for blindness. When she first saw him, Viktor was arriving late to dinner. His walk from the train had half frozen him, and he hadn't shaved in days. His hair—she'd thought it was the ice freezing it out like that in all directions. He sat next to her and said very little. She asked him for the salt without even looking at him—an elderly playwright was holding forth on hermaphrodites—and Viktor took her hand and uncoiled her fingers, tilted the shaker so the salt poured slowly into her palm. She turned, and he locked up her eyes in some kind of cage with his own, so that she couldn't turn away. Everyone began laughing and thought it a great joke, but really something far stranger was going on, something to do with her spinal column and her entire future. Her hand grew heavy. The salt began to spill over the edges and between her fingers. It was a long time—a minute? five minutes?—till he gave the container a last shake and set it down, and there she sat, dopey, buried under a mountain of a million small things. She pinched a few grains off the top for her casserole, and sat there eating the rest of her meal with her hand still outstretched, still laden. She said nothing at all, and this became a source of tremendous amusement for the rest of the table. They tried to remember which Roman goddess it was she resembled, and whether there might have been, once, a salt-bearing oracle. For the rest of that stay, the whole group called her The Oracle. She resumed talking the next morning, and found she had become such an object of fascination to the other artists that they all wanted to hear whatever she said. They wanted to ask The Oracle their futures. "How burnt shall dinner be?" "When will my poems ever be done?" "Which painting will sell?"

But she was caught up, meanwhile, in watching Viktor. His clothes were always too small or too large, or both. His eyes bugged out, so dark a brown that you couldn't tell iris from pupil.

She'd thought him tremendously ungraceful for a dancer at first, until she understood his problem: He was meant to move in empty and infinite space, not to interact with chairs and lamps and soup spoons. Still, every muscle engaged in whatever he did. No movement was isolated to just the hand, or just the leg. Each action had behind it the force and eloquence of his entire body.

The next night there had been a storm, one of those violent Midwestern ordeals she was still unaccustomed to. They'd been gathered in the library after dinner, and midway through the first round of drinks Zilla had confessed how terrified she was of the thunder, of the lightning hitting her in bed as she slept. Viktor had rested his cigar in the ashtray, and left the room. They'd laughed about where he'd gone—he felt a dance coming on!—but twenty minutes later he was back, soaked like a shipwrecked sailor, teeth clacking, hair improbably still erect. He extended his palm, a wet, black acorn in the middle. He said, "For your windowsill. To protect you." It was a tradition having to do with Thor, he explained, being god of both the oak trees and the lightning. The whole crowd had laughed again, but this time with— she thought she heard it—an edge of wonder and knowing and general romantic envy. This man must be in love with this woman. *But we haven't yet spoken!* she wanted to say. Later they would speak. They'd spend hours on the terrace, always with others, laughing about failure and rent parties and a thousand other things.

She hadn't thought of it till now, but this must be why she'd chosen oak leaves to paint. Of course. How dense, not to realize.

A knocking below.

"Yes!" she called. "Yes, yes, yes."

And here, hurrying up, were Samantha and Ludo, and trailing behind was Armand, the illustrator, the sweet golden one with the odd teeth.

Samantha's eyes were bright and wet. "We'll need to hide

Ludo up here. Tonight at dinner, and after. You know Gamby thinks he's gone. I swore."

"You no mind?" Ludo said. "I leave alone your paint." He appraised the room.

Zilla took Samantha's wrist and led her gently to the rolling stool. "Sit down," she said. "Breathe great slow breaths."

She found chairs for the men and a crate for herself, and they sat by an open dormer, where an electric fan fought a losing battle with the heat.

Samantha said, "I'll offer Gamby the extra bed in the director's house, but I'm sure he'll stay at the hotel. Either way, Ludo should be safe to sleep in his room. I mean, just at night. I don't imagine Gamby will stay more than a day or two. Unless he kicks us out and stays *forever*."

"He won't," Ludo said.

"He will. He actually will."

Ludo was a frenetic little man. It had been two years since he and Zilla had made love (*love*, ha!) in the composer's cottage, since Viktor had hit him in the mouth with a dinner plate the next day—also, not coincidentally, the last day Viktor had spoken directly to her—and she could remember nothing at all about the feel of Ludo's body, his smell, his tongue. He looked at her with equal vacancy.

Samantha said, "This morning I wrote to the board. Some are my friends, but most aren't. I don't know how much sympathy we have."

Armand, quiet till now, let out a loud breath, a dragon puffing contemplative steam. "What would he take from New York? The Broadway, or the Twentieth Century? Well, no, it doesn't matter. They both get to the city in the morning. Let's say he's there now, he'll have to switch to the local, maybe he'll have lunch first. We have a few hours."

"To do what?"

"I haven't a clue."

Ludo said, "I quote you Ovid, but I don't know in the English: Fortune is not helping those who pray but those who act."

"Didn't Ovid get exiled?"

Armand said, "Stay here." He vanished down the stairs, and they all stared after him, bemused, and then in seconds he came running back. He put something on the windowsill: a little monkey, carved from green jade. Loopy arms, a manic grin. "It's the Lord of Mischief," he said. "A relic of my dissolute years in the Orient. He'll be our totem."

Samantha stared at the thing. "I thought you'd be coming back with an idea."

"Well, no."

Zilla rubbed Samantha's neck. She said, "We could either seduce him or kidnap him. I believe these are our options."

Armand: "We'll charm him."

Samantha: "It won't work. And what then?"

"Then, anything and everything. Desperation."

VIKTOR IN HIS STUDIO: THE WINTER'S TALE

It is a dance to be done to a wall.

On the stage, it will be a dance to a statue, to the frozen Hermione. Leontes will dance his grief, his longing, for the wife he betrayed and killed, and then—then!—the statue steps down, Hermione lives, and there is to be the most exquisite *pas de deux*, all the more wrenching for their sixteen-year separation, for the age of the dancers. If only he can create the thing. But for now, in the Longhouse, he lives inside Leontes' dance of despair, the score spread around him on the floor like icebergs. His feet bare. The music is in his head, and he dances to the western wall. Zilla is through that wall (Armand Cox is through the other) and there are times when he knows she's standing not two feet away, facing him, brush in her left hand, a brush in her teeth, painting on her thin cloth. If there were no wall, if there were no cloth, she'd be painting the same air he is dancing in.

In sixteen years, he will not need a statue to remember her body, her face.

He dances as far as the dance is written.

He presses his hips to the wall.

Armand and Ludo, hunting down the other artists, giving them their roles.

Josephine at the window, to Fannie: "It's one of the last good places in the world, isn't it? One of the last."

Viktor, walking Marlon around to sober him up. Marlon: "Have you seen those photos of Zilla? The ones her husband took? And exhibited in public! They're—let me tell you. Let me *tell* you." Viktor: "Yes. I've seen them."

Zilla and Samantha in the kitchen of the director's house, giggling like children, tearing at the thin plaster of the wall around the small black hole, until chunks come away in their hands and the opening is two feet square between the counter and the icebox.

"There, see? That cross beam back there," Samantha says.

They reach carefully into the hole with the bottles they've brought from the library, and line them up along the exposed beam: gin, bourbon, rye, scotch, vermouth, all new and full from the bootlegger's drop.

Zilla: "That's the ugliest speakeasy I've ever seen."

"It'll do."

They nail the square board over the hole, as gently as they can, so the bottles won't fall.

Outside, sunshine and wind.

ARMAND AND EDDIE IN THE FLOWERED BEDROOM

He found Eddie under the desk, tucked in a ball, writing in a small black notebook. Armand understood instantly, and wanted to tell him so: that it sometimes felt better like this, tucked into something solid, hidden from the world. Instead, when Eddie scooted halfway out, what he said was, "You look like a turtle."

Eddie laughed and nodded, but he didn't come any farther, so Armand sat Indian style on the floor.

"I'm sorry to interrupt," Armand said.

"I'm glad you did. I didn't like what I was writing."

Eddie was so controlled, so careful. His eyes, though—the way they pulsed around the room and then back to your face—it was as if they were taking in everything with such tremendous force, such thirst. A good chance *this* was the reason for his quiet. There was so much pouring in that nothing could come out.

Armand told him his role for the evening, and said nothing would go into effect till Samantha gave the word. "We might yet be wrong," he said. "He might be paying a purely social visit. To absorb some culture, you know. Perhaps he wants to learn to paint. Ha." Eddie didn't say anything. "It's not a full plan, I know, but it's something. God, I'd love to draw you under there. The lines are fantastic. It's just the desk and your head and your knees."

Eddie blushed. Everyone blushed when you said you wanted to draw them. It was perhaps the most flattering thing in the world.

Not the suggestion that you were beautiful so much as the implicit revelation: *I see you. I really see you.*

Armand said, "You're so quiet." And without knowing he would, he reached forward and grabbed Eddie's jaw and popped it open like he was giving a dog a pill. He pulled a nickel from his pocket and stuck it on Eddie's tongue. Eddie closed his mouth. Armand let go of him.

Eddie managed to say, "Why did you do that?" The coin still in his mouth. Armand heard it click against his teeth.

"I thought if I paid the nickelodeon it would make some noise. And see? It worked."

THE WHITE RABBITS APPRAISE GAMBY

Mr. Devohr has requested dinner at five—a bad sign, surely. There will be no drinks before, no gathering in the library. When they enter the dining room at four-fifty, Gamby Devohr is already there, Samantha at his side. She's managed to put on a dress.

Fannie whispers to Josephine: "He looks like a starfish. Stuffed in a suit and fitted out with a black wig."

Josephine to Fannie: "He doesn't resemble his mother one bit."

Fannie: "Not a bit."

They glance to where Violet hangs on the wall, darkly regarding her endless stream of uninvited houseguests.

"He's terribly young."

"He's twenty-five."

"Keep your voice down."

"He can't hear."

"He flunked out of Yale, Samantha said."

"But I thought he left to marry the girl. And seven months later, wouldn't you know, a baby!"

"It's amazing how quickly they grow them, these days."

"Look, someone's folded all the napkins like little sailboats. How swank!"

The artists file past to shake Gamby's hand, to thank him for his generosity. Armand has traded in his knickers for ludicrous Oxford bags, a facetious nod to formality, and as he introduces himself Gamby stares, confused, at what appears to be a floor-length skirt. When Samantha introduces Marceline, Gamby turns red. "Miss Horn," he says. "It's a great honor. I watched you in *Old Kentucky*, and you were just swell. Wasn't that you in *The Statesman*? In the dress, you know, that dress? I'd love to—wow, I'd love to hear some of your stories!"

Fannie can't look at Josephine, or they'll both laugh. Gamby is nothing more than a little boy in a suit. The silly nickname fits.

Marceline accepts the kiss on her hand. "The honor is entirely mine."

Fannie, whispering: "His father's been trying to boot Samantha for years, Zilla said. Only the board wouldn't."

"Augustus? That's the father?"

"And he had a stroke last year."

"He's got something to prove, then, hasn't he? Gamby."

"Show up at the old man's bedside and give him back the house."

"Look how smooth his hands are!"

"And plump!"

They sit to eat.

Josephine to Fannie: "Wouldn't we love to sculpt him?"

Fannie to Josephine: "I'd do it in mashed potatoes. With a little butter hat."

EDDIE AT DINNER

The food was elegant, a stretch for the cook: consommé julienne, roast Surrey fowl with bread sauce, hearts of celery, new potatoes in cream. Eddie struggled to eat.

Gamby asked them each, cordially, about their work. Armand said, "You've probably seen my magazine covers and forgotten them at once. I did a lot of fadeaway girls, when that was the style."

"I suppose they model for you!" Gamby said. "The girls."

"Certainly."

"And why does it help to be here in the woods? Don't artists thrive in the city?"

Zilla said, "We are like flowers, Mr. Devohr. We might exhibit ourselves in the city, but we grow best in the wilderness." She touched his arm with two fingertips. She wore all white.

"Huh."

Fannie said, "We don't even have a proper studio right now, Josephine and I. We're trying to make enough pieces here this month to last the rest of the year."

"What, to sell?"

"That *is* how artists make a living." Samantha must have realized how sharp she sounded because she took a long drink of water and looked around the table. She wanted someone to rescue her.

Marlon said, "I've written a tremendous amount, this stay. A *tremendous* amount."

Gamby listened patiently, and soon enough he was focused in again on Marceline, asking about the talkies. "Von must speak from farther up in the throat," she was saying. "Or it von't record vell. You do as if you vere talking into the telephone."

He said, "I heard they can do gunshots now. Isn't it true, they invented a slow-motion pistol just so it'll record?"

"Yes," Marceline said. "It opens many possibilities." Brave woman, chatting so amiably about the death knells of her own career.

Zilla, seated to Gamby's left, was the one responsible for figuring out how serious he was in his mission, how doomed they all really were. If anyone could get a man to give too much away, it was Zilla—her palpable empathy, the way she leaned into everything you said. Even Eddie relaxed when he talked to her, and the chill vanished. Being near Zilla was being near a small, smooth lake.

Eddie forced a bit of bread. He'd lost weight here. If he stayed any longer, he might vanish entirely. He heard Zilla, her voice a bit higher, more emphatic than normal: "Oh, but we don't even *interact* with the town! It's like an invisible fairy castle! This is my third stay, and I haven't set *foot* off the grounds but once, when I cracked my wrist and was rushed to the doctor. I don't suppose they think anything of us at all!"

A minute later, Gamby laughed for all the table to hear: "It goes without saying that if I'd decided to be an *artist* or a *poet*, or what have you—my father would have sent me over Niagara in a barrel."

"Yes." Zilla said it through her teeth. "We're awfully lucky to do what we do."

Viktor was rotating all the food on his plate to the left. Choreographing his vegetables. What must it have meant, Eddie wondered, to be accustomed to young dancers he could throw around—literally throw in the air!—and then to fall in love with a woman like Zilla? A woman so grounded, so unflappable (so *married* too), that he, Viktor, would inevitably be the one to bend and break. It would be unbearable, surely.

Gamby was saying: "So when you start a painting, do you arrange all your fruit and whatnot on a table, or do you just make it up?"

Eddie watched Armand and Marlon pretend to talk to each other. Marlon had removed his smoking jacket for once, and he might even have been sober. His moustache was waxed. Armand, beside him, his hair combed into golden waves. Armand's teeth looked as if each had been collected from a different man's mouth, a sort of harlequin set. Eddie remembered a toy Roman arch where, when the keystone was pulled, the entire thing collapsed. He imagined that if he pulled out Armand's incisor, something similar would happen, the splendors of the ancient world giving way all at once.

Eddie excused himself from the table as the orange layer cake was served, and said he must lie down with his headache. It pained him to be so rude, but his one task tonight was to sneak Ludo his dinner. And then he'd pack his trunk. He wanted to leave as soon as possible in the morning.

In the kitchen, Eddie picked up the covered plate from the cook and wove past the sinks to the back exit. A small blonde girl, no more than four, sat at the counter on a stool, staring disconsolately at a plate of peas. Her milk glass was empty.

"Mr. Devohr's daughter, Grace," the cook whispered. "I don't know what I'm expected to do with her."

When he returned from the attic with the empty tray, she was there still, and she glanced up with hopeful eyes, until she saw he wasn't her father. He wondered if anyone had considered her in the midst of all the planning. He didn't imagine they'd found a maid to watch her, to put her to bed. He said, "I have an important job to do. There are hungry fish out back, and I'm going to give them their supper. I don't suppose you know how to rip bread very, very small."

Grace gave him a deep, appraising look, like an old lady's. "Oh yes I do!"

"Well, you'll have to help me, then. I'm afraid I'm not very good at it. The fish are always complaining. Will you come along?" She hopped from her stool, and the cook, winking, handed Eddie two slices of the dinner bread. He put one in Grace's hand and said, "This one's too heavy for me."

"Are your arms very skinny?"

"Yes, quite."

They sat on the two big rocks by the largest koi pond, and Eddie showed her how to tear tiny pieces and throw them in. They watched the fish come to gobble the crumbs, their round mouths impossibly large.

"The spotted one is my best one," Grace said. "What is his name?"

"Oh, that's Elwood. A terribly distinguished gentlefish."

"Does he love bread the best of any food?"

"*Almost.* Almost. Do you know what he told me the other day? He wishes, more than anything in the world, for a root beer float."

Grace looked skeptical. "It would fall apart in the water."

"That's precisely the problem. He'll never get his wish."

"But I know how to do it! Take him out with a big scoop, and put him *into* the root beer float. He can eat it from inside it."

"Ha! You are an exceptionally wise young lady. I might make a poem about you."

She threw another crumb and thought a moment. "Face."

"I beg your pardon?"

"That's what rhymes with Grace."

He convinced her, miracle of miracles, to lie in bed with a book. He read her the story of Rapunzel from the Brothers Grimm she'd brought on the train, and he changed her into her white night-gown, and he tucked her into the spare bed in Samantha's house, in the room behind the office that Gamby had surprised everyone by accepting. He drew the blinds against the evening sun—it was only ten to six—and told her that back in Toronto, it was nearly midnight.

"Can you remember what I just read you? You can look at the pictures all over again."

"I can read words. I can even read the big words!"

"I shouldn't have doubted it. Did you know, if you lie very still and read the same story ten times, you'll have magic dreams?"

"Oh, I knew that."

"So someone told you the secret. And Elwood will dream about root beer, and I will dream about you."

Grace giggled and kicked her toes under the sheet. Eddie moved her water closer and kissed the top of her head. She smelled like sun and grass.

MARCELINE AT THE END OF THE WORLD

Zilla dropped her spoon on the table with a clatter, and said, a bit too loudly, "Oh, how *clumsy* of me!" Confirmation. That Devohr was here on a euthanasia mission. That he couldn't be charmed. Marceline hadn't caught his exact words, but then she didn't need to—the man's intentions were clear. And so: They all braced themselves, ran through their parts, such as they were, and tried to continue their several conversations as if nothing had happened.

Zilla took a breath to say something, but just then there came a loud knocking above them. A series of small, hard raps that seemed to travel the whole length of the house, ending over the window.

Josephine laughed—a nervous burst.

It happened again: hard and fast, on the roof—the dining room did stick out from the rest of the house—and trailed off as if it wanted them all to follow somewhere.

Devohr scanned their faces, blinking his little eyes again and again.

Marceline wondered if this was the misfiring of some effect they'd arranged for Devohr's benefit—akin to all the fireworks shooting off at once, before the grand finale. She perceived nothing but confusion all around her, though, and concern. Fannie and Josephine grabbed each other's hands.

Samantha said, finally, "It's the acorns. They're early this year."

So it hadn't been the plan. What had been the plan? Zilla was to have spoken. But she just sat there, ashen, the only one not laughing now, the only one who didn't seem relieved, and whispered into her cupped hands: "Good lord."

Marceline had simply been told to flirt, and this she had done expertly. The high art of pantomime—quite possibly her last performance of that art. She was unfortunately hazy on other details. But she could flirt till dawn.

Mr. Devohr stretched and stood. "We should end this soirée. I'll be heading back to Chicago quite early in the morning."

Samantha said, "We're finished." But it was a question, and they all knew she wasn't referring to dinner.

He sniffed. "You've had a good run, Miss Mays. I always say, it's important to recognize when the party's over. There's a fine art to it."

Armand said, out loud: "What in the hell do you know about *art*?"

Marceline thought for a moment they might all erupt into violence or weeping. Instead the energy slowly left the room. A leak in the balloon.

Zilla should have taken over now, but she was still glazed, still spooked.

Marlon finally spoke. "Well, what happened to the booze? If we're giving up here, can we at least make a good night of it?" The poor man. He was twitching, positively twitching. Marlon hadn't been in on the plan—he'd spent the afternoon sobering up, not rehearsing—but he'd inadvertently cut to the chase, skipping over Zilla's forgotten invitation to visit the studios, skipping the slow progression that would lead them all to a nightcap and then another and another. Which would all lead, somehow or other, to Gamby Devohr's heart.

"He's only joking, Mr. Devohr," Fannie said. "We don't drink a drop here!" Marceline supposed this was part of the script, a displaced line. She felt herself back on a rooftop in Fort Lee, those embarrassing summer flickers of twenty years past, costumes pulled from theater trash, directors who'd never directed so much as bicycle traffic. Devohr was about to laugh. Marceline—finally she knew exactly what to do—Marceline stood up next to him and slid her hand down the outside of his thigh. She cocked her head and let her eyelashes fall slowly down. "Please do join us for a drink," she said. "For a last bacchanal. How often, back in Canada, do you live like the artists do? The night is terribly young." And she could see in his dopey eyes the affirmation of what she'd learned on her very first picture: Sex trumps a poor script and poor players any day.

Marceline walked with him, arm in arm, trailing Zilla and Samantha and Armand back to the director's house and up the stairs. Marlon followed at a distance, apparently even less sure than Marceline of what was happening. Alfie circled their feet. They found Eddie alone at the little kitchen table, his finger to his lips. The girl, he said, was in bed.

Samantha got a hammer from under the sink and, turning it to the prong end, began prying the nails loose from the ugly square board behind her. Marceline kept Devohr talking and laughing while Armand took a turn, and then Eddie. The board broke loose from the wall, and then there was a great clatter as Eddie and Armand reached in and pulled out an improbable number of liquor bottles.

Marceline guessed from the proximity of the hammer, from the loose way the board was nailed, that this unveiling had been part of the plan all along. If Devohr thought they were letting their guard down—if he thought they'd given up entirely and were revealing their true selves—he'd maybe let his guard down, too.

Armand said, "The terrace! I'll bring cigars!"

Eddie stayed behind to make sure the child was asleep. Marceline pulled Devohr by the hand—down the stairs, down the walk that circled behind the big house. The sun was still bright and high. When she was sure he'd been propelled in the right direction, she let go and fell back with Zilla and Armand, five bottles between them, the dog at their heels.

"How does the plan go now?"

"That *was* the plan. That's as far as it goes."

ALL OF THEM

More acorns covered the ground than should have been possible. The oaks all grew in front of the house—the smaller ones off to the left, the majestic one between the director's house and the big house—but even so their helmeted seeds carpeted the lawn and terrace and paths out back like hail. Green still, and dangerous: Josephine went rolling forward, and Fannie caught her under the arms. "They're good luck!" Marlon said.

"Well, we need plenty of that."

Hazy and hot, the air still and heavy.

Viktor said, "Shall we build a fire? Back on the pile?"

"Oh, yes, yes!" Fannie said.

Everyone made it to the terrace. Even Ludo, with nothing more to lose, came down from the attic to slap Gamby on the back and say he'd teach him to drink like an Italian.

Armand took over one of the long, high tables and started mixing drinks. Someone broke into the kitchen and brought out lemons, and soon Armand was squeezing them into a glass and picking out seeds with his fingers so he could mix the juice with the gin and the precious Cointreau to make White Ladies. ("How ghostly!" Josephine cried, and Fannie rubbed her hands together. "Ooh, shall we bring out the Ouija? It's still in the library!")

Gamby said, "You don't believe in ghosts, do you? Tell me this. Why'd they all die violently? Where's the ghost of the nice old lady who died in bed from a tumor?"

"Resting in peace! It's *energy* that makes a ghost, unfulfilled energy. Anger, or fear, or—or—"

"Love," Josephine said. "Unrequited love."

Armand said, "There are more things in heaven and earth, Mr. Devohr, than are dreamt of in your philosophy."

Marlon and Viktor decided they were in charge of the bonfire. Marlon slipped his smoking jacket back on and ran around gathering extra sticks, while Alfie the dog scampered after in joyful brotherhood. Viktor became convinced the quality of the fire would depend on the number of matches used to light it, and took donations from the men's pockets.

Marceline and Zilla reclined on the terrace wall, legs stretched along it toward each other. Sylphic bookends. Samantha put a chair for Gamby right in front of them, at eye level with the legs. And she sat too, and she asked Ludo to open the solarium windows and turn on the Victrola. Soon there was music, "A Shady Tree" and "Was It a Dream," and soon Ludo was back and handing out Armand's cigars, and Armand was passing drinks. Marceline said, "I vent to such a lofely garden party last month, at the house of Mary Pickford. Mister Devohr, do you know her films?"

"Heavens, yes!"

She lowered her voice. "And I vill tell you the real reason she cut her hair."

Behind them, Josephine leaned against the ivy, and Fannie leaned against her, on her soft shoulder. She said, "What would we do without this place? What sort of world would this be, without refuges?"

In the distance, the fire pile began to glow. Small spots around the lower edges first, then a few thin arms of fire. Now the whole thing, a consummation. Marlon ran back to the terrace, to view his creation from a distance. "A fine fire," he said. "The best work I've done here." And it was true, he saw that now. He shouldn't have let himself sober up. He could suddenly see his whole book, the shape of it, the bulk of it. It was a monstrosity, a tangle, a snake swallowing its own tail. He took a White Lady from Armand, and with the drink he walked slowly back down the path, back to where Viktor stood staring at the blaze.

Up on the terrace, Armand filled Gamby's glass before it could get half empty.

Gamby didn't seem to doubt that the high spirits were genuine. That these women would naturally want to surround him and regale him with stories. That these artists were simply dying to share their liquor.

Somone did find the Ouija board, and Marceline climbed down from the wall, pulled a chair close to Gamby's, convinced him to press his knees into hers with the board between them. Here was some hope: If Marceline was as gifted an improviser as they all supposed, she might manage to nudge the planchette toward some helpful message. Something about ghosts of artists past, or the ghost of his mother. Saying she loved the art created here and wanted the colony to stay. But all Marceline knew of his mother was that horrible attic story, nothing personal that would shock him into compliance. She couldn't even recall her name.

From behind Gamby's head, Fannie mouthed it: "Violet! Violet!"

Josephine whispered, "Watch, she'll spell it with a W."

Gamby's short, stout, pale fingers on the planchette, Marceline's long ones. She said, "I haf done the Ouija von time before. At a Hollyvood party, vith my dear friend Lon Chaney. I vill tell you, he used the board to proposition me!"

Back by the fire, Marlon and Viktor. Marlon said to him, "I might burn the novel. The whole thing."

"Don't."

"It's a doorstop. I've sat here six weeks and made a doorstop."

"Then burn it." Viktor regarded him with something like spite, a look Marlon hadn't anticipated. "Did you know, you can't burn a dance? There are quite a few things you can't burn, unless you burn yourself, unless you jump into the fire *yourself*."

"Let's step away from the fire."

"Look at her up there, offering herself like—"

"Who? Sobriety doesn't suit you. Good God." Marlon handed over his own drink. "It's delicious," he said.

Viktor looked down at it. "I don't drink."

"You don't?" Marlon thought through the past weeks, and took back his glass. "You mixed the vat last night. And you're always dropping things. You're the drunkest man I know."

"I've never touched the stuff. I couldn't dance."

"But when you were younger?"

"I started training when I was eight." Viktor poked the fire with a long branch and said, "Tell me something. Tell me why I could walk down a street in the city and see two faces in the crowd. And one of them—a stranger—it might be a beautiful woman—for one of them I feel nothing, I remain intact. And the other, no more beautiful, no more spectacular: When I see her, I fall through the universe. And only because of our past, only because of some promise my idiot heart made itself years before."

"Why don't you try a drink."

"The truth is, there's no such thing as love. There's only *history*."

Zilla was pouring her drinks off the far side of the wall. She needed to stay clear.

Alfie ran yapping between the terrace and the fire, the terrace and the fire.

"The Ouija dates to Pythagoras," Ludo said.

Zilla said, "Ludo's our encyclopedia."

Gamby laughed. "That's funny, it says here *William Fuld Talking Board Set.* Was Mr. Fuld a follower of Mr. Pythagoras?" Marceline smiled up as if the two of them alone were in on the joke. Gamby addressed the board. "What horse shall I pick at Saratoga next summer?"

"No, no," Marceline said, and she attempted to make even that one word flirtatious. "Let us ask the spirit's name."

She aimed for the V. She was halfway there when Gamby jerked the planchette down to the bottom, to the number 2.

"Hell of a name!" Gamby said. Pleased with his own joke. "You should get your money back from Mr. Pythagoras."

Marceline said, "It must mean there are two spirits!"

Samantha closed her eyes.

Gamby said, "Are you men or women?"

Before Marceline had time to think, the planchette slid to the sun face on the top left, with the word *YES* beneath.

"Well played, Miss Horn." Devohr waggled his eyebrows. "One of each, male and female! Are we ourselves the spirits, by chance?"

"I am not mofing the pointer, Mr. Devohr. Are you?"

Fannie and Josephine swayed to the music. Ludo changed the record, and, returning to the terrace, did a shuffling little solo dance to "I'm Saving Saturday Night for You."

Samantha, next to Gamby but silent, relied on Marceline's and Zilla's social graces. She wrapped her hands around the iron arms of the chair, let the metal cool her fingertips. Or rather, her fingers transferred their warmth, electron by electron, into the chair. An important distinction. And when she was gone, when there was no visible trace of her at Laurelfield, when the lawn was filled with matrons drinking tea, her electrons would remain in the chair. That was something, and she pressed harder. That was something.

Alfie slept, at last, under her.

Zilla watched Marlon lead Viktor back to the terrace. She said, "There ought to be marshmallows."

Viktor said nothing. He swayed a bit. Marlon had never seen a man sway from sobriety. He led him to Armand. He said, "We need to fix this fellow up."

Marceline had asked again for spirit's name. They all watched.

G

G

G

The planchette circled the letter like a bee on a flower.

"I think you are writing your own name, Mr. Devohr." She wanted to push back harder on the planchette, but then the whole idea was for him to believe it had moved on its own.

"No, too many G's!" he said. "Gagog. It sounds like a caveman. Gagog the Horrible. Gilgamesh!"

Fannie said, "Ask how she—ask how it perished. The spirit." And they did.

S

C

R

F

C

"Scarface!" Marlon called, unhelpfully. Josephine aimed a plump elbow into his ribs, but he didn't understand. "Maybe they're two of the fellows Capone got! Ask if they died on February the fourteenth! Ask if the last thing they saw was a warehouse!"

Marceline tried to think quickly. "Perhaps it means *sacrifice*. Perhaps—it is von who sacrificed a great deal for, for the colony."

But she was going off course, wasn't she? Violet hadn't had a thing to do with the colony. She felt the looks around her, a net of disappointment. She said, "Vhen did you lif?"—not certain where she'd aim the thing even if she could wrest control.

NO

Gamby said, "Well that's terribly uncooperative! Tell us, brave spirits, when did you walk the earth?"

NO

NO

NO

GOOD BYE

The planchette stopped and stayed on that "good bye" at the bottom as if its motor had run out. Gamby lifted his fingers.

"But *NO* was on the moon picture!" Fannie said. "I think it meant 'Many moons ago!' Don't you?"

Josephine said, "It's useless."

Marceline said, "Let's gif it von more go."

Gamby sighed and looked down. "Well," he said. "I suppose there is one person I want to reach. It's just that she's been gone a long time. And she—BOO!" He slapped the board, and it flew across the terrace with the planchette, and Gamby erupted into boisterous laughter at the same moment that Fannie and Josephine screamed and Viktor fell back into the ivy. Alfie awoke and barked disapprovingly.

Ludo scrambled after the Ouija set. Marlon poured his own drink straight into Gamby's glass while he was distracted, then fetched himself a refill.

By the time Eddie joined the party, the little girl at last asleep, or at least pretending, there was no appeal to joining the drinkers. He'd never catch up, and they made it look so tiresome. Flushed faces and stupid, shouted conversation. He ought to pack, but his room would be hot. He'd wait till the air had cooled. He leaned against the ivy, next to the White Rabbits, and together they watched Gamby.

Fannie said, "Look at him there, surrounded by beauty. What did he do to deserve any of this?"

Josephine said, "What if we murdered him? What if we threw him on the fire?"

"*Josephine!*"

"We could forge letters back to Canada. He'd say how he was joining the artists, how he'd always wanted to be a painter."

"There's that little girl!"

"Well, I'm only *joking*. Eddie, I'm afraid Fannie takes me *awfully* seriously. And I don't deserve to be listened to for a single word."

"She's all nonsense, it's true."

Meanwhile Gamby had grown loud and shrill. "That's *ace!*" he shouted.

"He's going to lick her shoulder," Armand whispered. "Marceline's."

"Do you suppose he's corked?"

"He's fried to the hat."

Eddie watched Zilla, still perched on the wall, watched the way she never fully looked away from Viktor. He'd understood half of it before, but now he realized there was something he'd absolutely missed, something about the way her eyes sunk into themselves: She was bereft, or broken, or grief stricken. She stared at Viktor the way a woman on a boat stares at a man drowning in the ocean.

Marlon and Armand leaned on the makeshift bar, and Ludo soft-shoed around the terrace, but Viktor sat now, Indian style, an empty glass by one knee. He was looking out, either at Zilla or the fire. Maybe to him they were the same thing.

In one breath Eddie fished his Waterman from his trouser pocket and grabbed Viktor's hand. Viktor didn't seem to notice at all. He wrote across the veins, in dark blue: *She loves you.* He stepped in front of Samantha, in front of Gamby, in front of Marceline, who was talking about Hollywood ghostwriters and the confessional craze. He grabbed Zilla's hand—she at least looked at him, startled—and wrote: *He loves you.*

He capped the pen. It was a service someone had to perform,

he felt. A translation service, in a way. What *was* all this, but a modern tower of Babel? Here was someone speaking nothing but dance, and someone else speaking paint, and someone speaking poetry, and someone speaking music. And what were they trying to express, but the inexpressible? If there existed words, regular words, to say what they were aiming at, then why would they even need to do what they did? Why were they all living here, knocking so ineffectively at the doors of the palace? The ink was insufficient as anything else, but perhaps it was a start. If he'd been a sculptor, he'd have sculpted it for them: Look! There! Love.

Someone had appeared at the edge of the terrace: a small girl in a white nightgown. No one but Marceline noticed at all, until Eddie sprang across the bricks and knelt in front of her and said, "Let's have one more story, shall we?" And he vanished with the girl, around the corner of the house. Gamby, his eyes closed in laughter, hadn't even seen.

The sun was lower in the sky. It hovered over the trees a long time, casting long shadows toward the house.

Fannie: "If we could only slow down time, we could accomplish an infinite amount of work before this place gets the wrecking ball."

Armand: "I'll move very slowly when I'm near you. And you'll believe it's come true."

Josephine: "You have such an honest energy, Armand. You live very close to the skin."

And off Armand bounded, to pour more gin in Gamby's cup.

Zilla and Viktor both squinted at the backs of their hands like confused palm readers.

Marceline, a laugh like an oboe: "Vell, can you belief, ve all thought the talkies vould mean more vork for *theater* actors. But instead they vant to pay youngsters something like seventy-fife a veek. And gif them leads! And star them!"

Zilla tried to focus on the same conversation: "But," she said, "*here* is a place—here we're so different from a place like Hollywood. They've built a city, an industry. And here we are in our studios. You understand it, don't you, Mr. Devohr? What it is we do here, and why it matters. A man like you, a man has everything he wants, autos and servants and land—what does he do next? He buys art!"

"I do!" Gamby said. His words were garbled. "I buy art! I'll buy it from you! You can paint me a picture of Marcelot. Of Marceline. Of—ha!—of Miss Horn."

Eddie returned. Things felt like they'd fallen apart—the Ouija long abandoned, even Marceline and Zilla's flirting strangely mechanical and overdone now. Samantha had turned to stone. He wished he could think of something to help. The magic words to save this place that he himself wanted nothing more to do with.

But Armand was staring at him, Armand was smiling at him, Armand was not looking away.

Any instinct on Eddie's part to hide had been wiped away by the catastrophe of Viktor and Zilla. Did he want to end up like them, made sick by what he wouldn't acknowledge? And so he stared back at Armand.

Ludo wove around them like a leprechaun. The music from the solarium was "Let's Fall in Love." Ludo pulled Zilla off the terrace wall with both hands, pulled her into a little waltz that didn't match the music at all.

He whispered: "Where is your camera? Don't you, somewhere, have a camera?"

"Marlon's got a Leica."

The August air, thick enough to climb.

Alfie, asleep again.

Eddie looked right at Armand. And—the bravest thing he'd done in his life—he slowly, slowly, stuck out his tongue to display the nickel he'd kept in his mouth since the afternoon, removing it only for dinner. Then he flipped it back in and closed his lips.

Armand did not look away. For the next five minutes, he did not look away.

Gin fractured the time. An encounter halfway down the lawn, Fannie tripping—how had they gotten there?—and one back on the terrace, surely later. Marlon would try to recall, the next morning. He'd had his smoking jacket, and then he hadn't. Eddie had been near, and then he'd been quite far away, and then there was a bathroom floor. And then there was the fire, still burning, though someone else was in charge. The sun was low but still hot, and Viktor was crying. Why was Viktor crying? What was wrong with the man?

Gamby stumbling down the lawn, grabbing at Marceline's chest. She was nimble. She held him by the elbow. Laughing and laughing.

Zilla had Marlon's camera.

"Everyone together! Quick, before the last of the sun—"

Fannie, trying. Josephine pulling at her arm. "Mr. De—Mr. Devohr. Your mother, and her death. Don't you think—don't you think, though, she'd have wanted all this? All this art?"

"Vell, the tap dancers are doing splendidly now of course. Who could haf guessed?"

"Eddie, what's wrong with him? Can you get Viktor some water?"

Samantha nodding to Armand. *Yes, go ahead, do it, whatever it is.*

"Miss Horn will join us, yes! And Miss Silverman as well! But—"

Armand's clothes off, Gamby's off, Zilla's off too. Marceline backing toward the house. The sun beginning to set.

"It's the way the natives fish!"

"Here, get your head up! Don't drown."

And the two of them, Armand and Gamby, out of the water. Who had kept the fire going? Laughing and laughing, and no one could stop laughing.

Armand, grabbing: "Look, I caught a fish!" Moving the other's plump hand: "Look, you caught one too!"

Laughter and the click of the Leica and the low red sun, and the light of the fire. No one could stop laughing.

It was dark so fast, and they couldn't remember how.

Viktor, somewhere out in the dark. No one could find him. They could hear him, but they couldn't find him.

In the humid night, some of them stumbled together, and some stumbled farther apart.

ZILLA IN THE DARKROOM, GAMBY IN THE DARK

First she points it at the back of the big house and clicks through the rest of the film. Thirteen photos of abandoned windows, lit orange by the setting sun. Up there, the room where she slept on her first visit, before there were beds in the Longhouse. The yellow room at the other end, where Viktor once stayed. The solarium studio, Fannie and Josephine's sculptures shining like living things. The dining room, where she's fallen in some sort of love with every artist and composer and writer who's ever sat across from her.

The sun is gone as she gropes her way down the path to the darkroom cabin. She's been developing Lemuel's prints for years, doing half his work, really, and even in this unfamiliar space it takes her little time to sort things out. All the chemistry she needs is here: a jackpot of not quite empty bottles left by departing photographers. Tanks and reels. An ancient ruby light, with a funny little door. But no photographic paper. No matter, if the negative is clear and convincing. She takes her time lining things up left to right on the counter. Developer, stop bath, fixer. She makes sure the sink works.

(At this same moment, back on the lawn: Gamby, somehow both drunker and more sober, lunges at Fannie. He says, "Hey, wait, where's your camera? Wait!" "Good gracious, it wasn't my camera," Fannie says.)

She turns off the electric lamp and feels her way back to the counter. It's a relief not to see her hands anymore, the upside-down script: *He loves you.* Well, yes. Eddie didn't know what he was doing, writing on them like that. He imagined he was point-ing out something they didn't both already know.

(It has started to rain again, to pour. Marlon wakes up on the terrace and wonders why he's in a pool, why he's underwater, how he can breathe underwater. He goes back to sleep. Gamby is look-ing for Armand. He's shouting.)

Her hands are shaking so that she can't get the film hooked onto the reel. She has no idea if the light was enough. She has no idea if the shutter clicked at the right moment. If everything's a blur. At last she gets it engaged, begins reeling. One long strip of gray. The images hidden under that gray, waiting. Backward through time. This first half will be empty house. Somewhere in the middle here will be Gamby and Armand, the four shots she managed. The last bit should be Marlon's shots—yesterday, and the day before, and the day before. She finishes, and traps the whole thing in the aluminum canister, and hopes, as she pours, that the bottle of developer is correctly labeled, that it isn't some-one's old supply of bathtub gin. It smells right at least. She closes the canister and turns the lamp back on. She sits on the counter to agitate. She goes by her watch to time the moving meditation—the front of her wrist, the back of her wrist—and the periods of rest.

(Eddie and Armand, behind the composer's shed, in the rain. The coin has been replaced by Armand's tongue. Eddie Parfitt, despite his considerable success, his poetry collections, his awards—Eddie Parfitt is twenty-one years old. He has lived a thousand years in those twenty-one. But he has never been in love.)

The stop bath, the fixer, the water. The water, at least, she can trust.

(Viktor, back in the house alone. Picking up the book Zilla

left in the library—Keats's letters—opening it to the middle: He smells it.)

She feels that Eddie broke something tonight. By writing it out, so starkly, so stupidly, on their hands.

(They are starting without her. Ludo walks Gamby in, drenched and confused, face like a mole forced above ground, and sits him in the solarium among Fannie and Josephine's sculptures.)

At last, she can allow herself to look at the negatives, to see the damage. She finds scissors first, a good sharp pair hanging from a nail. She opens the canister and slowly unspools the reel. The first frames, of the house, she snips off. A blurry shot of the two men, so unclear that they might as well be monkeys. The next one, yes, as she hoped: everything clearly visible, everything anatomical and precise. Gamby's face, as clear as a mug shot. And Armand's as well, and his body, and the sinews of his legs. The head of his penis, fat and soft.

(Samantha says, "You're a businessman, Mr. Devohr.")

She cuts the good shot loose and hangs it to dry. Then she spools back through the shots Marlon's been taking all week. A close-up of a daylily, meant to be artistic. Samantha on her balcony. The giant oak, the two houses, Armand smoking a cigarette. Eddie, smiling uncomfortably on the terrace. Fannie and Josephine walking by the fountain, but obviously posed. Perhaps because she's already in an agitated state, perhaps because of the awkward subjects, Zilla finds these photographs all unduly chilling. What should be so troublesome about two women walking the path? Only she can't shake the feeling that the photographs have existed all along, have been waiting in their canister for a thousand years, and that the people in them have lived their whole lives just to end up in these exact positions, just to hit their marks like dancers. Certainly this is what happened to Gamby, every moment of his life leading him right into this photograph, this trap. They got him to stand just so. They got him entwined with Armand. And he became the picture.

(Eddie's been summoned to the solarium as a bodyguard. All five and a half feet of him, arms like—well, like a poet's. Armand hiding in the library, for his safety. Eddie slips his coin back in his mouth, where it now belongs. Samantha, in a molten voice Eddie didn't know she had in her: "Mr. Devohr, Armand Cox is a known homosexual.")

Zilla realizes something, and it takes her a minute to wrap herself around the idea. She's always thought of Laurelfield as a magnet, drawing her back again and again. But that's just it: A magnet pulls you toward the *future*. Objects are normally products of their pasts, their composition and inertia. But near a magnet, they are moved by where they'll be in the next instant. And this, *this*, is the core of the strange vertigo she feels near Laurelfield. This is a place where people aren't so much haunted by their pasts as they are unknowingly hurtled toward specific and inexorable destinations. And perhaps it feels like haunting. But it's a pull, not a push. She doubts she can express it to anyone else, and she doubts she ought to.

(Gamby, no more blood in his face, sunken back in the chair, surrounded: "What in the hell do you people want?" Samantha still sitting, but she might as well be flying above him, Athena in the sky: "We want twenty-five years.")

Zilla hangs Marlon's shots next to the shots of Gamby. He'll be delighted that someone's done all the work for him.

(Grace, tossing in bed, turning the pillow to the cool side. Dreaming of Rapunzel and fish.)

But a moment later Zilla's sinking, and she realizes what's wrong, what it is. A lot of time has passed, and she's done her job, and Viktor hasn't followed her here. After Eddie wrote those words, there was a window of maybe half an hour when Viktor might have staggered through the dark, knocked on the door, called her name. But he hasn't, and the night air has hardened to impenetrable glass.

(Gamby's head between his knees. He says, "Twenty-five?" And he sits up to sign the paper they've made.)

Zilla and Viktor might pine for the rest of their lives, but that is *all* they will do. They will harden and soften into their old age, and she will paint him a hundred pictures and he will make her a hundred dances, but there will be no words, and there will be no coming together of bodies.

(It's not till Fannie has escorted Gamby back to the director's house that the solarium erupts in jubilation. Armand bursts in and says, "We changed fate! Do you realize what we did? It's—what is it? The victory of art over greed! It is! We reached in and we changed fate!" But Eddie says, "Did we?" Because this whole evening he's felt himself sucked into a whirlpool of inevitability. "Are you sure?")

Oh, stupid Eddie with his stupid pen. And stupid Zilla, too, and stupid Viktor. She sits on the floor and stretches her legs. Lemuel is waiting for her, back in Madison. She can feel him, lying in bed awake, waiting. A different kind of magnet.

(Samantha turns a cartwheel, a full cartwheel, into the hall. The skirt of her yellow dress falls over her head like a parachute.)

After a while, the rain lets up.

And a while after that, the negatives are dry.

Dear Miss Mays,

  Please, if it isn't too late, disregard my premature attempt to leave Laurelfield.

  (And do pardon my slipping this under the door. It's early, and I'd hate to wake you.)

  Everything felt wrong before, but now I know this is exactly where I ought to be, of anywhere in the world. I think I had hold of the place by the wrong end. Or it had hold of the wrong end of me. The point is, it's all changed now. It's right.

  The batch of poems I finished—they were too dark. I'm not going to write that kind of thing again. They were haunted. I thought I was haunted, or the house was, but it was only the work. I'm going to start over.

  Do you ever think of it, how as artists we can just start over? I don't suppose a businessman could throw out his business and start fresh. But we can begin again. And that's what I hope to do, if you haven't given away my spot.

  Sheepishly, thankfully,

  Eddie

THE GHOSTS

Samantha walked the grounds. She wanted to kiss everything. The grass was soaked.

She'd stayed hidden in her rooms when Gamby stomped out of her house at dawn. So it wasn't till noon, when she found Marlon smoking his pipe on the terrace, that she learned about the scene in the big house. Gamby had stalked in and dropped his little daughter off at the breakfast table, asking Josephine to tend to her. Josephine had told riddles, and Fannie went running around the house looking for things that might pass as toys: a pencil and paper, Armand's little jade monkey, a hair clip.

Gamby went through the house opening doors, startling Marceline half dressed. Marlon was heading back to his room for more sleep when he heard a noise above him on the attic stairs. A thundering, a crashing. He thought of the ghost. But no, it was Gamby, descending like an avalanche. Gamby braced himself in the doorway, panting. He said, "The attic may *not* be used for a studio."

"I'm a writer," Marlon said.

"Who the hell's been painting up there?" When Marlon didn't speak—he would have, if he'd known the answer—Gamby exploded. "The attic is a FAMILY space! It has not been offered to you!"

"I don't think it's a studio."

Gamby slammed the door and turned the key in the lock. He

regarded the key with a horror normally reserved for bloody knives. He slipped it in his pocket.

"I'm just a writer."

But by the time Marlon told this all to Samantha, Gamby was long gone. Beatrice, arriving for work, had been so cowed encountering him angry outside the director's house that she'd fetched him both the other copies of the attic key.

In the library that night, Zilla was disconsolate.

Samantha said, "We can pick the lock, I'm sure."

But this wasn't the problem. The problem was the acorns pelting her, the words fading on her hand, the sense that Viktor— look at him in the corner, folded up like an umbrella—was a fate she'd circumvented. And that she wasn't sure if this would be her salvation or her undoing.

Though, yes, the unfinished painting bothered her as well. She hadn't been able to work all day. She'd sat on the fountain, nearly overflowing from all the rain, and stared at the attic dormers, and considered that part of her soul was locked up there, as surely as Violet Devohr had been locked up there. Violet, Violet, dragged here against her will. Was *that* the magnetic force behind her haunting? She was pulled, and so she pulled others. Toward ruin, toward redemption, toward love, away from it. Why? Because she could.

Fannie: "Doesn't he recognize the irony? In *locking* the *attic*!"

Josephine: "I think he's truly that dense."

Outside, the storm was back—violently this time, lightning at all the windows. Marlon said, "In the English department, this is what we would call the objective correlative. Storms of all kinds, outdoors and in."

And on cue there came a shattering thunder unlike any they'd heard before. The glasses clattered on the table.

When the rain finally thinned, when they could count ten seconds between the lightning strikes and their crashes, a

delegation ventured out front: Zilla and Armand and Fannie—
and Alfie, who needed to relieve himself. At first they saw nothing.
Then Armand realized. "The oak," he said. And he pointed to
where the giant oak, the oldest oak, had stood, west of the director's house, taller than any building at Laurelfield, older than the
oldest living turtle. It was utterly gone. A ragged stump stood
maybe four feet high, and a thick mulch of branches and bark and
leaves had formed a carpet for yards and yards around. But there
was no piece thicker than an arm bone, no piece longer than a leg.
Alfie sniffed through it, barking and whimpering.

Fannie said, "Holy mother of God."

Zilla leaned forward at the waist as if she were retching,
though she wasn't. The rain hit her back.

Very late that night, when they were all asleep, she left Laurelfield
without saying anything. Since she hadn't worked in the Longhouse for days, those paintings were dry enough to roll. In the
morning they would find her studio empty, but for a little pile on
the table: rocks, a feather, a dead bee inside a Mason jar.

The attic would not, in fact, be reopened until August of 1954,
when, in those last, calamitous days of the colony, someone called
a willing locksmith and the able-bodied hefted the desks and office machines and cabinets with forty-two years' worth of files up
the stairs. A few files were expunged at that time. Ludo's, for one.
Eddie's, for another.

Zilla came the next year, to visit Laurelfield's grave. She got up
in the attic when Grace and George were out, but her oak leaf
painting—the one held prisoner all those years—was neatly
tacked beneath a window. Its absence would be noticed, and
there was no telling who'd be blamed. And so she decided it
ought to stay. If she couldn't return to Laurelfield, at least part of
her could always remain.

Out on the terrace at midnight, Marlon, terribly soused, his head finally clear: "Only oaks will do that. They always split or explode. And they draw it, they actually draw the lightning to them. *Beware the oak! It draws the stroke!*"

Josephine told him, fondly, to shut his mouth and write a book about it.

Viktor refused to speak.

In 1933, Zilla would watch him dance Albrecht in *Giselle*, his last performance before he vanished. She would sit in the second-to-last row and dart out at intermission.

From 1929 to 1954, forty novels, seven symphonies, fifteen dances, around three hundred stories, and over five thousand poems were completed at Laurelfield. Six times as many of each were begun or continued. Which isn't to mention the concertos and memoirs, the photographs and charcoal sketches. Seventy love affairs were begun, and forty-two were ended. One woman died in the bathtub. A poet hanged herself in the woods. A violin was hurled from the roof. Eight children were conceived. Between 1938 and 1945, seven Jewish artists from western Europe were allowed indefinite stays.

Some of this is a matter of record, the Laurelfield archives having been made public in the fall of the year 2000. Other stories, other sequences of events, are known only to Edwin Parfitt's Olympian gods (if they have survived our neglect) or to the fates, or to the ghosts who keep watch. Count it as the universe's cruelest irony that the ghosts, who alone could piece a whole story together, are uniquely unable to tell it.

One such tale: On October 18, 1944, Lieutenant Armand Cox, a photographer with the Army Signal Corps, climbed onto a barricade in the street outside the Hotel Quellenhof, in the bloody heart of the Battle of Aachen. His interest in the shot was journalistic, not tactical: just a German soldier up in the window. The frame, never developed, captured the soldier's arm mid-motion. The grenade killed Lieutenant Cox, not the eighteen-year-olds below him on the street. His camera landed near his right leg and was, in any event, crushed soon after. In the window boxes of the hotel, there were still geraniums.

A year later, sorting through Armand's things in their Rush Street apartment, Eddie found, in a box in the closet, a photograph of the love of his life, naked, laughing, on the night he first fell in love with him. One of the five copies Samantha had spread throughout the world to prevent Gamaliel Devohr from simply burning Laurelfield to the ground. That night Eddie made his way up Route 41 to Laurelfield, where he stood out back, at the edge of the woods, with a pistol to the flesh behind his chinbone.

He stood there an hour, until he couldn't feel his legs, until he'd become part of the earth, until he thought he might grow leaves. The upstairs lights came on, one by one, as the artists finished their drinks and returned to their work or their trysts. Someone staggered back to the Longhouse. It was a revelation to him, those lights, the shadows behind the curtains: There were artists still up in those rooms, making art. There was good in the world. And the world was worth living in, it truly was. It just wasn't worth being Edwin Parfitt. He had nothing left to write, and he had no one left to love, and he had nowhere left to go. His editor at Holt, himself just returned from the Pacific, had telegraphed that the public awaited his next work, his response to the war. The only thing that could make his grief even less bearable was feeling stared at, waited for. When all he'd ever wanted was to hide inside of something, to crawl inside a piece of furniture and become a mouse.

He wondered if he could move his finger on the trigger.

But look at those lights.

He lay on the ground and put the gun in the leaves. He slept, and as he woke at dawn he remembered a woman he'd met on his last stay, in '41. Armand was already off at training, and it was Eddie's first visit to Laurelfield without him. Her name was Alma Nellis. Hair like grapevine tendrils. This woman would shatter plates against the fountain lip, then mortar them back together in completely illogical ways. The final plate would be vaguely round, but jagged and jumbled. She destroyed and reconstructed an entire tea set this way. Cups no one would dare drink from. "Is it always china?" he asked, and she said, "Next will be a chair."

He wondered if a man, a broken man, could be reconfigured in the same way.

When the sun was up, he knocked at Samantha's door. She held his face in her hands as if he were returning from the dead, as if his had been the dog tags and left arm sent back from Aachen.

Her hair was longer now, wispy. She was softer somehow. She made him toast, and they sat at her table, and they talked about, of all things, the White Rabbits, and Josephine's new solo work, and how she'd taken over the same seventh floor studio in the Fine Arts Building where Armand had once camped out. "She's a worthy inheritor," Eddie said.

Samantha said, "Eddie, I'm dying. I have cancer in my breast."

He had nothing left—the night had drained him—but she understood. She didn't expect anything. After breakfast they walked the grounds. Eddie said, "You'll have to move the fish in soon."

"Eddie, it should be you. The board would hire someone awful. Why can't it be you instead?"

Eddie thought again of the smashed-up plate. He thought of Proteus, shifting shape and evading capture.

"Wouldn't you want to? Wouldn't you want to live here?"

When they finally stopped, at the bench by the pond, he said,

"We've pulled two tremendous stunts here. The Chippeway raid, and the trapping of Gamby Devohr. Let's do one more great and ridiculous thing."

"I doubt I have the energy."

"It's called The Death of the Poet Edwin Parfitt."

On October 29, a small circle of poets and artists and writers—some in residence at Laurelfield at that very time, some farther flung—gave testimony to the police about a drowning by suicide in Lake Glinow, Wisconsin, and the perverse funeral that followed. The artist Zilla Silverman and the composer Charles Ives together paid the hefty fine to the town hall that was all the police could come up with by way of penalty, after their fruitless inquest.

"Proteus Wept," published posthumously in *The American Mercury*, drew quite a bit of attention, as did the man's extraordinary suicide note.

Before her death the following spring, Samantha wrote a letter to Gamby reminding him of the poet Max Perry, "whose acquaintance you made in the summer of 1929. He was the one who took such fine care of your daughter Grace when you were incapacitated. I'm afraid he hasn't made much of himself as a poet since that stay," Samantha wrote, "but he is devoted to the arts, and would be an exceptional steward for Laurelfield. He also has possession of a file of particular interest to you. I expect his guaranteed employment and lodging as caretaker through at least the end of our agreement on September 1 of '54."

As for the artists who stayed there over the next ten years—a very few were friends who recognized him, but most were not. One writer, having been acquainted with Parfitt in Chicago and having mourned his death, wasn't sure if his heart would recover till halfway through his stay. No one left talking about him, though—they all understood the charge of silence, and admission was, after all, selective—and so to everywhere that was not Laurelfield, Edwin Parfitt remained dead.

Zilla Silverman, on the other hand: Zilla's was a real suicide. In February of 1956, a note from Lemuel, saying simply that she'd poisoned herself. Eddie knew it had nothing to do with Viktor. By then there had been other men. She'd flung herself at other closed windows. The windows never broke, but her heart, at the end, was in splinters. (Nor had Viktor's breakdown had anything to do with Zilla Silverman. Except that had he found one love, one great love in his life, she might have kept him off the street, kept him warm and fed and sane. And Zilla might have been that love.) Eddie never learned what had changed for Zilla that particular February morning, beyond the obvious, beyond what one can assume about every suicide: that her unhappiness, in the end, had outweighed all the beauty of the world. Lemuel brought the ashes to Laurelfield. Josephine Lizer carved the statue of a bear that served as Zilla's only headstone—the sculptor's last completed work.

Eighty years after the oak tree exploded, the ground where it had stood was an especially fertile bed for all those small flowers that thrive in shade and rich soil: lily of the valley, trillium, Jack-in-the-pulpit, dog violet, wood sorrel. And there was a little girl named Emma Grace Herriot, whose mother and father ran the place. When her parents worked late in the director's house she'd gather whatever was blooming and tie it together with string and, on tiptoes, leave the bundles outside studio doors. She had her mother's curls, her father's half smile. She believed herself to be in charge of the koi. She ran away silent from the studios, as she'd trained herself to do. She hoped the surprised artists would believe the flowers were a gift from the ghost.

———

But it was still 1929. And we were in the middle of saying: The oak tree had been blown to toothpicks. When Fannie came back to the library, drenched to her slip, she tried to tell Josephine about it. "You'll see for yourself in the morning. I've never been so startled before by an *absence*, by a shaft of thin air! I wish we could sculpt it. But how do you sculpt something that isn't even there?"

SAMANTHA AT HER WINDOW

There went Ralph and John, on a *Sunday*, bless them, carting wheelbarrow after wheelbarrow of oak shreds back to the fire pile. Hours earlier there had been just a circle of ash, and now already there was a whole new heap to burn. Eddie was down there, for some reason, poking at the pile and talking to the men. He'd seemed utterly changed yesterday, pink and energized.

She plucked a ladybug off the windowsill and dropped it gently onto the leaf of her hydrangea, where it might be happier. There was a lot to do. The hole in the wall was still open, and she ought to give the maid the sheets from Gamby's and Grace's beds. The White Rabbits were leaving tomorrow, and three new residents would arrive the day after. She ought to telephone Zilla and make sure she was all right, that something hadn't happened to Lemuel. And with Zilla gone she'd need to make prints from the negatives herself, the ones they'd told Gamby they already had. At the very least she could wash out the Mason jar from Zilla's studio. She poured the dead bee into the dustbin, rinsed the jar, and left it to dry.

After lunch, as she walked Alfie through the mud, she noticed what looked like a water lily. A folded white flower, at the edge of a puddle. When she got close she saw it was paper. A poem, or part of a poem. Typed, with a few penciled marks. A marvelous line about a tree cased in ice. She smoothed it and took it with her to find Eddie—there were no other poets, it must be his—and then she remembered what he'd said about starting over. But he'd finished twelve poems, and surely he couldn't mean he'd abandoned all of them.

And then, as she and Alfie continued behind the house, she thought of the fire pile, the way Eddie had been lurking there. She trudged off the path and all the way back, till she saw, like ornaments on a Christmas tree, the white rolls stuffed between the splintered oak branches. She glanced around the grounds and saw no one—she could hear Viktor's phonograph, too loud, from the Longhouse—and began pulling them out. Some were hard to reach, and they were all damp, but she couldn't leave them. Eddie was prone to changing his mind, after all, and in a week he might be in tears over their loss. There were more than twenty pages. The endings were signaled by his initials and the date, the beginnings by hand-penciled titles now smeared with the wet. She found one more page off by the composer's cottage, and one by the catalpa.

She let them dry on her kitchen table, and when they were dry she resisted the urge to take them back to Eddie. She clipped them together and set them on the counter.

The next afternoon, when John and Ralph came in to nail the board back to the wall, she told them to wait a moment, and on a whim she folded the stack in half and rolled it to fit in Zilla's Mason jar. She screwed the lid on tight and set the jar in the hole, on the beam where the liquor bottles had been.

John held the board and Ralph nailed it. They'd seen enough strange behavior at Laurelfield that they'd stopped asking questions years before.

PROLOGUE

1900

Virgin land is a fine and great thing. The Irish farmer who'd sold it did nothing with this part, letting decades of decomposing leaves richen the soil. Augustus and his architect, Mr. Ross, walk apace where the trees will let them through. Where the way is narrow, Mr. Ross follows Mr. Devohr.

This plot feels auspicious, not like a place he's seen before but a place he's always been meant to see. What is the opposite of memory? What is the inverse of an echo?

"It's flattest just beyond," Ross says. They are less than a quarter mile back from the road, and Augustus originally imagined even more seclusion, a long ride down a private drive. Ross is right, though, about the space. They've stopped by a massive oak, a tree stately enough to anchor an estate. "Most of your landscape would sit behind the house, then," Ross says. "We might clear a whole pasture, or we might put trails through the woods."

"Violet will want some ornamentals."

A scrawny rabbit stares at them, petrified. Augustus claps his hands and the creature darts away. The snow is long gone, but the mud cracks in brittle, icy sheets under both men's boots. The century is only six weeks old.

Violet, after the long ride from the city, refused to leave the station. He left her sitting on the bench with her travel case, hunched against the cold, and tipped the stationmaster a dollar to keep watch, to see to her lunch. After his visit to Mr. Ross's office, the two men stopped to see that she was still there, a seated statue, hands in her muffler. She insists he's building her a prison in the wilderness. And isn't he? What other choice has she left him?

His own idiocy: the failure to realize, when she abruptly stopped referring to Billy, the boy she'd left behind in Surrey, the boy who'd given her daisies for her fourteenth birthday and swam across the river for her—that it might not be a good sign, an acquiescence to marriage, but a very bad sign indeed. A Dr. W. H. Lambert showed up in Toronto that same year, a fellow Briton, and Violet saw him for her heart, and her women's troubles, which were several in that year after the wedding. Her parents were dead before the newlyweds had even returned from Paris, and there was trouble in the grain market, and Violet lost two babies in the womb, and in short there was so much worry that Augustus was left apologizing for the Devohr curse, not thinking he ought to watch for more bad luck. It was at the Ambulance Association Ball last summer that Violet's brother, back in town, sidled up to Augustus at the punch bowl and nodded at the doctor across the room. "Imagine old Billy Lambert showing up here in Toronto." Augustus was a drowned man.

Mr. Ross is counting his paces, walking what he thinks might be the perimeter of the main house.

"I'd want a wall," Augustus calls. "If we're so close to the road."

"And you'll have neighbors eventually."

When he returns to the station he'll tell her the house will be perfect. He'll tell her that in this new century, on this untouched earth, they will start something noble and good. What will Billy Lambert be, but a memory? What will the babies be, but things that never lived? *For man is man and master of his fate.* All boys ought to memorize that one in school.

And he has made the money that has made escape possible.

Money is freedom, and he will explain it to her again, how this move is the triumph of money over fate and memory—which is, in turn, the triumph of hard work. For what is money but work made tangible and put into the bank?

He imagines he'll take her back to Toronto just for the spring, for the packing of the house, and then they'll stay in Chicago while the new estate is built. They might look, tomorrow, at the homes along Astor Street. Yesterday she said he wants to lock her up. And he said, "Would you rather I had your dear doctor shipped back in a barrel? I'm doing things the proper way."

She looked at him level and said, "You may shut me in, but I can shut you out. There are two sides to every door, Augustus." Her eyes were dark and sharp, and he felt, in that moment, like a lion tamer. Like a man who is only in charge because for now, for a few days more, the lions will still allow it.

He must forgive her. Billy Lambert had the prior claim on her heart. She cannot see Lambert for what he is, a fellow who deals in blood and urine all day, whose coat sleeves are always too short. And Augustus is not without sin.

Violet, maps of blue veins inside her wrists. But where can he follow them? Her eyes, too: windows to what, precisely? He thinks of the Sargent his father briefly owned—a small painting, not a great one, Mrs. de Somebody—how he himself, age twelve, would stare at her eyes, just dark and imprecise daubs of paint, and yet he *knew* her, he felt she might see that he alone loved her truly. And he knew what she was thinking, which changed daily. And now that he possesses a real woman, all her flesh, her eyes are nothing but opaque glass. He is slowly learning there might be greater honesty in art than in woman.

Ross has circled back. He says, "You couldn't do better. It's a fine plot."

"I thought you'd be chalking it off somehow. Something official."

Ross smiles, indulgent. "Why not break a branch to mark the front door?"

He shows Augustus the spot, and a scrubby little tree, leafless, doomed to die with its cousins when ground is broken. Augustus takes hold of a low branch, level with his own face, thin enough to snap but thick enough for the men to find again later.

"I ought to say auspicious words. Aren't we meant to throw wine and salt?"

Ross raises his hand as if lofting a goblet. "A full moon on a dark night, and the road downhill all the way to your door!"

"That should do." The branch breaks cleanly down with an echoing snap and hangs there, swinging, by a strip of skin. It is decided.

Ross says, "I'll come back to mark it. A red ribbon."

He pulls out his watch and shows it, grimacing, to Devohr. It is nearly half past three. The men sprint for the horses, and the horses, cold and unprepared, hurry as best they can back to town.

At the station, Devohr throws his bridle to Ross and dismounts and runs, but he sees, as he nears the platform, that the train is not inching to a stop but to a start. Men who have just disembarked hold their hats to their heads and wait to cross the track. And Violet is not on the bench where he left her. Instead there is a row of brown acorns down the bench arm, lined up and evenly spaced. She hoards small things, collecting them in columns and stacks: coins and pebbles and beetle wings. Once, he found it charming. Now he wonders what strange math she's doing with the trinkets. The world is her abacus. She is calculating against him.

He searches frantically for the stationmaster, but then he sees, gliding past above, more slowly than if she were walking, Violet's face in the window.

He shouts her name, and she looks down, but just a bit, and he isn't sure she's seen him. He refuses to run along the platform like a fool in a French novel. He can keep pace by walking, for at least a moment, and he thinks what can be done. He could take Ross's horse, but it's more than thirty miles to the city. He might track down an automobile. If nothing else, he can wire the Palmer House and make sure she arrives, make sure she's seen to.

The train picks up a bit of speed, and he'll trot, but just barely, not for much longer. Above him, she has put her white knuckles to the window and is knocking, slowly, listlessly. Looking straight at him now, with no expression at all. A cruel and pointless knocking: not to get out, and not to call him in. As if to demonstrate, simply, that the glass is thick.

He can almost hear the knocks, above the hiss of steam and the sound of the pistons. But he can't, he knows he can't. It's in his head. The train only gets louder, and it only moves forward.

He will see her tomorrow, in the city, but this feels for some reason like the last glimpse of her he'll ever get: staring through him, pale and inscrutable behind the glass.

Oh Violet, Violet, Violet! He wants to shout it, but he won't.

Let me in.

Let me in.

Let me in.

ACKNOWLEDGMENTS

This is a novel about, among other things, how much artists need a community. These are a few of the communities that have sheltered me during the writing of this book:

The wonderful people of Viking and Penguin: Kathryn Court, Lindsey Schwoeri, Scott Cohen, Veronica Windholz, Nina Hnatov, Nancy Resnick, and Kristen Haff; as well as Josh Cochran, who gave Laurelfield the red sky it needed.

The stupendous Nicole Aragi (the Queen of Pentacles) and Duvall Osteen.

A phalanx of early editors: the writers M. Molly Backes, Alex Christensen, John Copenhaver, Tim Horvath, Brian Prisco, and Emily Gray Tedrowe; and the readers (the world needs more readers like them) Shelley Gentle, Margaret Kelley, and Pamela Minkler.

The friends who let me bother them about technical details (and aren't responsible for my errors): the writer David M. Harris on series ghostwriting; the writer Margaret Zamos-Monteith and the photographer Matthew Monteith on photographic history and 1920s darkrooms; Edward McEneely on WWII history (so much work for so few words!); and my social media hive-mind for everything from the drying time of oil paint to oak stump decomposition to pry bars.

The Sewanee Writers' Conference, where the first chapters were encouraged, and where Christine Schutt's kind read convinced me to keep working on this book.

The colleges on Chicago's North Shore that have been kind enough, in the time since I originally drafted the first part of this novel, to welcome me to campus or let me teach. The college in this book is explicitly *not* based on any of those institutions.

The Ragdale Foundation and The Corporation of Yaddo, and everyone I met at both, whose work—from sonnets to paintings to smashed teacups—has inspired my last few years. What sort of world would this be, without refuges?

My family—Jon, Lydia, Heidi, Mom—who have been, variously, great editors and/or less requiring of diaper changes than they were three years ago.

Also, all five of the people I've forgotten.

This book started as a short story about male anorexia. I have no idea what the hell happened.

Read on for a story from

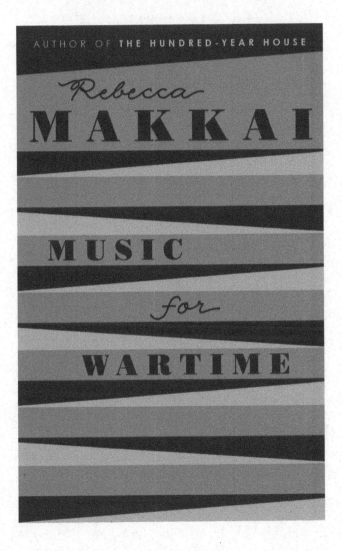

THE BRIEFCASE

*H*e thought how strange that a political prisoner, marched through town in a line, chained to the man behind and chained to the man ahead, should take comfort in the fact that all this had happened before. He thought of other chains of men on other islands of the earth, and he thought how since there have been men, there have been prisoners. He thought of mankind as a line of miserable monkeys chained at the wrist, dragging each other back into the ground.

In the early morning of December 1 the sun was finally warming them all, enough that they could walk faster. With his left hand, he adjusted the loop of steel that cuffed his right hand to the line of doomed men. He was starved, his wrist was thin, his body was cold: The cuff slipped off. In one breath he looked back to the man behind him and forward to the man limping ahead, and knew that neither saw his naked, red wrist; each saw only his own mother weeping in a kitchen, his own love on a bed in white sheets and sunlight.

He walked in step to the end of the block.

Before the war this man had been a chef, and his one crime was feeding the people who sat at his tables in clouds of smoke and talked politics. He served them the wine that fueled their underground newspaper, their aborted revolution. And after the night his restaurant disappeared in fire, he had run and hidden and gone without food—he who had roasted ducks until the meat jumped from the bone, he who had evaporated three bottles of wine into one pot of cream soup, he who had peeled the skin from small pumpkins with a twist of his hand.

And here was his hand, twisted free of the chain, and here he was running and crawling, until he was through a doorway. It was a building of empty classrooms—part of the university he never attended. He watched out the bottom corner of a second-story window as the young soldiers stopped the line, counted ninety-nine men, shouted to each other, shouted at the prisoners in the panicked voices of children who barely filled the shoulders of their uniforms. One soldier, a bigger one, a louder one, stopped a man walking by, a man in a suit, with a briefcase, a beard. Some sort of professor. The soldiers stripped him of his coat, his shirt, his leather case, cuffed him to the chain. They marched again. And as soon as they had passed—no, not that soon; many minutes later, when he had the stomach—the chef ran down to the street and collected the man's briefcase, coat, and shirt.

In the alley, the chef crouched and buttoned the professor's shirt over his own ribs. When he opened the briefcase, papers flew out, a thousand doves flailing against the walls of the alley. The chef ran after them, stopped them with his feet and arms, herded them back into the case—pages of numbers, of arrows and notes and hand-drawn star maps. Here were business cards: a professor of physics. Envelopes showed his name and address—information that might have been useful in some other lifetime, one in which the chef could ring the bell of this man's house and explain to his wife about empty chains, empty wrists, empty classrooms. And here was a note from that wife about the sandwich she had packed him. There was no sandwich left. Here were graded papers, a fall syllabus, the typed draft of an exam. The extra question at the end, a strange one: "Using modern astronomical data, construct, to the best of your ability, a proof that the sun actually revolves around the earth."

The chef knew nothing of physics. He understood chemistry only insofar as it related to the baking times of bread at various elevations. His knowledge of biology was limited to the deboning of chickens and the behavior of bread yeast. What did he know of moving bodies and gravity? He knew this: He had moved from his line of men, creating a vacuum—one that had sucked the professor in.

The chef sat on his bed in the widow K———'s basement and felt, in the cool leather of the briefcase, a second vacuum: Here was a vacated life. Here were salary receipts, travel records, train tickets, a small address book. And these belonged to a man whose name was not blackened like his own, a man who was not hunted. If he wanted to live through the next year, the chef would have to learn this life and fill it—and oddly, this felt not like a robbery but like an apology, a way to put the world back in balance. The professor would not die, because he himself would become the professor, and he would live.

Surely he could not teach at the university; surely he could not slip into the man's bed unnoticed. But what was in this leather case, it seemed, had been left for him to use. These addresses of friends, this card of identification, this riddle about the inversion of the universe.

Five cities east, he gave his name as the professor's, and grew out his beard so it would match the photograph on the card he now carried in his pocket. The two men no longer looked entirely dissimilar. To the first name in the address book, the chef had addressed a typed letter: "Am in trouble and have fled the city. Tell my dear wife I am unharmed, but for her safety do not tell her where I am. If you are able to help a poor old man, send money to the following postbox.... I hope to remain your friend, Professor T———."

He'd had to write this about the wife—how could he ask these men for money if she held a funeral? And what of it, if she kept her happiness another few months, another year?

The next twenty-six letters were similar in nature, and money arrived now in brown envelopes and white ones. The bills came wrapped in notes (Was his life in danger? Did he have his health?), and with the money he paid another widow for another basement, and he bought weak cigarettes. He sat on café chairs and drew diagrams of the universe, showed stars and planets looping each other in light. He felt that if he used the other papers in the briefcase, he must also make use of the question. Or perhaps he felt that if he could answer it, he could put the universe back together. And, too, it was something to fill his empty days.

He wrote in his small notebook: "The light of my cigarette is a fire like the sun. From where I sit, all the universe is equidistant from my cigarette. Ergo, my cigarette is the center of the universe. My cigarette is on earth. Ergo, the earth is the center of the universe. If all heavenly bodies move, they must therefore move in relation to the earth, and in relation to my cigarette."

His hand ached. These words were the most he had written since school, which had ended for him at age sixteen. He had been a smart boy, even talented in languages and mathematics, but his mother had needed him to make a living. He was not blessed, like the professor, with years of scholarship and quiet offices and leather books. He was blessed instead with chicken stocks and herbs and sherry. Thirty years had passed since his last day of school, and his hand was accustomed now to wooden spoon, mandoline, paring knife, rolling pin.

Today his hands smelled of ink, when for thirty years they had smelled of leeks. They were the hands of the professor; ergo, he was the professor.

He had written to friends A through L, and now he saved the rest and wrote instead to students. Here in the briefcase's outermost pocket were class rosters from the past two years; letters addressed to those young men care of the university were bound to reach them. The amounts they sent were smaller, the notes that accompanied them more inquisitive. What, exactly, had transpired? Could they come to meet him?

The postbox was in a different city than the one where he stayed. He arrived at the post office just before closing, and came only every two or three weeks. He always looked through the window first to check that the lobby was empty. If it was not, he would leave and return another day. Surely one of these days, a friend of the professor would be waiting there for him. He prepared a story, that he was the honored professor's assistant, that he could not reveal the man's location but would certainly pass on your kindest regards, sir.

If the earth moved, all it would take for a man to travel its circumference would be a strong balloon. Rise twenty feet above, and wait for the earth to turn under you; you would be home again in a day. But this was not true, and a man could not escape his spot on the earth but to run along the surface. Ergo, the earth was still. Ergo, the sun was the moving body of the two.

No, he did not believe it. He wanted only to know who this professor was, this man who would teach his students the laws of the universe, then ask them to prove as true what was false.

On the wall of the café: plate-sized canvas, delicate oils of an apple, half-peeled. Signed, below, by a girl he had known in school.

The price was more than a month of groceries, and so he did not buy it, but for weeks he read his news under the apple and drank his coffee. Staining his fingers in cheap black ink were the signal fires of the world, the distress sirens, the dispatches from the trenches and hospitals and abattoirs of the war; but here, on the wall, a sign from another world. He had known this girl as well as any other: had spoken with her every day, but had not made love to her; had gone to her vacation home one winter holiday, but knew nothing of her life since then. And here, a clue, perfect and round and unfathomable. After all this time: apple.

Once he finished the news, he worked at the professor's proof and saw in the coil of green-edged apple skin some model of spiraling, of expansion. The stars were at one time part of the earth, until the hand of God peeled them away, leaving us in the dark. They do not revolve around us: They escape in widening circles. The Milky Way is the edge of this peel.

Outside the café window, a beggar screeched his bow against a defeated violin. A different kind of leather case lay open on the ground, this one collecting the pennies of the more compassionate passers-by. The café owner shooed him away, and the chef sighed in guilty relief that he would not have to pass, on the way out, his double.

After eight months in the new city, the chef stopped buying his newspapers on the street by the café and began instead to read the year-old news the widow gave him for his fires. Here, fourteen months ago: Minister P——— of the Interior predicts war. One day he found that in a box near the widow's furnace were papers three, four, five years old. Pages were missing, edges eaten. He took his fragments of yellowed paper to the café and read the beginnings and ends of opinions and letters. He read reports from what used to be his country's borders.

When he had finished the last paper of the box, he began to read the widow's history books. The Americas, before Columbus; the oceans, before the British; Rome, before its fall.

History was safer than the news, because there was no question of how it would end.

He took a lover in the city and told her he was a professor of physics. He showed her the stars in the sky and explained that they circled the earth, along with the sun.

That's not true at all, she said. You think I'm just a silly girl.

No, he said and touched her neck, You are the only one who might understand. The universe has been folded inside out.

A full year had passed, and he paid the widow in coins. He wrote to friends M through Z. I have been in hiding for a year, he wrote. Tell my dear wife I have my health. May time and history forgive us all.

A year had passed, but so had many years passed for many men. And after all what was a year, if the earth did not circle the sun?

The earth does not circle the sun, he wrote. Ergo: The years do not pass. The earth, being stationary, does not erase the past nor escape toward the future. Rather, the years pile on like blankets, existing at once. The year is 1848; the year is 1789; the year is 1956.

If the earth hangs still in space, does it spin? If the earth were to spin, the space I occupy I will therefore vacate in an instant. This city will leave its spot, and the city to the west will usurp its place. Ergo, this city is all cities. This is Kabul; this is Dresden; this is Johannesburg.

I run by standing still.

At the post office, he collects his envelopes of money. He has learned from the notes of concerned colleagues and students and

friends that the professor suffered from infections of the inner ear
that often threw off his balance. He has learned of the professor's
wife, A———, whose father died the year they married. He has
learned that he has a young son. Rather, the professor has a son.

At each visit to the post office, he fears he will forget the combination. It is an old lock, and complicated: F1, clockwise to B3, back
to A6, forward again to J3. He must shake the latch before it opens.
More than forgetting, perhaps what he fears is that he will be denied
access—that the little box will one day recognize him behind his
thick and convincing beard, will decide he has no right of entry.

One night, asleep with his head on his lover's leg, he dreams that
a letter has arrived from the professor himself. They freed me at the
end of the march, it says, and I crawled my way home. My hands are
bloody and my knees are worn through, and I want my briefcase.

In his dream, the chef takes the case and runs west—because if
the professor takes it back, there will be no name left for the chef, no
place on the earth. The moment his fingers leave the leather loop of
the handle, he will fall off the planet.

He sits in a wooden chair on the lawn behind the widow's house.
Inside, he hears her washing dishes. In exchange for the room, he
cooks all her meals. It is April, and the cold makes the hairs rise
from his arms, but the sun warms the arm beneath them. He thinks,
The tragedy of a moving sun is that it leaves us each day. Hence the
desperate Aztec sacrifices, the ancient rites of the eclipse. If the sun
so willingly leaves us, each morning it returns is a stay of execution,
an undeserved gift.

Whereas: If it is we who turn, how can we so flagrantly leave
behind that which has warmed us and given us light? If we are moving, then each turn is a turn away. Each revolution a revolt.

The money arrives less often, and even old friends who used to write monthly now send only rare, apologetic notes, a few small bills. Things are more difficult now, their letters say. No one understood when he first ran away, but now it is clear: After they finished with the artists, the journalists, the fighters, they came for the professors. How wise he was, to leave when he did. Some letters return unopened, with a black stamp.

Life is harder here, too. Half the shops are closed. His lover has left him. The little café is filled with soldiers. The beggar with the violin has disappeared, and the chef fears him dead.

One afternoon, he enters the post office two minutes before closing. The lobby is empty but for the postman and his broom.

The mailbox is empty as well, and he turns to leave but hears the voice of the postman behind him. You are the good Professor T———, no? I have something for you in the back.

Yes, he says, I am the professor. And it feels as if this is true, and he will have no guilt over the professor's signature when the box is brought out. He is even wearing the professor's shirt, as loose again over his hungry ribs as it was the day he slipped it on in the alley.

From behind the counter, the postman brings no box, but a woman in a long gray dress, a white handkerchief in her fingers.

She moves toward him, looks at his hands and his shoes and his face. Forgive me for coming, she says, and the postman pulls the cover down over his window and vanishes. She says, No one would tell me anything, only that my husband had his health. And then a student gave me the number of the box and the name of the city.

He begins to say, You are the widow. But why would he say this? What proof is there that the professor is dead? Only that it must be, that it follows logically.

She says, I don't understand what has happened.

He begins to say, I am the good professor's assistant, madam—but then what next? She will ask questions he has no way to answer.

I don't understand, she says again.

All he can say is, This is his shirt. He holds out an arm so she can see the gaping sleeve.

She says, What have you done with him? She has a calm voice and wet brown eyes. He feels he has seen her before, in the streets of the old city. Perhaps he served her a meal, a bottle of wine. Perhaps, in another lifetime, she was the center of his universe.

This is his beard, he says.

She begins to cry into the handkerchief. She says, Then he is dead. He sees now from the quiet of her voice that she must have known this long ago. She has come here only to confirm.

He feels the floor of the post office move beneath him, and he tries to turn his eyes from her, to ground his gaze in something solid: postbox, ceiling tile, door. He finds he cannot look away. She is a force of gravity in her long gray dress.

No, he says. No, no, no, no, no, I am right here.

Of course he does not believe it, but he knows that if he had time, he could prove it. And he must, because he is the only piece of the professor left alive. The woman does not see how she is murdering her husband, right here in the post office lobby. He whispers to her: Let me go home with you. I'll be a father to your son, and I'll warm your bed, and I'll keep you safe.

He wraps his hands around her small, cold wrists, but she pulls loose. She might be the most beautiful woman he has ever seen.

As if from miles away, he hears her call to the postmaster to send for the police.

His head is light, and he feels he might float away from the post office forever. It is an act of will not to fly off, but to hold tight to the earth and wait. If the police aren't too busy to come, he feels confident he can prove to them that he is the professor. He has the papers, after all—and in the havoc of war, what else will they have the time to look for?

She is backing away from him on steady feet, and he feels it like a peeling off of skin.

If not the police, perhaps he'll convince a city judge. The witnesses who would denounce him are mostly gone or killed, and the others would fear to come before the law.

If the city judge will not listen, he can prove it to the high court. One day he might convince the professor's own child. He feels certain that somewhere down the line, someone will believe him.

The Great Believers

A Novel

It's 1985 and Yale Tishman's career begins to flourish, even as the AIDS epidemic grows around him. Soon the only person he has left is Fiona, his departed friend's sister. But it will be years before Fiona finally finds herself grappling with the devastating ways AIDS affected her life. The two intertwining stories take us from the heartbreak of Chicago in the eighties to the chaos of the modern world in contemporary Paris, as both Yale and Fiona struggle to find goodness in the midst of disaster.

"Stirring, spellbinding, and full of life." —Téa Obreht,
New York Times bestselling author of *The Tiger's Wife*

PENGUIN BOOKS

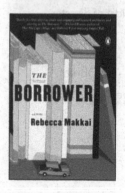